I0594961

Veilfall
Book One:
The Veiled Prophecy Series
By Ali Wren
The Wren's Hollow

Table of Contents

Dedication

To my family, for your endless love and encouragement, you are the
foundation of every story I dare to tell.
To my husband, for believing in my dreams even before I fully
believed in them myself. Your support makes the impossible feel
possible.
To my children, who inspire wonder in my heart every single day.
Thank you for reminding me that magic is real if we dare to see it.

This book began as a dream, shaped by imagination, and made real
because of you.

The skies above Sylvaeris bled fire.

Ash drifted like cursed snow over fields once lush with wildflowers and singing grass, now nothing more than scorched ruin. The earth, torn and blackened, drank deeply of fae blood. Elemental magic had left the air warped, thick with ozone and smoke. Where once fae warriors had carved light from storm and flame, the land now lay silent, nothing left but ruin.

Lucien Caelith knelt beside a fallen soldier, the forest-green armor of the Head Guard gleaming faintly beneath layers of soot and blood, silver runes along its surface pulsing weakly as if absorbing the dying light of battle. The ceremonial mask shadowed his face, but his fingers trembled as he pressed them to the warrior's throat. Nothing. No pulse. No flicker of life. His jaw clenched. Another gone.

Around him, the remnants of the Sylvaerian elite fought like cornered wolves. Screams of the wounded and dying split the air. Magic cracked and howled through the sky, lightning laced with grief, fire screaming its last breath. Beside him, Prince Lucan Thornevale, moved like a storm embodied. The two men fought back-to-back, blades singing, magic crackling between them as they carved through waves of werewolves and vampires that had breached the outer wards.

"Right flank!" Lucien shouted, ducking under a swipe of claws.

Lucan responded instantly. A wave of raw energy burst from his palm, incinerating the creature mid-leap. The two didn't speak after that, didn't need to. Their rhythm was forged through years of brotherhood. Step. Strike. Breathe. Block.

When the battle ended, the silence was worse than the screams. The smoke lifted just enough to show what remained. Bodies strewn like discarded dolls, weapons forgotten in blood-soaked mud. The first light of dawn crept over the horizon, casting a sickly gold hue across the battlefield.

Lucien staggered forward, eyes scanning the ruins. His soot-streaked face was drawn with exhaustion. His armor hung unevenly, torn in places. His dark hair, usually neatly kept, was matted with sweat and ash. Lucan stood near the edge of a crater, one arm clutching his side. Blood ran down his ribs.

"You're hurt," Lucien said hoarsely.

Lucan didn't look at him. "It's not mine." A pause. "My father..." He didn't have to finish it. He could feel the pain emanating from the man he was sworn to protect.

Lucien's breath caught. "No."

Lucan nodded once, the motion tight. "I couldn't get to him in time." The crown, shattered with the man who wore it, would now be reforged for the son who survived him.

Lucien's voice was rough. "I'm sorry."

Lucan gave no answer, just turned his gaze to the smoldering horizon. "We need to assess the losses. Reverence Hall still stands. We'll regroup there."

They began the slow walk away from the battlefield. Somewhere beyond the carnage, a faint cry echoed, a baby's cry. Lucan paused, his face softening.

"They're safe?" Lucien asked.

Lucan gave a nod. "Viviana, Ilyra and the twins are at the Grove. Thalina kept them hidden in the deep warding. No one made it past."

Lucien's shoulders eased slightly. "Then it was worth it. Vivi will be furious she missed the battle." He tried to laugh. It came out hollow.

"Lucien! Come quick! It's Viviana!"

Thalina's voice pierced the stillness, breathless, joyful. Lucien didn't wait. He broke into a sprint, boots pounding through ash, toward the untouched heart of the realm, the Grove of Stars. Lucan followed.

The Grove shimmered with peace that felt stolen. Silver-leaved trees swayed gently as if unaware of the death just beyond their roots. Here, the Veil between realms was thinnest. Stars glimmered even in the pale daylight, their light refracting off the sacred pool at its center.

Lucien stopped at the edge, catching his breath. The still water reflected the canopy above, glowing like molten glass. He didn't speak. He couldn't.

Viviana was resting inside the guardian home nestled into the roots of the ancient trees, cradling their newborn daughter. And just an hour after her birth, Veralyn's fate had been sealed.

The seer had come. Silent. Uninvited. Lucien had met her eyes and knew. He hadn't told Viviana. Not yet. Not until he was sure. She had whispered of a darkness. A rising shadow that would seek Veralyn. That his daughter barely minutes old, was already hunted by something vast and vile.

He looked up as footsteps approached. Lucan stepped into the clearing, regal even with blood on his boots, his war cloak dragging through leaves still glowing with magic.

"You summoned me," Lucan said.

Lucien nodded. "Before the coronation. I need to speak with you in private."

Lucan's brow furrowed. "This sounds ominous."

"It is." Lucien's voice dropped. "I saw the Pontivar. She found me after Veralyn was born." Lucan stiffened. "She said something is coming for my daughter. Something old. A shadow wrapped in prophecy." Lucien's voice cracked. "We must go into hiding. No one can know. Not even the Order."

Lucan stared at him in silence. "You want me to let the Head of my Royal Guard vanish in the middle of a power shift?"

"I want to save my daughter's life." Lucien stepped forward. "Give my position to the runner-up, Rowain of Duskmere. He's strong.

Loyal. He's already here with an update from their border. He won't ask questions."

Lucan's mouth tightened. "You ask too much. You've already taken the oath, we will always be connected."

"I ask only what I would give you, if our roles were reversed."

Lucan looked to the pool, voice cold. "If I agree, I do it as your king."

Lucien's voice softened. "And I thank you, as your friend."

A long pause. Then, Lucan nodded.

"If you ever call for me," he said, "I will come. I swear it."

Lucien's smile was faint but real. "That's all I could ask."

Later, under the fading starlight, Lucien stood over the cradle carved from ancient root and moss. His daughter glowed faintly, her magic already humming beneath her skin. Her eyes, though closed, seemed to shine with starlight.

"She's perfect," Viviana whispered beside him.

"She's not safe," he murmured, placing a kiss on her temple.

Viviana's expression turned grim. "Then we go. Wherever we must. We will find the others." Lucien nodded, eyes never leaving his daughter.

"Tomorrow," he whispered, "we disappear."

Valerian nodded once. "The rite is sealed."

A knock broke the silence. "Enter," he said, his voice steady, without turning.

The door creaked open. Rowain of Duskmere stepped inside, tall and grim, the polished black of his armor dulled by blood and ash from the final border skirmish.

"Your Highness," Rowain said, bowing low. "The southern border is secured. Duskmere stands ready."

Lucan turned to face him fully, gaze unreadable. "And Lucien?"

Rowain hesitated only a breath. "He's gone."

Lucan's nod was slight but final. "Then you're Head Guard now."

Rowain blinked, caught off guard. "As you command." Nobody but Ilyra or Lucien ever questioned him.

Lucan gave a faint wave of dismissal. The door shut softly behind Rowain, leaving the king alone once more.

He crossed to a side table and poured a measure of amber liquid from a crystal decanter, watching it catch the light. Then he returned to the window, glass in hand, and gazed out over the endless stretch of forest beyond the palace. The trees whispering secrets only the wind could carry.

His voice was low, almost a breath. "Be safe, little one."

Lucan stood before a wide arched window, the morning light casting long shadows across the stone floor. His robes of mourning had been traded for a deep forest cloak, embroidered with threads of gold that glinted like distant stars. The weight of the crown was absent from his brow, but its burden lingered in his eyes.

He and Rowain stood together in silence, both facing the figure cloaked in shadow.

Pontivar Valerian of Varethos, seer of the old blood, moved like a drifting veil as she stepped into the center of the chamber. The air grew colder with her presence, as though the veil between worlds had thinned. Her hands, bony and etched with ancient ink, held a delicate porcelain cup filled with a dark, steaming draught.

Lucan's voice was low and steady. "You understand what this binds you to."

Rowain, towering and grim, gave a single nod. "To you. To the crown. Until death."

Pontivar Valerian's voice rose like a chant carried on wind. Ancient words in a forgotten tongue spilled from her lips, soft and reverent, but threaded with power. The magic in the room stirred, subtle but undeniable, as if the stones themselves remembered the rite.

She offered the cup to Rowain first. He took it without hesitation and drank. Then to Lucan, who followed in kind. Reluctant, as Rowain was never meant to be his guard. He hesitated his mind now on his missing best friend.

A beat passed. Then a ripple, like a quiet pulse of energy, hummed between them. It wasn't overwhelming but it *was* present. A new tether, delicate yet binding, unseen yet irrevocable.

"You are linked now," she said, her ash-colored eyes flicking between them. "Not in thought, not in sight but in fate. If one falls, the other will feel it. If the crown is extinguished, your strength will break."

Lucan looked to Rowain. "You are my shadow now. My shield. My vengeance, if need be."

"I will not falter," Rowain answered.

The seer extended her hand, and from beneath her cloak, an object was revealed, a mask of gleaming blackened metal, stylized with sharp lines and solemn grace. Its design echoed the helmets of ancient Sylvaerian warriors, evoking the empire's long-forgotten roots: faceless, eternal, unyielding.

"This is not a decoration," the Pontivar said as she placed it in his hands. "It is who you become from this moment forward. You are no longer just a fae." Rowain bowed his head, then lifted the mask and placed it over his face.

When he straightened, silence pressed in. His presence was no longer familiar. He had become something more and something less. The final protector of the throne. The first to bleed if it fell.

Lucan watched, jaw tight. "Then it is done."

Pontivar Valerian nodded once. "The rite is sealed."

Chapter 1: Truth. Trust. Safety.

Vera

I should've known something was wrong when the birds went silent.

It's Friday, and the crisp bite of October is already in the air. I graduated high school this past summer, but today feels like a fresh start, the beginning of something new. My parents are taking me to a show in the city tonight, something we only do once in a while. They usually prefer to stay home, quiet and tucked away. Routine. Safe.

We've spent the last few months tossing around ideas for what comes next. College applications, maybe even a gap year to travel, ancient ruins, bustling markets, stories carved into stone. Most parents would push for the fast track into school. Not mine. They appeared to be more nervous, not sure what I should do.

I don't understand but I think they want to travel, we have never had a family vacation before. Other kids in my school would talk about their vacations even summer beach trips, the only thing we did was take trips to the city to see shows.

They said they had a surprise for me and I am excited. I don't know what it could be, even a weekend off of training would be appreciated. Every day, my father had me outside training—running, sparring, tackling the obstacle course he built himself. At first, I thought it was just something fun for us to do together. But the older I got, the more intense it became. He was determined that I'd be able to take down someone his size.

The sky above me is heavy and swollen, thick gray clouds bruising the horizon. The air is sharp and electric, the way it feels right before a storm tears open the sky. A cold breeze snakes through the trees, lifting the fine hairs on my arms. I tug my jacket tighter and push the unease down.

Our house isn't far from town, I like to walk to the library some days and find new books to read. As soon as I'm out of sight, I break into a jog. My dad always says, "Stay sharp," like life's some kind of battleground waiting to jump out at you. Sometimes, I think I was raised to be more cautious then I needed to be. Nothing bad happened in this small town in Maine. When I round the final corner and see my house, my steps falter.

Something's wrong. I feel it. I open my senses that my parents tell me to never use but for some reason I can't feel anything. Where are they?

The porch light is off. The curtains are drawn. Not a single glow slips through the windows. It's too quiet, an unnatural hush, like the whole world is holding its breath.

Normally, I'd hear the faint clatter of pots in the kitchen, smell the buttery warmth of something baking, hear my mom's humming drifting out through the windows.

Today? Nothing. Only the low moan of the wind through the trees.

I push open the front door. It groans on its hinges, the sound scraping against the silence like a warning.

"Mom?" I call out. "Dad?"

No answer.

A metallic tang clings to the air, sharp and wrong. Like iron and rain and something else I can't name.

My sneakers squeak faintly on the wood floor as I step inside. Shadows press in from every corner. The narrow hallway stretches out before me, the familiar photographs on the walls seeming to watch me as I move past. I catch a flash of my own reflection in the hallway mirror, wide eyes, bloodless face.

The kitchen is deserted. The back door swings open on its hinges, creaking with each gust of the growing wind. It wasn't locked. My mom always locks the door. The dread in my stomach curdles like sour milk.

I set my backpack and phone on the counter with trembling fingers, not even sure why. Instinct. Habit. My legs move me forward, out into the backyard. The air feels thicker out here, heavier, like something unseen is pressing down on me.

That's when I see it. Blood. A broken trail smeared through the grass, dark and vivid against the pale green blades, leading toward the forest. My stomach twists into a hard knot. My breath stutters in and out.

No. No, no, no.

I want to run. I want to pretend I never saw it. But my feet betray me, carrying me toward the trees, following the grim path. The forest closes in around me, dark and damp. The scent of wet earth rises up, mingling with the coppery tang of blood. Twigs snap underfoot. A crow caws in the distance, harsh and jarring.

And then—

I find them. My parents lie crumpled beneath the gnarled limbs of an old oak, their bodies entwined as if my dad had tried to shield my mom even in death.

Their skin is pale. Their clothes soaked in crimson.

"Mom!" I choke out, falling to my knees beside them. "Dad!"

I scramble to check their pulses, my hands trembling uncontrollably. Nothing. No warmth. No breath.

The scream tears out of my throat, raw and animalistic, echoing into the woods. The cold breeze from earlier swelling into a sharp wind. Branches groan and whip above me, carrying the storm I had sensed before, now here, now raging, as if the sky itself grieved with me.

I don't know how long I stay there, sobbing, clutching at them, as if somehow the force of my grief could anchor them back to life. My tears soak into the earth.

But then, a sound. A faint crunch of leaves behind me.

I freeze, my whole body tensing. Slowly, I turn.

A woman steps into the clearing, moving like a ripple through the misty trees. Her hair, long and wild with silver streaks, tumbles around her shoulders as the wind teases the strands. She's dressed in gear unlike anything I've ever seen, dark green, fitted close to her body but reinforced with plates along her shoulders and chest. Straps cross her torso, holding blades that gleam even in the muted forest light. At the center of her chest, etched into the armor, is a strange symbol: a sword crossed with a curling spiral, like a tornado caught mid-surge. The whole look is sharp, efficient, and dangerous, but when her eyes find mine, there's something almost familiar in the way she studies me.

Light seems to cling to her, like the mist itself bows around her form. There is something about her, she feels familiar to me. Like I have met her before, but I have never met her. I shield my parents the best I can. Ready for any fight that comes my way.

"Veralyn," she says softly.

The name feels like a ghost brushing against my skin, familiar and strange at the same time.

"Who—who are you?" I manage to whisper, stumbling to my feet.

"My name is Rina. I'm your aunt." Her voice cracks as her gaze drops to my parents. "You look just like your mother."

Aunt. Flashes of faded photographs. Half-finished stories. It's just us, my parents would say. *Safer that way.*

"I'm sorry we're meeting like this," Rina murmurs, her voice trembling. "Are you okay?"

No. No, I am shattered. But I nod anyway.

"I'm here to help," she says, reaching out with a trembling hand. "You need to pack. I'm taking you home."

"Home?" I whisper. "I am home."

Rina's eyes soften. "I know, sweetheart. But you're not safe here anymore."

She steps closer to my parents' bodies and pulls a small vial from her coat. She sprinkles a fine, shimmering powder over them, whispering strange words that seem to buzz at the edge of my hearing.

Slowly, their bodies begin to fade, dissolving into sparkling light. The blood-stained earth, the twisted leaves beneath them, everything becomes more visible as their physical forms vanish.

Gasping, I stumble back. "What are you doing?! What's happening to them?!"

"It's okay," she says quickly, coming to steady me. "I'm sending them home, to our land. They'll have the funeral they deserve. Your mother wanted it this way."

Our land? Coming home? Confusion roils in my gut. I reach out with the senses I was always told to hide, reaching for the unseen currents around her.

Warmth wraps around me like a summer breeze. Bright, muted gold light shimmers just out of sight, gentle and steady.

Truth. Trust. Safety.

"I can feel you, sweet girl," Rina whispers. "I promise, I'll keep you safe."

I gasp softly. Only my mother and father could ever sense when I did that, how can she?

"How?" I rasp.

"There's no time now," she says urgently. "We need to go. Pack quickly."

She steers me toward the house. My limbs move automatically, like I'm underwater. The grass under my feet, once soft and comforting, now feels slick and cold. Above us, the clouds boil and churn, the first fat raindrops spattering the ground.

Inside, the house yawns around me, empty. Silent. Echoing with memories that already feel like ghosts.

I climb the stairs slowly, the wooden steps creaking under my weight. The hallway stretches dark and unfamiliar before me. My bedroom door, painted a deep green, looms like a gateway to another life.

Inside, I grab my suitcase and start stuffing clothes inside, shirts, my old worn leggings, a worn hoodie. My hands tremble as I grab keepsakes: ticket stubs from plays and concerts, museum postcards, a necklace my mom gave me last Christmas.

Last, I grab my favorite photo. The three of us, laughing in front of a ridiculous dinosaur backdrop at a museum. My dad's arm around my shoulders. My mom's smile radiant.

I place it gently on top of the pile.

I'm reaching for the photo album when a chill races down my spine. I freeze.

The air around me pulses strangely, like the world just exhaled something dark. I reach out with trembling fingers and brush the air in front of me. A faint reddish glow stains the space. Danger.

I jerk back, heart hammering.

A hand lands on my shoulder and I flinch, a yelp escaping.

"Shh, it's me," Rina whispers urgently. "We have to go. Now."

She pulls another vial from her coat, sprinkling its contents in front of us. She murmurs something under her breath, soft and rhythmic, ancient-sounding words that make the air vibrate in my chest. Then it happens.

The space in front of us ripples, a distortion that looks like heat rising off stone, then tears open with a soft, resonant hum. A swirling veil of silver light spirals outward, shimmering like liquid moonlight. It's beautiful and terrifying all at once, a doorway cut into the fabric of the world. She grabs my suitcase and my arm, dragging me toward it.

As I step toward the opening, I glance back. A shadow figure stands at the top of the stairs, moving toward my door. Cloaked in the dark, I can just make out the broad shoulders, wide stance and the hilt of a sword poking out above his left shoulder.

My breath catches in my throat.

Rina yanks me through the portal just as the figure reaches for me.

The world blurs into mist and light. We move through a tunnel of shimmering fog, the air thick with the smell of earth and magic. A low hum vibrates in my bones, resonant and alive. Tingling rushes through me, prickling at my fingertips, curling down my spine. My limbs feel… longer, stretched by unseen hands, as though the air itself is pulling me taller.

A strange warmth flickers along the sides of my head, sharp and insistent, and for a heartbeat I swear the shape of me isn't what it was. The hum grows louder, pressing against my skull, until all I can do is breathe and push forward.

Then a bright light. When the mist parts, a small stone cottage emerges from the haze, its windows glowing like lanterns against the night. Nestled at the base of a towering, forested mountain, it looks as though it grew from the earth itself. Ivy clings to its stone walls, and smoke drifts from the chimney in lazy spirals, carrying the faint promise of warmth.

But it's the sky that steals my breath. The full moon hangs impossibly close, so bright and vast it feels like I could reach up and touch its silver-cratered face. Behind it, a massive tilted planet glows, painted in bands of sapphire, indigo, and molten gold, its colors shifting like liquid in the heavens. Threads of starlight weave through the sky, not fixed like constellations but moving, flowing as if the stars themselves are alive. Hues of violet, rose, and emerald ripple faintly in the atmosphere, like an aurora that never ends.

It's beautiful. Unreal. Like stepping into a dream spun from color and light.

The cottage looks safe, inviting, like a storybook illustration brought to life. But this is no fairytale. When I glance back, the portal is gone, no shimmer, no trace, only shadows where it once stood. And with it, the figure cloaked in mist.

Who was he?

Chapter 2: Impossible to Breathe

Vera

"This is my home," Rina says softly. "We're safe. For now."

I shudder. "Th-there was a guy," I whisper hoarsely. "Coming up the stairs…"

"I felt him too," Rina says grimly. "But hopefully he won't find us. Not yet."

Inside the kitchen, no bigger than my bedroom at home, a wooden table sits in the center with two chairs tucked neatly against it. Her house feels strange but oddly comforting.

Dried herbs, lavender, rosemary, and others I can't name, hang from the ceiling in neat bunches. Crystals nestle in the corners of window sills, glowing faintly when the sunlight touches them. A vine creeps along one of the kitchen walls, and for a second, I swear it shifts like it's breathing.

I step carefully into a small sitting room surrounded by shelves. Books line every inch, some so worn their titles have disappeared, others etched with symbols that look ancient and hum with energy when I get too close. One book's cover twitches, and I stumble back before convincing myself it's just my imagination.

In the center of the living room sits a shallow bowl of water with flower petals floating across its surface. The colors of the petals are familiar, deep purple, fiery orange, muted gold and my chest tightens with memory.

It's not creepy. Just… strange. Like she lives by a set of rules the rest of the world forgot.

"Veralyn."

Her voice pulls me back. Turning, I find Rina standing by the kitchen, the sword gone and some of her gear now shed, revealing more of herself.

She's about the same height as me, my mother was just a little shorter but there's something more substantial about her. Her auburn hair has strands that seem to catch the last rays of the sun, glinting like live embers. Stormy gray eyes, dusted with silver flecks, study me with a piercing, almost too-knowing look.

Her skin has a faint silvery shimmer, like moonlight trapped just beneath her surface.

She wears a black, form-fitting tank top, the kind meant for training. And peeking out from the left side, curling around her ribs and shoulder, I catch a glimpse of something. A tattoo.

The part I can see looks like the thick trunk of a tree, the lines bold and flowing like the tree is alive on her skin. The branches stretch upward, thicker and fewer than the wild tangled trees I'm used to, their ends weaving into a shape that almost looks like… a crown. It's so subtly worked into the design, it could almost be missed if you weren't looking closely, like it grew there naturally.

Rina follows my gaze and just smiles sadly, as if she already knows the questions racing through me. They must have used the same artist, my parents had tattoos like that. Sometimes I swore they moved when they held each other.

"Why do you keep calling me that?" My voice cracks. "My name is

Vera."

"Okay, you're right. I'm sorry." She moves quietly around the tiny kitchen, filling a hand-painted tea kettle and setting it on the stove. "I know this is a lot. I can't imagine what you're feeling right now. When you're ready, I'd love to explain everything."

I shift, my fingers picking at the worn wood of the table, the grain and color too much like the trees I left behind, where my parents had laid, cold and gone. The pain rises so sharp I almost choke on it.

Rina moves with quiet efficiency, grinding dried herbs in a stone bowl as the kettle begins to hum. She doesn't press me, just lets the silence stretch.

Finally, in a voice so small it barely feels like mine, I whisper, "Where are my parents?"

Without responding, she walks over and sets a mug in front of me. The faint clink of ceramic against the wooden table feels too loud in the stillness between us. I pour a little honey into the steaming tea, the golden ribbon disappearing as I stir.

I watch the tea swirl around, colors bleeding together in slow, lazy spirals. The scent of lavender, chamomile, and lemon rises up in a soft cloud, wrapping around me, wrapping around the ache lodged deep in my chest.

"Your parents were brought to the Reverence Hall," Rina says gently, her voice a whisper over the rim of her cup. "It's a sacred place for guard members to be held until families are ready to give them a Guardian Honor funeral."

The spoon clinks against the side of my mug as I set it down, my fingers trembling slightly. She's really not making a lot of sense.

"Can we visit them?" My voice is so thin it feels like it might break apart.

Her eyes soften, the stormy gray of them calming to a heavy mist. Unshed tears gleam in her lashes, making it harder for me to hold back my own.

A lump forms hard in my throat, making it almost impossible to breathe.

"Of course, when you're ready, whenever you want," she says, her voice soft but heavy with sorrow. "Where they're resting, you can visit anytime. When it feels right, we'll plan a proper farewell, a grand one, the kind they deserve. The Veilfire Grounds aren't far from here, it's where Guardians are honored, their spirits carried home through the Veilfire."

I didn't even know what to say to that. The silence stretches between us, thick and heavy. We sit with it, slowly sipping our tea that grows cold in our hands. The mug feels too heavy now, the floral taste turning bitter on my tongue.

"Your mom and I were like best friends growing up," Rina says after a long moment, her voice soft and faraway, like she's talking more to herself. "Of course I was younger, so maybe I just idolized her. But we were inseparable." She smiles faintly, her eyes distant.

"We moved to this cottage when we were little girls. It's hard to imagine really. We were only ten and twelve when our father sent us here. We lived here, just the two of us."

"Just the two of you? Why would your father send you away?"

"That's the thing, no one knew. He said we were in danger." Her fingers trace the rim of her cup absently. "Our mother passed away when I was born. Then one day our father changed, he was paranoid and worried. After that he sent us here and we never heard from him again."

The faint hum of the refrigerator kicks on in the background, the sound oddly grounding.

"But your mom? She was a rock," Rina continues, her smile turning bittersweet. "She took care of us. We enrolled in school under fake names. It was always just us, trying to piece together what happened, but we never found the answers. We never traveled back to our home to find out. Life stayed the same until your mom turned eighteen, enrolled in Auravale Academy and met your dad."

"She always said it was love at first sight," I say, my voice catching, "that they just knew."

Rina laughs, a bright, tinkling sound that cuts through the sadness like a bell.

"She did. She tried to push him away, of course. Tried to keep us safe. But your dad?" She shakes her head fondly. "He was relentless. Nothing—not even your mom's stubbornness—was going to keep him away."

She smiles wider. "When they passed the Order, your father was sworn into his position, and they got married. I know I have pictures somewhere."

"I would love to see them," I rasp out, my throat raw around the words.

Rina moves quickly, a flash of movement as she crosses the room to the bookshelves.

She pulls down two thick books with cracked leather covers, worn soft with age and use. She handles them like they're treasure.

Settling back beside me, she opens one. We flip through pages filled with moments frozen in time.

One photo catches my breath: my mother, looking about my age, her face lit up with a carefree smile. She stands next to a younger version of Rina, a bustling market behind them, colorful vendor tents flapping in the breeze.

In another, my dad gazes down at my mom like she hung the stars just for him. I reach out and run my finger over the photograph, the glossy surface cold and smooth under my touch.

Then there's a picture taken at night, a fire burning behind them, painting their faces gold and crimson. They're locked in an embrace, the flames casting long shadows behind them.

"That was their Veilfall Festival," Rina whispers, her own voice thick with memory. "They were embracing as they felt their fated marks forming."

"Their… fated marks?"

She nods. "Yeah. Their tattoos? The ones on their arms?"

I shake my head slowly. "I thought they just got matching tattoos when they were younger."

"No." Rina closes the album gently, like sealing away something sacred. "Those appear when you meet your fated. And on the night of the Veilfall Festival in your eighteenth year, you get your mark, who you are meant to be. And when you meet your fated, another mark appears."

Fated.

Veilfall.

Marks.

The words swirl in my mind, foreign and frightening, like they're part of a language I was never taught.

Rina sighs, the sound tired and sad. When I look up, I catch something in her expression: pity, yes, but also fierce sympathy. I hate both.

"Vera, I know this is confusing," she says gently. "Your parents were meant to tell you everything. I don't know why they didn't, but if you'll let me, I'll explain. You can ask anything you need. I'll tell you everything I know."

Her voice is so kind, so real, that something inside me softens. That same warm golden breeze brushes against me, the strange sensation deep in my chest that tells me: she's telling the truth.

"What happened? Why are they dead? Who killed my parents?" My voice shakes as the words tumble out.

"I'm so sorry," Rina says softly. "I don't know. But we'll find out, I swear it. I know that doesn't make the hurt easier right now."

"Who was that? Who was in my house, coming into my room?" The whisper scrapes from my throat.

"I don't know," she admits. "Whoever he was, he was tied to your parents. If he came for them… he'll come for you too. We need answers, Vera, and we'll find them. There's so much more I need to tell you, I just—" Her voice falters. "I only wish I had their help to do it."

"I think, for now I want to go lay down." I don't think I can hear anymore even if I really need to.

"Of course, just tell me when you're ready to hear more." The chair scrapes quietly against the floor as she stands. She picks up my bag and leads me down a narrow hallway lined with faded pictures in dusty frames.

There are three doors. She stops at the first one and opens it slowly.

The room is small, tucked under a low window where light filters in weakly. A twin-sized bed sits beneath it, the blanket worn thin and faded green. A battered wooden dresser stands against the wall, the knobs mismatched like they were replaced over the years.

She sets my bag down carefully, almost tenderly.

"This was your mom's room," she says softly. "I know it's not much, but we can go into town tomorrow and get anything you need. The bathroom's right across the hall. Feel free to shower. I'll start dinner. Just call if you need anything."

I nod, but it feels mechanical, like I'm moving through water.

When she leaves, the room is swallowed by silence. I plop down onto the bed, the mattress stiff and unyielding, pressing into my back. I stare up at the cracked ceiling, trying to hold myself together.

The scent of old wood and dust is thick here, filling my lungs and coating my tongue. The images of my parents flash behind my eyes, the way they used to laugh, the way they always made the world seem safe.

Now all I feel is the hollow space where they used to be. Was this the surprise they promised? Coming here? Being left alone?

Chapter 3: Fae? Like the Mythical Creatures?

Vera

A sharp knock jolts me upright. My heart stutters against my ribs. The door, slightly yellowed with age, shudders faintly in the frame.

I scan the small room again. The chipped paint, the dresser with only three drawers, the closed door that must lead to a closet.

"Sweet girl, dinner is ready," Rina says softly. Not Mom. Not the familiar voice that would float up the stairs every night calling me to dinner.

The sob breaks free before I can stop it. Tears pour down my face, hot and unrelenting, soaking into the scratchy blanket beneath me. I bury my face into the pillow, but it does nothing to muffle the raw, aching sounds tearing from my throat.

I don't even hear Rina come in. I only feel her arms wrap tightly around me, her hand stroking my hair.

"I'm so sorry," she whispers, voice shaking with her own grief.

I don't know how long we sit like that, my body wracked with shudders. When the storm finally passes and the sobs taper into quiet hiccups, I lift my head. Rina's eyes are red and swollen too, her own tears drying into salt tracks on her cheeks.

We sit in silence, grieving together, two pieces of the same shattered family.

"Come on, dinner will get cold." Standing up, we both wipe the tears from our faces. My skin feels tight and sticky from crying, my head pounding with exhaustion. I trail after her out of the small room, the creaky floorboards beneath our feet groaning with every step.

The moment we step into the kitchen, I'm hit by a wall of warmth and the rich, savory scent of something hearty and familiar. A pot bubbles gently on the stove, sending out waves of rosemary, thyme, and something smoky I can't quite place. My stomach growls loud enough that I know Rina hears it, but she doesn't say anything, just gives a small, understanding smile.

Rina pulls a couple of chipped ceramic bowls down from the cupboard. They clink softly as she stacks them on the counter. I watch her stir the wooden spoon through a thick stew, the hearty contents swirling in the cast iron pot, releasing more mouth-watering aromas.

She scoops the stew, chunks of tender beef, bright orange carrots, soft potatoes, and bits of onion swimming in a dark, fragrant broth into the bowls and sets one in front of me. The heat rises up, fogging the edges of the bowl and warming my chilled hands.

She places a small plate of buttered rolls between us, the golden tops glistening. The scent of the fresh bread mingles with the stew, and for a moment, I just breathe it all in, grounding myself in something normal, something real.

Rina sits across from me, her chair scraping slightly against the old wood floor.

"You know," she says, tearing a piece of her roll and dipping it into her stew, "this is the first time I've cooked for anyone since your parents left. Not that I was ever a big fan of cooking, but..." she shrugs, her voice soft, "it's almost therapeutic. Brings back memories."

I manage a smile, swirling my spoon through the broth. "My mom wasn't a huge fan of cooking either," I say quietly. "But she used to say the same thing. She would cook most afternoons while I trained with my dad. Then she'd call us in for dinner, hearing you call me earlier, it just…" I swallow hard, blinking against the sting in my eyes. "It reminded me of her."

Rina reaches out and brushes her fingers lightly over my knuckles, grounding me again. "Don't ever be sorry for feeling your emotions," she says, her voice steady but warm. "You just went through something unimaginable. You have to let yourself feel it, Vera. Just don't drown in it."

I pause, spoon hovering over my bowl. My eyes lift to meet hers, those same stormy gray eyes my mother had.

"My mom used to say that," I whisper.

A soft chuckle rumbles from Rina. "I know," she says. "She told me the same thing when we were growing up."

We eat in silence for a few minutes, the only sound the clinking of our spoons and the quiet crackle of the old heater kicking on in the corner. The warmth seeps into my bones, dulling the sharp edges of my grief just enough to breathe again.

After a while, Rina sets her spoon down with a soft clink and leans back in her chair. Her fingers tap a slow rhythm on the table, like she's trying to find the right words. I sense the shift before she speaks, like the air itself is holding its breath.

"There's a lot you don't know, Vera," she says at last, her voice low and careful. "About your parents. About why they left, why they were planning to bring you back."

I set my spoon down, heart thudding so hard I can feel it in my fingertips.

"I think it's time you knew the truth. There is so much, I don't know where to start."

Surprise. Shock. I think those are the only things I am feeling right now. But mostly I feel betrayed.

"You were born here. In Sylvaeris. Your father was the Head Guard sworn in to protect the current king."

"King? Sylvaeris? Are you making this up?" I demand. This is insane.

"No, it's not made up. I talked to your mom, she got a hold of me a few months ago, that was the first time I have heard from her in over 17 years." She chokes up a little. "She explained that they didn't teach you anything about where you came from, mostly because they didn't want you accidentally sharing anything but then they didn't know how. I know they felt guilty for keeping it from you for so long. She was worried about how you would take the news. They should have told you."

I sit there quietly staring at her. Waiting for her to start laughing. Like this is some joke.

"You were born Veralyn Caelith, but when you moved they just shortened your name so no one would find you as easily. I know it's a lot. Your mother knew it would be a lot to explain. Her and I went by the last name Cale when we first came here. So they kept that name thinking people would be looking for Caelith. I wish they hadn't withheld everything from you. Obviously you know about some of your gifts, she told me that she would make you Veilbrew Elixir every night?"

Veilbrew Elixir? "Umm, I don't know what that is. Why would you need to hide you're identity?"

"It's a type of drink kind of like tea. Not very many fae even know about it. We had to hide because something bad happened to our father and the King thought that maybe someone would come after us. Your mother would take care of us and make us tea, especially the Veilbrew Elixir to help conceal us. Over time it felt like no one was even paying attention to us so we slowly stopped taking it."

There is too much to unpack here. I don't know where to start asking questions.

"She did like to make tea every night. She would do this weird thing as she would make it, like talking to it. I never heard what she said but when I asked her she would say, 'just thinking out loud."

"That was probably it, I was thinking we would continue making something like it, maybe a little weaker."

"Why would I need it?"

"Your parents were going to bring you home. Since it's your 18th year, they wanted you to join Auravale Academy to get your full fae calling. Plus it being your 18th Veilfall, so you will get full access to your powers and your marks. The Veilfall is always more powerful when in Sylvaeris."

"None of this is making sense. You don't make sense, is this all a joke?" I demand, standing so abruptly my chair scrapes across the floor, nearly toppling backward.

Rina startles, eyes widening before sympathy fills her stormy gaze.

She exhales slowly, fingers threading into her auburn hair as she twists it into a ponytail. That's when I see it—points poking out over the crown of her head. My breath catches. Her ears. I never noticed until now. They're longer, sharper, unmistakably inhuman.

"Your ears! They're pointy!"

Her hands fly up instinctively, then she smiles, almost sheepish. "Yeah, my hair's too thick you don't see them unless my hair is up. They always poke out, more obviously like this."

"But… they're pointy."

"Yes," she says with a soft laugh. "Just like yours."

The world tilts. My skin prickles. "Mine?" My hands fly up to feel my ears. I slowly slide my fingertips up and there they are. Two points that were never there before.

"How?"

"Because your fae. When we cross the border into the human realm they disappear so we can blend in with the humans. But when cross back into our realm they come back."

"Seriously, this is all some kind of joke." Rina's smile fades into something gentler, steadier. She shakes her head, her voice quiet but firm.

"No, it's not a joke. I wish more than anything your parents were here to explain this to you, to help you through it. I'm sorry you're hearing it from me instead. I know it's too much, too fast, and it isn't fair—but you're not alone in this."

"Fae? Like the mythical creatures? Faeries? I'm supposed to believe that?"

"Well not mythical but yes. We are faeries, this is why you have truth sense and sense people's abilities and you seem to do it well even though your not 18 yet. That was something that your mother and I could do as well, it runs strong in our family bloodlines."

I get up and look at the pictures of my parents I was looking at before. There they are the pointy ears, how did I miss that? I was just looking at their faces, the way they looked at each other. A kind of love that was timeless, never fading.

"This is too much." I storm off to my room, slamming the door behind me.

Throwing myself face down onto the dusty, uncomfortable bed, I scream into the pillow, muffled and raw.

Fae. Royal. Gifts. The words echo in my head like they belong in a fantasy novel, not my life. And yet I can't shake the feeling that she's telling the truth. Every part of me feels it. I just don't understand how any of this is possible, how everything I thought I knew about myself could be so wildly, irreversibly wrong.

Needing something familiar, I pull open my bag and start digging through the few things I brought. A pair of worn ticket stubs from plays I saw with my mom. Postcards from museums, corners bent and faded. A simple necklace she gave me last Christmas, silver, with a tiny crescent moon charm. I let it dangle between my fingers, grounding myself in the pieces of a life that suddenly feels a world away.

Lastly, I pull out the picture. The three of us, laughing in front of a ridiculous dinosaur backdrop at a museum. My dad's arm slung heavy and warm across my shoulders, like he always did, as if he could anchor me to the world with one hand. My mom's smile is so radiant it seems to light up the whole photo, her lilac hued eyes just like my own are shining brighter than any flash could capture.

I trace their faces with my thumb, remembering how my mom made us pose with the T. rex even though Dad groaned about how cheesy it was. I'd laughed so hard when he tried to mimic the dinosaur's claws. We'd ended up doubled over, laughing until our stomachs hurt, Mom snapping the photo at just the right second.

Now it's only me, staring at this frozen moment, the echo of their laughter stretching across a lifetime that feels too short. The paper crinkles in my hands as my chest tightens, the memory equal parts warmth and ache.

Chapter 4: This Is All So Crazy

Vera

It's been almost twenty-four hours since I lost everything I thought I knew. My entire world had flipped upside down, and it hadn't even been a full day.

I didn't know what to do or think. I felt frozen. I felt lost. But I could almost hear my dad's voice in my head: Push forward.

And my mom's gentler reminder: It's okay to feel, just don't drown in it. We're fighters. Always have been. We don't quit. We turn pain into strength. After a tense, silent breakfast, Rina finally broke the quiet.

"We need to do some shopping," she said briskly, setting her coffee mug down. "You start school at Auravale on Monday, and you can't wear just training clothes."

As we drive into town, I notice several things all at once. First, this whole region is swallowed in thick forest. Green stretches endlessly, a living sea of pine and oak broken only by the winding ribbon of road beneath us. The scent of damp earth and resin drifts through the cracked window.

Second, the sky. At first it looks almost normal—blue and clear—but the light is softer, tinged with a faint rose-gold hue. Their star burns closer than the sun I knew, a red dwarf that stains the daylight in subtle warmth, as if the world itself has been brushed with watercolor. And there, looming in plain sight, is the massive tilted planet I glimpsed last night. Even under the day sky, its bands of cobalt and bronze shimmer faintly, like a mural painted across the heavens.

Third, the town itself looks like something out of a storybook.

The town felt surreal as we stepped out of the car. Quaint and impossibly charming, like it had been plucked straight from a painting. Old brick roads, uneven with age, wound between colorful storefronts. Balconies draped with flower boxes leaned over the streets, their iron railings curling in delicate patterns. Wooden signs in elegant, swirling calligraphy swung in the mild breeze, their paint faded just enough to suggest they'd been there for centuries.

Shops like *Lily & Laurel*, *Everhart Books*, and *The Stitched Fable* lined the street, their windows decorated with hand-drawn gold lettering and displays of woven scarves, rare books bound in strange metals, and carved trinkets that seemed to hum faintly when you walked past.

Further down, the buildings shifted—newer constructions blending with the old. Sleek condos of dark green and deep wood rose above the shopfronts, their facades softened by ivy and delicate silver blossoms that shimmered faintly in the fading light.

The air smelled faintly of fresh bread, blooming jasmine, and something woodsy, like cedar and sage. The soft murmur of conversations and the clinking of dishes floated from cozy cafés tucked between shops, where lanterns already glowed warm despite the daylight.

As we walked, something caught my attention. Almost everyone was tall. Women, girls, even older men, graceful, long-limbed, impossibly elegant. It wasn't just a few people; it was everyone. For once, I didn't feel like a giant. Instead, I felt like I belonged,   until I looked closer.

Pointed ears peeked through cascades of hair, auburn, silver, black, every shade glinting under the sun. Some faces were too symmetrical, cheekbones cut high and sharp, eyes luminous like polished glass. They moved with an ease that made me stumble in comparison. My chest tightened as I stole glance after glance, trying not to gawk.

Maybe I had stepped into another world entirely. Maybe I wasn't dreaming at all.

We ducked into a boutique that smelled like lavender and clean linen. I stuck to practical choices, comfortable dresses, comfortable leggings I loved so much and a few tops in soft, earthy colors. Nothing flashy. I'd never been the mini-skirt or designer-label type. Just clothes that felt like me.

On the way to lunch, a ripple of loud laughter caught my ear. I looked up, and my heart stumbled. A group of boys about my age lounged against a stone wall, their easy grins and broad shoulders making them stand out like they owned the street.

One of them locked eyes with me. Sandy-blonde hair, tousled like he lived in the sun but styled just enough to look intentional. His ears, sharper than mine, more defined, caught the light, a subtle reminder that I wasn't the only one carrying the strange new feature. Did that mean something? Did it mark him as different somehow?

Then his eyes, so vivid a green they almost glowed. He didn't just glance; he studied me. His gaze swept down my body before snapping back to my face, like he'd been caught but didn't care. Something about the way he looked at me, intent, unblinking, like I was a puzzle he needed to solve, sent a shiver racing down my spine.

Before I could think too much about it, Rina tugged my arm, steering me into a small restaurant. The door chimed softly as we entered, the scent of roasting meat and spices enveloping us.

The waitress, a plump woman with silver hair and a kind smile, greeted Rina like an old friend.

"And who's this?" she asked, eyeing me curiously.

"Vera," my aunt answered simply, her voice clipped. Something she told me might happen. People are curious. Nosy. We decided it would be best to say she is a guardian hosting me, that sometimes guards do that for students coming here for the academy and didn't have anywhere to stay.

The rest of lunch passed in a blur. After we ate, we retraced our steps through town. The boy with green eyes was gone, though part of me searched for him anyway, feeling strangely hollow when I didn't see him.

Rina led me into a tiny shop tucked between two ivy-covered buildings. The sign above the door reading: *The Verdant Nook*. The smell of dried herbs, wax, and something sharper, almost metallic, hung heavy in the air. Inside, bundles of flowers and leaves dangled from the rafters, brushing my shoulders as we passed.

Rina pulled a folded list from her pocket and grabbed a wicker basket, moving efficiently between shelves.

I trailed her, reading the hand-lettered signs:

Lunar Bloom Petals – for muting eyes.

Ashenmint – for cloaking auras without compromising internal strength.

Helleaf – for shielding magical signatures.

Lindenflower – for soothing the body.

Starroot Shavings – for syncing herbs together to strengthen a fae's magic.

I stayed silent, just observing as she selected handfuls of each. The elderly woman behind the counter watched us curiously but said nothing as she rang us up, the papery crackle of the bags sounding loud in the quiet shop.

Back in the car, I turned to Rina. "What was all that for? I've never heard of any of it."

"It's for the Veilbrew Elixir. They'll help conceal your true identity without taking away your gifts," she explained.

"Your mom would have been giving you similar potions most nights. Whatever she could have found in the human realm. It would have protected you without you even knowing. This way, at school, no one will be able to sense who you are."

I frowned. "But how would people even know?"

"Most wouldn't. But those who knew your mother would recognize you immediately. And those with gifts in aura reading, they'd sense that something was different. We can't risk that while you're still training."

I stared out the window as she spoke, the dense forest swallowing the narrow road ahead. My chest felt tight, my heart a tangled mess of confusion and longing.

"I don't understand any of this."

Rina's voice softened. "I know you don't. And I'm sorry. Hiding who you are, it's a heavy burden to carry. I had your mother by my side when we first went into hiding. But you—" she shook her head, voice thick with emotion. "I can't imagine how hard that must be. But you're not alone. I'm here, Vera. I'm not going anywhere. We'll figure this out together." I didn't answer. I just stared out at the blur of trees and cottages flashing past.

We passed a hand-carved sign that read:

The Grove of Stars – 2 Miles.

"What's the Grove of Stars?" I asked.

Rina smiled faintly. "It's the name of the castle. It's where the royal family lives. They hold council meetings there and sometimes they host events for the kingdom. The head guard has a home on the property, but the rest of the Guard, like me, live over here."

"Did my parents live there?"

"Yes," she said after a beat. "After your father was sworn in, they lived there until you were born."

I could feel her holding something back, but I didn't push. Not yet. I had a million questions swirling in my mind and somehow, none at all. Back at Rina's cottage, I unpacked my bags methodically, like staying busy could anchor me.

I tossed new clothes into the washer, sorted fresh bedding, and stacked my books neatly on the desk she'd cleared for me.

History of Sylvaeris.

Herbal Infusion.

Known Gifts.

She had told me that these were the kinds of things every fae child grew up learning. She wanted me to be ready. She wanted me to fit in at Auravale Academy, even if it broke her heart to have to prepare me like this. I brushed my fingers across the worn covers, feeling a surge of anger, confusion, and heartbreak. Why hadn't my parents taught me any of this?

Why had they hidden who I was? I wished for answers. But more than that, I wished I could still ask them myself.

Later that night, Rina came into help me put away my new things and make my bed. I finally asked, "So this academy… what's it like?"

Rina sat on the bed, her gray eyes thoughtful. "Think of it like a university. You'll study elemental magic, of course but also history, combat, diplomacy, and magical theory. For those who qualify, there's the Veilbound Order, an elite program within the Guard."

My heart skipped. "That's what you did?"

She nodded once. "It's where your mother and I trained. And your father, he was there to be the Head Guard."

The air left my lungs in a whoosh.

"Then that's what I want. If it can help me figure out what happened, who did this, then that's all I want. I want to find out who killed my parents."

Rina's eyes softened. "You'll have to work harder than you ever have. The Order is grueling physically, and mentally. Not everyone makes it through." She doesn't know that I have been training all my life. That I spent my entire life of mornings and afternoons training. I didn't have a life outside of school.

"Good," I said fiercely. "Then it's exactly where I need to be."

She studied me for a long moment, then gave a solemn nod. "Then we'll make sure you're ready. You start on Monday. But you must keep your true identity and your abilities secret."

Something inside me shifted then. A steely thread weaving into my heart.

"This elixir we're going to make will dull your eyes," Rina explained as she measured out shimmering powders and dried herbs into a ceramic bowl. "Your mom had purple eyes, too. Very unique in our world. They would be identifying. This will keep them purple, but not so vivid. It should also mask the gold specks." The scent of crushed herbs and something metallic filled the small kitchen, tickling my nose. I leaned closer, fascinated.

"It will also dull your aura. Some fae can read auras like open books, and others can sniff out magical abilities before you even cast a spell. We don't want anyone seeing what you're truly capable of yet. As for your abilities, they'll be unaffected. If anything," she smiled, a bit mischievously, "it might even sharpen them. Especially now that your back home in Sylvaeris."

"You said at the festival I'll get access to more powers?" I asked, curiosity stirring beneath the weariness clinging to my bones.

"Yes. Every fae, on their eighteenth year at the Veilfall, gains full access to their gifts. Auravale is meant to teach us how to wield those gifts properly, and help choose career paths. Many enroll just to train for the Veilbound Order, passing their tests is an honor."

"If I do that, will I have to be part of the guard?" A tight knot formed in my stomach. I wanted to make my family proud, but was that the right path for me?

"No. Many do it purely for the training. And honestly, Vera," Rina's voice softened, "I just want you to be able to defend yourself if anything happens. That's all that matters right now."

"So, my dad was the head of the guard. What about my mom?" I asked, voice barely above a whisper.

Her stormy gray eyes filled with warmth. "She was head of recruiting. I took over that position after they left."

A lump formed in my throat. "Back home, I was always bigger and stronger, even against the boys at school. I never understood why my parents made me sit out of sports or made me hold back in gym class. My dad would just say, "it wouldn't be fair."

Rina laughed, a rich, rolling sound that filled the small room with light. "No, I imagine it wouldn't be fair at all, the poor human boys when you're faster, stronger, and more agile." Her laughter was infectious. Despite everything, I found myself chuckling too. The heaviness lifted, just a little.

"My dad worked out with me every day. He built this crazy obstacle course in our backyard. Every morning—rain, snow, or shine—I had to run it. After school, self-defense lessons."

"He was preparing you," Rina said with a proud nod. "Preparing you for the Order all along. We'll continue the tradition, morning and after-school training. You'll be ready."

"This is all so crazy," I whispered.

Her eyes softened again. "Yes. It is. I am truly sorry. But you're not alone, we're going to figure this all out together." She squeezed my shoulder gently, and I felt the weight of her words.

We said our goodnights, and later, I lay in bed staring at the ceiling. The moonlight spilled across the rough wooden floor, painting everything in ghostly silver. The room smelled faintly of fresh linen and the lingering sweetness of herbs.

I could hear the distant rustling of leaves outside the window and the occasional creak of the old house settling into the night. I pull out my box and slowly sift through the ticket stubs and museum postcards, each one an echo of the life I lost. These are all I have left, all that still ties me to who I was before. I miss my parents fiercely. I wish I could ask them everything. I wish they were here to tell me what to do next.

As I finally fell asleep, it wasn't my parents I was picturing. But those vivid green eyes I seen in town. I've never seen eyes like that before. The way they were assessing me, just remembering creates little goose bumps all over my flesh.

Chapter 5: Okay, Let's Go!

Vera

There was a soft knock at the door. "Vera, time to get up for training," Rina called gently. "I'll get the tea ready."

My heart stuttered. For a moment, half-asleep, I'd wished it was my dad's voice. I forced myself out of bed, muscles stiff, and stumbled toward the bathroom. The tile was cool under my feet, the water from the faucet cold and sharp on my skin, helping me wake up a little more.

Back in my room, I threw on fitted black leggings and a simple tank top. Practical, easy to move in. I braided my hair tightly down my back, keeping it out of the way. The house smelled like mint and something earthy.

I wandered into the kitchen and found Rina at the counter, her back was to me. She turned just as I stepped in, handing me a mug without a word. The steam curled up in soft, lazy spirals, wrapping around my face like a gentle touch. Whatever was in the cup smelled earthy, calming, something between spiced tea and sun-warmed moss.

Rina was dressed simply, yet somehow she still looked like she belonged on the cover of a nature magazine. A pair of fitted charcoal leggings hugged her legs, and a dark sage sports bra revealed the kind of strength that doesn't shout, just quietly exists. The early morning sun glinting off the silver streaks in her hair and her hair was pulled up, a few strands escaping in soft waves that framed her face with her pointy ears poking out.

Then I saw it. The ink. Drawn across her left side, where her ribs curved into her waist, was a tattoo unlike anything I'd ever seen. It wasn't just a design, it felt *alive*. At its base, where the lines rooted deep like a tree pressed into her skin, ancient-looking symbols were etched with striking precision. I didn't recognize the characters, couldn't name them, but I *felt* them. Earth. Air. Water. Fire. Each element hummed at the edge of my senses as if my blood remembered even if my mind didn't.

The ink itself wasn't a flat black, it shimmered subtly with color, like old magic caught in light. Threads of soft gold glinted like sunlight through leaves. Forest greens whispered through the roots and branches. Ocean blues curved like hidden currents. And flickers of fire-orange burned through it all, dancing when she moved. It looked less like a tattoo and more like the essence of something wild and sacred woven into her flesh.

Encircling it all was a thick border of braided vines and blooming flowers, interlaced with thorns. The vines weren't uniform, they wrapped around each other in careful chaos, stronger together than alone. The whole design felt *protective*, like a living ward. Something meant to shield and honor, not just decorate.

I couldn't stop staring.

The tattoo didn't scream power. It radiated it. Quietly, patiently. Like the kind of strength you never question because it doesn't need to prove itself.

Rina caught me looking and gave me a knowing smile and turned back to the stove, as if this magic she carried was no big deal. As if it hadn't just completely redefined what I thought a person could wear on their skin.

"This is my mark," Rina said softly, her fingers brushing the glowing ink as if it were an old friend. "I received it at my Veilfall. Every fae does. It's part of our coming of age, when the veil between who we were and who we are meant to be thins, and the truth of our magic settles into our skin."

Her gaze flicked toward me, gentle but steady. "The mark carries our bloodline, but it also becomes uniquely ours. A reflection of the magic within us, our strengths, our place in the world. Some marks reveal their lineage first, then blossom into their full form at Veilfall. Others emerge all at once. No two are ever the same. They're as singular as our souls."

She turned back to the stove with a quiet shrug, as though it wasn't extraordinary at all. But the way the vines shimmered when she moved, the way the colors seemed alive, told me otherwise.

"Drink up. It's Starleaf Tea," she said. "It'll sharpen your focus, give you steady energy."

I took a tentative sip. The taste was clean like the first breath of fresh air after a rainstorm. Hints of sweet mint danced on my tongue, and something else too, something golden and warm, like swallowing sunlight. Almost immediately, warmth unfurled in my chest, spreading through my limbs. For the first time this morning, I felt truly awake. This is going to be my new daily routine, I love it. No more being dragged out of bed, cursing the morning.

"Okay, let's go!" Rina said with a bright smile.

We stepped outside, the morning air crisp and slightly damp with dew. The grass beneath my boots was slick, and the faint scent of pine from the surrounding trees hung thickly in the air. The yard wasn't big, more of a clearing carved out of the woods but it had a flat stretch of packed dirt, perfect for sparring.

"First, we warm up. Always," Rina said.

She led me through stretches, deep lunges, shoulder rolls, neck rotations, loosening stiff muscles. The air was chilly enough that my breath puffed in front of me in tiny white clouds.

Next, we moved into basic footwork drills.

- Guard up (hands protecting the face and ribs).
- Knees slightly bent, weight balanced.
- Eyes always on the opponent's center, not their eyes.

"Balance is everything. If you lose your footing, you lose the fight."

We practiced shifting weight quickly from one foot to the other, pivoting on the balls of our feet, moving forward, backward, side to side. The dirt shifted underfoot, and I had to work to stay nimble.

Then she demonstrated basic hand-to-hand stances.

"Watch the chest," she said, tapping her own sternum. "That's where the first twitch of movement happens. Not the face."

She came at me slow at first, light jabs toward my ribs, sweeps toward my knees, mock punches toward my face. When she jabbed I pulled, slipped and threw a hook that landed like a lighting strike. She came at me with a quick right left combo and managed to land her left hook, catching me right in the liver. I came back with an uppercut where I held back only gently hitting her chin.

The sounds of punches filled the small yard, the slap of hands meeting forearms, the soft shuffle of boots on dirt, the occasional grunt of exertion. Sweat started to bead on my forehead despite the cool air. After a few rounds, she upped the speed. Quick strikes, fakes, testing my reflexes.

"Good!" She praised when I sidestepped one particularly tricky feint.

She even threw in some grappling moves, teaching me how to break holds, lock joints, and sweep legs. Rina wasn't pulling her punches but she wasn't cruel either. Every movement was purposeful, meant to teach not to punish.

"You're strong," she said between bouts, slightly out of breath herself. "Stronger than most girls your age. Don't shy away from it. Own it."

By the time we finished, my muscles were singing, tired but alive. The clearing smelled of crushed grass, earth, and sweat. Birds chirped in the canopy overheard, and the sunlight had warmed the chill from the air.

"You did well," Rina said, clapping a firm hand on my shoulder. "We'll do it again tomorrow. Every day until you can take down someone twice your size." I didn't bother telling her the truth: I hadn't been training to win matches, I'd been learning how to be stronger than my father.

The first time I deflected one of his punches and flipped him to the ground, his face lit up like I'd just handed him the moon. I hadn't even realized my mom was standing in the doorway until I heard the slow clap behind me. Back then, I didn't know they were preparing me. I thought it was just a game. My dad's obsession. But now… now there was something more. A spark of purpose. A path I couldn't ignore. I would learn. I would train. And I would find out who was hunting me.

And when I did? They'd regret ever laying a hand on my family.

I wonder if I will make any friends. I wonder if I will meet someone at school that I could practice with. Maybe if I meet some others there training like me I could ask someone at school, someone much larger than me, preferably. I need the challenge, the preparation. Especially when I don't even know what I'm up against. The memory of the shadowed figure flashes in my mind. He was definitely large, that much I know. I don't even know if he's the one after me, or if he's the one who killed my parents, but every instinct tells me he had something to do with it.

The heavy clang of steel comes back to me. A broad sword had hung from his hip, the kind you'd expect in an old-world kingdom. Which, I guess, is exactly where I've landed.

"Rina, how many people carry swords here?" I ask, bending into a stretch beside her, feeling the pull of my hamstrings.

She hums thoughtfully, rolling her shoulders until they pop. "Hmm, I really don't know. I guess a lot of fae have them."

"So it's not just people in the guard?"

"No, anyone could have one. It's a common gift to congratulate those who finish the Veilbound Order. Not everyone gets into the guard."

"Okay." My palms press flat against the cool wooden floor as I fold deeper. "So I guess we can't narrow it down to just the guard."

"Why do you ask?"

"Because that shadowy figure had a sword. I was hoping we could narrow it down."

Rina exhales, stretching her arms overhead until her back arches. "Oh, yeah, I'm sorry, Sweet Girl. Lots of people have them. And as far as I know, the vampires and the shifters use them as well."

My head snaps up. "Shifters and vampires?!" The words tumble out sharper than I mean, bouncing off the walls.

Her head had been bowed in a long leg stretch, but she jerks up at my outburst. Her brows knit.

"Veils," she mutters, scrubbing a hand down her face. "I'm really trying not to spring everything on you. Everything's a shock. There's too much to explain." Her voice is as tight as mine, the frustration equal on both sides. "There are shifters and vampires, but they have their own realms. We don't see them, only the occasional rogues that somehow make it here."

Questions flood my mind like a dam breaking. My throat tightens. "I have so many questions. Why didn't they just tell me?" The heartbreak is clear in my voice, tangled with anger.

"I'm sorry." She shifts closer, her arm curling around me, pulling me against the warmth of her shoulder. Her scent is faintly floral, like crushed petals and smoke. "We're going to figure it all out, I promise. Just keep asking questions."

I nod against her shoulder, though my chest still aches.

"Rina?"

"Yes?"

"What is 'veils'?"

She bursts out laughing, the sound light and unexpected, breaking the tension. "It's a swear word, I guess. People use it when they're frustrated. It relates to our underworld, where the dead go."

"Oh." It slips from me hollowly. I feel untethered, lost in the dark, drifting with nothing to hold on to, and no clear place where I fit.

Chapter 5: Okay, Let's Go!

Chapter 6: Remember Who You Are

Vera

I walked the path through a sunlit forest, where towering trees arched overhead in a canopy of vibrant green. Strange blossoms I didn't recognize spilled along the edges, their colors brighter than any flowers I'd ever known, glowing faintly as if the forest itself was alive and watching. Above it all stretched a sky that stole my breath—blue, but brushed with a faint rose-gold cast from the red dwarf burning closer than the sun I grew up with. Its light made every leaf glimmer, every petal flare like stained glass. And there, hanging impossibly close, was the tilted planet I had seen the other night, its swirling bands of cobalt and bronze so massive they seemed to tilt the whole world beneath them.

It felt like walking through a dream, one I could never conjure on my own.

The school, if you could even call it that, loomed ahead like a fortress cloaked in shadow. Most of the massive structure was built from weathered brick that seemed to drink in the early morning light, making it feel older than time itself.

A newer building jutted out behind the school made of dark, polished woods that bled seamlessly into the forest just beyond its edges. Its steeply slanted roof bore the word *Echoforge*, carved in curling script into a wooden plaque above the entryway, as if the trees themselves had branded it.

And then there were the words above the main entrance, staring down at me like a verdict: Auravale Academy.

The whole school radiated a brooding elegance, tucked up in the crook of the mountains and half-swallowed by the forest. It looked less like a school and more like a castle, a place where secrets were kept and maybe born.

Students brushed past me without pause, like I didn't belong, which obviously, I didn't. A few shoulders bumped into mine without apology, while others stared openly like I had grown an extra head.

Great. Guess it's obvious I'm the new girl.

I sucked in a slow breath, my father's voice echoing in my mind, calm and sharp like flint: *"Remember who you are... but never show anyone the real you."*

I never knew exactly what he meant. Not really. But it kept me at arm's length from everyone I'd ever known. Steeling myself, I started up the wide stone steps. They stretched out before me like the path to something irreversible.

Inside, the school caught me off guard. Bright sunlight streamed through towering windows that reached nearly to the vaulted ceilings. The walls were pale, but splashed here and there with vibrant bursts of color, student paintings, tapestries, or maybe even enchantments, I wasn't sure. For a place that looked like a haunted manor on the outside, the inside pulsed with life. The life seemed to hum faintly beneath the surface, like it had soaked into the very stones of the building.

But something about it didn't feel right. The air was too still. The way students moved. Silent, too sure of themselves, too polished, it was like walking into a dream someone else had scripted.

The corridor branched wide, with offices on either side and a long hall stretching toward rows of lockers. As I made my way toward the one marked *Front Office*, I accidentally collided with a girl.

Tall. Pretty. She matched my height, which was rare. Her blue eyes narrowed at me with calculated disdain, platinum blonde hair spilling down her back like liquid silver.

"Watch it!" she snapped.

"Sorry," I mumbled, face heating.

I didn't want trouble. Not on the first day, anyway. I just want to get through this program. This Order. She strutted off, hips swaying in designer heels that had no right being that high or that graceful.

The office was quiet, save for the rhythmic hum of a printer and the soft slurp of coffee. The air smelled faintly of peppermint and paper. Behind the polished oak desk sat a middle-aged woman, her soft golden-brown skin catching the light from the stained-glass window behind her. Her chestnut hair was swept up into a practical twist, not a strand out of place, and her moss-green robes shimmered faintly with silver thread whenever she moved, like sunlight filtering through leaves.

Small, round glasses perched low on her nose, and warm hazel eyes peeked over them, sharp with intelligence and glinting with a hint of mischief. Despite the serene, orderly space around her, there was something earthy and grounding about her, like she belongs in a grove rather than behind a desk.

"Good morning, Dear. I see you've already met Cassia," she said, her melodic voice both soothing and amused. "Don't let her rattle you. You must be Vera."

I nodded, stepping forward. "Yes, I was told to stop here to get my locker number and schedule?"

Senara's eyes softened as she studied me, a knowing smile touching her lips. Then she leaned forward slightly, as if inspecting something invisible, something only she could sense.

"Wow, your eyes are beautiful," she murmured. "I haven't seen eyes like that since—"

"Good morning, Senara." A deep, velvety voice cut in from behind me.

Chills prickled down my arms. I didn't turn, but warmth blossomed in my chest without permission.

Since when? What was she going to say? I thought Rina said no one would be able to see the true color. As far as I knew, only my mom had these eyes. My chest tightened, grief flaring up like a flash fire. I shoved it back down. Did she know my mom? Does she know who I am?

Senara's smile lit up even more. "Good morning, Dear. How can I help you?"

I shifted aside instinctively, not daring to glance his way, though I felt the weight of his gaze tracing my frame like a touch. I stared hard at the papers in front of Senara. I don't know what this sensation is, but it is deeply unsettling. The day has barely started and I'm already drawing attention.

"You were here first," he said, his voice like thunder muffled by silk. It slid over me, warm and comforting. I kept my eyes down, determined not to blush. I don't understand this affect he is causing me to feel, I haven't even looked at him.

Senara looked between us, blinking like she'd forgotten where she was. "Right! Here is your locker number and combination. Come back in a few minutes and I'll have your schedule ready. I just need to finalize it and print it."

"Thank you," I said, taking the slip from her, my fingers brushing hers.

Still avoiding eye contact with him, I ducked out of the office. I found my locker quickly and opened it with a sigh. At least that seems to go my way easily. Pulling out a magnet and a worn photo of my parents, I stuck it inside. The ache returned, sharp and constant.

I will push through. For them. As I headed back toward the office, a group of guys loitered by the lockers, their easy laughter echoing down the hall.

One stood at the center without even trying. Everyone seemed to just gravitate around him. The kind of person who didn't just *occupy* space but *commanded* it.

Tall, broad-shouldered, and unmistakably confident, he moved with the loose, relaxed power of someone who knew exactly who he was. His sandy blond hair looked like it had been spun from sunlight, windswept and effortless, catching every flicker of light as he shifted.

But it was his eyes that truly caught me, sharp green threaded with gold, so bright they seemed to cut straight through the noisy hallway, straight through *me*. My steps faltered. It was him. The guy from town, the one I couldn't stop thinking about. The one I will never admit that I was fantasizing would come to my window and save me from this unknown threat.

For a moment, it was like the world narrowed to just those eyes, to the way they glowed faintly in the afternoon light, unsettling and mesmerizing all at once. My skin prickled, heat rushing to my cheeks, my ears, my fingertips. I didn't know if I should wave, smile, or *run*. Before I could decide, a girl bounded up, the same pretty blonde from this morning, and threw herself at him with an easy, possessive kind of affection.

He caught her without hesitation, laughing low in his throat as he staggered a step back to steady them.

The spell shattered. I looked away, heart hammering painfully against my ribs, my footsteps awkward and too loud in the suddenly too-bright hall. I ducked my head, cheeks still burning, and hurried the rest of the way to the office, embarrassment prickling across my skin.

When I returned, Senara handed me my schedule, full of strange classes. I can't believe any of this is real.

> *Veilbound Lore & Legacy*
> *Elemental Symmetry & Control*
> *Truthsense & Future Sight*
> *Kingdoms & Bloodlines: A Political History*
> *Runes & Relics*
> *Battlecraft & Elemental Synergy*

I wandered toward my first class in a daze. The hall narrowed, becoming more like a winding passage than a traditional school corridor. I passed doors etched with runes, some glowing faintly, others humming under my fingertips when I brushed against them. A prickling sensation crept up my spine.

This isn't right. This can't be real. It's all so strange.

The classroom was small, barely big enough for a dozen students. No posters or whiteboards, just stone walls and wooden desks carved with sigils and initials. It felt less like a school and more like a forgotten library or a sanctum.

I slid into a seat at the back, praying no one would notice me. The classroom smelled faintly of parchment and something herbal, maybe old ink or whatever strange things this academy used for writing supplies.

The bell rang at the same time, the door creaked open. I glanced up and the world seemed to shift. A man entered, moving with a kind of slow, deliberate grace that didn't belong to a classroom. Tall and lean, he carried himself like a shadow slipping through twilight, every step unsettlingly silent on the stone floors.

He wore a long robe of deep charcoal, embroidered with faint, archaic symbols that shimmered when he passed through a beam of light. His skin had a pale, muted glow, like he'd lived too long under cloudy skies. Even from where I sat, I could see the gloves, black leather, perfectly molded to his hands. Not a single patch of skin showed beneath his sleeves.

But it was his face that truly caught me. Sharp cheekbones, a jawline that looked almost sculpted, and a mouth set in a neutral line that hinted at secrets he'd never tell. His hair a dark brown so deep it looked black, was tied back neatly with a thin leather strip.

At the base of his neck glowed a mark, faintly silver in the light, an eye caught in a circle of mist. I couldn't stop looking. Something in it shifted, or maybe I only imagined it, the trailing lines curling into the shapes of hands. Reaching. Wanting. I had the uneasy sense that if I stared too long, it might start staring back.

Then there were his eyes. Pale gray, but not flat, alive with shifting flecks of silver that caught the light like water under the moon. They missed nothing. And gave nothing back. The temperature in the room seemed to dip when he walked in, a crisp bite to the air that had me pulling my sleeves down instinctively.

Around me, the low murmur of students dimmed, like a collective instinct to be quieter. Even the boy next to me straightened in his chair. I swore, out of the corner of my eye, I caught the faintest flicker of movement behind the man as if something unseen followed just a pace behind him. But when I blinked, there was nothing.

He paused when he walked in front of my desk, gently setting his things down. He nodded once to himself before he sat in the chair behind the desk. I let out a breath I hadn't realized I was holding. My heart was beating too fast, as if the air itself had grown thinner.

The sandy-haired guy from this morning slipped in right after, his tousled hair and easy grin a jarring contrast to the heavy presence that had just entered. His emerald eyes skimmed the room and landed on me. One corner of his mouth tipped up in a way that felt, intentional. Like he knew I would be in this room.

I looked down immediately, scribbling nonsense in the margins of my notebook.

"You're in my seat," a voice said.

My heart skipped again. But when I glanced up, he wasn't talking to me. He was addressing the boy beside me, who rolled his eyes and shifted. The sandy-haired guy dropped into the newly vacated seat next to mine with a low grunt, his shoulder brushing the edge of my space.

I stared hard at the front, where the teacher finally seemed to remember he had a job to do.

"Okay, guys. We're starting our discussion on the history of the Veyari," the professor said, his voice cutting through the quiet like a blade. No introduction. No warm-up. Just straight into it, like we were all supposed to know what *Veyari* even meant.

I scribbled notes furiously, my hand trembling slightly from the rush of anxiety. What if I missed something important? I could feel the sandy-haired guy beside me glancing over now and then, but I kept my head down. Letting my hair fall like a curtain between us, a thin veil of focus and pretend confidence.

He listed them off in one breath, like the four points of a compass: "Witches. Shifters. Vampires. Fae." There was a pause after the last word, as if he expected us to feel the weight behind them. And I did. I looked around briefly to see if he was joking and I was the only one falling for it.

"Each Veyari race," he explained, "had once ruled their own corner of the world, distinct, powerful, and deeply mistrustful of one another. Shifters bound to the moon and beast, vampires to blood and shadow. But it was the witches that seemed to make the Veyari's tense.

"They practiced an older craft," the professor continued. "Magic drawn not from nature, but bent to will. Alchemy, curses, hexes. What some fae historians deemed *unnatural manipulations* of life itself."

I stopped writing, just for a second.

"The fae," he added, "were born of the land. Our magic flows through stone and stream, wind and flame. It exists because the world allows it. But witchcraft, witchcraft *takes*. And so, long ago, a rift was formed. One not easily mended."

There was no hatred in his tone. Just fact. Old, bone-deep truths spoken aloud like warnings passed down in hushed voices. I looked down at the notes I'd been taking. My pen still hovered above the paper, unmoving. If witches were still out there, what happened to them? Were they hidden? Hunted? Or were they waiting? I wrote those down in my notes, something to think about later. Add to my ever growing list of questions.

Toward the end of class, the teacher's eyes found mine. He hesitated for a heartbeat, his expression unreadable. Before he could say anything, a throat cleared sharply next to me.

The teacher blinked, as if waking from a trance. "Right. Okay, class dismissed. I expect you to have read the first two chapters before next time." What next time? Tomorrow?

Chapter 7: One Dimple

Vera

As I am walking into the next class, Elemental Symmetry and Control, that same tall blonde girl from this morning waved in my direction, I panicked and took a seat near the front. I toss her an apologetic glance and it wasn't until a moment later that I realized she wasn't waving at me at all, she was waving to the guy behind me. The same one I keep bumping into. My stomach twisted. Of course she wasn't waving to *me*. I rolled my eyes at my own ridiculousness.

"Cae! Over here, I saved you a seat." She said with a sugary voice. It sounded fake to me but he must like it cause he smiled and walked right over to her. Taking the seat directly behind me, I can feel his gaze on the back of my neck, shooting tingles up my spine.

Cae. That name suited him. I felt this strange tingling when he passed by me. Another boy slid in next to me. He seemed to be bigger than the other one. More muscular and seemed to emit darkness.

"You must be new." He said, barely sparing me a glance. I am not even sure he is speaking to me. But then he turned my way and his eyes were so dark, a black like the night sky and his hair was just as dark.

"Oh, um, yeah. Is it obvious?"

"Only because I am too. My name is Nero. I'm from Duskmere."

I give him my hand to shake. "Vera." I replied.

"And?"

I looked at him questioningly. "Where are you from?"

"Oh, I'm from here. My aunt homeschooled me." I say quickly. Then I turn to the front quickly, that is not what we practiced. But I panicked, I didn't think people would ask where I am from. What the hell I mean veils is Duskmere? He looked a little confused but the teacher starts class and he doesn't get a chance to ask.

The teacher walks in just as the bell chimes, a whirlwind of energy wrapped in a cropped golden blazer and flowy green trousers that somehow still seem professional. She's a little shorter than I expected, barely taller than me in boots and looks to be around Rina's age, maybe early thirties. Her hair is a soft copper-brown, tied back with a thin ribbon that floats like it has a mind of its own.

I tug the folded paper from my pocket and glance at my schedule again. *Professor Liraen Virelle—Elemental Studies.*

I can't wait to show Rina my schedule and ask her more about the classes and the teachers. Especially this one.

"Good morning!" the woman beams, her voice ringing out like chimes. "Welcome to your first official day at Auravale Academy! What an exciting time to be alive, am I right?" A few students chuckle, some roll their eyes but I find myself smiling.

"I'm Professor Virelle, and this is Elemental Synergy, the foundational course that will prepare you for elemental magic if it's part of your gift. If not…" She shrugs cheerfully. "You'll still need to understand how the elements move through our world because, like it or not, they move through *you.*"

She claps her hands together, eyes twinkling. "Let's dive in. We're starting with a bit of history today. You'll hear this again, probably in several other classes but the first fae queen was said to be blessed by the moon goddess herself, and with that blessing came a rare gift: all four elemental affinities. Fire, water, air, and earth."

Professor Virelle begins pacing lightly as she speaks, her steps soft but intentional. Her enthusiasm is contagious. I find myself leaning forward in my seat, actually interested in what she's saying.

"She had a particular strength in *earth,* which many believe tied her more deeply to the land of Sylvaeris itself. It's said her presence caused the forests to bloom and the rivers to sing." She winks playfully. "Whether or not that's a bit of poetic exaggeration, I'll leave for you to decide."

My pen is already flying across the page, scribbling notes as fast as I can write.

"We'll spend time with each of the four elements this semester," she continues, "but this week…" She grins. "We begin with *fire.*"

Fire? I glance around, half-expecting someone to spontaneously combust.

Professor Virelle keeps talking, sliding seamlessly into the history of the royal bloodline and their rare ability to control all four elements. Apparently, it's a trait that's passed down only through certain fae lineages. Each member of the royal family has one dominant element, something innate, like a pulse in their magic.

She draws an intricate diagram on the board with a flick of her finger, flames sparking in the air as she sketches. Literal flames. They hover, curling and twisting into the outline of a family tree glowing with ember-like names.

I stay mesmerized. Not because it's fire. But because this doesn't feel like school the way I've known it. It feels… real. Like magic isn't a secret anymore, it's something I'm allowed to touch.

My next class is just a short walk down the hall. I double-check my schedule—*Truthsense & Future Sight – Professor Thessa Oryll*—before stepping inside.

The room feels quieter than the last, the kind of quiet that makes you instinctively lower your voice. Long windows line the far wall, casting sunlight in slanted golden beams that dust the rows of desks. It smells faintly of old parchment and dried lavender.

That boy, Nero, is already here, slouched in his chair with one leg stretched out like he owns the place. I hesitate for a second before sitting a seat over from him. Not too close, but close enough that I don't feel entirely alone.

I glance around the room, wondering, *Do they know I have this gift?* Is everyone here like me? Or worse, are they more advanced? There are others in the room, I lock eyes with another boy who is glaring in our direction, he has black hair and equally dark eyes. I track where his eyes are looking and they are at Nero beside me. He looks like he could be equally as big.

"Don't worry about him, he's just an asshole." Nero says beside me.

"Oh." Is all I say. I look back at him and he is assessing me now.

A minute later, the door opens again, and a tall older woman walks in. Her silver hair is braided and coiled at the back of her head, not a strand out of place. She wears deep plum robes lined with navy trim, and her presence feels... commanding, but not cold. There's something wise in the way she scans the room, like she's seen it all, twice.

I straighten in my seat.

"Good morning, class," she says with a warm, worn voice. "You get the pleasure of having me just before lunch, which means I expect at least a *little* focus while you all daydream about pastries and roast potatoes."

A few students chuckle. She smiles like she's used to holding the attention of distracted minds.

"I'm Professor Oryll—Thessa, if you must and this class is for those with truthsense, future sight, or anyone who wants to understand how those gifts work. You don't have to be Gifted to be here but if you are, I promise you'll learn how to use it responsibly."

I shift in my seat. *Responsibly*. The word sticks in my chest.

She continues, pacing slowly as she speaks. "Now, as with most gifts, the roots trace back to our first fae queen. But unlike elemental affinity, truthsense and foresight didn't remain confined to one lineage. Over the centuries, they scattered, woven through bloodlines, shaping entire provinces."

She pauses near the window and rests one hand on the sill, eyes flicking across the room.

"Duskmere, for example, has long been associated with truthsense, those who can feel or hear lies like static in the air. While in Varethos, foresight runs strongest, some are born with glimpses of what's to come. Others learn to listen."

At the mention of Duskmere, I glance sideways at Nero. He doesn't react. Just keeps lazily spinning his pen between his fingers, unreadable as ever.

Then the door swings open again, and that same guy, Cae, walks in.

He looks irritated. Tense in the shoulders, his jaw clenched tight. But the second his eyes find mine, his whole face softens, the hardness melting into something quieter. The look lands heavy in my chest, too intense, too direct. My pulse stumbles, and I glance away, suddenly wishing I hadn't met his eyes at all. The furrow in his brow disappears like it never existed.

"Well, Mr. Thornevale," Professor Oryll says, her tone dry but not unkind. "Nice of you to join us. Try not to make a habit of it?"

"Wouldn't dream of it, Thessa," he replies smoothly, flashing her a charming grin like it's a private joke. "Won't happen again."

He moves through the rows without hesitation and slides into the empty seat between me and Nero. Of course he does. I keep my eyes fixed on the front of the room, determined not to react. But I can feel him, his presence buzzing like a current next to mine. Every so often, I sense his gaze flick toward me, brushing against my cheek like a whisper.

The other guy with black eyes is turned towards us again and now he is glaring at me.

I grip my pen tighter and focus harder on Professor Oryll's lecture. Truthsense. Foresight. Keep your head down. Try to blend in. Too late for that now.

At lunch, the cafeteria buzzed with noise and laughter. I spotted him instantly, sitting with her. The same pretty girl that also seems to be everywhere. Smiling at a girl whose hair was as light as his. Surrounded by girls, flanked by other guys, their table was a whirlwind of energy, everyone talking over each other like it was the most exciting moment of the day.

Of course he was popular. Of course he was good with girls. I feel stupid for even being attracted to him. Not that I was, I tell myself it's just because he was in every one of my classes. Before anyone noticed me, I spun on my heel and went searching for the library.

It took me ten embarrassingly long minutes to find the library. My hands were shaking more than I wanted to admit, and my breath kept catching in my throat. But at least here, tucked between towering shelves and away from too many watching eyes, I could finally breathe.

What *is* all of this?

I felt like I'd been dropped into someone else's story, like everyone else had been handed a rulebook I didn't get. The unease curled in my stomach like smoke, spreading until I couldn't tell if it was fear, anger, or just exhaustion. Probably all three.

I wandered the aisles, trying to look like I belonged. Waiting for the bell to ring. My fingers trailed along spines etched with strange symbols and titles that made little sense to me. It was beautiful, in a way but also overwhelming. Like the books themselves were keeping secrets I wasn't meant to understand.

I don't think I belong here. Not really.

In this place of gleaming halls and whispered magic, I felt like a walking question mark. I wonder if others can sense how out of place I was. Maybe it wasn't just nerves. Maybe this whole academy, this world, wasn't safe for someone like me. The thought came quiet at first, then louder, more persistent: *Maybe I shouldn't be here at all.*

I started running through a list of excuses. Reasons I could give Rina, why I wasn't a good fit for this school. Reasons that might actually convince her, like I don't understand anything of this world for one. Maybe if I explained how out of place I felt, how wrong this all seemed, she'd understand. Maybe she'd even agree I didn't need to be here.

But beneath every excuse was the truth I didn't want to say out loud, I feel untethered, like I've been dropped into a life that isn't mine. Lost in a place that should feel like home but doesn't, and terrified someone will see how little I belong.

He walked into class, the guy with blonde hair, Cae, just before the bell rang and dropped an apple and a granola bar on my open notebook. I'd been doodling again, half-listening to the pre-class chatter. Mostly, I keep drawing the planet in the sky, I want to get it perfect. I still can't believe it's real.

I looked up at him, caught by the green of his eyes. His pupils dilated as he stared at me, and then his smile tugged crookedly at one side, one dimple deepening and that was enough to make me blush.

"You didn't eat lunch," he said.

"What?" I asked, brilliantly. His eyes were like a nebula that had just gone supernova, and I'd lost all sense of language.

"Lunch." He repeated it slowly. God, he must think I'm an idiot. "I didn't see you in there, so I brought you something." Oh. How could even tell I wasn't in there. Is he watching me? He must think I am some kind of charity case?

"You can keep it. I already ate," I lied, well, half-lied. I've had enough practice to know how to bend the truth. It comes with the gift, when you can *see* someone's truth and intentions.

His eyes narrowed. I placed the snacks back on his desk quickly before facing the front again.

"You need to eat," he said quietly. "I know you have Battlecraft last period. You'll need your strength."

Wait, how did he know my schedule? Well, it's apparently the same as his, but still. Something in his voice made the hairs on my arms rise. Was that a threat? Or just a warning?

I tried to read him, tried to catch the flicker of his intent but for some reason, I couldn't. That was new. I didn't think he meant harm, but I couldn't be sure.

"Why will I need my strength?" I asked, watching his eyes. His eyes that always appear to be assessing, like he's looking through me.

"Because it's physical activity, and you need calories to keep up," he replied evenly. But again it felt ominous. And I still couldn't *read* him. Was he trying to read me? I wonder what gifts other people, *fae*, had around here.

"Well, thanks," I said finally, "but like I said, I ate earlier."

He looked at me a little too long, and I got the sense he knew I wasn't telling the whole truth. But I turned back to the front, dismissing him just as the teacher walked in.

A movement next to me had a shadow forming around me. I look up to find Nero sliding into the seat on the opposite side of me. He gives me a small smile and a nod. He has been in almost every one of my classes, just like the other guy, he doesn't speak just listens. I didn't look toward the sandy haired guy but I could sense his irritation. I hope I didn't make him mad along with his girlfriend. I am trying to float under the radar. It doesn't seem to be working. And it's only the first day.

Mr. Valeis, the same one from this morning, set his coffee on the desk. His eyes locked on mine again, assessing. Measuring. Green eyes on the other side of me clears his throat. Mr. Valeis smirked and launched into his lesson about Runes.

Thankfully, he started with the history of runes, something I could at least *pretend* to follow. I don't know what's going on here. If all these people are crazy or if I am. Still not sure this isn't some kind of bad dream. A nightmare I can't escape from.

After class, I stuffed my notebook into my bag, the lingering chill from earlier still clinging to my skin like a shadow I couldn't shake. Students filed out around me, their conversations hushed and careful, as if even their voices were afraid to disturb whatever strange energy had settled in the room.

I slung my bag over my shoulder and turned only to nearly crash into someone. Nero stood just inches away, grinning like the near collision hadn't fazed him at all.

"You surviving your first day?" he asked, his voice light, a little teasing.

I managed a weak nod. "Barely."

I hesitated, chewing the inside of my cheek. Then, before I could stop myself: "Hey—um—who was that? The guy, that teacher?"

His grin faltered for just a breath. Blink and I might've missed it.

"You mean Professor Valeis?" His tone was casual, but something behind his eyes sharpened. "He teaches two classes. And, uh, a few other things. Advanced stuff. You'll probably run into him sooner or later, outside of class."

"Is he..." I struggled to find the right words. Creepy? Inhuman? Something not meant to be here?

Nero chuckled, low and amused, like he knew exactly what I was getting at but wanted me to work for it.

"Intense? Mysterious? Maybe cursed?" he offered, ticking each off on his fingers. "Depends who you ask. Some people say he's marked by the dead. Others think he just enjoys being creepy."

I swallowed hard. "He didn't seem normal." Not that I really knew what "normal" even looked like anymore.

"That's because he's not," Nero said, still smiling, but his voice had lost the teasing edge. "He's different. He just started this year as far as I know. No one really knows how old he is or what he did before Auravale. But whatever it was, it definitely wasn't boring." How does he know this information if he's not from around here?

I hesitated again. "They offer advanced classes?" The question slipped out, casual on the surface but inside, I was tense. Curious, yes, but wary. I didn't want to make it obvious how little I knew. Or worse, what I was.

"It's specialized classes for after the Veilfall. When most fae's get their gifts." Nero said with a shrug. "There's also stuff for those who've found their fated, classes about the bond, how it affects your magic. Those kinds of things." What the heck is fated?

"Oh." I tried to sound unaffected. "That sounds helpful. Like they teach you how to use your gifts better?"

That could be good. Necessary, even. But what if it revealed too much? What if I couldn't hide how different I was?

"You could ask the front desk lady about the extra classes," Nero said, his voice even. "But they'll want to know what gifts you've got." Something in his tone made my stomach twist. He *knew*.

Or at the very least, he suspected I was hiding something. And I wasn't sure if that scared me or made me feel seen in a way I hadn't in a very long time. *Am I not hiding well enough?*

Nero adjusted his bag, then gestured toward the hallway. "Come on, new girl. I'll show you the way to the courtyard. You'll want to see it before you get buried in assignments."

I followed him, my footsteps echoing softly beside his. But just before we turned the corner, I glanced back at the classroom one last time, half-expecting the air to shimmer where Professor Valeis had stood, like it had been burned into the space. But it was just a room again. Normal. Or at least pretending to be.

Chapter 8: Remind Me Not to Bet Against You

Vera

The locker room buzzes with low conversation and the soft clatter of students changing. I tug on the school-issued gym clothes and catch my reflection in the mirror. They gave us all the same uniform, black from head to toe. The base layer clings close, a moisture-wicking spandex fabric that fits like a second skin, tracing the lines of muscle I didn't even know I had. Over it, a light combat shirt, elbows reinforced but cut slim so it doesn't bunch when I move. The pants are the same, sleek, flexible, built for motion, with vents along the thighs that keep them from feeling suffocating. The boots are light but firm, gripping the ground with every step.

It's not flashy, not meant to be, but there's no mistaking the intention. This isn't about looking good, it's about stripping you down to what you can do in the field. And yet, the way the fabric molds to my body, the way it moves when I move, I can't help but feel…sharper.

For once, I'm not the tallest girl in the room, or even the tallest person in the school. I don't feel as self-conscious. Like I can blend in more, I've never had that. That's what I need. To blend in more, to be able to fly under the radar.

I tugged at the edge of my training uniform as I stepped through the arched walkway that linked Auravale Academy to the Echoforge. The second my boot crossed the threshold, the air shifted, denser, heavier, almost like it carried a charge. I swore I could taste iron and cedar on my tongue, and something else beneath it all, something older that vibrated low in my bones.

The building looked like it had been standing for centuries. Massive oak beams arched overhead, carved with runes that faintly glowed when the torchlight brushed them. The walls were lined with tall windows, panes of glass that caught the morning sun and fractured it into strange, shifting colors across the floor. The sconces flickered not with fire but with silver flames that never seemed to die. Even the floorboards creaked like they knew exactly who was walking across them.

This place felt alive. Watching.

The hall split into two wings, one marked by a towering set of double doors carved with twisting vines and blades. Above one door way read: The Gauntlet of Ascension. The other curved into shadow where I caught the gleam of polished wood, with the name—The Rite of Steel.

I followed the others toward the Gauntlet first, my chest tightening as the doors swung open on their own. What should have been just a gymnasium opened into something else entirely. I expected something like back home just a big open areas with hard wooden floors that squeaked constantly from everyone's tennis shoes.

The chamber stretched impossibly high, so far I couldn't even see the ceiling, just platforms disappearing into gloom. Ropes spiraled into beams of light that blinked out halfway up, vanishing into nothing. Wooden bridges swayed though there was no wind, and narrow poles gleamed with faint runes as if daring us to balance on them. This can't be real.

Back home, I'd trained on obstacle courses. Real ones. Dirt tracks, climbing walls, ropes that burned your palms raw. My dad built a huge one in the backyard, I could practically run it with my eyes closed. But this? This wasn't training. This was something that shifted and breathed, waiting for you to step forward so it could twist against you.

It didn't just test strength, it hunted your weakness. I could feel it, like the course itself was already sizing me up. Does it already know my weakness?

And at the far end, looming like a promise or a threat, was the final wall. Mist curled over its face, and its surface flickered from stone to glass to steel as if mocking anyone foolish enough to try.

A shiver ran down my spine.

When we turned down the other wing, the world narrowed into something simpler but no less terrifying. The Rite of Steel. A massive round platform sat raised in the center, built of dark wooden planks polished smooth by generations of blood and sweat. Students had to step up into it like crossing a boundary, like saying yes to whatever waited.

A narrow ring circled the platform just wide enough for someone to walk, sharp-eyed and silent.

The air hums with a different energy here. No whispers, no judgmental glances. Just a sharp, buzzing tension: competition, raw and clean. I exhale, tension slipping from my shoulders. This, I can handle. Physical challenges make sense. People are predictable when they're pushing their limits.

"Alright, gather around," a voice boomed, deep enough to rattle the beams above.

I turned, and there was a mountain of a man, broad and towering, his bulk packed into dark forest-green field gear that clung to him like a second skin. The fabric was reinforced at the shoulders and chest with hardened plates that caught the torchlight, and over his heart, a sigil was stitched in silver thread, a sword cleaving through a spiral of wind. It looks just like what Rina was wearing that first day I met her. His presence was heavy, commanding, the kind that didn't just enter a space but swallowed it whole.

"I'm Halric," he said, dipping into a mock bow that was all sharp edges, no softness. "Your charming guide through Phases One and Two of the Veilbound Order. Before we roll out the welcome mat, we'll run assessments to see if you're even vaguely competent, or if I should start digging graves now."

His voice carried like thunder, low and vibrating through the stone beneath my boots.

"The first phase," he went on, pacing with his hands locked behind his back, "is The Gauntlet of Ascension. Don't let the name fool you, it's alive, crawling with old magic. Platforms rise higher than your stomach will want to climb. Ropes that seem solid vanish into shadow halfway up. Bridges sway like they're daring you to fall. You'll bruise, you'll bleed, you'll curse my name—but if you're lucky, you'll make it through."

A grin tugged at the edge of his mouth, but his eyes stayed cold.

"Phase Two is The Rite of Steel. Simple enough. No tricks, no illusions, just you and your opponent. Step into the ring, prove you can fight, and more importantly, prove you can control yourself. The arena's enchantments will keep you alive. Don't expect them to keep you unbroken. Bruises, cracked ribs, split lips, that's the price of entry. If you can't stomach it, you don't belong here."

He stopped then, shoulders squared, his gaze cutting across us like a blade. When he spoke again, his voice dropped, almost reverent.

"And then there's Phase Three: The Heart of the Crucible. That one…" He let the pause stretch, dark and deliberate. "That one you face alone. No opponent, no obstacle course, just yourself. Your greatest fear, your deepest weakness, the secret you'd bury in the dark. If you can't conquer that, nothing else matters."

Halric's gaze swept over the students, sharp as a blade. "So. Welcome to the Order. Still eager?" A pause. "Today's test? Stamina and teamwork. Translation: running in circles and not tripping over each other. Track and field."

He paced in front of us, boots scuffing the polished floor, each step as measured as if he were already deciding who'd make it and who'd cry trying. Halric's dark ash-blond hair was pulled back into a rough half-knot, strands escaping around his temples like they'd tried to flee but failed. Steel-gray eyes scanned the crowd, sharp, unblinking, clearly unimpressed.

Deep scars carved across his tanned skin, including one that dragged along the side of his neck like someone had once tried to remove his head and gave up halfway. Nothing about him looked polished or ceremonial; he carried himself like someone who had spent a lifetime drilling others into shape. The air around him smelled like leather, iron, and the warning before a storm. When he spoke again, it sounded like gravel had a grudge.

"You'll work with assigned partners. Strength alone won't get you through. Neither will speed. We're looking for those who can think on their feet and not hurt each other by accident or worse, our feelings."

His gaze flicked to me for a beat too long. I stiffened, unsure if I'd been weighed, measured, or marked for death.

"Meet me at the starting line in five minutes. I hope your all wearing something you don't mind bleeding in. And hydrate I'd hate for you to pass out before I've had the chance to break your spirit properly." A few uneasy chuckles trickled through the group.

Halric didn't crack so much as a molecule of a smirk. He pivoted and strode out, the faint clink of his axe shifting as he moved. The room held its breath until he was gone. It's hard to know if he was joking or if he was serious, I am worried it's the latter.

Stepping out onto the sprawling track field, the afternoon sun is sharp against the muted gray of the buildings. My eyes have to adjust the sun after being in the Echoforge. The breeze carries the smell of crushed grass and old stone. I drift toward the outer edge, not exactly blending in but not inviting conversation either. A comfortable nowhere space.

Then a shadow falls across me. I glance sideways and there he is again. Same guy from every class. It's getting weird now. Stalker-ish. What are the odds we'd be in every class together? He has plenty of friends, they are somewhere behind him. Laughing and shoving each other nearby and a girlfriend who's magnetic. Yet here he is, hovering just inside my space like he thinks he belongs there.

I look up at him fully this time, expecting some smirk or teasing comment. Instead, his eyes meet mine. The lazy charm he wore earlier is gone. He's assessing me, not in a creepy way, not even in a flirty way, but in a way that feels like he's reading a language written across my skin that I can't see.

The training gear fits close to his frame, all black, sleek and utilitarian. It should look the same on everyone, but on him, the fabric stretches in all the right ways, broad shoulders, lean muscle, power coiled just beneath the surface. My gaze lingers a beat too long on the flex of his chest and the narrow taper of his waist. Heat blooms low in my stomach, sharp and distracting, before it rushes to my cheeks.

His eyes flicker, catching me. And then—there it is. The subtle lift of his lips. Not a full smirk, but the kind that says he knows exactly where my attention wandered. The kind that makes my pulse stumble and something molten curl inside me.

The air between us feels charged, almost too heavy to breathe in. My skin prickles like it's waiting for him to touch me, though he doesn't move. I break eye contact first, pretending to tighten my shoelaces, but it doesn't steady me. He doesn't say a word. Just stays there, silent and steady, like he's daring me to look back.

The other girls are already starting to gather by the track. I start moving that way so I can be ready.

"I'll see you out there, Brightstep." His silky voice calls as I move away. Brightstep? I turn to look at him and my gaze gets trapped by his, he has a sexy smirk that just oozes confidence. I think my heart stops beating for a moment.

Then Cassia appears bright, bold, possessive. She leaps up and hooks herself to his arm, tugging him close. Pulling me out of my trance, I really need to stop staring at him. I force myself to focus, stretching alongside the others. Not without thinking that I hate how good she looks in the uniform. Trying not to be too obvious about watching him. I focus on assessing everyone else. Everyone here looks strong. Like they belong.

Something flickers in my chest, nerves, maybe. But also excitement? I used to run with my dad in the early mornings, just the two of us. We'd cut through foggy trails, our breath clouding in the cold air. After school, he'd drill me on footwork, speed, self-defense. He always said he just wanted me to be safe. But now it felt like he was preparing me for something more.

"Alright, this is the beginning of a series of tests. This week will assess whether you will continue into training for the Veilbound Order. Look around, we're starting with 30 students, but only about half of you will make it through. Over the next two weeks, I'll be calling you out in groups and teams. We'll be watching how you perform, and based on that, you'll be paired with someone at your level. No excuses, no complaints, you earn where you land." Okay, so don't hold back. I remember my dad's words, "don't show the real you." They can't see the real me, but I don't need to hold back anymore. It's time to make him proud.

Okay. This I can do. This, I understand.

Halric calls out the teams. Of course, I get stuck on the same team as her, Cassia Corvina. Her glossy platinum hair is pulled back in a tight braid, and she's already glaring at me like I stole her crown. The other two on our team giggle when she fake-whispers, "Try not to trip over your own feet."

Whatever. I've dealt with worse, no one really liked me in the human schools. Cassia volunteers to go first and places me second, right behind her. Which would be fine, if she hadn't handed off the baton before she crossed into the exchange zone. On purpose.

We got disqualified in the first round.

"I'm so sorry," she says, with a sugary voice and a smile that feels like it's made of knives. "I thought you'd know how to handle a simple handoff."

Before I can reply, Halric looks at Cassia deadpan. "Nice teamwork. Remind me not to assign you to any mission that involves other people or objects." There are a few chuckles around us. Cassia looks like an angry kitten. I guess her plan to make me look bad backfired on her.

"Let's mix it up," he says, scribbling on his clipboard. "Vera—you're with Caelum now."

The same guy with blonde hair that's been my shadow all day, looks up at me and smiles. Caelum. So that's his full name. I repeat his name, testing it, it felt right, the name suited him somehow. He gives me a little wave from across the field, like he already knew this would happen. When I jog over, he tosses me my water bottle. "You ready?"

"I guess," I say, twisting the cap. "I haven't done this in a while." I tell the little white lie.

"Something tells me you'll be fine. Just let me lead and I will get you through it." He says with a wink, his voice is smooth, low and way too cocky. And then he smiles, crooked, dimpled, and far too confident. But my heart flutters all the same.

He's up first. When the whistle blows, he's a blur. Fast and fluid like he's floating above the ground. When he hits the handoff zone, his baton slides cleanly into my fingers.

I run. The wind tears at my clothes, my breath syncing with my strides. The world blurs. I feel the rhythm of my feet pounding the track. Feeling a warmth spread through my chest, I'm *faster* than I remember. Way faster. Maybe faster than I should be. I reach the next runner seconds ahead of the next team, and as I pass the baton, I catch a glimpse of Cassia on the sidelines, her mouth tight and arms folded.

We won the round.

Then I was assigned with Nero, he gave me a nod as we got into position. I see the look in his eyes that says I can do this, push myself. So I do. When the baton slides into my hand again, I run. I felt the wind ripple through me, pushing me. By the final heat, the class is buzzing. Whispers ripple through the crowd, and even Halric is watching me like he's trying to figure out what box I fit in.

"You've got serious speed," Caelum says after the last run, wiping sweat from his brow. "Where'd you learn to move like that?"

I shrug, trying not to let my heart hammer too hard in my chest. "My dad. Early morning runs. Nothing special."

He grins. "Well, it's special now."

The words are light, teasing, but his eyes aren't. They drag down my body with a slow, deliberate weight that feels like a touch. Heat blooms under my skin everywhere his gaze lingers, shoulders, chest, thighs, as if he's memorizing me piece by piece. My breath stumbles, shallow, and tingles spark to life low in my belly, racing outward until I feel like my whole body is on edge, waiting.

The air between us tightens, heavy with something I don't want to name but can't ignore. His grin deepens like he can feel it too.

Halric's clap cracks through the moment, loud and sharp, shattering the pull. I jolt, dragging in a breath I didn't realize I'd been holding, the flush still hot on my skin "Vera, that was impressive." A pause. "Didn't expect it, but I'll take it. Remind me not to bet against you. Again."

Before I can answer, I catch Cassia approaching from the corner of my eye. She moves in behind Caelum like she's trying to reestablish territory, sliding a hand along his bicep with a laugh that's just a little too loud.

I clear my throat. "Thanks." Halric gives a nod and turns to yell at a group still tangled in a hurdle.

Chapter 9: It Felt Intentional

Vera

Heading to the locker room, I feel the sweat sticking to me again, as nice as these training clothes are they don't for a lot breathing.

Cassia and her two shadows step in front of me. "Listen, new girl," she says, tone suddenly ice cold. "He's mine. Stay away."

"Who?" I ask, playing dumb.

"Caelum," she snaps. "Don't act like you don't know."

"Ohhh," I say, blinking. "Sorry, I'm not great with names yet. But don't worry. I'm not interested." I flash a polite smile and walk past her before she can reply.

By the time I finally stepped out of the academy, my head was spinning. Too many new faces, too many secrets I still didn't understand. I needed air. I couldn't wait to be among the trees and fresh air, this is where I have always done my best thinking.

When I was back at my parents house in Maine, whenever I had a bad day I would go sit in a small clearing in the forest. It was my personal safe place. The forest path waited for me like a release, and I let my feet carry me into the green. The trees stretched tall and endless, their leaves whispering above as if they knew how much I needed the quiet. Each step away from the school loosened something tight in my chest.

As I made it outside, I spotted Caelum heading toward a sleek black car with a friend. I'd seen them together throughout the day. His friend was tall and lean, not as muscular, with chestnut brown hair that looked soft and perfectly styled. They were laughing, their voices light and easy in the warm afternoon air.

I slipped onto the trail I'd taken that morning, my shoes crunching lightly over the gravel. A now familiar shadow fell across me again. I looked up and there he was. Nero. My other shadow of the day. His face was unreadable, the same stoic expression he'd worn all day.

"I'll walk with you," he said quietly.

"I don't need anyone to walk with me," I replied, a little too sharply.

"Well, I live this way too. We don't have to talk." I can hear the amusement in his voice.

And we didn't. The silence between us stretched, but it wasn't uncomfortable at least, not for him. For me, it left too much room for thinking. I kept sneaking glances at him, trying to get a read, trying to feel something. Anything. But Nero was a wall of calm. No hostility, but no warmth either.

It was strange. With humans, reading intentions had always been instinctual. Effortless. Fae are different. Stronger, maybe. Better at guarding their emotions. Maybe that was part of why I felt so unmoored today.

The trail wound deeper into the woods, tall trees casting a dappled shade over us. The earthy scent of moss and damp bark filled the air. A breeze tugged at my hair, whispering through the leaves. I wanted to run, to let my muscles burn and my mind go quiet. But I kept pace beside Nero, not wanting to be rude.

Something about today felt different. Like I'd finally been seen but not in a way that made me feel safe. Then there was Cae with his bright green eyes that just held my attention. Then the way my body just felt alive when he looked at me, I can't say I ever felt that way before, never experienced that feeling before.

Everyone else at Auravale moved through the day like they belonged, like they *knew* this world inside and out. And me? I felt like I was playing dress-up in someone else's life, waiting for the seams to split.

"How was your first day?" Nero asked, his voice breaking the quiet.

I had to crane my neck to look up at him. He had to be taller than my dad and a lot broader through the shoulders. I'm not used to people so much taller, he would be a giant in the human realm.

"I thought we weren't talking," I pointed out.

He chuckled, the sound low and rough. "I said we didn't *have* to. Doesn't mean I didn't want to."

"It was fine. How was yours?" I asked, more out of politeness than real interest.

"It was good. I'm happy this is finally starting." There was something in the way he said it, an invitation to ask more. But I didn't. I wasn't here to make friends. I was here to survive. To figure out who was hunting me. And maybe to find a way to go back to the life I understood.

'Don't let them see the real you.' I kept my dads words in my head all day, but I don't know if I was able to keep myself hidden the way I was meant to. How am I supposed to prove I can do the Veilbound Order, if I am trying to pull back and not show how strong I am?

Today had been weird. First Nero, who seemed to pop up everywhere. Then Caelum, who was in every single one of my classes. Always around, even when he wasn't talking to me. And I couldn't shake the feeling that Caelum knew more than he let on. The woods began to thin, the guards' houses coming into view through the trees. I slowed.

"Okay, well I live this way," I said, pointing down a side trail.

He nodded. "I'll meet you here tomorrow morning. We can walk in together."

"That's not necessary. I can manage just fine on my own."

He just smiled slightly. "Right. It can't hurt to have friends." And with that, he turned and walked away. I stared after him, frowning. Was he flirting? It didn't seem like flirting, not like in the movies. No one ever flirted with me back home for me to learn how it works. All the guys were intimidated by my size so they stayed clear of me.

Besides, he didn't give me butterflies. Not like when Caelum looked at me, then it was like my whole body might lift off the ground. Not that I am thinking about that. I shook my head and started down the trail toward home.

Home. When had I started thinking of it as *home*? The house was quiet when I stepped inside. Too quiet. The kind of silence that feels thick, like even the walls are holding their breath. Rina wasn't here yet, so I headed straight to my room. I kicked off my shoes harder than necessary, frustration burning under my skin. My mind running through the day.

There was Caelum. In every class. Always somehow nearby. Auravale didn't even have standardized classes, it wasn't like in human schools where everyone had the same schedule. Which meant his being in every single one of mine wasn't an accident.

It felt intentional. It *was* intentional, I could feel it.

And Cassia. Of course, there was Cassia. All flowing silver-blonde hair, high cheekbones, and that infuriatingly smug smile. She and Caelum made sense. Shiny. Perfect. Probably powerful. She was way more confident not to mention prettier than me.

I wasn't sure where that left me. How had Caelum known I hadn't eaten lunch? It was only a half-truth, but he saw right through it. Like he could see right through *me*. I should ask Rina about all this. About him. About everything. But when I heard the door open, I shoved the thoughts aside. Stuffed them deep down where they couldn't reach me.

"Vera?" Rina called, her voice warm.

I leaned against the doorframe. "Yes?" She was shrugging off her jacket, nearly tripping over my abandoned shoes, laughing at herself.

"Come out here. Tell me about school! How was your first day?" she asked, cheerfully bustling around.

"Umm…confusing," I admitted.

We decided to warm up before training, and I followed her outside into the cooling dusk. The yard opened up beneath a sky tinted strange and beautiful, the red dwarf sun bleeding copper light across the horizon. Because of the planet's tilt, shadows stretched at odd angles, long and skewed, like everything was just slightly off from what my instincts are used to. The air carried that in-between chill of early evening, cool against my heated skin.

We stretched side by side, the boards of the porch creaking softly under our weight. I told her about the track course, leaving out names, but trying to capture the fire in my chest, the burn in my muscles, the wind cutting at my face. The words tumbled out faster than I meant, like the light slipping lower with every heartbeat. I even told her about my strange classes, the ones that still left me feeling like an outsider.

When I mentioned trying to read someone and failing, it came out in a rush, like I was bracing for a scolding the way my parents used to. Instead, she listened quietly, her expression unreadable but patient, the strange sunset painting her hair in ribbons of gold and crimson.

"I could always feel others' intentions, you know? But I struggled with it. I couldn't always read them, and I swear one or two of them smirked like they knew what I was doing."

"That's because there are others that can," she said softly. "Especially if they have the same gift. There are many that can see auras, have truthsense, and can sense people's intentions. There are a lot of other gifts too, but those with those gifts—well, as soon as they manifested, they would have been trained how to use them. To read others and to know when others are reading them."

"Oh. I didn't know. My parents never showed me that."

"I'm sorry," she said, her voice gentler now. "Both your parents had the ability to read auras, and your dad could sense intentions. Your mom had truthsense. It seems you got those. Can you see auras too?"

"Umm, no? I mean… sometimes I see colors when I sense when people are lying, or I can see colors when I sense their intentions."

"Maybe that one will come with your Veilfall," she murmured, tilting her head, the copper light catching her eyes. "You already seem powerful with your gifts. I can start training you how to hone in on them."

Something inside me loosened at her words. Beneath the strange and beautiful sky, in the odd slant of red light and shadow, I felt a flicker of something almost like belonging.

"Why couldn't they just teach me?" I say exasperated.

"Veralyn, I think your parents just wanted to protect you," she said softly. "Not because they thought your gifts were wrong, but because you needed to understand how to wield them first. Some fae can feel it when you're trying to read them. If you encountered another fae and you didn't know when you tried to read them, they could have known. But you have every right to protect yourself."

There was something she wasn't saying. I could sense it, but I didn't press. I can only take so much everyday.

Instead, she shifted, her voice steady but gentle. "When I start to feel overwhelmed, like my mind is spiraling, I ground myself. I focus on something real, something I can touch or hear. The sound of my breath, the feel of the grass under my hand, the rhythm of my pulse. Little anchors that bring me back to the moment. It reminds me I'm here. That I'm safe."

Rina's kitchen smelled like rosemary and something buttery and rich. I dropped into a chair at the table, picking at a loose thread on the tablecloth. At dinner, conversation was sparse. My thoughts kept circling, looping back to the same place: This isn't real. It can't be real.

Later, curled up with a book about elemental symmetry, I found myself staring at an illustration of an earth elemental. Vibrant green energy swirling from the ground, wild and beautiful.

It reminded me of his eyes. Caelum. His sharp green eyes, flecked with gold. Like the forests back home in Maine.

Home. I always knew where my home was. It turns out it wasn't the place where we lived but with my parents. They were my home and now it's gone. My old life. My chest tightened. It had only been a few days since everything changed. It felt like a lifetime.

A knock on the doorframe broke the spell. "Vera, want some ice cream?" Rina called.

"Yeah, coming." In the cozy living room, Rina handed me a bowl piled high with mint chocolate chip.

"Did you make any friends today?"

I shrugged. "Not really. I talked to a few people I sat next to in my classes but mostly just introductions. I am used to keeping to myself." Back in the human realm and here.

She smiled knowingly. "I bet you stood out anyway."

I laughed, surprising myself. "Yeah. I always do. At my old school my height and strength made people uncomfortable."

"You definitely have your dad's height advantage," she teased. It felt good to laugh but it also felt wrong. Good to feel *something* that wasn't fear or uncertainty or sadness. It feels wrong to feel anything other than complete loss right now.

"Maybe now's your chance to show your real strength," she said. "To be who you're meant to be." Maybe. If I could just figure out who that was. My dad's words echo again. 'Never let them see the real you.'

"Did you find anything out about my parents?" I whisper.

"No, not yet. I was trying to see if there was any logs for anyone traveling to the human realm, but there wasn't anything obvious. Mostly it's fae that go there to buy items to bring back to sell here.

Regular visits. I will keep looking though I promise."

"Thank you." I didn't know what else to say. What could I say. I don't know where to look either.

75

Chapter 10: Like Pulling Teeth

Cae

I am walking out of the school with Sylas, he is talking about something and I laugh right on cue but I don't really hear him. I usually drive him to and from school, Sylas has always been my best friend since we were little. Always together, he's one of the few people I can trust.

Getting in my car, I start the drive home. Letting the day replay in my mind. Vera lingers there like a song I can't stop humming. There's something she's hiding, something that keeps her guarded, but every once in a while, her walls slip and her eyes shine a little brighter.

When I first saw her in the office this morning, something inside me shifted. Even though she kept her head down, avoiding attention, I was drawn in. She wasn't trying to impress anyone, no designer clothes, no makeup. Just natural beauty, quiet and confident in her own way. Her scent enveloped me, bright and clean, like lilacs after a spring rain. From what little she allowed me to see, it was enough to unsettle me in the best way.

There's something strange about her aura, though. I've always been able to read people. It was the first gift I ever manifested, and my father made sure I sharpened it until I could see through any lie, any façade. Being prince of Sylvaeris demands that kind of clarity. But Vera... her aura is muted, cloudy, like something's cloaking it. I can't get a full read, which unsettles me more than I'd like to admit. Her lilac eyes, rare enough around here, don't feel entirely real, either. I don't mean fake, just veiled. I'm going to find out what she's hiding.

Then she spoke, and it was like everything clicked into place. Like finding my true north. For the first time in a long while, I felt content. Like maybe I'd found home. She could be my fated. But if that's true, I need to find a way to talk to her without getting interrupted.

Cassia, kept appearing out of nowhere. I never stopped her before, she was easy enough when I didn't have any other options. I know she's only after the status I can bring her. I was only with her that one time and she immediately started turning it into something more than it was. Chasing away any girl that would come near me, not that it worked. I was never with a girl more than once, they were a diverting pastime, I knew I wasn't going to have a girlfriend because I wanted to wait for my fated.

Of course all the girls lingered, hoping I would change my mind. Hoping by chance maybe they were my fated but I would have sensed something. But now? Now, I need Cassia to leave me alone so I can get to know Vera.

She's clever with her words, careful with her truths. She doesn't know I can sense when someone's holding something back. But I know. She's not lying, not exactly. She's just not telling me everything.

"Is everything okay?" Sylas asks. I forgot he was even in the car with me. I zoned out and ran on autopilot. I slow down to start turning towards his street.

"Yeah, I am fine. It's just been a long day and now I need to prepare for a council meeting." I lie smoothly. Then he launches into some of the girls he was talking to today. Like me he's never had a girlfriend, but unlike me he will sleep with whoever, more than once. I don't know if he's waiting for his fated. But for now he's just having fun.

"Dude, seriously. Usually you respond." He says bringing my attention back to him.

"Sorry, just a lot on my mind."

"What's the deal with Cassia? Are you guys back together?" I glance over at him quickly. He's got a sour uncomfortable look on his face. Yup, I can't stand her either.

"No, we're not. I don't know, it's like she's staking a claim she never had. You know how she is. Her parents are trying to get us married off to each other." I give a mock shiver, trying to play it off like a joke. I don't add that there was once an arrangement. That doesn't need to make the rounds at school.

He looks at me worried for a second before schooling it again. I wonder what that's about but before I get a chance he changes the subject and we're pulling into his driveway.

"Hey, can you drive tomorrow? I got to meet with my dad in the morning."

"Yeah, no problem. I might be having a girl over late tonight anyway." He says with a laugh as he's getting out. His parents are often out late, his father is on the council. But most nights they are out partying. He never got along with his father. A lot of times growing up, Sylas would be spending the night at the Grove with me and my dad would bring us to school. That is until he really discovered girls.

After he gets out I head back towards my place, he is in the opposite direction of school, it never made sense to ride together but we wanted to anyway. Maybe it's time for him to start meeting me there so I can get a certain dark hair beauty in the seat next to me. I can imagine her beautiful lilac scent filling the space between us, and my cock starts to react.

Veils, it's been too long since I've been with someone. I wonder what I can do to convince her to spend some time with me. I can tell she's guarded. I can already feel a bond and I wonder if she can too.

I ease up to the front gate, the familiar stone arch etched with runes of protection and legacy. The guard nods and waves me through without a word. Everyone knows this car, this face, this weight I carry.

As I turn into the main drive, the towering spires of our ancestral home rise before me. The Grove of Stars, both fortress and sanctuary, a relic of ancient fae glory. Its towering graystone walls have endured for centuries, a steadfast relic of all the Shattering could not take. My sister's car is already parked near the ivy-covered column by the side entrance. Of course she beat me here. I pull up beside her care before getting out.

Thalina is waiting at the entrance beneath the carved stone arch, her silver hair braided back tight against her head, though a few stubborn curls have already escaped to frame her sharp, knowing face. Her warm bronze skin glows softly in the afternoon light, and the muted earth-toned gown she wears is partly hidden beneath a worn apron, the familiar stack of keys at her waist jingling softly with every subtle shift of her weight.

Her piercing amber eyes, eyes that seemed to see straight through any excuse or half-truth, fix on me as I approach. Her expression balancing that usual mix of stern disapproval and quiet amusement. She doesn't even have truth sense she just knows me that well. She may be the housekeeper for the Grove but she is also like a mother. She certainly helped take on that role after my mom passed away. Taking care of the three of us when we were all lost.

"Good afternoon, Thalina," I offer, voice low, matching the solemn air that always seems to hang over this place. The scent of cedarwood and old parchment curls around me as I step inside. It smells like history. Like home.

"Father's waiting," she says, but not unkindly. She knows I have been struggling with him lately, so she will warn me to prepare when she can.

I nod and take the stairs two at a time, muscle memory guiding me through the palace's winding halls. The second and third floors are reserved for family, our sanctum away from the politics and performance of the lower levels. My room sits in the northern wing, where the wind carries the mountain chill and the view stretches over the Veil like a painting that never fades.

Inside, I let the door shut behind me. I quickly changed into my dress pants and dress shirt before I drop onto the edge of my bed. The tension in my shoulders refuses to ease. Lying back on the bed, I let my legs dangle off the corner. I scrub a hand over my face, telling myself I just need a moment to myself before the meeting but my thoughts stray the moment I close my eyes.

Lilac eyes. Gods, her eyes. Like starlight trapped in glass. I shouldn't be thinking about her, not with everything going on. But she ran that track like the Veil had whispered its secrets directly to her. Like the wind and the earth were fueling her every move. And I'd watched.

Too long, too closely.

"Son." My father's voice cuts through my thoughts like steel. Always direct. Always calm. I sit up straight, forcing my mind to focus. When did he even get in my room?

I turn toward him and find King Lucan Thornevale standing near the doorway, a familiar yet distant figure. There was a time when he felt more like just *Dad*, all warm laughter, strong arms, and quiet encouragement. Now, that warmth seems buried beneath the weight of the crown, hidden behind the stoic mask he wears so easily.

Today is no different. His suit is impeccably tailored in deep charcoal tones that speak of power and formality, the rich fabric catching the low light of the hall. He stands tall, imposing, with broad shoulders squared and a deliberate stillness in the way he holds himself, like even his silence commands obedience. His shoulders are draped in his deep forest green cape that matches our royal guard. The same cape that was his father's and will get passed to me. His dark hair is neatly combed back, the streaks of silver at his temples sharper than I remember, and his piercing amber eyes, so much like my own, catch and hold mine with quiet authority.

"We're meeting with the council shortly. Walk with me." His tone leaves no room for argument.

"I'm ready," I say, smoothing my hands over my clothes before stepping into line beside him. As we head for the stairs, he glances at me, the edge in his voice unmistakable.

"Is everything okay? I knocked and called for you." He says it in a way that makes it clear he's not pleased to have to come find me, rather than meeting in his office like I usually do.

"Yeah, everything is fine. Just a long day, I just needed to close my eyes and refresh before the meeting." No way am I telling him about Vera, not yet.

As we descend the stairs and turn the corner toward the private offices and conference room, the weight of expectation settles heavier on my shoulders. The room itself is grand in the understated way that only true power can be. Polished obsidian floors reflect our steps like still water.

A high, vaulted ceiling catches the afternoon light in delicate crystal strands, scattering it across the carved walls like starlight. And at the center, the great obsidian table, etched with the crest of House Thornevale and the sigils of the other provinces, wait like an altar.

The elite guard is more than title. It's a legacy. One I was born in.

One I'm expected to lead. Our Head Guard, stands like a shadow come to life in the far corner of the room. Towering, still, and cloaked in the back and silver ceremonial armor that reflects no light, only depth. Upon his face rests the mask—a relic of vow and duty. Forged from ancient alloy, faceless and expressionless, it carries the faintly gleaming lines of Sylvaeris' forgotten age, sharp and solemn. It is never removed in the presence of others, a living oath made visible. Around others, he does not speak. Does not move. He is the kingdom's sentinel, the blade behind the crown. A reminder of what we've lost and what we're willing to protect at any cost.

But I know him.

Beneath the mask and the silence is Ro, the man who once taught my sister and me to hold a sword steady with shaky hands. Who makes terrible tea but insists on brewing it for my father anyway. Who, when it's just us, will tell stories and even laugh, though never loud, never long.

He has never removed his mask in front of anyone else. Only within our family's walls, where duty softens just enough to allow memory in. I never understood the custom completely, but I know this: the mask is not for him. It's for the world. And it is deeply, profoundly imposing.

I never understood the vow. Allowing someone to completely disappear from life. They should be able to be proud of the position they fought for. Something I might change when I take over.

The council falls silent as we enter, every gaze sharp and assessing.

We begin with Veilfall plans. The festival looms large on the calendar, both culturally and strategically. Then we move to the Veilbound initiation. As student body president, the logistics fall to me, the ceremony, the dance, the symbolic oaths. Another performance. Another test.

My father raised me with a sword in one hand and a ledger in the other. Discipline and duty, never questioned, never avoided. And I've done well. I know I have. But lately, something feels… off. Vera's arrival changed something in me. Watching her on the track earlier, it was like seeing power wrapped in wildfire. Controlled. Dangerous. Beautiful. Her body gliding through the course was beautiful, making me wonder what else her body can do. It didn't hurt to see how the training uniform perfectly molded to her body. Her long, powerful legs carried her with effortless strength, each muscle flexing beneath the sleek black fabric. The leggings hugged her hips perfectly, accentuating the curve of her ass, every movement drawing my eyes like a magnet. It was impossible not to notice.

"Caelum." My father's voice cuts clean through the memory. I blink. The room has gone quiet again.

"Apologies," I say quickly. "Could you repeat that?"

"Has training begun for the Order?" He doesn't smile. Lately it just feels like I am just a disappointment.

I nod, slipping seamlessly into the practiced rhythm of command. "Yes. Preliminary assessments started today and will continue all week. We've already identified four standouts. Council coordination with faculty is going smoothly. Festival logistics are under control."

After battlecraft each day, I'll meet with Halric to review our assessments. Next week, Ro will join the class to give his evaluations as well. Then the last couple of weeks our head of recruiting Rina, will be there to see who they will offer positions to join the Royal Guard. The room eases as I speak. I know what I'm doing. I always have. But even as the meeting resumes around me, I feel the weight of eyes still on me. Especially Mr. Corvina's. He's waiting for something.

"Prince Caelum," he says with a slight bow.

I barely resist the urge to roll my eyes. "Just Caelum. How are you, Mr. Corvina?"

The Corvina clan has always served on the council, but something about Solenar Torvyn Corvina sets my teeth on edge. He's polished in a way that feels unnatural, his platinum blonde hair slicked back too perfectly, not a strand out of place, and his sharp blue eyes too cold, too calculating. Too much like Cassia's. His smile is a touch too smooth, like everything he says has been weighed and measured long before he speaks. There's a coiled quality to him, like a snake dressed in silk, hiding venom behind pleasantries.

Solenar is the head trusted council to the leaders of each province. The Corvina's have held that seat for generations, but since he didn't produce a male heir they won't continue. I have chosen Sylas to take that seat and he's been going through extra political training and classes to make sure he's ready. His father sits on the other end. Next week he will start sitting in on meetings. It will be interesting to see how they interact in meetings when they barely talk to each other as is.

Behind me, I feel Ro shift, so slight no one else likely notices, but I do. A tension radiates off him, not defensive, but alert. Focused. I glance back just in time to see his masked gaze turned directly toward Mr. Corvina. Still unmoving. Still silent. His slight shift is enough to tell me he is suspicious of Torvyn. A flicker of unspoken guardian history, sharpened by years and veiled by protocol.

Torvyn's smile tightens just a fraction. "Your Head Guard is a fine figure of loyalty," he remarks casually, eyes flicking to Ro's imposing form. "It's remarkable, really, how some roles stay in the bloodline… while others are better left buried."

A strange beat of silence follows, delicate and charged. My father's jaw tightens. I don't know what that meant. But my father seemed to know. But it lands like a blade slid beneath the table.

Ro doesn't move. Doesn't speak. But I swear I feel it again, the air around him drawn taut like a bowstring.

My father tolerates him. I endure him. Barely.

"I'm doing well. And you? And Cassia?" Torvyn continues speaking through the silence around him.

"There is no *me* and Cassia," I say for what feels like the thousandth time. But it doesn't matter. Her parents and my parents, keep pushing for a match. It's exhausting. My father is mostly indifferent, which almost feels worse, because he should be supporting me.

"Oh, you're still young. Time will tell." He waves it off like my words are nothing more than a breeze stirring the leaves. "But she mentioned a new girl? She must not be from Sylvaeris."

My shoulders tense. "Yes, we got a lot of new students, some from the other lands. You know how it is with Auravale, fae come from all over to learn and join the guard." I reply carefully. Instinctively, I know he's talking about Vera. But I won't mention her.

My father appears beside me, placing a firm hand on my shoulder. A reminder to relax. To never let anyone see a reaction out of us. But I don't like him bringing up Vera. I don't like Cassia talking about her.

"Torvyn, how are you?" My father asks.

"Oh, great," he says. "We were just discussing our young prince and Cassia." And there it is again. Maybe I should start keeping a score of how many times I have been asked or they mention us together. It would already be close to a thousand.

"Have you asked her to the festival?" he asks.

"No, I'll be busy running my booth," I answer.

"Well, I'm sure she'd love to help," my father adds unhelpfully.

"Don't worry. I'll ask who I want to help," I say, already imagining Vera's face as she'd glare at the idea of being volunteered. Not that she'd say yes. Still, I'd like to be the one to ask. My fathers hand subtly squeezes my shoulder again.

Mr. Corvina finally departs, and I sit with my father as the rest of the council files out.

"What's going on, Cae?" he asks, studying me.

"With what?" I deflect.

"You've been distant lately. And spacing out during meetings? That's not like you. Also being disrespectful to Torvyn. People expect you to lead, son." Like you've been leading? I think, but don't say.

"What did he mean that some bloodlines should stay buried?"

He sighs, long and tired. "He was talking about my first Head Guard. My best friend. I don't know why he's bringing him up, what did he say before that?" Torvyn is plotting something, he's just been too checked out to care.

"He mentioned that our Head Guard was a fine figure of loyalty." We grew up knowing he had a best friend and that they had to leave. But we were to never talk about it, not even around Ro. It stayed just in our family and Thalina included.

Maybe now he will tell me the story. "Yes, Ro does a great job. But this does not negate your behavior today."

"I'm sorry, *Father*. I will watch my words, but I want you to stop forcing me to be with Cassia."

"Watch your tone, son. Cal is already drawing up a contract, it will be good for the kingdom and good for you."

I feel my anger flare up. "May I be excused."

He sighs heavily, regret flitting across his face. "Yes, I will see you at dinner. Cae, it will be good, just give it a chance." I nod my head and walk out. Going to find my sister.

Chapter 11: Something Vast. Something Ancient.

Something Waiting.

Vera

The cottage smelled faintly of chamomile and old wood, the kind of scent that clung to soft things; wool blankets, pages of worn books, the corners of memory. Morning light filtered through gauzy curtains, casting golden lines across the polished floorboards. The hearth had gone cold, but the embers still held a low red glow.

I stood at the window, arms wrapped tightly around myself. My breathing fogging up the glass before me. Beyond it, the mist rolled low across the hills, softening the edges of the world. Behind me, Aunt Rina moved quietly around the kitchen, the soft clink of porcelain, a comfort I was coming to depend on. There was something steady about Rina. Like a pillar half-buried in the earth, worn by time but unmoving.

"I packed your satchel," Rina said gently, setting it on the table near the door. "I don't want you rushing. Yesterday was hard." Turning slowly. My heart thudded unevenly. Auravale Academy. I can't believe all of this is real.

"Are you sure this is right?" My voice was barely above a whisper. I asked her last night, too. I hate feeling so unsure, so indecisive about my life. I thought I always had a plan, knew somewhat how my life was going to end up and now? Now, I don't even know if I will live beyond the next year.

To think that I really wanted to be a book editor. Cliche I know. I was going to get my degree and read books, I mean what else was I supposed to do, I've always been a misfit. I always drawn to my fantasy romance novels. I wish I had brought some of them with me, I really want to compare.

Rina's eyes, a warm faded gray. They were tired. Wary. But warm. "You've been in hiding long enough, sweetheart. I know you're scared. But your father would've wanted you to learn. To do the Order. To grow strong."

What if I can't? What if I'm not like them? But the words tangled in my throat. The truth was, I *felt* different. Had always felt different. The way people's emotions tugged at my chest like invisible threads. How my skin tingled when someone lied. The way storm clouds made my heart race, not with fear, but recognition.

I don't know what that meant. Only that it had to mean *something*.

"I don't want people looking at me," I admitted. "I don't want to be known."

Rina walked over and brushed a lock of hair from my face, tucking it behind my ear. Her touch lingered, reassuring me.

"You won't have to tell them anything you're not ready to. Auravale is a place for all kinds of people. Some go to learn. Some go to forget. Some go because they're searching."

I let out a shaky breath. "Which am I?"

"I think," Rina said softly, "you're all three."

There was a pause between us, heavy and sacred.

"I'll be nearby," she added, her voice firmer now. "Watching. Protecting. But you'll have to choose who you want to be, Vera. No one else can do that for you."

The satchel felt impossibly heavy when I finally picked it up. So did the future. Did I get to choose? It feels like I'm being thrust into something impossible.

When I leave the cottage, the early morning mist clings to the ground like a living thing, curling around the roots of the towering silverwood trees. Their leaves shimmer faintly in the low light, casting shifting patterns across the narrow dirt path that winds its way toward the academy. The air smells of damp earth, cedar, and the faintest trace of something sweet and wild, like honeysuckle after rain. Those slightly glowing flowers yesterday seemed to be a little brighter.

But my steps falter when I see the tall, shadowy figure standing dead center in the path.

My heart slams against my ribs, the memory of the intruder flashing through my mind like a blade of panic. Every time I close my eyes, I still see that shadow, looming, cold, waiting.

"You going to stand there staring, or are we walking to school?" Nero calls out, his voice breaking the spell. Relief rushes through me so fast it leaves me dizzy. My breath whooshes out, and I force myself to move forward. As I approach, Nero falls into step beside me, his stride easy and relaxed.

I keep my gaze fixed ahead, but I reach out gently with my senses, feeling for the threads of his aura beside me. Warmth blooms against my skin, golden streaks swirling lazily around the soft pulse of his energy. He means no harm. Not today. Why couldn't I feel that yesterday?

"Why'd you look so freaked out when you noticed me?" he asks, his voice low and gruff, though there's a gentleness underneath it, like he's trying not to scare me.

"I thought we didn't have to talk," I remind him, repeating the words I said yesterday.

He chuckles, the sound rough but not unkind. "We don't. Just, if you need help, you can come to me."

"I don't even know you. You don't know me."

"No. But something tells me we'll be good friends." I glance at him from the corner of my eye, but he's already facing forward, as if it was nothing. We fall into a comfortable silence after that. And maybe— maybe he could be someone I could trust. Like a brother. Maybe he's someone I can ask to help practice sparring with, he's definitely large like my father was.

As we crest a gentle hill, the school comes into view. Auravale Academy. It rises out of the forest like it was carved from the shadows themselves. Its dark stone walls veined with silver, the spires reaching toward the misty sky like fingers. Vines drape over the old stones, their leaves a deep violet that only darken the façade. In the heavy morning gloom, it looks almost abandoned, swallowed by time.

Only the windows betray the truth, warm light spilling out from within, golden and inviting, as if daring you to step inside. A living heart inside a sleeping beast. As we draw closer, I notice the same sleek black car from yesterday parked near the entrance, its polished surface glinting under the weak sunlight.

I spot Caelum. He's sitting in his car but his eyes are unmistakably trained on me. Sharp and unblinking.

Nero slows, nudging me gently with his elbow. "See you later," he murmurs, then veers off, disappearing toward one of the side entrances. I barely have time to brace myself before Caelum is standing in front of me. There's something magnetic about him that sets all my nerves alight, the easy confidence in his stance, the casual way he runs a hand through his light hair, the way his piercing green eyes seem to see right through me.

"Good morning, did you sleep well?" He asks with a light tone.

"Yes. Thank you. I need to get to class." I pick up the pace, but he easily falls in step beside me like it's nothing.

"I did too, thanks for asking," he says with a sexy grin that I really want to hate. "Though I kept seeing these stunning lilac eyes every time I closed mine." And when he speaks, when he flashes that slight, knowing smile, my heart stutters.

I halt and glare up at him, voice cold. "That is inappropriate. You have a girlfriend." Now I definitely hate that grin. Hate that he makes me feel that way when he's with someone else. I'm not someone he can just use.

I manage to escape thanks to Cassia's sudden interruption, her high, sharp voice slicing through the tension like a blade. Grateful, I slip away, weaving into the crowded hallways. But not before I hear him curse, "Veils."

The main corridor is massive, its high, arched ceilings held up by dark beams carved with symbols I don't recognize. Hanging lanterns sway gently overhead, casting pools of golden light across the slate floors. To my right, a grand staircase sprawls upward, splitting into two large staircases that curve toward the second floor. The air buzzes faintly with magic, like the building itself is alive, watching. There are a lot of students milling around, some with cups of coffee. I wonder where they get it from, I miss coffee.

Most of my classes are on the second floor, but I know from the ornate plaques that the library, the lunchroom, the gymnasium and my locker are all on the first. I haven't yet dared venture to the third or fourth floors. There was no need to. But I'm curious what is up there, I do see lot's of students go up there.

I get to class earlier than yesterday and slide into the same seat in the back corner where my back can rest safely against the wall, and I have an unobstructed view of the door. I like it. I *need* it. I feel really uncertain in this moment. The classroom smells faintly of parchment and lavender. Valeis, arranges his notes at the front. When he finally looks up, his smile is kind, if a little unsettling.

"Hi, Vera. Did your first day go well?" he asks.

"Yes, thank you. I..." I almost say *my aunt is helping me* but catch myself. *Don't reveal anything, Vera.*

"I read the first three chapters." He gives me a slight, approving nod but his sharp eyes linger a beat too long, as if weighing the parts of me I haven't revealed.

Then he walks in. Caelum. The air shifts the moment he enters. My spine straightens. My heart leaps stupidly in my chest. I can feel him glance at the teacher and then slide into the seat beside me closer than yesterday. His presence hums beside me, distracting, impossible to ignore.

I refuse to look at him. Refuse to notice how he leans in slightly, like he might whisper something. Refuse to let my heart pay attention to the low rasp of his breathing or the subtle scent of him, cedarwood and something sharper underneath, like cracked lightning.

"Hi, I didn't get your name yesterday." He says.

"I didn't give it," I say quickly, eyes flicking up for only a second before dropping back to my notebook. I purposely keep my head down. My pencil moves in slow, absent-minded loops, sketching symbols in the margins.

Grumbling under his breath, he keeps pushing. "What's your name?"

"You didn't hear it when Halric said it yesterday and you were standing next to me?" I say irritated that he's still trying. He scrubs his hand down his face and mumbles "Frustrating." I can't contain my smirk. Glad I am getting to him.

"Fine." He grumbles. "Vera, that's a beautiful name. My name is Caelum. My friends call me Cae." I roll my eyes and I can sense his irritation growing. Still he doesn't give up.

"Nice to meet you, Caelum." I say still looking at my notebook.

"Please, call me Cae." He prompts. I swear I hear him grumble, "It's like pulling teeth." But just quiet enough I can't be sure.

"We're not friends. Now please, I am trying to listen." I say quietly. But clearly class hasn't started yet and I hear a "Ha" come from the front of the room.

"He's not even teaching yet." He points out, ironically.

"Yeah, well he will be. Like I said, it was nice meeting you." The bell rings finally, preventing him from speaking again.

I spend the entire class focused on the page in front of me, even as he scoots his chair a fraction closer, the scrape of it loud in the otherwise quiet room. Butterflies riot inside me. As soon as the bell rings, I bolt for the door, slipping through the flood of students. I don't know what Caelum wants from me. I don't know if I can trust him. I don't know if I can trust *anyone.*

The next class, I wait until the very last possible moment to slip inside, heart hammering. The wide, arching doorway leads into a room with soaring ceilings and tall, narrow windows etched with symbols I don't recognize. The sunlight filters through them in hazy colors, splashing faint patterns across the dark stone floor. The room smells faintly of parchment and something sharper, magic, maybe, clinging to the walls like a memory.

I spot an empty desk near the front, beside Nero, and quickly slip into it, my bag hitting the floor with a soft thud. A moment later Caelum claims the other seat beside me but I don't look at him. Even as I keep my eyes forward, I can *feel* Caelum's stare burning into the back of my head. It's like a tangible thing. Alive, thrumming with some unreadable current. Heavy in the best and worst way, unsettling and magnetic all at once.

I sigh audibly without looking up. Wanting him to hear my annoyance. "What's it going to take for you to leave me alone?"

"Nothing. I told you, I want to get to know you."

"There's nothing to know. Now go back to your girlfriend, or whatever flavor-of-the-month you're on, and leave me alone."

"She's not—"

The bell cuts him off, and Cassia struts in like she owns the place, daggers flashing from her eyes.

"Are we sitting up here now?" The other guy Caelum was with yesterday, Sylas I think, drops into the seat on his other side, smooth as ever.

"Yeah. Just wanted to be closer to the board," He replies, casual. That alone tells me that whatever he is trying to do with me isn't important for him to mention to his friends.

"Uh-huh. You're chasing the hot girl. Just find out if she has a friend for me." Sylas says quietly but I still hear it. Cae also chuckles quietly. My shoulders tense and the anger starts rolling off of me. They just help each other chase girls, there were boys like that in my old school. It's easy to hear what others are doing when they mostly pretend you don't exist. I feel a bump on my left shoulder and I look at Nero. He gives me a reassuring smile and I know I need to breathe and calm myself. Remembering what Rina told me. To ground myself, bring me back to the moment.

In Truthsense & Future Sight, Professor Oryll stands at the front explaining the day's lesson. The class where I'm finally supposed to understand the gift I've had for as long as I can remember. The one that made me different. *Other.* Here, the ancient art is studied, sharpened like a blade passed down through generations. She starts discussing truthsense and my mind is lost. I remember the moment like it was yesterday.

Just before my fifth birthday, in a little house tucked at the edge of the human world. My parents pretending they'd forgotten my cake, their voices lilting with false regret. I had known, even then. I'd planted my tiny hands on my hips and declared, "You're lying!" Their laughter had filled the room, rich and proud, their eyes shining with something I hadn't understood until much later.

A tear slips down my cheek before I can stop it. I swipe it away quickly, pressing my palm harder into the cool, carved wood of my desk. *Stay grounded, Vera.* Close your eyes. Breathe. Anchor yourself. I do. The sounds around me sharpen, the faint scratch of pens, the murmur of a spell humming from the walls themselves. I breathe in… and there it is again. *Him.*

The subtle, wild scent of cedarwood. Caelum. It winds its way toward me, stealing my focus, but also calms me. I try to push it aside, reaching for the Truthsense, calling it like a tendril of smoke curling through my mind.

But something else stirs. A thread of connection, so faint I might have missed it if I wasn't already reaching. It pulses, steady, like a heartbeat just beyond my own. I follow it, instinctively, pressing deeper.

Warmth. It spreads through me, golden and alive, and for a dizzying second, it feels like I'm standing on the edge of something vast. Something ancient. Something waiting. A tether. I don't know what it means, and before I can chase it further—

"Okay, class dismissed. We'll begin future-sight exercises tomorrow," the teacher's voice cuts through the spell.

My eyes flutter open to a half-empty room. Students are already packing up, laughter and murmured conversations spilling into the corridors beyond. I blink, dazed, my hands trembling slightly as I close my notebook.

When I glance up, Caelum is watching me. That half-smile of his plays at the corner of his mouth. Crooked, knowing and it steals the breath from my lungs. His eyes, deep green laced with gold starbursts, catch the fading light like they're alive, like they know something I don't. Heat rises to my cheeks. I duck my head quickly, shoving my things into my bag with shaking hands. I don't even remember where I'm supposed to go next, but I fumble out my schedule and bolt for the door.

"Are you okay?" Nero asks, appearing at my side.

"Yes. I'm fine," I mutter without looking up, my voice tight.

I clutch my bag to my chest as I hurry down the long hallways, the heavy stones echoing every step like a drumbeat against my ribcage.

Chapter 12: Do Fae's Have Wings?

Vera

The next class is already filling up by the time I reach it, a smaller room with rounded windows overlooking a courtyard tangled with vines and flowers that seem to shimmer faintly under the sun. The walls inside are painted with soft colors, calming, and a kind-looking older woman stands at the front, her silver hair pulled into a loose braid.

Gratefully, I slip into a seat near the front, pulling out my notebook and pen with hands that are still unsteady. The seat next to me scrapes back. I inwardly groan. Why does he have to keep sitting next to me.

I don't need to look. That warmth unfurls through me again, chased by the rich, earthy scent I now associate with him. Caelum. Still, I pretend he isn't there.

"Ah, Mr. Thornevale." The teacher's voice brightens. "I'm so happy to have you in my class this year. It's been a long time since your father sat in that seat."

"Kailis," he says, respectful and smooth. "I'm honored to be here and eager to learn from you." She blushes. Blushes.

"Oh, please. I'm sure your father already taught you more than I ever could." There was a weird expression on his face, like disappointment but he quickly hides it.

With that, the rest of the class quiets down and settles in. And I find myself holding my pen, staring straight ahead, pretending I'm not on fire from the inside out. Pretending I don't feel his gaze on me or the warmth spreading through me.

Today, I brought my own lunch and went straight to the library to study. I ate quickly, I was able to bring some fruit and a sandwich. Shoving my garbage back into the bag, I focus on my notes. A shadow comes across my table and looking up I see Caelum, he gently places the apple in front of me.

I look at it and then at him. Does he really think I need his help?

"Hey, I didn't want you to be hungry. I am glad you brought lunch."

"Is there a reason you're here?" I infuse the attitude again a bravado I don't really feel. Seriously, I am not interested in being one of his conquests. He must think because I am new that I will fall prey to his charm. I will admit he is persistent when he wants something.

"Just trying to get to know you." He says smoothly, putting his hands in his jeans. Jeans that seem to form perfectly to his body.

"Okay, well like I said earlier we're not friends. I am just here to learn."

"Maybe I could use a friend." I roll my eyes so he can clearly see, and he chuckles.

"Okay, where are you from?" He tries again.

"Listen, *Cae*." I love saying his name. It sounded right. "Just go back to your friends, I am just trying to study so I can learn about the magic and the Veilbound Order." That was the wrong thing to say. He clearly took that as an invitation because he pulled the chair out opposite me.

"I can help. We have all the same classes, you know." I glare at him and then ignore him and I continue to read and then make notes and use my highlighter. He sits there quietly. Even when the bell rings he stays quietly near me as I gather my things and we make our way to our last classes.

He seems to quietly stay by me the rest of the day and sits next to me in the rest of our classes. Until we go to Battlecraft, that is to which Cassia notices and is glaring at me. Making it just as awkward if not more. I change quickly, and when I reach the rest of the class I avoid Caelum's gaze as I make my way to the Echoforge. The lights above flicker, and the air smells like sweat, rubber, and something faintly metallic.

Halric's voice rang out across the training field like a thunderclap.

"Gather around, everyone! Today we begin the path of the Veilbound Order. First challenge is physical. Second, combat. If you can't run without wheezing or throw a punch without crying, I suggest you start praying to your ancestors now."

He clapped his hands once, the sound sharp as a crack of lightning.

"Pair up! Yesterday was speed. Today, I want to see who can actually survive the course without becoming one with the dirt. We'll run it together first, timing starts next week." A pause. His eyes scanned the group like he was already making mental cuts. "And make no mistake, we *will* be watching. If you're wasting our time, we'll cut you faster than a rusty blade through butter. You want to stay? Prove you belong." I didn't move. Just stood, waiting. Someone always chose first, and I'd learned long ago not to expect it to be me. Sure enough, Cassia latched onto Caelum's arm before I could even glance in his direction.

"You're with me!" she chirped. "I'll need all the help I can get." Her tone dripped sugar, but her eyes were all steel and sharp edges. A sting of jealousy flared in my chest. I shoved it down.

"Come on, partner. Don't let her get to you," Nero said, appearing at my side like he'd always been there. I straightened my shoulders, nodded once, and followed him toward the course. I'd trained for this my entire life. I didn't know that, I just thought my dad loved fitness. Or it was a way I could workout and train since I couldn't join any sports.

"She's not getting to me. I don't care about either of them." I tell him even though it does bother me.

I get a smirk from him. "Okay." That's it, just the one word. He doesn't believe me, I guess I wasn't convincing.

The first team, a pair of girls, struggled with the rock wall but encouraged each other the whole way. They finished in just over five minutes, breathless and grinning like they'd won a war.

Halric barked, "Vera, Nero, you're up. Let's see if all that brooding translates to results."

I jogged to the starting point without hesitation, though my stomach twisted at the sight of the chamber stretching impossibly high above me. From the outside, the building had seemed no larger than a gymnasium, but inside, platforms spiraled upward into shadow, shifting when I looked away as though the walls themselves were breathing.

Nero fell into stride beside me, his grin quick, sharp, unbothered. My muscles moved before my brain caught up, instinct, drilled into me by years of running when survival was all I knew. But survival had never looked like this.

The rock wall rose before me, runes pulsing faintly across its surface. My fingers gripped the stone, and it shifted under my hands, smooth as glass one moment, jagged the next. My foot slipped, scraping skin, but I dug in harder and climbed anyway, dragging myself to the top.

The monkey bars stretched ahead, gleaming silver, too bright. When I swung forward, the metal jolted like a living thing, vibrating beneath my palms, trying to throw me loose. My breath caught. For a moment, I dangled, one hand slipping but then Nero's voice carried up from below.

"Focus forward. Don't fight it, flow with it."

I forced myself to stop clutching, stop resisting. I swung in rhythm with the bars, let the motion carry me, until I hit the end and flipped onto the next platform. My chest burned, but I refused to pause.

The rope climb spiraled upward, disappearing into light. I grabbed hold, arms straining. Halfway up, the fibers unraveled beneath my grip, thinning to threads. My pulse jumped. My hands nearly slipped free, but Nero's presence at my side—steady, relentless—pushed me higher. I gritted my teeth, ignoring the sting in my shoulders, and hauled myself to the top.

The beam waited. Barely wide enough for my foot. Shadows yawned below, and the illusion of a raging river roared in my ears. I faltered, balance tipping. My heart lurched but Nero's hand brushed mine, quick and grounding, before he shot ahead. Just enough contact to steady me. Just enough to remind me I wasn't alone.

I sprinted. Jump. Descend. Leap the logs. My body moved faster than I thought I could, muscles catching up to fear. The obstacles twisted under me, alive with enchantments, but I pressed through. I launched myself ahead of Nero.

And then, the final wall. Slanted, slick with mist, transforming from stone to glass to steel with cruel rhythm. My hands slipped once, twice, nails catching against nothing. My legs screamed, every muscle raw fire, until finally, I clawed myself over the top. I dropped onto the last platform, landing hard enough to rattle my bones.

Silence.

My chest heaved. Sweat stung my eyes. I staggered toward the water station, lungs burning with both triumph and disbelief. A heartbeat later, Nero landed beside me, stride perfectly matched to mine, as if he'd been pacing me all along.

But the moment I stopped moving, I felt it. The weight of it. Silence, thick and charged. Eyes. Everyone was staring. Nero. Even Caelum. They both held varying expressions, not shocked, exactly. More... intrigued. Impressed. And something else I couldn't place. Curiosity, maybe? Crap. Maybe I shouldn't have gone all in. I wasn't even thinking just moving. I don't even know our time. It felt much longer in the Gauntlet, but when I looked at the timer it shows four minutes exactly.

Then Halric's voice cut through the silence like a blade. "Well, damn. Remind me never to race you before breakfast." He strode over, his expression unreadable but the faintest twitch of amusement pulled at the corner of his mouth. "That was clean, efficient, and disturbingly fast. If you're hiding wings under that training shirt, now's the time to confess." Wings? Do fae's have wings?

A few quiet laughs rippled through the group. Halric didn't smile. He never smiled. "But don't get cocky," he added, deadpan. "That was the easy round." I think I nodded. I didn't even think it was that smooth, I messed up a few times. Nero is the one that helped get me through it.

I'd let frustration get the better of me, the weird tension between Caelum and Cassia had lit a fuse. My dad used to say emotions made things messy. Especially on your worst days. I backed away from the group, keeping to the edge. A couple guys came up, asking how the veils I'd done it so fast.

"Just luck," I said with a shrug, taking a long sip from my bottle to avoid further questions.

When Caelum and Cassia's names were called, I pretended not to watch but I felt the flicker of his frustration. Not from what he said or how he moved... I could *feel* it. That wasn't normal. Not for me. Is that something I could do now that I am in this realm?

Cassia messed up on the rope climb, clearly struggling with her balance, but still managed a decent time. Caelum, on the other hand, barely looked like he was trying. He strolled through the course, effortless as usual. When he passed me, his gaze lingered just long enough for Cassia to notice. Her scowl said it all.

By the time everyone finished, I knew I'd done better than any of the girls by a long shot and faster than all the guys. Next time, I'd have to dial it back. Pretend to mess up. Blend.

As I was sipping more of my water, pretending to keep busy. Someone steps up to me. Based on their height I thought it would be Nero. When I looked over, it was another boy. That same one from yesterday that was glaring at me. His midnight hair and his eyes that matched were assessing me. Trying to read something. I shift uncomfortably. He wasn't classically handsome, his nose looked crooked like it's been broken many times, maybe it had been. Sharp cheekbones that lead to thin lips that are shaped into a weird half-smile, half-sneer. Like he's trying to appear nice, but he's missing the mark.

"You must be Vera," the voice came like gravel, low, sharp, and just a touch amused. "That was impressive. Where did you learn to move like that?"

His words were technically a compliment, but they felt more like a challenge. My instincts prickled. This guy was massive, maybe even the same height as Nero but broader through the chest, like he was carved from obsidian and combat drills. The kind of person who carried power like armor. His gaze dragged over me like he was assessing a threat or a weakness.

I didn't answer. "Who are you?" I asked, my voice clipped, sharp. He was definitely sizing me up.

"Ryven. From Duskmere." His voice curled around the name like it was meant to intimidate. "Here to be the next Head Guard for the prince."

He said it like it was already decided. Like the crown had already been passed to him in secret.

Footsteps crunched behind me, and the air seemed to shift. "Ryven," Nero's voice was quiet but tighter than usual. "I see you met Vera." So they knew each other. That should've made me feel better. But it didn't. I can feel the animosity and tension between them.

"Yes," Ryven said, his tone laced with a smirk. "Just sizing up my competition."

I glanced at Nero, and for the first time since I met him, I saw tension coiled in his frame. Like he was waiting for Ryven to make the first move in a fight that had been brewing for years.

"Yeah, she sure is something," Nero replied. But the words were quiet, laced with caution.

"How do you two know each other?" I asked, regretting it the second it left my mouth. Of course they knew each other, they were both from Duskmere. But the way Ryven was watching me now, like I was some half-interesting puzzle, made my stomach twist.

Nero shot me a quick glance before answering. "We've trained together most of our lives. Both here for the guard. Hoping for the head position."

"Not we," Ryven snapped. "You don't stand a chance. You've always been too soft. Too concerned with protecting people to be a real guard." Ouch. I didn't know their history, but that cut deep. Isn't that the guards job though?

Before I could respond, another voice slipped in low and close, the kind of voice that made your heart skip whether you wanted it to or not. "Where did you learn to do that?" Caelum. His breath brushed the back of my neck, stirring loose strands of my hair and setting goosebumps dancing down my arms. I turned slightly, careful not to meet his eyes. Not now. Don't look. Don't fall.

Ryven's tone shifted instantly. "Ah, nice run, Caelum." Syrupy, suddenly polite. I blinked at the sudden flip. So fake it was laughable.

Caelum gave a diplomatic nod, his lips pulling into a small, tight smile. "Thanks. Yours was great too, steady pace." But the way he said it? Like he'd rather be anywhere else.

"Yes," Ryven continued. "I've been training my whole life for that Head Guard position."

Nero rolled his eyes beside him, subtle, but I caught it. I tried to hold in a laugh, but it slipped past my lips anyway, a quiet bubble of amusement I couldn't smother in time. Nero's lips twitched. Caelum looked at me like I'd just handed him the sun.

Ryven, looked like he wanted to incinerate me on the spot. I swallowed hard. Wait. Fire could be his gift. Note to self: *maybe stop laughing at people who could set things on fire. Like myself.*

He stormed off, boots crinkling over the mat and thudding over the hard wood floors in the open area where everyone is gathered. Nero followed more slowly, shooting me a calm, reassuring smile before turning his back. There was something about him, steady, warm in a way that didn't demand anything from me. I wondered why he was so kind. Maybe it was a trap. Keep your enemies close, right? I didn't want the Head Guard role. Especially not for some stuffy prince.

"Thanks for your help!" I called to Nero as he walked away.

He gives me a weird finger salute off the top of his head as he keeps walking but doesn't turn back around.

Caelum's voice pulled me back. "So…" he said with that slow smile, "where did you learn to run the course like that, Lilac? It looked almost effortless." The nickname curled around me like silk. I knew I wouldn't get out of answering this time.

"My aunt likes to train," I said, my voice steadier than I felt. I ignore the butterflies in my belly from the nickname. Wait, no I was supposed to say guardian, she was hosting me. He just unsettles me, I don't think right when he's near me. I keep slipping up and it's only day two. Both with him and Nero. I need to get my crap together.

"Mm." A thoughtful sound rumbled from him. "Who's your aunt?"

"Rina," I answered, just as the bell rang, sharp and blessedly loud. I don't know why I told him the truth again it just slipped out.

"Next time, I want to be the one running it with you." The way he says it isn't casual, it's a claim, soft but unmistakable. I don't respond to that, because I don't even know this guy.

"Can I ask you something?" I ask him quietly. He looks at me surprised.

"Of course, Lilac. You can ask me anything." I almost roll my eyes but I hold back this time.

"Umm, do some fae's have wings?" I whisper. He stopped and looked at me, surprised. And now I feel stupid. Maybe I shouldn't have asked. Maybe that was too telling that I'm not from here. I should have asked Nero, I felt like he wouldn't have judged me.

"Uh, we used to. A few generations back some fae mostly the most powerful were gifted them, mostly from the Elarindor region, but it slowly faded away. No one alive has them, that we know about. It's thought that maybe since the realms of shifters and vampires are kept separate that we didn't need that anymore." He says kindly. I can feel the truth coming from him. He's purposely being nice and patient which is appreciated, there is still so much to learn about this life I have been thrusted into.

"Oh, right. Of course, thanks!" Before he could ask more, I was already moving, slipping through the crowd and making for the locker room. But when I pushed the door open, I pulled up short. Cassia and her little clique lounged in front of my locker like they were posing for a portrait, casual, fake smiles firmly in place.

Chapter 13: I Was not Broken

Vera

"What kind of freak are you?" Cassia sneered, her voice sweetly venomous.

I took a deep breath, refusing to rise to it. "I'm not sure. I guess I never thought to look into it," I said coolly. "Now if you'll excuse me, I need to get my things." I tried to move around them, but they spread out, blocking my path. The only way out was *through*. Cassia's eyes glittered with something cruel.

"I thought I told you to stay away from him," she said, stepping forward.

"You can have him," I said evenly. "Now can I leave?"

The air shifted. She moved closer, so close I could see the flecks of silver in her ice-blue eyes. Her intent was clear. She wanted a fight. I could feel her through my gift clearly. A cool breeze flowed around and a hint of red.

"Grab her," she snapped.

Before I could process the command, two of her bimbo twins seized my arms, their nails biting into my skin. I could break free, easily. But I didn't. Not yet. I wanted to see what they would do.

They forced me down to the floor, the cold stone biting into my knees. Around us, other students watched from the corners of the room, silent, detached. The first kick came fast, slamming into my ribs and ripping a groan from my throat. Pain flared white-hot through my side. I braced myself, ready to move, but another kick slammed into my hip, driving me back down.

Cassia pulled her leg back for another kick but I was faster.

I used my body weight to hurl Posse Number One into Posse Number Two. Their shrieks echoed off the metal lockers as they tumbled together. Before Cassia could land her kick, I lashed my leg out, sweeping hers from under her, and spun into a crouch.

She hit the ground hard, a *sharp crack* of bone against tile. I didn't wait to see if she got up. Pain flared sharp and hot under my ribs, but I pushed through it, sprinting for my locker. I yanked it open, grabbed my things, and bolted into the hallway, my bag barely zipped.

Everything was too bright, the buzzing fluorescents overhead, the chatter of students, the sharp smell of floor cleaner still clinging to the air. Every breath was a stab through my right side. Every step jarred the bruises blooming under my skin. I ducked my head, weaving through the crowd. I needed out. I needed air.

But then I saw him. Caelum. He leaned against the brick wall near the entrance to the east wing, one foot propped against it, arms folded. Waiting. *Why is he always there when I don't want him to be?*

What do I need to do to get him to leave me alone? He doesn't get it, I guess I will make it more clear.

I glared at him, fury and humiliation burning hotter than the bruises on my skin. I veered away, trying to move faster, but my body betrayed me, stiff, limping. A sharp stab of pain lanced through my ribs and I gasped, clutching my side.

"Are you okay?" Caelum asked, pushing off the wall to fall into step beside me.

"I'm fine," I said, the words brittle, snapping like dry twigs between us. "Now please, for the last time, stay away from me."

I surged forward, trying to escape but his hand caught my shoulder. I stiffened at the contact, a fresh bolt of pain flaring through my ribs. I flinched, barely suppressing a sound. But then warmth flows through me. He gasped, his eyes widening as he gazes down at me. The surprise on his face clear, but he looks something else. Pleased? Concerned? Amazed? I'm too frazzled to think straight.

Where his hand met my skin, a strange, tingling heat bloomed outward, soft and golden, like the first breath of sunlight after a storm. It spread through my veins, warm and real and terrifying. I shuddered, trying to shake it off.

"What happened?" he asked, voice low and rough, scanning me with those piercing green eyes.

He saw the bruises on my arms, the dark purple already forming. His jaw tightened until the muscle ticked along his cheekbone. A rage rolled off him, thick and heavy, the air between us practically vibrating with it. His gaze flicked back toward the locker room, then returned to me. Harder now, deadlier. I took a step back, that look screamed predator.

"Nothing happened," I said stiffly, swallowing down the hot lump rising in my throat. "I need to go. My aunt's expecting me home."

"Please," he said, voice a rough whisper. "Don't lie to me."

The way he looked at me, with such intensity, such *knowing*. It almost broke something loose inside me. Almost. But I couldn't. I couldn't fall apart now. Not here. Not in front of him.

"I'm not lying, now please leave me alone. I want nothing to do with you." I bit out, more viciously than I intended. He let me go. I stumbled forward, barely catching myself before I fell. I didn't look back.

My locker. I needed my locker. I needed to get out of here. I shoved everything into my backpack without thought, my hands shaking. I didn't even care that I was still in my training gear. The polyester, nylon and spandex mixed with my sweat is clinging to my skin. Tennis shoes tight. Muscles primed.

Fight or flight roaring in my ears. I chose flight. I burst out into the corridor and sprinted down the hall, ignoring the shocked stares. Through the side door and out into the trees that lined the back of the campus. The air hit my face sharp and cold. I pushed harder. Every breath was a knife in my ribs. Every step screamed through my battered side. But I didn't stop. *I couldn't stop.*

Hot tears blurred my vision, but I blinked them away furiously. I wouldn't cry. Not for them. Not for anyone. But the pain, not just the physical, but the ache in my chest, threatened to tear me apart. I ran faster, faster like I could outrun it all. The shame. The fear. The memory of Cassia's designer tennis shoes slamming into my ribs. The wind is whipping around me, I can feel it fueling me as I run. Right now I don't even feel the pain that will surely be excruciating when I stop.

The feel of Caelum's hand, warm and solid, like an anchor I couldn't afford. I couldn't want. The wind tore at my clothes, my hair, but I welcomed the sting. I *needed* it. I needed something real. Something that wasn't bruises or lies or almost-tears.

Footsteps matched mine. I snapped my head to the side, heart hammering in my chest. Nero. He was there, running alongside me with effortless grace. He didn't say anything. Just ran. That silence, that simple act of staying without asking. It steadied me more than any words could have. So I kept running. Not away. But through. Through the anger, through the hurt, and through the wildfire burning in my chest that refused to be tamed.

Because I was *not* broken. I would *not* break. Not now. Not ever. They couldn't break me in the human realm and they won't here, either. At least there they probably knew they couldn't hurt me, not physically. I will always be the outcast. I don't say anything to Nero, though I'm grateful for his steady presence. Without a word, I veer off toward home, slowing to a light jog once I'm out of sight. The run didn't do my ribs any favors, the bruises throb in time with my heartbeat. Although, it helped clear the chaos storming inside me.

Not healed, not really. Enough to hold the pieces of myself together.

By the time I reach the cottage, my body feels like it's stitched together by sheer stubbornness. The porch creaks under my weight as I climb the steps and slip inside. I head straight for the bathroom, stripping out of my sweat-soaked clothes and stepping under an ice-cold shower. The water hits my skin like a thousand tiny needles, shocking me back into myself. The pain comes back tenfold but I don't regret the run. I needed it, even if I was trying to outrun my problems.

I don't have long. Rina will be home soon, and she'll want to train. I scrub quickly, wincing every time the washcloth grazes my side. Wishing I could scrub away the bruises and the pain. I dress in loose clothes to hide the worst of it, but the second the door swings open downstairs, I know it won't be enough. Rina is a force. Sharp-eyed and sharper-willed. And she knows me too well already. Heavy footsteps thud up the stairs, and the next thing I know, she's standing in my doorway, arms crossed, brow furrowed.

Her sharp intake of breath says it all. "What happened?!" she demands, rushing forward and grabbing my arms before I can dodge. Her hands are gentle, but the look in her eyes is fierce as she scans the bruises painting my skin in ugly shades of purple and blue.

"I fell in battlecraft today," I say smoothly, keeping my voice casual. "We started training on the obstacle course. I'm not used to that and I fell off a beam." Rina's dark eyes narrow. She's silent for a beat too long. I can tell she doesn't buy it.

"Then why do the bruises on your arms look like fingerprints?" she asks, voice low and dangerous. I shrug, ignoring the sharp pull of pain.

"When I fell, a couple of girls tried to grab me. It got messy." Not a full lie. But enough of one to keep her out of it. Hopefully. The last thing I need is her storming into the Academy and making things worse.

Rina stares at me, like she's trying to read between the lines. Finally, she sighs heavily, the fight leaving her shoulders.

"Okay," she says reluctantly. "But if your ribs are cracked, you're skipping training this afternoon and tomorrow morning. Plus, I think you need to miss a day of battlecraft. Non-negotiable." I open my mouth to protest and she gives me a sharp look telling me it's futile to argue. I nod, keeping my face carefully blank.

What she doesn't know is that by tonight, I'll already be healing. I always do. It's not the first time I cracked ribs. But if she found out just how fast, it would lead to questions I'm not ready to answer. That I don't know how to answer.

Rina moves to the tall cupboard near the hearth, pulling open the creaking wooden doors. The scent of lavender, cedar, and something fresh and citrusy spills into the room, thick and soothing.

Bundles of dried herbs hang from the shelves like trophies, and rows of glass jars catch the fading sunlight, their contents glittering gold, green, and deep violet. She sifts through them with practiced hands, finally pulling down a small jar filled with a shimmering cream that seems to pulse faintly under the light.

"This should help," she murmurs, unscrewing the lid. The smell is different, earthy and sweet, with a bite of something wild underneath. Moonflower and Starroot. Two rare herbs that thrive in moonlight and speed healing beyond normal means. I've been learning a lot from the books she bought me and from my textbooks from school. But it still feels as though, there is a lifetime of knowledge that I will never fully understand, not having grown up in the fae realm.

She dips her fingers into the balm and gently rubs it into my bruised side. The coolness bites at first, but then a slow, tingling warmth spreads under my skin, easing the worst of the ache.

"Thank you," I whisper, barely able to meet her eyes. She just nods, her hands steady, her touch careful.

Chapter 14: This is a Day From Veil

Vera

"You can't train physically, but we can work on more of your gifts.
Let's get some water and we can head outside."

I follow her silently. I know I need to learn. I know this is important.
But my body feels like lead, and my mind, my mind is drowning in
everything I've seen, everything I've felt. This new life is already
pulling me in so many directions, and today… today felt like a battle I
didn't know I was walking into. A day from hell, *or the Veil,* as the fae
so poetically put it. I inwardly roll my eyes, frustration seeping
through me.

We step outside into the fading light, the last fingers of sun brushing the tops of the trees. The grass is cool beneath us as we sit, and I let out a breath I didn't realize I was holding. For a moment, I just listen. To the whisper of the wind through the leaves, to the hum of something ancient in the air. This world is so alive, even in its quiet.

Rina watches me for a beat, then says gently, "Let's start simple. With your truthsense."

I glance over, brows pinching. "I've always had it. Since I was a kid. I can just… tell."

She nods. "Exactly. You feel it, but you've never trained it. You've let it happen, like a reflex. But if you learn to focus it, hone it, you'll be able to control when and how it comes." I shift in the grass, curious despite myself.

"It's like having a blade you've never sharpened," she continues. "Still useful. But not nearly as powerful as it could be."

"Wait. You have truthsense?" I ask her worried.

"Yes, and before you ask, yes I know you haven't been telling the truth."

"Why didn't you say?" I'm so embarrassed! I feel so dumb, I should have known.

"Because I want you to feel comfortable coming to me about things. I won't push you, I don't know what happened today but if you have someone attacking you then you need to report it. I am here to listen and remember I went through the Order, I know it doesn't result in that and definitely not broken bones."

I really don't know what to say so I settle on, "okay." I won't report it, because I just have a feeling that reporting it won't do anything.

Clearing her throat she pulls a paper from the folds of her cloak, she pulls out a small stone, smooth and glassy, etched with a single line down the center and places it in my hand.

"Close your eyes," she says softly. "This is just focus. Nothing else. I'll speak, and you tell me what you feel." The stone is cool and solid in my palm. I let my eyes fall shut, steadying my breath.

She begins, random phrases, statements, confessions. Her voice is even and rhythmic, but the words hit differently. Some land sharp, sudden like a splinter beneath the skin. Others drift by, weightless.

Then one sinks like lead in my chest, wrong and cold.

"That one," I murmur, opening my eyes. "That one was a lie."

Rina's mouth curves in approval. "Very good."

I glance down at the stone, surprised to feel its warmth against my skin, like it absorbed my pulse. "I've always felt something," I admit, rubbing my thumb over the etched line. "But I never tried to sense it. It just happened. Like breathing."

"Well," she says with a spark in her eye, "you're about to learn how to breathe on purpose." And somewhere, beneath the fear and fatigue, something sparks.

We eat dinner in silence. The only sounds are the scrape of forks against plates and the low crackle of the fireplace. The warm, herb-scented air wraps around me, making my eyelids heavy. But I can't rest.

I bury myself in schoolwork, hunched over my notes at the battered oak table, the dim light from the overhead fixture blurring as exhaustion pulls at my vision. The ink smudges where my hand trembles slightly, but I grit my teeth and push through it. Focus. Keep moving. Don't feel. Don't think.

Eventually, my body gives up before my mind does. I gather my books into a pile and drag them over to the worn-out couch where Rina sits, flipping through one of her old worn books. I settle onto the cushion beside her, close enough that our shoulders almost brush. I didn't want to be alone. I needed to feel her steady presence beside me, even if we said nothing.

I crack open one of the books she bought me, History of Sylvaeris and pretend to read. Anything to keep my mind busy. Anything to not think about... I sigh heavily and lean my head back against the cushions, staring up at the low wooden beams overhead.

My thoughts betray me anyway. I remember the way Caelum had inched closer during Mr. Valeis' lecture, his arm brushing mine by accident or maybe not. The way my whole body had gone still, hyper-aware of the heat radiating off him. The way the space between us had snapped tight, invisible but real.

Just then, that same warmth spreads through me again, low and steady, blooming from somewhere deep inside.

It's like a piece of me had been missing all along, and now, just for a moment, it's whole. I glance up, scanning the darkened windows. Outside, the night has swallowed the world, nothing but endless trees and shadows. I can't see anything. But I *feel* him. A thrum, low and insistent, vibrating through my chest like a second heartbeat.

I know Caelum is out there. Watching me. Reaching for me somehow, without even touching me. The sensation lingers, heavy and comforting and terrifying all at once. The same feeling I get when he is near me. And then, just as quickly, it fades. The loss punches the air from my lungs. I swallow hard and shove the feeling away.

I imagine his stupid, perfect face, the way he smiled, a little crooked, like he knew exactly how dangerous it was. And damn it he *was* dangerous. To me, anyway. Tall, infuriatingly handsome, with those green eyes that seemed to cut right through me. The kind of smile that could make you forget your own name if you weren't careful. Too bad I know better. I know what people like him are. The Cassias of the world don't let their trophies wander far. I'm the new girl. The challenge. Maybe even the joke.

Maybe he was even in on the attack. It's hard to get a read on him, it was never hard when I was back home. At this school, I didn't feel people as much. I never tried to read my parents, of course sometimes it slipped through. During heightened emotional times. I smile fondly at the memory. They were trying to surprise me with a trip to the city, to go see a new exhibit at the museum. I was thirteen, they told me we would have to stay home again.

It's safer that way and I lost it. They never said why it was safer. Was it because I was a freak? So different then all of the other children. Sick of staying home, sick of never getting to experience anything outside this house. When they tried to calm me down, I sensed it then. They had been lying and I felt foolish for my outburst. But now I am wondering if I couldn't as easily as I could with humans and I never really tried.

And if the other students are worried about how high I'm climbing on the Veilbound rankings. If they think they can scare me off, they're going to be sorely disappointed. I'm not naive. Not stupid. I know people like that Ryven guy isn't happy with me. Is it because I am doing better than him? If anything, this just solidifies my resolve. I *will* reach the top. I *will* find out who killed my parents. I *will* survive whatever this place throws at me. I don't have a choice, I will fight or literally die trying.

Deciding there's no way my brain can absorb anything else, I start stacking my books, shoving my notes into my satchel for tomorrow. As I reach for the last one, I hear a sharp gasp. I look over. Rina is staring at me, her mouth parted in shock.

"Your bruises," she breathes, crossing the space between us in two strides. "They're… gone."

Well. So much for hiding it. Her hands are already lifting the hem of my shirt, searching for the bruises that had marred my ribs and back just hours ago. There's nothing left but smooth, unmarked skin. I can feel the cracked ribs knitting together too, still sore, but healing at a rate that should be impossible. Like a light tingling running through my ribs.

"How?" Rina demands, her voice a mixture of awe and disbelief. I scramble for an answer, my mind racing.

"W-we don't know how," I rush out, the words tripping over themselves. "At least, my parents never told me. They seemed like they didn't understand either. I—I don't get hurt often, but after sparring with my dad, any bruises would disappear in about an hour." I bite the inside of my cheek, hoping the half-truth will be enough.

"You have the gift of healing?!" she exclaims. I shrug helplessly, feeling suddenly very scared.

"I guess? I don't really know. I never had anyone explain it to me."

Rina studies me for a long, heavy moment, like she's piecing together a puzzle she didn't know she was holding. Her eyes are soft when she finally releases me, but there's a new sharpness there too, a thousand unspoken questions. But she doesn't press. Not yet.

"Okay, this is definitely something we will need to do more research on. Do you know if you can heal others? Have your parents talked to you about the Virelai gift?"

I shake my head, "No, at least I have never tried. Never had a reason to, really. My parents thought it best to not talk about it yet, I guess. Like everything else in my life." Frustration leaking into my voice. I am getting sick of all these secrets and lies.

She nods her head, telling me she is listening, but her eyes are glazed over looking off into the distance. "The Virelai is rare, so rare, most think it's a myth. It's not like other healing magic. It's deeper. Old. Tied to emotion, memory, even bloodlines. Most who had it could only ever use it on themselves. But there were stories, long ago, of a few who could channel it outward, to heal others. It originated from the very first fae queen. They say she came from the Nareth Peaks that surround Elarindor. When she traveled to Sylvaeris the gods blessed her with many gifts. But it came with a cost." She snaps back to focus and stands. "Okay, we're going to get books about this."

I sink back into the couch, feeling more exposed than I have in a long time. Eventually, I get up and say good night. Heading to my room, exhaustion heavy in my limbs. When I slide into bed, I try not to think about anything, just wanting to sleep.

What does this all mean? Can I just heal myself or will I be able to heal others too? The more I learn about everything the more questions and secrets pop up. I try to clear my mind to think of something else so I can fall asleep, but when I close my eyes. It's *his* gaze I see. For a moment it's like I can sense him nearby again, but then it goes away so quickly I think I imagined it.

Those burning eyes with golden flecks, so much like mine, shining too brightly, pulling me in against my better judgment. And it terrifies me more than I care to admit. I remember the soft, startled gasp he gave when our skin touched. The flicker of something raw, something real, before he masked it. I know what I felt. The warmth sliding over me, tying me to him in ways I can't explain.

The real question is, did he feel it too?

Chapter 15: The One Girl That Won't Talk To You

Cae

I stand there, fists clenching and unclenching at my sides, as Vera disappears into the main part of the academy. Every fiber of my being screams to go after her, to pull her into my arms, to protect her. The warmth still thrums through my chest, blooming outward from where I touched her. My hand tingles like it's been branded.

In that instant everything had changed.

When my skin brushed hers, her aura exploded to life, no longer the soft flicker it had been. A radiant violet flame engulfed her, wild and untamed, nearly blinding in its beauty. I sucked in a breath, staggered by the sight. Her life-thread, once invisible to me, blazed into view, silver spun with streaks of amethyst, reaching out like a living thing to entwine with my own. A perfect match.

Her lilac eyes locked onto mine, deepening, catching the golden flecks in my gaze and reflecting them back tenfold. The connection was undeniable. I felt it hum in my bones, in the very air between us.

The sheer force of her aura hit me again, a dazzling swirl of violet laced with hints of other colors, sapphire for wisdom, emerald for healing, gold for courage, all waiting under the surface to awaken. My chest tightened painfully at the sight. This girl wasn't just powerful. She was extraordinary.

And she was mine. Even if she didn't know it yet. I don't understand why everything had been muted before. Why hadn't I seen her thread until now? Whatever the reason, it didn't matter. Now I could see her clearly. I wanted to know everything, every secret she hid, every scar she carried. If only she would stop pushing me away.

Since my Threadkeeper gift had appeared a few months ago, I had only told my sister. I'm still fumbling through understanding it, still learning the ancient magic humming in my blood. And yet, some truths are too clear to deny. She's my fated. And I can't even tell my father. Not anymore. The thought coils darkly in my gut. Distrust sharp and heavy, heavier than I want to admit.

Movement out of the corner of my eye snaps me out of it. Cassia limps out of the locker room, flanked by her two wolves, both already sporting fresh bruises. I can't help the smirk that tugs at my mouth. They thought they could corner Vera and walk away unscathed? Idiots. It's clear Vera is strong and well trained.

The way Cassia moves, favoring her left side, holding her ribs, tells me Vera didn't just survive. She fought. Fought hard enough to leave a mark. Pride stirs in my chest.

A few other girls file out behind them, heads down, a sickly yellow shame curling through their auras. Cowards. They either watched or stood aside. I shake my head in disgust but say nothing. Let them stew in it. One last girl files out. Her head is down and shoulders slumped. There is an aura of blue surrounding her and a little bit of green. I can sense she feels guilty, sad.

Cassia catches sight of me standing there. For a split second, genuine shock flickers across her face before she schools it into a glare. I grin wider just to spite her. She *hates* that Vera fought back and won.

I turn toward the heavy wooden doors, pushing them open to let the crisp, earthy air outside wash over me. The scent of pine and damp moss fills my nose, grounding me for a moment. I know I should head to Halric's office to report the mess in the locker room, but I can't. Not yet. Especially, since I don't really know what happened.

I need to see Vera. Need to make sure she's okay. I take a few steps outside when a voice, low and steady, cuts through the stillness.

"You know," it says, rough as gravel, "you might want to do something about that situation with Cassia."

I glance sideways and find Nero standing there, arms folded across his chest. He's broader than I realized, muscles coiled tight beneath his uniform, his deep golden eyes scanning the area like he's ready to take down a threat at a moment's notice. The distrust rises immediately, unbidden. What does *he* want?

"What situation?" I snap, sharper than intended.

He shrugs one massive shoulder. "The one where Cassia keeps trying to claim you. I don't know your dynamic. Don't care, really. But if you let it keep happening, Vera's never gonna trust you." Something inside me snarls at his words. He doesn't know Vera. He doesn't know *me.*

"What do you know about her?" The jealousy bleeds into my voice, and I can't hide it. I narrow my eyes, studying his aura. Golden brown, steady. Threads of bright gold weave through it, truth, loyalty, purpose. I know he's allowing me to see it, in Duskmere they are trained to hide their aura's just another way to protect themselves.

He chuckles, rough and humorless. "Relax, lover boy. I don't want her like that. She's just a friend. It's obvious from your aura your connected to her. And you should thank the stars someone's looking out for her, because she's guarded. Real guarded. She's hiding something big."

"I know that." I grit out. He doesn't need to tell me about her. "How can you see her aura?"

"I can't really. I get small glimpses, but yours lights up whenever your together." I thought I was able to hide mine well, I guess I haven't been keeping mine concealed. I been trying to allow her to sense me. I know she doesn't trust anyone. My dad always taught us as royalty we need to be neutral, never let people know what your feeling, I need her to sense me, my intentions. To know she can trust me. I don't know if she can see auras.

Before I can say anything else, Vera bursts through the main doors, boots thudding hard against the worn stone steps. She doesn't even glance at us, just bolts down the trail leading toward the guard houses, her hair a dark banner behind her.

"I'm going after her," Nero says simply. "You? You better start coming up with a damn good game plan." And then he's gone. Vanishing into the trees after her with long, effortless strides. I stay frozen for a moment, staring after them. It should be me with her, me running after her. With her.

The cold bites at the back of my neck. Was he right? Will she ever trust me if I can't cut Cassia loose? The thought settles heavily on my chest, colder than the night air. I need to get my dad on my side.

Pulling up beside El's car, I cut the engine and hurry up the front steps.

The Grove looks imposing as always. High stone arches, ivy winding like veins across the grey façade. The setting sun throws long, gold-edged shadows across the grounds, making the place feel both magnificent and lonely. Inside, the warm scent of baking spices and tomatoes immediately wraps around me like a hug. Thalina, our housekeeper, is dusting a side table near the entry, her worn apron fluttering as she moves.

"Caelum!" she says brightly, her smile a little oasis in the too-formal hall. "Good to see you home. I'll have dinner ready after your meeting —your favorite!" The rich, savory smell makes my stomach rumble.

"Lasagna?" I ask, grinning.

"Of course!" she says, giving me a playful pat on the back before bustling off toward the kitchen, her humming trailing behind her.

It's Thalina and El who make this place feel anything like home anymore. The Grove used to be filled with life, with laughter. Before our mother died, before father grew so distant it felt like an invisible wall had dropped between us. Now the halls feel too big, too cold, despite their beauty.

I make my way down the long corridor, the polished floor cold under my boots, the old portraits on the walls watching silently as I pass. At the end of the hall, light spills from the Grove's private library. I step inside and immediately spot El, curled up at the heavy oak table, a book open in front of her. Dust motes dance lazily in the golden sunlight streaming through the tall windows. The familiar scent of old parchment and lavender polish lingers in the air.

I try to approach quietly, grinning to myself, but—

"I know you're there, Cae," El says without even looking up. I straighten and huff, sliding into the chair across from her.

"How? I was seriously quiet this time." She smirks, her pale lavender eyes, so like mine, glinting with amusement.

"I can always sense you. I've been practicing." She closes her book and leans forward, elbows on the table. "Have you?" Like me, El can see people's aura's truth seeking and manipulate all the elements. Unlike me she seems to have an affinity for kindness and patience. She also seems to have an incredible affinity for learning new things, she doesn't think those are magical but Thalina and I do.

"Yeah." I shift uncomfortably. "Testing it. Also, I've been looking into the threadkeeper thing." At the word, she leans in closer, eyes darting around to make sure we're alone. Ever since both our new gifts emerged after our eighteenth birthday, we've been careful. We don't talk about it around our father. Not when we no longer trust him to look out for us the way he once did.

"What would I do without you? What did you find out?" I whisper. She smiles slightly, pride flickering across her face.

"It's rare. Like, really rare. It's always been in our bloodline, but no one else outside it's ever had it. It enhances your aura-reading and truth-sensing. And for people you're deeply connected to, you can use the thread to *find them*. Like me, your future Head Guard and your fated." The words hit me like a physical blow, leaving me breathless.

The way my thread flared to life when I touched Vera, the way it *wrapped* around hers. It wasn't my imagination. My expression must give me away because El narrows her eyes.

"What's that look?" she demands, voice suspicious.

"What look?" I mutter, glancing down at my watch. My next meeting is creeping up too fast. She leans over the table, whisper-yelling like we're still kids hiding secrets under the heavy library tables.

"Oh gods, you found her! Didn't you? It's that new girl, Vera! The one you always watch at school!" I gape at her, stunned by how easily she saw through me. Of course she did. She's my twin. My best friend since we could toddle across these halls in matching boots. I nod, feeling my face split into a grin I can't suppress. It feels stupid and giddy and right.

"Yes. It's her," I say, voice dropping low. "But don't tell anyone yet. I need to convince our father to back off Cassia first. And convince Vera to even talk to me." El throws her head back and laughs. A pure, tinkling sound that fills the dusty old library with life.

I groan. "It's not funny."

"Oh, it's *hilarious*," she teases between gasps. "The one girl in this whole kingdom who *won't* talk to you is your fated."

"Yeah, yeah. Laugh it up." I grumble, pushing back from the table. She grins, not the least bit sorry, as I rise to my feet.

"I gotta go. The council's meeting soon. Dinner after?"

"Wouldn't miss it. Good luck convincing Vera you're not a complete idiot," she calls after me.

I flash her a mock scowl over my shoulder before heading out the door, her laughter following me down the long hallway.

My dad is already seated in his chair in the conference room. I take the seat next to him, pulling out my pen and notebook. I can feel his eyes on me, heavy and expectant, but I straighten my back and wait for the others to arrive.

"How was training today?" he asks.

"It was great. We're moving along with the selection of who will continue into the Veilbound Order."

I glance at him quickly, polite but closed off. I won't invite more conversation than necessary. He hasn't cared much for the last year. He didn't even bother with our eighteenth birthday. It was Calindra who decided we'd have a big celebration once I'm crowned. As if that was the only thing that mattered.

That night, I took El to dinner instead. Just the two of us. At the Ember Glass a newer, nice restaurant built in town. We exchanged gifts something small, something meaningful. Her forlorn expression gutted me, but I was determined to make sure she knew she was still the most important person in my life.

"That's good. I'm glad to hear it," he says, but the words fall flat between us. Silence stretches heavy, awkward, suffocating. A knock at the door has both our heads snapping up. Thalina stands there, looking between us with a slight frown.

"Your guests have arrived, sir." She dips into a low curtsey more formal than usual. Around others, Thalina puts on the act. It always makes me smile. She's just as likely to cuff me upside the head when no one's looking.

Chapter 16: Destined to be Great and Powerful

Cae

The Caezars from Duskmere walk in first, commanding the room with sheer size and presence. Dareth is a wall of a man, broad-shouldered, he always has an intense look on his face, I don't think I have ever seen him smile. His tactical cloak a deep navy almost black, the fabric reinforced but fluid, embroidered with silver thread that caught the chandelier's light like faint starlight. The Thornevale sigil gleamed on his chest plate, subtle, but unmistakable. Every fae that is part of the guard wears the Thornevale sigil but the colors of the uniforms differ for each region.

Duskmere is named for its sky. Where Sylvaeris knows the full rhythm of night and day, Duskmere lingers at the edges of both. Resting just far enough from our star, its horizon is almost always caught in the colors of sunrise or sunset. The province drifts in longer hours of twilight, touched only briefly by bright daylight. Every time I've visited, the sky has taken my breath, the whole land bathed in that fleeting moment when the star dips low, painting the land in shifting hues.

His son, Auren, follows him, and immediately, I want to groan.

He looks like a soldier straight from a recruitment portrait, gear cut to fit him perfectly, his Duskmere armor a twilight shade of navy with brushed steel accents, the same sigil is etched into the plates over his ribs. Even his scabbard, slung over his back, has been polished until the faint runes shimmer. His blond hair is a little too perfect, tousled just so, and the smug curl of his mouth makes it worse. His tactical rig was spotless, every strap lying flat, every buckle gleaming, as though he had stepped off a parade ground instead of a battlefield.

When he smirks across the table at me, I know exactly the kind of problems he's going to cause. Auren is a year older than me and already acts like the world and every fae woman in it is his for the taking. We're both constantly picking fights with the other, especially since every time I see him he likes to ask about my sister. Just to push my buttons because he knows I will react, but no one will say anything about El. They take the seats across from me at the long, polished table.

Next comes the Pontivar from Varethos, Valerian, her presence making the temperature in the room seem to drop a few degrees. She's a smaller fae, nearly swallowed by the heavy dark cloak she wears. She moves like a whisper, deliberate and unhurried, and takes the seat next to me.

Varethos itself is nothing like the main city of Sylvaeris. It is an ancient, enigmatic province shrouded in perpetual mist, tucked away in a secluded region untouched by time. Unlike our monarchy, it is governed by a Council of Seers, a circle of powerful oracles who read the threads of fate and guide their realm through prophecy. Those who come from Varethos are said to carry the weight of visions in their very bones, and Valerian is no exception.

When she lowers her hood, her skin gleams pale as moonlight, etched with deep wrinkles carved by centuries spent in shadow. Varethos knows only darkness, its land lit by moon and stars alone. The old legends say it was by choice, that they pushed the star away, drawing it instead over Sylvaeris, because they thrived in the dark. Her eyes are a faded gray, almost white, like the remnants of ash. If I hadn't known her all my life, I'd be terrified. No, I'm still terrified.

"Dareth. Auren. It's nice to see you both. I hope all is well in Duskmere," my father says, his voice dipping into formal politeness.

"Things are going well," Dareth replies, his tone clipped but respectful. "I am to ask you about my Solenar's son. She couldn't come with for the meeting today. She misses him greatly, he's in the Order this year."

"That might be something to ask my son here," my father says, gesturing to me with a slight nod. "He's at the academy as well."

"Ah, yes. How is that going, son?" Dareth's sharp gaze fixes on me, evaluating, testing. He's the kind of man who doesn't waste words, but when he speaks, you listen. Him and my father have always been cordial but never friends.

"Things are going well," I answer evenly. "We have a strong group going through the Veilbound Order this year."

"Ah, yes. Our boy Nero is among them. His mother is my Solenar. He's always done well in school," Dareth says with a rare flicker of pride. "Plans to become Head Guard." No wonder Nero is already so observant and disciplined. He was raised training for the position.

"I've met Nero. He's doing great, passing through with flying colors," I say honestly. As long as he stays away from Vera. Across the table, Auren stretches back in his chair, lacing his fingers behind his head.

"Figures. Duskmere breeds them tough," he says with a lazy grin, flashing a dimple at Valerian as if he thinks he's charming. Valerian doesn't even blink. If anything, she looks through him. I find it unsettling, I don't know how Auren doesn't.

My father clears his throat, dragging the conversation forward. "Valerian, how are things in Varethos?"

"Things are well, King Lucan," she answers, her voice so thin and dry it sounds like leaves scraping over stone.

We continue on through the meeting smoothly, the topics flowing from trade to patrol schedules and upcoming festivals. Thankfully, it ends quickly. My father begins speaking with Dareth about something military-related—something I'm sure will take a while so I stand, stretching slightly. That's when Auren saunters over.

"How are things going at the Academy?" he asks, his tone casual but with an unmistakable undertone of arrogance. He's always been nice enough, but I can tell, he likes hearing himself talk. He thrives on attention, the weight of the room shifting when he walks in. His light hair is perfectly styled, falling just past his shoulders, and his eyes, rich brown and full of calculation. Scan me like he's weighing whether I'll respond with something interesting enough to hold his attention.

"They're going well. Just starting," I reply, keeping my tone carefully neutral.

He tilts his head, the corners of his mouth lifting with that signature Duskmere grin, sharp, polished, and a little too practiced. "Will you be coming back for the Veilfall Festival in a couple of weeks?"

"Yes," I say, matching the energy with a nod that's cool and unreadable. "My family will be there."

"Good," he says, his voice smooth. "My father and I will be attending, of course. Next month is my official ceremony. Caezar of Duskmere. It would mean a great deal if the Thornevale family was present." His words are laced with importance, but the smirk underneath is undeniable.

"I'm sure we'll be in attendance," I reply. "Looking forward to it. I haven't been to Duskmere in a long time."

Auren's eyes gleam like he knows something I don't. "I do hope your sister can make it as well."

There it is. He always brings up Elowen. Every damn time I have seen him for the past year. It's deliberate. Measured. Like he's tapping at the one place he knows might make me crack.

"She's quite the radiant presence," he adds, just to twist the knife a little deeper.

I bite back a sharp response, jaw tightening. Auren's reputation with girls precedes him, charming on the outside, but I've seen enough behind that smile to know exactly the kind of mess he leaves in his wake. No way in hell is he getting near my sister.

"Of course," I say flatly.

He seems pleased with my restraint, his smirk lingering as he takes a slow step back. The moment stretches, taut and vaguely uncomfortable, like a thread pulled tight between us.

Auren clasps his hands behind his back and studies me for a beat longer, then finally nods. "Until then, Thornevale."

He pivots and walks away, leaving behind a faint trail of Duskmere arrogance and whatever storm he came in with. I exhale, not quite realizing I'd been holding my breath. He's not my enemy. But I'll be damned if I ever let him think he's a friend.

"King Lucan." The familiar, aged voice of Valerian cuts cleanly through the air. We all glance toward her.

"Yes, Val?" my father asks, amused. We may be royals, but there's history here, decades of shared war councils and festivals, of youthful rivalries turned into uneasy alliances. Formalities are usually discarded, but there's a quiet respect that lingers.

"May I borrow your boy for a moment?"

My father looks at me with a flicker of curiosity but nods once. "Of course."

The room suddenly feels too quiet. My heartbeat picks up.

I walk her down the hall into an empty office, the old stone beneath my boots cool and echoing with each step. The door creaks closed behind us. The moment I turn, she's closer than expected, ghostlike in her movements and before I can react, her gnarled hands close around mine.

A jolt slams through me. My lungs hitch. Her eyes roll white. A chill skates over my skin.

"Ah yes," she murmurs, voice suddenly distant, as if layered with something ancient. "Just as I suspected. You found her." My breath catches, and the room feels like it's pressing in on me. "She is destined for great things. If she succeeds, she will bring all the lands closer together again. She must find the others. If she fails, the kingdom will fall."

I can't move. Her grip tightens, her skin that is as cold as frost, digs into my arm.

"There will be hard times coming for you, my boy. You must keep her close. Help her. Protect her."

Then, just as suddenly, her eyes clear. Gray once more. The cold leaves me, like a wind sucked back into the earth. My hands burn where she touched them, the ghost of her magic still tingling in my fingertips.

"Who?" I manage to choke out. My voice sounds far away, like it doesn't belong to me.

"Your girl. Your fated. Together, you are destined to be great and powerful. Apart, and everything will fall."

"Vera?" I whisper, because I already know the answer.

"Yes." She turns toward the door, her cloak whispering against the stone. "I will not be here for the Veilfall Festival. When I return in a month, I would like to meet her. Please arrange that. And do not tell anyone you cannot trust with her life."

She disappears down the hall before I can say another word. I stand there for a moment, the silence pressing against me like a second skin. When I return to the conference room, my dad and Thalina are already cleaning up. The warm, familiar scent of old books and polished wood helps ground me, but I still feel off-kilter.

My dad looks up, his brow furrowed. "Everything alright?"

"She just wanted to tell me that phase three of the Order will be challenging," I say quickly, trying to keep my voice even. "If I think with my mind instead of relying on my physical training, I'll get through it."

He nods, believing me. Thalina doesn't. I can tell by the slight tilt of her head and the knowing look in her eyes. But she doesn't push.

"I'm going to find El," I say. "I'll meet you at dinner."

I bolt upstairs, two steps at a time. My heart still hasn't slowed. What was that? Protect her? Is she in danger now? In my room, I shut the door, leaning back against the solid wood. I walk to the window, pressing my palm against the cool glass. The direction of the guardhouses is obscured by trees, but I know Vera is there. Somewhere.

Closing my eyes, I take a deep breath, and reach. Just faintly, I feel it. A soft thrum. Her tether. Her thread. It's not strong, but it's real. El had said it might work. That I might be able to track her with it. So I try something new.

I shift my focus, searching for the familiar pink thread that connects me to my sister. A softer energy, lighter. I tug on it gently. It strengthens. Guided by it, I walk through the Grove, the thread growing brighter. It leads me to the library, then toward the tall French doors that open onto the garden.

"Hey, El." She jumps, spinning around, startled. I laugh, just a little, relieved that I can still surprise her. But my smile fades the moment I see her tear-streaked cheeks.

"What's wrong?" I demand, voice sharper than intended.

She rolls her eyes but it doesn't hold its usual sass. "Nothing. I was just missing Mom. I wish I could talk to her."

"Yeah, me too." I swallow hard. "I could really use her help."

"Oh, Trouble Twins. It's time for dinner!" Thalia's voice shouts from somewhere inside the library. It's uncanny, she always knows exactly where we are. El and I exchange a look. That small smile returns to her lips, and I feel something ease inside me. But the weight of Valerian's words still lingers like a storm cloud waiting to break.

When we get to the dining room, I take my seat next to my father while El slides in on my other side. The familiar scent lasagna fills the air, my favorite but tonight it only makes my stomach twist. The large wooden table stretches before us, enough seating for ten, though it somehow feels suffocating. My father, as always, sits at the head, his presence steady, a silent force.

But today, something feels off.

The table is already set, more than usual. Extra plates glint under the low golden light of the sconces, polished silver catching every flicker of flame. A faint, metallic tang lingers in the air, though I can't place where it's coming from.

Before I can ask, Calindra sweeps into the dining room like a storm wrapped in silk. Her dark gown ripples behind her, midnight fabric that clings to her figure before spilling to the floor. The sleeves brush her wrists, where a single bracelet gleams, black metal etched with a symbol I've never seen before, sharp and curved like something alive. My guess its a rune designed for protection or who knows with her maybe even wealth and power. Her heels strike the marble in a measured rhythm, precise, echoing.

"Guess who's joining us!" she sing-songs, spreading her arms as though unveiling a long-awaited surprise. The jewels at her throat catch the light, blood-red stones that flash like embers when she moves.

My jaw tightens the moment I see who trails in behind her. Cassia and her parents glide in, all smiles and polished charm, but none of it reaches their eyes. Whatever appetite I had evaporates, leaving only the hollow ache that always follows when Calindra decides to *play hostess.*

"Elowen, dear. Can you move a seat down so these two lovebirds can sit together?" Calindra's voice drips sugar, but the command beneath it is sharp and unmistakable.

I feel El stiffen beside me. I know without looking that she won't move. She won't leave my side not when she knows exactly how I feel about this sham they're trying to force. Rather than make her the target of Calindra's inevitable displeasure, I shove back my chair and stand. The legs scrape sharply against the stone, loud in the sudden silence.

"Actually, I'm not feeling well," I say smoothly, voice low but firm. "I think I'll go take a bath. If you'll excuse me."

"Son, you are to eat with us. We will not be rude to our guests." It's been instilled in us, to be gracious to any guests. Make them feel welcome. I will not entertain this with them, not anymore. I will just as soon walk away from the crown before I am forced to marry Cassia.

"Please, excuse me. I hope you all enjoy dinner." I throw an apologetic look towards El and walk out. My father doesn't protest again, but I know it will be a fight later.

I don't wait for anyone's reaction. I turn on my heel and walk out, forcing my steps to stay even, even though everything inside me is coiled and burning. The moment I reach the corridor leading toward the stairs to our living quarters, I hear the sharp click of heels behind me, too fast, too frantic. I know it's not my dad or El. Before I can react, a hand grabs my shoulder.

"Cae, wait up!" I stop, my body going rigid, and turn my head just enough to see her. Cassia stands there, breathless, a flicker of pain flashing across her features before she masks it. Vera must have gotten her ribs good earlier. A grim part of me is satisfied.

"Do not touch me, again. You are not anything to me, nor is it allowed to touch royalty without their permission." I say, voice quiet but sharp as a blade. She smiles too sweetly, clearly ignoring everything I said. Tilting her head in a way I'm sure she thinks is endearing. It only makes my skin crawl.

"If you're not feeling well, I can draw you a bath," she says, syrupy and insistent. Clearly, she's decided to ignore every boundary I've ever set.

"I will not tell you again, do not touch me. You will not like the consequences. I do not need your help. Stay away from me."

I turn and jog up the stairs without waiting for her reply, her desperate footsteps fading behind me. It feels like a nightmare that won't end like I'm trapped inside a life someone else is scripting for me.

When I reach my room, I slam the door and lock it with a click that feels far too small for the weight in my chest. The air inside is heavy and still. I walk straight to the balcony, shoving open the doors. Cool night air rushes in, brushing over my skin, clearing some of the suffocating tension.

I don't care if it's late. I need to see her. I need to know she's safe. I need her. Valerians words echoing in my mind, I can't tell anyone about that I don't trust. She's someone important and not just to me. She is everything to me. Closing my eyes, I reach inward searching for the thread that connects us, that fragile lifeline only I can feel. There. A soft pull at the edge of my awareness, a heartbeat against mine.

Without another thought, I swing my legs over the balcony railing and climb down, the rough stone scraping my palms. My boots hit the ground with a soft thud, and I take off running, the cold night air biting my face. I don't stop. I *can't* stop. Every step brings me closer to her, drawn by the invisible tether humming in my chest. Through the trees, down the familiar winding path toward the guard homes, toward her. Toward the only person who makes the chaos inside me quiet.

Chapter 17: This is Too Much

Vera

Reluctantly, I drag myself out from under the covers like I'd been buried there for days. Sleep had been impossible. My mind a whirlwind of questions, doubts, and memories that refused to quiet.

I kept replaying everything that had happened yesterday on a feedback loop. Every glance. Every moment. Every strange flicker of energy inside me. The sun had just begun to rise, the red dwarf's glow spilling over the horizon in soft copper and violet. It didn't burn like the sun back home, it smoldered, slow and strange, painting the sky in colors I'd never seen at dawn before.

The healing. The warmth. The way *his* bright green eyes looked when he touched my arm, soft, surprised, like he'd felt it too. Like something inside him recognized something inside me. But what did it mean?

I hate not knowing. Hate the way my thoughts spiral. There are too many unknowns, and every time I reach for a solid truth, it slips through my fingers like mist. Nothing is getting answered only more questions. If Rina is right, then everything changes on my birthday. Full access to my gift, whatever that means. Does that mean there's more inside me I haven't even begun to understand?

The not-knowing is what scares me most. The not being able to ask questions causes undeniable grief. I'm frustrated, but then I remember why I can't ask my parents for the truth and that hurts the most. Everyday Rina looks for answers but right now we're at a dead end. There's nothing to go on, no clues as to who did this or who is after me.

Rina was already up, unsurprisingly. She noticed right away that I was moving better and declared that we'd return to training. So we sparred, not hard, not full speed but it was enough to shake the rust off. I moved fine. The pain was gone. My body felt healed. But the exhaustion clung to me like wet clothes.

I dressed in one of my favorite workout outfits from the human world. Black, tight-fitting and flexible enough to make me feel powerful and confident, even if I didn't today. I layered a flowing purple tank over it, the same shade as my eyes, not that anyone could actually see their real color here. I didn't want to impress anyone. I just wanted to feel confident, to feel *ready*.

Because Cassia? She wasn't going to let yesterday go. I probably embarrassed her—publicly, no less—and now, she'd make it her mission to put me in my place. If only I could get Caelum to stay away from me, maybe she'd see there's nothing to worry about. But that's the problem, isn't it? He keeps insisting on being where I am and I clearly can't control that.

A small, stupid, traitorous part of me *wants* him to stay close. I hate that part. Because there are so many reasons I shouldn't even consider it. He's popular. Charming. Practically royalty or a celebrity, with the way everyone treats him. People tend to just revolve around him. I'm still trying to *hide*. Also, Cassia would never let it happen.

And beyond all that, I don't even know if I *have* a future. So why get attached? Feeling heavy with thoughts I don't want to carry, I met

Nero on the path that led to the academy. He stood waiting beneath a cluster of evergreens, dressed in his usual black combat gear, dark, efficient, serious. Just like him.

The morning sun filtered through the trees, golden beams streaking across the path. It was quiet, except for the occasional rustle of wind in the pines and the muffled crunch of gravel beneath our feet.

He glanced at me as I approached, his eyes scanning my face. "Why did you look so sad when you walked up here?"

Instead of answering, I nod toward his arm. "What does your mark mean?"

He raises his right wrist, studying it before looking at me. The black ink seemed to glow against his sun-warmed skin. A crescent moon cupped three interlocking circles, and flames crowned the top like a silent blaze. The design felt ancient. Powerful.

"It's the insignia for Duskmere," he said, voice low. "The moon represents our shadowed realm always on the cusp of night. The chain links stand for strength, loyalty, and duty. The fire crown shows my gift. Fire magic, strength in battle. I got it when I turned eighteen."

I swallowed, awe curling inside me. "Wow. It looks really cool."

He smiled, nudging me with his shoulder. "Yeah, I like it. I bet yours is going to be badass."

We kept walking. The academy appeared ahead, its towers silhouetted against the rising sun. He looked at me again, this time with concern.

"You're moving easier today. Are you feeling better? Will you be able to do battlecraft today?"

"I'm fine. I'll be ready."

He nodded once, then peeled off toward his side entrance, disappearing with a wave. I wonder why he goes that way, I think it leads to the Echoforge. And as if the universe wanted to ruin my mood again, Caelum falls into step beside me. His presence buzzed like electricity in my skin. He didn't even need to say anything, his silence was too warm, too confident.

"I hope you slept well, Lilac." I ignore the butterflies that erupt from the nickname. The same one he called me yesterday.

I blinked. "Lilac?"

"Yes, my Lilac." He said it like it was obvious. "Like your eyes. That soft purple. Beautiful, like the flower. And you *smell* like it too. Like freshly bloomed lilacs in the spring."

His voice dropped an octave, his eyes half-lidded. I nearly lost all sense of gravity. My pulse roared in my ears. We had stopped walking. We were standing way too close, right in front of the main doors. Sunlight spilled across the stone beneath us, golden and romantic in the worst. Possible. Way.

I scrambled for words, but they slipped away. "Umm. I don't—uh —" He grinned, slow and devastating, clearly pleased I was flustered. That smug, sexy grin set my blood on fire, for the wrong reasons. He thinks he's charming but he's missing the mark.

I stepped back, glaring. "That is incredibly inappropriate for someone who has a *girlfriend*, to say to someone else. You should really keep your distance. It's better for everyone that way. Excuse me."

I turned on my heel, jaw clenched. Behind me, I heard him inhale, like he was about to protest. But right on cue, Cassia's voice cracked through the air like a whip.

"Caelum!"

I glanced over. She was limping slightly, holding her side. Good. Maybe she'd back off for a few days. Maybe in that time he will get bored with me and leave me alone. I ignore the pang of hurt from that thought but continue on. While he was distracted, I ducked inside the school and headed straight for the main office, heart thudding like a drum line in my chest. I leaned against the wall just inside the door, hoping I was out of view. My cheeks burned.

Ms. Wrenfell looked up over her teacup, steam curling around her face. Her soft, hazel eyes met mine.

"Ms. Cale. How have your first couple of days been?" Her voice, kind, helped settle my nerves. I exhaled.

"It's going well," I said, trying to smile. "I'm learning a lot. Meeting a lot of people." Not necessarily a good thing. But she didn't need to know that.

"How can I help you, dear?"

"I was told by a friend there are options for advanced classes. I was wondering if there's a course catalog?"

"Ah, yes," Ms. Wrenfell said with a knowing smile. "The way it works is we wait until after the Veilfall Festival. That's when most young fae gain full access to their gifts." She stood, the chair creaking softly as she moved, and reached behind her desk to retrieve a thick, glossy booklet. The scent of spiced tea clung to the air around her, warm and slightly sweet.

"For those who've already begun sensing their gifts, they're welcome to explore certain courses early. Some will feel the shift during the night of Veilfall itself, it's intense for many. The magic is strong, and it tends to awaken what's been dormant. Currently, we start with some introductory classes for all the students and let them get used to the academy. And for those who meet their fated that night…" she paused, her eyes gleaming like she knew more than she let on, "there are resources to help navigate that connection." She handed me the booklet. The cover shimmered faintly in the light. Auravale Academy framed by twilight skies, stars like pinpricks of silver overhead. Across the top: Course Catalogue.

I accepted it carefully. "Thank you. That could be, helpful."

"Take your time looking it over. You've got until the end of the month to decide. We like to know what gifts our students have so we can assign the correct courses." She gave me a gentle nod, just as the bell rang overhead.

I rushed to my locker, heart still thudding, not from nerves this time, but something else. Something bigger. Something ancient. *Veilfall.* I'd heard the word whispered with awe and reverence, but now it felt like it was pressing in on me. Like the word itself was alive.

I will need to ask Rina more about the festival and what it means. I hate being so lost, being thrust into an entirely new world. On top of that, I have to try to hide my existence and not draw attention to myself. So asking anyone else questions? Impossible. Others would wonder why a fae wouldn't know anything about their own heritage and customs.

Moments later, I slipped into class behind Mr. Valeis and sighed in quiet relief. No Caelum. Thank the stars. I picked a seat in the back, letting my shoulders drop as I opened my notebook. The reprieve didn't last. The chair beside me scraped sharply against the floor, and that scent of cedarwood and something electric, wrapped around me like a net.

My body tensed. Of course. I wish I could just be indifferent or at least act like it.

"Lilac," he murmured low, voice rough like velvet worn thin. "Just give me a chance to explain."

I didn't answer. Didn't look. Just stared ahead, as if ignoring him would make him disappear. I could feel the attention on us like heat against my skin. I hated it.

"I don't have—" Mr. Valeis began class, cutting him off. Caelum let out a breath, frustrated. The sound made me clench my jaw.

Curiosity tugged at me. I opened my senses, hesitantly, like cracking a door to peek through. Instantly, that familiar warmth unfurled around me like sunlight through fog, soft but undeniable. Gold light shimmered at the edge of my perception. When I focused, I felt his emotions: sharp frustration laced with amusement?

What could he possibly find funny? Why can I sense what he is feeling? Is something I can do with all Fae that I couldn't do with humans, or is it him specific.

Mr. Valeis paced the front of the classroom, his voice grounding me. "With Veilfall approaching, we will begin our unit on the history of the Veil and the myths surrounding the Night of Thinning." He paused, letting the words settle like dust. "Veilfall, called the Night of Thinning in the old tongue, is the point in the year when the veil between realms grows weak. It marks the turning from light to shadow, from harvest to hush. It's a time of reverence, but also danger."

The room quieted. Even the ever-chatty twins in the front row stilled.

"Ancient fae believed it was the one night a year the Veil could thin enough to let things slip through. Spirits. Memories. Power. It's why we light fires in the Firewatch. Why we cast protective spells, offer fruit and flame at the forest's, edge. The fire keeps what belongs in the Veil *out*, and it helps guide those lost fae souls *home*."

A few students shifted uncomfortably in their seats. I gripped my pencil tighter. Will my parents be there?

"The Veilfall is also when the threads of fate pull the strongest. Some believe the Fated Bonds can only begin to awaken on this night. That under the stars, souls meant to find each other will always do so."

I dared a glance at Caelum. His eyes were already on me, glowing softly beneath heavy lashes. I turned away, heart pounding. I didn't want this. Didn't want him to look at me like I was something he had a right to. *Fated Bonds.* That word again. The heat in my chest tightened, making it hard to breathe.

I scribbled nonsense in the margin of my notebook just to stay grounded. If this night could really pull fate into the world, what did that mean for me?

Chapter 18: Balance first. Power second.

Vera

Elemental Symmetry & Control—a class that lets me learn to use the elemental gifts—was my second class of the day. I slip into the seat next to Nero. There was only one seat open between him and another student so I think I am safe from Caelum. He glanced at me once, then leaned forward with his elbows on the desk, giving me the silence I didn't know I needed. My heart was still pounding from the last class, and the flickering nerves in my fingertips hadn't quite settled.

The classroom was arranged in a wide semi-circle, tiered so each row had a clear view of the practice floor in the center. Crystalline sconces glowed gently on the stone walls, giving the room a warm amber hue. In the center stood a platform ringed with elemental markers. One each for fire, water, earth, an air.

Cassia arrived a minute later, trying to play it cool but clearly favoring her right side. Her posture was off, her steps stiff. She was hunched protectively, an arm tucked subtly around her ribs. I guess she didn't heal as fast as I did. Satisfaction curled low in my belly. Good. Maybe now she'd think twice before lunging at me like a rabid dog.

She glared at me as she passed my desk, her lips pressed in a thin, bloodless line. I barely withheld my smirk, and from my left, I heard Nero chuckle under his breath.

She *knew* how much damage they did yesterday. Would they wonder why I healed so quickly? Or assume they hadn't done much damage to begin with?

The door swung open again, and in walked Caelum like he had all the time in the world.

"Cae!" Cassia called, too loudly.

He gave her a lazy nod, then continued past her desk without pause and stood right in front of the student on my other side.

"Would you mind moving, please?" His tone is polite enough, but there's a tightness under it, a command dressed as a request.

The boy stands without a word, and I bristle. Of course. People just move for him. What makes him so special that he can clear a seat with nothing more than a look and a clipped sentence?

He drops into the empty chair beside me, as if the whole exchange was inevitable. Cassia's huff of frustration echoed through the room like a badly muffled sneeze. Great. Now she will certainly be coming after me again, I doubt she is someone that will let this go.

He drapes an arm over the back of my chair. "You can't keep denying us. I can feel how curious about me." He whispers into my ear and I shiver. I look at him and his eyes are peering into mine, only inches away.

My mouth parts and I mouth "stop it." And he gives me a sexy half smirk before leaning back. I grip my pencil in my hand and I snap it just as the low murmur of students fade. Professor Oryll steps inside, her crimson robes catching the light with every deliberate movement.

"Good afternoon, class," she said, voice clipped, like the steady pop of a contained fire. "Today, we begin working directly with elemental ignition. We'll focus first on *fire*—the most volatile and the most misunderstood. For those of you that are not well practiced you will use the sparkstones. They are said to have been forged from the hollow flame. It is incredibly rare and some of these stones have been around for millennia for the Hollow Flame is hidden behind a veil of magic that only the marked may pass. Now, who among you has a fire affinity and would like to demonstrate?"

Silence. A few students shifted awkwardly. One boy coughed. Even the girl across from me who wore bright red gloves tucked her hands under her desk.

Professor Virile's gaze swept the room. "No volunteers?"

Then her eyes landed on Caelum.

"Mr. Thornevale, would you give us a small demonstration?"

He stood with a graceful ease that made my stomach twist. He makes everything seem effortless. "Of course."

He strode to the center of the classroom, his presence alone seeming to shift the air. Every movement was deliberate, unhurried, like he had all the time in the world and nothing to fear.

"Now," Professor Virile said, turning to the class, "remember: we begin with symmetry. *Balance* first. *Power* second. Fire without balance is destruction. Fire *with* balance is transformation."

Caelum extended his hand. He didn't so much as glance at the sparkstone sitting on the pedestal beside him. Golden-orange light coiled at his fingertips, lazy at first, like smoke drifting on a breeze. Then it sharpened, flaring outward in a controlled arc.

A hush fell over the room. The flame suspended midair, no fuel, no match—just him and raw intent. His eyes fell to me, only briefly but I saw the gold specks flaring to life in his eyes.

Then, slowly, deliberately, the fire began to *move*. It swirled like calligraphy drawn in midair, a glowing ribbon of light. With each pass, the glow deepened.

L-I-L-A-C

My breath caught in my throat. The flames shimmered as the final letter hung in the air. The smoke slowly drifting together into a heart. I felt every gaze in the room swing toward me, but I couldn't look away. Because his eyes were on me, again. The fire flickered once… and vanished, leaving nothing but the faint scent of smoke and stunned silence behind.

Nero let out a low whistle beside me. Cassia's pencil snapped. I guess everyone is snapping pencils today. This is too much. As he lazily, cockily walked back to his seat and he just places his arm back over my chair. I feel a strong urge to hit him. Or run away, I don't know which was stronger right now. If he hadn't painted a target on my back before, he certainly did now. Why was he doing this?

"Okay, now I will pass out a few sparkstones for those who need it. I want you to practice igniting a spark. We don't need full fires. When you have the stone in your hand, I want you to use it to ground yourself. Feel it, feel for the fire or the warmth." I am certain she keeps talking but the blood is pumping in my ears.

She walks around and sets the stone on my table, she pauses to assess me. I don't know what I look like but she keeps walking. I take that as a sign that I must not look like I'm panicking. I hope. Silently, I look down at the sparkstone, feeling unsure and lost in this moment. I was excited to try when she first started talking about it but now? Now, I felt apprehensive, my skin was tingling from the stares.

A throat clears to my left and my gaze swings up to Nero. "Breathe." He murmurs. Dragging in a much needed breath I didn't know I needed, I relax my shoulders.

I grab the sparkstone in my hand. Just feeling the weight. It smells like smoke and is warm to the touch. I feel that familiar warmth flow around me and I know Caelum is assessing me. Or maybe helping me, I really can't tell. I feel his gaze wrap around me, calming me. I focus back on the stone in my hand and imagine a flame. Living, breathing.

Balance first. *Power* second.

I start with the imagining the fire, the bright blue center and expanding into orange and yellow. The smell of campfire smoke.

Suddenly, the stone starts sparking. Startling me I gasp and drop the stone onto the table in front of me.

"That's a good start." Caelum says softly. I glance up at him and his eyes are soft. I hear a snort from behind me but don't look back.

"It was good, but next time when you feel the spark, try to flow into it. Imagine it wrapping around the stone." Caelum tells me. He grabs the stone in front of me and gently holds it in his palm. In an instant there are little sparks all around it.

Watching in awe he gently moves his hand in front of me. "Hold out your hand."

I hold out my right hand with my palm up. He slowly lets it slide onto my hand and it dims slightly and then continues. He rests his hand under mine. While it's there I try to feel the sparks. The warmth, the little jolts against my palm, the smell of the smoke.

There is a strong wave of warmth passing between us. I am

concentrating on the rock so I don't try to see the warm amber hues that sometimes appears between us but I feel it all the same. What does it mean? The sparks start forming into little flames. I gasp but this time I don't drop it. Not with his palm resting under my hand. I chance a glance at him and the flame sizzles out of the stone. But his eyes are doing that shining thing again. The gold specks look like they are dancing in a flame.

I can feel the tingles flowing through me that has nothing to do with the fire or sparkstone. He makes my body react in ways I didn't know it could. I feel heat flowing right to my core and I can't help but squeeze my thighs and squirm. Something that doesn't go unnoticed by Cae. His eyes drop to my thighs and slides slowly back to my eyes and the fire in his eyes are enough to set me ablaze.

The bell rang forcing us to look apart. My cheeks feel warm and both of our hands drop. I quickly start gathering my things, my chair scrapes back against the floor harshly as I stand. I start rushing out from behind the table, squeezing past Nero's large frame, not nothing to look at him and return the sparkstone to the teacher. As I walk to the door I see Caelum still sitting in his chair watching me. There is an easy sexy smirk on his face, he's enjoying the way he makes me react.

I trip over something in the door but I right myself before I fall. I look over and Cassia is leaning on the wall outside the classroom. She has a small smile that doesn't reach her eyes.

"This isn't over. I don't know where you came from, or why you're really here. But I know something isn't right and I will figure it out."

I try to sidestep her and keep moving but Cassia is already there, stepping into my path. All smug smile and narrowed eyes, I can see the twinge of pain she is trying to smother. "You're don't even belong here," she said, voice syrupy and sharp. "Eventually, he'll see that."

I don't flinch. "Good," I said, tilting my head. "Maybe then he'll finally stop wasting his time." My heart thudded harder against my ribs in response to my words, it hurt to say. It's the way it has to be.

I brushed past her, spine straight, pulse thudding too hard. But the truth buzzed beneath my skin. Cassia wasn't going to give up. And I wasn't sure I could keep pretending I didn't care.

Not when every look, every moment, pulled me deeper into something I couldn't afford to want. Not when the future demanded all of me and he was becoming a distraction I couldn't risk. Not when girls like Cassia played games I wasn't raised to lose.

Chapter 19: It Feels Like Home

Cae

This morning Vera moved easier. The stiffness is still there, but it's not pain, at least not physical. The bruises on her arms are completely gone. Either she's good at hiding pain, or she heals abnormally fast. Like me. Another gift that developed that only El knows about. Luckily my sister is doing a lot of research into my new found gifts. I will need her help, especially with my focus on my stubborn girl.

Cassia was still moving stiffly, struggling after the events yesterday. I know she also stopped Vera outside the classroom. I don't know what was said, but I could see the tension in Vera's shoulders.

Exchanging a glance with Nero, I get up to interfere between Cassia and Vera. But I was too late, Vera was already strutting away, looking like she didn't have a care in the world. But I could see her aura. Tinged in red with hints of blue, I just wish I knew what made her so angry and sad.

She avoids me again in the next class. No chance to talk. Thankfully, I planned ahead. After breakfast this morning, I packed my own lunch. The library is technically off-limits for food, but no one dares tell me no. And for some reason, they don't stop her either.

When I step inside, the hush settles over me like a welcome cloak. I spot her immediately at a table near the fireplace, a few books scattered around her, food untouched. Her shoulders go rigid when I approach, like she senses me before she even sees me. Our threads glow faintly, responding to each other again. The threads want to connect, but can't quite reach yet. I wonder if anyone has ever been fated like this before the Veilfall. Is it because of my royal bloodlines, or because of what Valerian said. Together we are powerful.

"Hey, Lilac," I say as I slide into the seat beside her.

"Seriously? I can't have *any* alone time?"

"Now, now. No need to be angry. I come in peace."

"I know that," she snaps, then her eyes widen. That's interesting. A reflex. Did she feel something? *See* something? I file that fact away for later.

"Just talk to me. We can eat lunch and get to know each other." I need to find a way to get her to talk to me. Make her understand that she is the only one for me. That Cassia is nothing to me.

She glances around, scanning for anyone nearby, then sighs like I've crushed what was left of her spirit. That *look*, I hate that look. I'm not trying to trap her. I just want her to see me. To *see* that I see her. She picks at her food, eyes never leaving her notes. I don't even know what to say. No one's ever made me this off balance.

"So... how old are you?" Gods, that was stupid. She has me flustered and that never happens to me. I was raised being able to hold conversations with anyone.

"Seventeen." Her one word is clipped, like it was tortured out of her.

"My twin sister and I just turned eighteen in June," I offer with a half-smile. "Thanks for asking." I say coyly. Delighted when she gives me a small giggle. A giggle I feel shoot right through me.

"When is your birthday?"

"It's in November." She whispers quietly.

"Oh, so it's coming up next month. You live with your aunt?" I ask, hoping it's a safe topic.

"Yes," she replies, short and cautious. She glances up at me, eyes narrowing slightly. She's reading me now, I can feel it. She must not realize other fae can feel it when they are being read. Does she not feel it when I read her?

"Do you guys train together every day?" I ask gently, softening my voice and pushing out my intentions like a warm breeze. Her shoulders ease a little. Interesting. That's definitely her gift.

"Yes. Every day. I like to work out." The truth hums around her words, but there's more there, layers she doesn't want to open. With my threadkeeper gift, I have been able to use the truthsense and auras to detect deeper into peoples words and intentions. She's telling me the truth, but there is definitely more to it.

"Did you get to work out a lot where you lived before?" A flicker of sorrow crosses her face. She lowers her gaze to her notes.

"Yes, some. My dad also liked to work out." Her dad. So where are her parents? She's only mentioned an aunt.

"What does your dad do?"

"He died. With my mom." Her voice is quiet, flat. A whisper that holds a storm. Shit. No wonder she's been so guarded. Her aura is always tinged a little in blue, grief that would explain it.

"I'm so sorry," I say, meaning every word. "That can't be easy. I lost my mom ten years ago." Something shifts in her. I reach out, almost without thinking, and gently take her hand. Her fingers tense, then soften as our skin touches.

She gasps softly. Emotion floods her, and her tears well up, making the gold in her eyes shimmer even more brightly. One tear slips down her cheek. I catch it with my thumb... and without thinking, I bring it to my lips. A jolt of something powerful shoots through me. Our threads flare, a bright tether between us, they reach ever closer.

"Your eyes," she whispers, awe lacing her voice.

I focus on hers. They're glowing now, almost otherworldly. And yet... it feels like home. I want to kiss her. Gods, I want to. But I hold myself still, anchoring the moment. When I release her hand, everything dulls, the threads, the glow. But I can still just barely see the golden flecks in her irises... and her thread still reaching, softly, for mine.

The bell rings, jarring the magic away. She pulls back quickly, gathering her things without looking at me. She doesn't speak to me again for the rest of the day.

Why did it dull? Every time I touch her it flares, and when I let go it dulls again. I need to know why it does that but I also know I can't push her. She already keeps me at arms length, refusing to even talk to me. I am happy she talked to me today, now I need to work on convincing her that she is the only one for me.

I don't know if she is just naturally shy, just doesn't like people, or if she is hiding something. My gut tells me she is hiding something. I just need to get more time with her, get to know her. She won't stop pushing me away long enough to make a difference. Now I just have to figure out how to get her alone again and where I could take her that no one will interrupt.

In class earlier I couldn't help but write Lilac in the fire. I've been learning to control the fire for so long, it comes naturally like breathing. I needed Vera to know my intentions, that I am not going away. I thought writing Lilac would be safe, no one would know but somehow they did. Probably because my eyes were locked on her. It did not help my case when they all turned to look at her. This was also me claiming her, to keep others away and telling her I'm not going anywhere.

Cassia was sitting behind her so luckily she didn't see the glare coming from her. I know she is plotting something, I can sense that much. I need to figure out what. It's clear that Vera can take care of herself, but she also doesn't know the power Cassia's parents have. Not powerful in gifts but power in politics. To everyone else they're known for hosting charities and helping others, very few fae know how truly slimy they are. Not even my father seems to really know. I've only recently learned how corrupt they are and I now know that Calindra is a part of it. I just need to figure out what their plan is.

I change quickly in the locker room, the sharp scent of sweat and soap clinging to the air. The faint squeak of sneakers against polished floors echoes as I step onto the gym floor. My eyes scan instinctively, looking for her. Vera.

Halric is standing near the large rectangular platform. Some students meander over to him, I'm guessing some are realizing we will start sparring today. I will start with a demonstration with Nero. There are fresh blue lines painted on the canvas, showing where people are to stand. A couple of totes off to the side full of training gear to wear for protection. Padding hanging over the side of the buckets.

I keep looking around, she's not here yet. But Cassia and her pack of ever-present shadows stroll in like they own the place, perfume cloying in their wake. A ripple of tension climbs up my spine. The moment I realize Vera isn't behind them and almost all the girls have walked in, anxiety follows, coiled tight in my chest.

Just as I consider walking straight over to Cassia to ask if she's seen her, Vera appears. And just like that, the gym narrows, sound dulls, and my pulse roars in my ears. She walks in like she owns the place, strength and power in her every step. Even if I know she doesn't quite believe that yet.

Her training uniform should've looked plain, just standard all black, same as everyone else's. But on her, it was lethal. The fitted top molded to every curve, outlining breasts that strained against the thin barrier of her sports bra, like the fabric was fighting a battle it had no hope of winning. My hands itched just looking at her, imagining how perfectly she'd fit against me.

My eyes dragged lower, to the black spandex hugging her hips and thighs, short enough to show off the endless line of her legs. Long, strong, sculpted, made for speed and power, but right now, all I could think about was how badly I wanted them wrapped around me. Even the way she walked felt deliberate, her hips swaying with a confidence she didn't seem to notice, each step pulling me deeper under.

But it's the flicker in her eyes that stops me from completely losing myself in the view. She's scanning. Not obvious, no jerky movements or shifting weight. It's subtle. Intentional. Practiced. She's always watching. Always calculating. What could she be searching for? I remember what Valerian said, she had to find the others and that she's in danger. I don't think she could have been more cryptic if she tried.

Even as I let my gaze drift down again, taking in the way she moves, smooth, unbothered, effortless, something doesn't sit right. She's not stiff. Not sore. There's no sign of strain from yesterday's fall.

Fae heal fast, sure. But this fast? A quiet thread of suspicion slides through me. I wonder again if it's a gift, the Virelai is incredibly rare. Something I've never seen before, but something we might both have in common. This must be one of the things that makes her powerful. Something else I need to protect. Whatever it is, it makes me want to know more.

She stops a few feet away, close enough that I can see the rise and fall of her chest, the soft sheen of exertion on her collarbone, the faint smell of lilacs and something sharper, like ozone before a storm. She stretches, arms high above her head. Her shirt lifts just enough to reveal a toned stomach, and for a breathless second, I forget how to be subtle.

My fingers ache with the urge to reach out, to touch her, to anchor myself in that skin, that body that pulls me like a tide I can't resist. She shouldn't affect me like this. But she does. Every single time. A low throat clear slices through the fog in my mind. I turn to find Sylas smirking like a jackass.

"Dude," he says, voice dripping with amusement. "You're making it *really* obvious." I blink, caught. No point denying it. I want her. I don't know how to hide that anymore, not when she's standing there like the moon itself, and I've spent my whole life chasing shadows.

Before I can respond, Halric's voice bellows across the gym, commanding attention. I glance at her once more. Her expression is tight, jaw clenched, brows drawn. Watching Halric, yes, but something else simmers beneath the surface. Nerves, maybe. Or disappointment?

She could be nervous about sparring with someone else, I know many girls don't train like that. My sister always did, but she's one of few female fae that does. I don't know if it's about sparring or me. Either way, this might be my chance. Sparring could be the perfect excuse to get close and gods help me, I'm not going to waste it.

"Listen up!" Halric's voice boomed across the sparring grounds, cutting through the morning haze. "Today we're sparring. Teams have already been assigned. Now, before anyone gets too confident. Yes, I'm talking to you, Sylas—" a few chuckles rumbled through the group, "we'll be doing a demonstration first." He clapped his hands once, loud and sharp. "No, it won't be me. I don't want to embarrass you kids the first time we spar. Morale's important."

Another ripple of awkward laughter. Vera tilted her head slightly, brow raised. I could tell she wasn't sure if he was joking.

"Instead," Halric continued, drawing out the moment with theatrical flair, "we're watching our superstar, Cae, spar with— drumroll, please." He tapped his own thigh. Silence. He sighed dramatically. "Alright, no drumroll. Way to make it awkward for *everyone*, thanks."

My jaw ticked, and I barely held back a smirk. Halric might be a hard-ass, but he had a dry sense of humor that almost made you forget he could take you down with a flick of his wrist.

"Cae will be sparring with Nero." The air shifted. I felt it immediately. The tension, the excitement, the spark of something unspoken. Nero looked over at me and smirked, all slow confidence and steel edges. He started walking toward me, calm and measured.

"Good luck," Vera whispered to him, just loud enough for me to hear.

"No luck needed." His voice was gravelly, steady. His face, normally carved from stone, softened slightly when he looked at her. It bothered me more than I cared to admit.

"Where's my good luck, Lilac?" I asked, eyes locking with hers. I meant it to sound teasing, but I needed to hear her say something. Anything.

Her lips quirk up, and there was a glint of amusement in her gaze. "I would say good luck, but I don't think it will help." Her eyes scan down my body with a false look of pity. It wasn't much. But it was enough. Her voice curled around my ribs like a thread, pulling tight. This was the first full sentence she'd directed at me that wasn't laced with challenge or silence and it was flirting. Actually flirting, even if she was teasing. I swallowed the smile threatening to form, winked, and turned toward the center ring.

Progress. I'd take the win.

Nero and I stepped onto the sparring ring, the polished boards smooth beneath our boots, faintly warm where runes pulsed just under the surface. The wood smelled of oil and iron, carrying the ghosts of a hundred matches fought before ours. Around us, the others lingered at the edge of the platform, their shifting footsteps and low murmurs pressed close, watching, waiting.

"I won't take it easy on you," Nero said quietly, just for me.

"I don't need you to." My voice was just as even. "I can handle anything you throw my way."

Chapter 20: If You Lose Your Footing, You Lose The Fight

Cae

Halric stepped between us, hands behind his back like a bored general. "Alright, boys." His voice carried effortlessly across the expanse of the cavern echoing off the vaulted beams. "This is for demonstration, technical skill and tactical awareness. We are *not* doing damage. I know how much ego both of you are carrying right now, but this isn't a territorial piss-off."

A few laughs echoed from the sidelines. I didn't take my eyes off Nero.

Halric's eyes flicked between us, one brow arched. "If either of you starts throwing real punches, I'll break your kneecaps and call it a teaching moment."

Then he stepped back and gave a lazy two-fingered salute. "Begin."

We dropped into our stances immediately. Feet shoulder-width apart. Knees bent. Weight on the balls of our feet. My guard came up instinctively my hands raised, elbows tight, ribs protected. Nero's eyes were sharp, unreadable. He didn't go for the obvious. I appreciated that. We circled each other, silent but for the shuffle of canvas beneath our boots.

"Watch the chest," I heard Halric call out to the class. "That's where the first twitch of movement happens. Not the face."

The first strike came fast, a jab toward my ribs. I deflected with my forearm and countered with a quick pivot and sweep. He blocked with ease, twisting to avoid the hit. The rhythm picked up quickly. Strikes, blocks, counters. Dust rose around our feet. Grunts of effort echoed. Sweat beaded along my brow, slipping down the side of my face. Nero was fast. And strong. But I wasn't slowing down either. The crowd was gone for me, no Cassia, no Sylas, not even Vera. Just motion, impact, and the crackle of combat energy.

Halric called, "Balance is everything. If you lose your footing, you lose the fight." Nero feinted left, then aimed a low strike at my knee. I spun out, landing a mock elbow to his chest that would've winded him if it were real.

He grinned slightly. "Not bad."

"You haven't seen anything yet."

When he goes to throw a kick to knock me over, I dodge it. "What's your deal with Vera?" I grit out.

He smirks at me, only serving to make me angry. When I get ready to throw a right hook, he blocks it easily. "It's kind of ironic, you getting mad with just me talking to your girl but yet there is another girl all over you, telling anyone who will listen how you two belong together." Fuck, I am doing my best to get rid of Cassia, I can't help the shit she is spewing when I am not around.

Nero goes to throw a punch and I block it. "So while Vera is dealing with whatever she is dealing with and denying any feelings she may have for you she's also watching that girl keep grabbing you and threatening her."

"You don't think I know that?" This time I land a punch and it was harder than I intended. He spit the blood out of his mouth and smiled. This does not bode well for me.

"Boys, don't make me come up there." I hear Halric call but I am too focused on Nero in front of me.

"Listen, she is mine. You need to back off, I am doing the best I can to get rid of Cassia, but it's also politics. There's other things I am working on figuring out for the kingdom too." I glanced quickly to the side, Vera looks concerned as she watches the two of us. That guy from yesterday, Ryven is standing by her. Way too close for my liking. While I was distracted he lands his punch. Shit that hurt.

"That's payback for hitting me. I'm just saying I don't want your girl. I will be her friend, just like I will be your friend. I will be your Head Guard and with that I will also protect her. That is if you can get your shit figured out and win the girl. Now enough talking let's finish this."

We exchanged a few more practiced hits and kicks. Nothing serious, just enough to make it look like a demonstration. My mind reeled with every movement, a dozen thoughts colliding behind the rhythm of combat. The air between us felt tight, charged.

My skin was slick with sweat under my training gear, the fabric clinging to the curves of my spine. I caught the sharp scent of iron every time we shifted on the platform. Nero moved with coiled precision, like a predator holding back, and I matched him, strike for strike, refusing to flinch.

As I stepped down from the platform, heart still pounding, I opened up my truthsense. There it was, his thread, a tightly bound line of fire barely visible. Hidden beneath his training. He was skilled, practiced at shielding it. But I'd been trained better. I knew how to see through the cracks. He'd been telling the truth.

Everything about him was calm, restrained, but focused. Protective. Around her. It didn't make me like him more. But it helped. The thread faded as I released my focus, the world of the sparring field rushing back in around me just in time for Halric to clap his hands once.

"Alright, well that was interesting." His voice echoed across the sparring field. "Now we're going to move on. I want to see what *everyone* can do. And unlike those two" he shot me a pointed look, "we're not trying to hurt each other." A few students laughed nervously.

Halric started calling out the names of sparring partners, I moved back toward the sidelines, arms folded tightly across my chest, trying to rein in the leftover adrenaline. I walked closer to Vera. Ryven, one of the candidates for Head Guard, was standing by her, that sneer on his face has morphed into a different kind of smile. I don't know if it would be classified as a smile, he's obviously not practiced at it. My truthsense is still open and I am feeling for his intentions. Towards me, it's respect but towards Vera he seems angry, jealousy. I can sense his aura ebbing, hints of green and red.

"Are you okay?" Vera's voice was soft beside me, brushing against me like a breeze before a storm. I looked down to find her lilac-veiled eyes peering up at me, concern flickering in their depths. Her fingers touched my arm, a light almost hesitant touch, but the spark between us flared like it always did.

Just for a second, her eyes flashed that deep, vivid violet before she blinked it away and dropped her hand. I wonder in these moments where our skin touches and her aura flashes if others could see it, too. Or if it was just reserved for me. I subtly look around but only Cassia glares at us and I know she can't see auras.

"I'm alright, Lilac." My voice came out rougher than I intended, I can feel the bruise forming under my eye. "Are you ready for the sparring?" Ryven's attitude changed as soon as I called her Lilac. Now he knows she means something, he must not be as adept at reading auras like Nero is. However I already sensed his dislike for Vera, he's someone I cannot trust to be around my fated. But I have to play the game with the Order, pretend to give him a chance.

"Yes. I can handle it." Her chin lifted slightly, that steel spine showing itself again. Good. At least she had training. She seemed confident, but if she still has lingering bruises or worse after yesterday, it would hinder her. Halric will notice, maybe that was part of Cassia's plan. Too bad that's another plan that seemed to backfire on her.

"Great job, Caelum." He says politely. A hint of sarcasm laced in there, very subtle if not for his aura I don't know that I would have known. His aura is giving off a completely different vibe than what his face and words are telling me.

"Thank you." I responded. He gives a small head bow and starts backing away. I hope he will leave Vera alone, now. There are a lot of excellent students here, so why is he singling her out? She's not even in the running for Head Guard.

"Are you in any pain?" I lowered my voice, stepping a fraction closer. Her shoulders tensed at the question.

"No, I'm okay," she whispered, and glanced around as if she thought someone might overhear. Her fingers brushed the hem of her black training top, nervous. That protective instinct in me surged hard enough to make my jaw clench.

I wanted to pull her into my arms, tuck her against my chest, and keep her there until the fear left her eyes. She didn't even know what she was yet. What she could be. But I plan to find out.

"Okay, good. Get up there and make me proud." I gave her a wink, and she gave me a quick smile before walking away. She didn't look back but I didn't need her to. My eyes stayed glued to her the whole way to the platform. My eyes roaming over her curves as her hips sway, the black spandex curves perfectly to her body. I'm certain she is doing it because she knows I'm watching.

I joined Halric and Nero at the edge, arms crossed again, trying not to show how tightly I was wound.

"What crawled up your asses?" Halric muttered as the rest of the group paired off. Some looked stiff, tentative. But Vera? She launched into her stances like she'd been doing it all her life. Fluid. Controlled. Light on her feet. Definitely better than her partner. Her partner was nervous and didn't know what she was doing. I realize it's the same girl as yesterday, the one that felt bad after the fight in the locker room. This girl was trying to mimic Vera and Vera was obviously holding back. I kept one eye on her to be sure she didn't mean any harm to Vera.

"Nothing. We're cool," I said, glancing sideways at Nero. He gave a slow, solemn nod. Yeah. I believed him. I didn't like how easily she'd let him in but I trusted his intentions. If he knew she was my priority, then he was as good as my future Head Guard.

"I don't believe you," Halric muttered. "But I hope you *are* cool. Nero's the best we've got. If you two can get your heads out of your egos, he'll be on track to guard you." We didn't respond. Just watched.

After Battlecraft ended, I found Vera near the edge of the field. She must have wandered out here after class.

"You did phenomenal," I said, voice low so I didn't startle her. "If you'd like, I could give you pointers for all the phases of the Veilbound. That way you're prepared. We could spend a little time in the Echoforge after class." Hope snuck into my voice, damn it. I tried to rein it in.

"Umm, I don't know," she said, eyes flicking around.

"Just an hour after class," I added quickly. "That's all I've got before meetings with my father."

She hesitated, then gave a little nod. "Okay. It would be nice to get some different perspectives." Victory. I wanted to fist pump the air like an idiot, but I kept it together. Gave her a casual nod instead. My smile must've been a little too pleased though, because she rolled her eyes at me.

We made sure everyone left before we started our stretches, wanting to be alone with her. She stretched, slow, methodical, graceful, and I… didn't. I just watched her. The way her spine curved, the length of her legs, the way her braid swayed across her back when she bent down. She must've felt it. Color bloomed from her collarbone and crept up her cheeks. I reached out and ran my knuckles across her flushed cheek before I could stop myself. Shit. I needed to think of something boring. Like council meetings. Or goblin foot fungus. Anything.

"You ready?" I asked, once the last pair exited the hall.

"Yes," she whispered, voice barely above a breath.

"What do you know about the phases?"

"Umm, not much." She glanced toward the door like she was afraid someone might hear.

"Okay. No worries." I kept my tone light, smooth. I could tell she was nervous, her breathing hitched, shoulders tight. I couldn't see her aura, but I didn't need to. She was radiating tension.

"There are three phases, as you know." I began. "This week is about testing abilities, see how well everyone can run through the track, the Gauntlet of Ascension and The Rite of Steel. The track is meant to help with stamina and speed. Something we will need for both the Gauntlet and the Rite. Next week, the current Head Guard, will arrive. By the end of next week, they'll make the first cuts. Only a few will move forward into the official program."

She nodded slowly, processing.

"The following four weeks are prep. We'll be pushed hard, training, combat, magic control, mental discipline. Then we start sparring again, this time in matched pairs. Halric and the Head Guard will decide who we face."

"That doesn't seem so bad." Her voice had a little more strength to it.

I hesitated. "What do you know about the final phase?"

She blinked. "Nothing. Why?"

I exhaled. "That's the part no one really talks about. And the one you have to be ready for."

"Each phase will have its own day of assessment. If you pass the first two phases, you'll report to the edge of the Verdant Veil, the ancient forest that encircles our kingdom. There, you'll find the Sablewatch, a sacred observation stronghold where only the highest officials; my father, the Head Guard, Halric, and the recruiting guard Severina Elowen and once I pass I will be up there, are permitted to witness what comes next.

"Before we enter the forest, each of us will drink the Draught of Reveris, a rare and enchanted tea that opens the mind to its deepest, most buried fear and secrets. Once inside the Veil, you'll be forced to face that fear alone. There will be no help, you can only use your training and a sword. Just you and whatever truth the forest decides to show you.

"If you survive it, not everyone does, you'll emerge changed. You'll earn your Verdant Mark, a living sigil that appears on your skin, visible proof that you endured the final trial and were found worthy of the Veilbound Order."

"When you say not everyone survives, does that mean you could die?" She asks looking horrified.

"There may have been a couple of instances a long time ago, but no. We step in and stop it if it gets to that point."

"Okay, what is this fear we have to face?"

"It's different for every person. You won't know until it happens. The best we can do is prepare for anything. Get good at fighting both physically and mentally."

"So each day we have to pass, what if we fail the first day? How do you know you fail?"

"It has to be a near perfect run under a certain amount of time. You get docked points for any missteps and if you're over the five minutes. For the Rite of Steel you have to get your opponent to submit or knock them out. We don't do that during training, but we will move partners so everyone has a chance to practice with everyone."

"And the Heart of the Crucible?" She whispers.

"That one is simple, you just have to defeat whatever is conjured with the Draught of Reveris, the tea that is almost mixed with the magic of the Verdant Veil."

"Oh." Is all she says.

"Okay, let's get started. I want to run the course with you. I wish I could have yesterday." I tell her truthfully. Earning me a bashful smile. I follow her back inside, my eyes glued to her perfect ass the whole way. I am happy to see it empty, I want this time alone with her.

I take a step towards her and she takes off. I hear her laugh just before she jumps up to the course. I don't stare long, I start running behind her and easily catch up. She eats up the course like it's nothing.

Like this is just second nature to her, who is she?

Vera climbs the rope and I am right behind her, mostly staring at her perfect body as we climb. Launching herself off the platform she lands perfectly and I follow suit. She is not even winded, while I feel my breath coming in quick pants. Though, I am distracted.

We stare at each other for a moment and she blushes again. I reach out gently running my thumb over her cheek and her blush spreads. It can't be a coincidence that every time I touch her, I can fully see her. I don't know if it's like that for everyone or just because we're fated. No one else better be touching her.

"Your eyes are so beautiful." I whisper, my lips a breath away from hers.

"I love your eyes, too. The gold in your eyes shine, like mine." She says it curiously. I don't think she knows we're fated. I want to blurt it out.

"Yes, they will only ever shine like that when we're near each other." I hint. I want to know if she knows. I need her to know.

That must have been the wrong thing to say because she suddenly backs away and jumps down.

"Vera." I call for her, but she doesn't turn. Just tosses out something about getting home even though we haven't used our hour together.

"She's fast, it's like everything she does in here is second nature." I turn to see Halric coming back into the gym. How long has he been watching us?

"Yeah, I definitely think she will make it all the way. Should we go over the class today?" I ask to get his attention off my girl. We launch into it, discussing who might not be making the cut before I leave to go home. Trying to figure out how else I can get her to trust me.

Chapter 21: What More is There?

Vera

It's only the fourth day at Auravale Academy, and already my brain feels like it might short-circuit. There's so much to learn here, more than I ever imagined. Elemental Symmetry, Truthsense and Future Sight, Runes and Relics, Kingdoms and Bloodlines. Some of the names alone sound made up. But it's real. All of it.

The building itself is just as strange and wonderful. It feels like each area of the school is just a little different. Some warm and sunlit with greenhouses, others humming with static energy, or echoing softly with falling water. It's hard to believe this place is real, like something out of a dream I wasn't supposed to wake up in.

Yesterday at lunch, Caelum sat with me in the library. Just casually, like it was the most normal thing in the world. He was nervous. About me. And I found it endearing. We played twenty questions, his voice low as if afraid someone would overhear. Which begs to question if he was attempting to be secretive so Cassia didn't find out? I don't know if I can trust him. I don't know his intentions or why he is trying to talk to me and that worries me.

He didn't ask any further questions about my parents or where I'd come from, thank the stars. Instead, he asked about books, colors, food preferences, what kind of animal I'd be. (A hawk, I said, because they see everything.) He slowly warmed up and the nervousness went away the more we talked. His shoulders relaxed and he seemed in control, like he was used to asking questions. I guess he probably did this a lot with girls. I tried to not show my uneasiness after that thought but I think he caught it when he looked at me questioningly. I think he assumed it was a question he asked because then he switched to something else.

But then after Battlecraft when he said my eyes were beautiful, I felt myself light up from the inside out. Then to say his eyes only do that around me, is that a line or is it something else? I don't want to know, it's best I don't get close to anyone. I have nothing to offer him. No name. No family. No legacy worth anything in this world. All I have is purpose: survive, uncover the truth, and stop looking for softness in green eyes with golden starbursts. Still, there's something about him that pulls me in like gravity.

But today, I've done everything I can to avoid him. Pretending I don't notice when he looks at me. Pretending I'm not curious. Pretending his gaze doesn't linger like it's searching for something I forgot I had.

He keeps watching me. Trying to figure me out. And stars help me, I'm doing the same. Even though I shouldn't.

Today at lunch, I went to the library. I found a more secluded seat in the back, hoping he wouldn't find me. A large leather couch sat in front of the fireplace, quiet, cozy, hidden. I even laid down a little, head dipped so it wasn't visible over the cushions.

But then he slid into the seat beside me. He dropped his bag of food on the table with a thud. I looked up, startled.

"What's going on?" he asked.

"What do you mean?"

"What I mean is, we had a good time yesterday, and then you ran off on me. Then all day today you have been avoiding and ignoring me. So, what happened?"

"Nothing. Happened." I bit out. "Listen, I'm not looking for any complications." He was glaring now, sharper than I'd ever seen him. I instinctively leaned away, trying to read him. What was he feeling?

He sighed and scrubbed a hand over his jaw. "That's fine. But we're still friends. More than friends but we can start there."

"I'm not interested. You already have a girlfriend, probably more than one. And plenty of friends. Why don't you just leave me alone?"

"I already told you I don't have a girlfriend. Not one. Certainly not more than one." His voice dropped, lower, more intense. "And I don't *want* to leave you alone. I want you to give me a chance."

He reached for my hand and kissed the back of it, his lips resting warm against my skin. His green eyes lit up with those golden flecks, soft and unguarded. And there it was again. That damn smirk, that has my heart started thumping like a drum-line. Before I could fall straight into him, I yanked my hand back.

"So," he said, casually grabbing his sandwich. "What do you think of Auravale so far?"

"It's fine." The words came out sharper than I meant them to, frustration brimming beneath my skin. I focused on my food, jaw tight. *Breathe.* In and out.

My parents used to say I could sense people's intentions if I really tried. I never did. Hiding my gifts had become second nature. But now. I wanted to know. I imagined the violet orb they taught me to picture. My energy expanding, stretching until it brushed against Caelum.

And then I *felt* him. Frustration, same as mine. Curiosity. And then it seemed to change into something new. Something warm, startlingly clear. Romantic. Sexual. I gasped, eyes snapping open, heart pounding. *No, no, no.* Panic surged in my chest. I scrambled to pack my things, refusing to look at him.

"What's going on?" His voice was sharp, confused. Looking around for a possible threat.

"I have to go," I mumbled, bolting from the couch, dumping the rest of my food into the trash as I fled the library.

I hid in the bathroom, breathing fast, on the verge of a breakdown. *What just happened?* How did I do that? My emotions were spinning wildly, and my head was caught in a storm. When the bell rang, I rinsed my face quickly, hands trembling. But when I turned the faucet on—

The water didn't flow. It *sprayed* upward, wild, and then bent away from me. I stumbled back, eyes wide. *What the hell. I mean Veils!* Now I need to figure out how to dry my shirt.

By the time the next bell rang, I barely made it into class. Caelum was already there, watching me with a look I didn't want to decipher. I avoided his eyes, sliding into a seat far away.

That same guy from earlier, Sylas, I think? Dropped into the seat beside him, carefree and grinning. I did everything I could to focus on the lesson. But I could still feel Caelum. His confusion. His attention. The weight of his gaze. I didn't look his way once.

In Battlecraft, Halric tells us we're doing more sparring. Of course. My heart starts pounding again. Panic claws its way back in. I need to talk to my aunt.

Thankfully, most of the class is just Halric explaining the rules. Then he assigns us in pairs. Based on how well I did yesterday, I'm matched with the same girl as yesterday. I try to focus, pretending to fight a little harder but sloppier. It's not hard, since my mind is still spinning from lunch. I barely ate, and with feeling his emotions, it shook me.

Yesterday when I sparred with her, I barely had to try. Today it took a little more effort just to stay concentrated. My mind a jumbled mess, but I could also feel Cae's and Nero's eyes on me. She wasn't skilled, I just couldn't focus.

"Are you okay?" She whispers.

"Yes, I am okay."

"I am sorry about the other day with Cassia. I should have stopped them somehow. Or went for help, I hope you are okay." Her eyes were big and round. I could see the tears brimming. I don't think she could have stopped them even she wanted to.

"It's okay. Truly. I am fine, next time I won't let them get so far." I say with a sly smile. She gives me a smile and I know she is feeling better now.

When the bell rings, I bolt to the locker room, grab my things, and don't bother changing out of my gym clothes. I just need to get out.

As I reach my locker, I snatch what I need and hurry out, ignoring the looks from the others. I hear the rumble of an engine. A sleek black car pulls up beside the building. The passenger window rolls down. Caelum. I glance at him, then to the trees behind me.

"I'll give you a ride," he calls, his voice calm. Too calm for the storm raging inside of me. I shake my head and break into a sprint. Still in my gym clothes, perfect for running, so I push myself. The cold air bites at my cheeks, but I keep going. Then I feel his emotions. Worry. Frustration. It almost makes me stumble. Part of me wants to stop but I don't. Instead I try to outrun the panic clawing up my throat.

But I don't. I disappear into the trees. This time Nero never catches up to me, for which I am grateful. The forest feels different today. Colder. Still. No birds. No rustling leaves. Just silence. Like the woods are holding their breath. It reminds me of that day after school, when I first walked through those trees and found my parents.

'It's okay, to feel just don't drown in it.' I hear my mom's voice over and over again.

By the time I get home, I throw my things down and race straight to the backyard, desperate for air, for space. My heart won't slow. Panic claws up my chest, choking me. I drop to my knees, palms pressed into the grass as if the earth itself could anchor me.

But something's wrong.

The wind stirs, sharp and sudden, whipping strands of hair across my face. Beneath me, the ground hums with a low vibration that sinks into my bones. It isn't just sound, it's alive, pulsing through me like a second heartbeat. I close my eyes. In the distance, I feel it, pressure building, air thickening, the charged breath of a storm gathering strength on the horizon.

My pulse spikes, but not from fear. Recognition floods me, fierce and undeniable, as if the storm isn't coming toward me at all. As if it's answering. My breath catches, ragged and shallow. A gasp breaks from my lips.

What is happening to me?

"Vera?" Rina's voice cuts through the noise in my head. She stands at the edge of the porch, her face etched with concern.

I turn, my throat tight. "Are you okay?" she asks, her voice soft and steady.

I shake my head. "What's happening to me?" My voice cracks.

"Take a deep breath," she says, her voice like wind through leaves. I do. Cool, pine-scented air fills my lungs. I focus on the grass, on the earth grounding me, on Rina's voice. Another breath. Slower. I meet her eyes, hers a few shades lighter than mine.

"What was that?" I ask, quieter now.

"Have you ever played with the elements with your parents?" she asks gently.

"The elements? No. We thought it was just those two gifts."

"Moving the earth and wind, what you just did, have you ever done that before?"

I shake my head slowly. "That was me? We have been using sparkstones in my class but I've only gotten a spark or two, I didn't think I had elemental gifts."

"Okay." Her voice is steady now. "We have a lot to talk about. Come inside. I'll make us some tea."

Inside, I sit at the table, fingers tapping restlessly. She moves through the kitchen with too much malm for how fast my thoughts are racing. Finally, she sets the kettle on and turns to face me.

"Some fae have elemental gifts, earth, wind, fire, water," she begins. "Others, like you know, have sensing gifts, truth, auras, intentions. Some are gifted with strength."

"Okay but why? Is it just our family?" I ask. "My mom could sense intentions, but she never said anything about it being magical."

"No," she says. "Every fae is born with gifts. But only the royal family—or those like your father, from ancient protector lines, carry *multiple* gifts."

My breath catches. "My dad?"

She nods. "He had strength, could detect truth, and command the earth."

I stare at her. "They never told me. I just thought… he was strong. I figured all dads were."

She offers a soft smile, though her eyes stay sharp. "It's rare, Vera. Your parents must've passed their gifts to you but having *so many*? That's almost unheard of. Even in the royal line."

My head spins. "Why do we even *have* these gifts?"

Rina exhales slowly, and then everything changes.

"Because your mother and I are from another province, Elarindor, like I told you the other night. There is something sacred and ancient about the Nareth Peaks. There was never a clear answer as to why aside it being connected to the first fae queen. Somehow our lineage comes directly from her and she married the king which is where the royal line comes from. When we were children, someone tried to take our home from our father. He sent us here to keep us safe. He died defending it. The kingdom fell, and we never found out who was behind it. Since then, we've hidden our true abilities and who we are. But then your mom met your dad. We told him our lineage and he along with the king kept us protected, safe."

My heart stutters. "He always kept us safe."

"On the night you were born, there was a seer visiting the Grove of Stars for a council meeting, they don't come often. But it was also the day of the Veilfall Festival so lots of people come here to celebrate. When she saw your dad she said there was something he needed to know. She told him,

> *'Three daughters born beneath the same shifting stars.*
> *One of moon and flame, one of fang and thorn, one of blood and shadow.*
> *Beauty will crown them, and power older than the realms will stir within*
> *their veins.*
> *Before their nineteenth year, the darkness will seek their end —*
> *for if one falls, the balance breaks, and the realms shall bleed.*
> *Yet if they stand united, bound by choice not birth,*
> *they will awaken the first light again —*
> *and through them, dawn will rise,*
> *and the fractured lands shall become one.'*

Of course your dad demanded who, but they could not see who it was."

I'm still just staring at her.

Is this why he was always training me? It wasn't just to pass the Veilbound Order. He was adamant that I know how to fight and defend myself. I open my mouth, then close it again, completely at a loss for words.

Rina takes that as a sign to continue.

"After you were born, your father told the king he had to leave with you and your mom—to protect you. He said it was for your safety, but he never mentioned the part about the kingdom falling. Your parents and I are the only ones who know the truth." Her voice softens. "And now you." I glance around, half expecting someone to jump out and yell *gotcha*. She can't be serious.

"What?" It comes out barely louder than a breath. A chill slides down my spine.

"I need to get in contact with the king," Rina says. "But it's not easy. He's gone quiet. I haven't heard from him."

I just sit there, stunned. So many secrets. So many lies. My entire life, built on half-truths and omissions. What else don't I know?

"I—I…" Words slip through my fingers. She waits patiently, her eyes soft and sad.

"Three?" I finally manage. "Darkness? So, what you're saying there are *two others*? That we have to find them?" My voice cracks, half disbelieving, half terrified.

"We think so," she says. "Your parents searched, and I tried too. All we can assume is one's vampire, one's shifter, and one fae. You. But since the Shattering, the lands have been divided. Travel between them isn't simple. That's why we need to speak with the king."

I blink at her, incredulous. "If my parents didn't trust him with the whole truth, why should we? And why did you keep this from me?" The anger in me burns sharp and fast, fear disguised as fury. "I'm so tired of everyone deciding what I should or shouldn't know."

"I wasn't trying to keep it from you," she says quietly. "I just didn't want to overwhelm you. When you ask, I tell the truth. I'm doing my best to remember everything in the right order. As for the king, yes I think we can trust him. But I need to reach him first."

I exhale, shaking my head. "No more secrets. If it's about me, I deserve to know." She nods, regret shadowing her expression.

I stand abruptly, needing air, needing *space*. My thoughts are a tangled mess of prophecy, danger, and the gnawing ache of not knowing who I really am. I try to distract myself with schoolwork, but it's useless. Every word on the page dissolves into questions.

By dinner, I can barely force down a bite. I swirl my pasta around, staring at the flickering candlelight. *Three girls. Three realms. All hunted.* Are they just as lost as I was? Hidden away by frightened parents?

"Did something happen today at the Academy?" Rina's voice is gentle, perceptive as always. I nod.

"Yes," I murmur. "There's a boy. He's been talking to me for a few days. Today I tried to focus, like my father taught me, to sense his intentions. And it worked. But it wasn't just his intentions. I felt his emotions too, like they were my own. It startled me. I tried to get away, but even then, I could still *feel* him."

"Has that ever happened before?"

"No. Never."

She leans back, thoughtful. "Then for now, this stays between us. We'll start researching quietly. In the meantime..." Her voice trails off, her gaze distant.

"In the meantime?" I prompt.

She draws a slow breath. "We keep your powers concealed. No one outside this house can know what you can do. We'll keep training as usual, but also privately, away from the Academy. And if you feel overwhelmed again, ground yourself. Anchor your breath. You're not powerless."

I hesitate. "Do you think someone wants me—*us*—dead because of our powers? How would killing me threaten the kingdom? Or the other realms? I don't even understand what I'm supposed to be."

Her eyes meet mine, and for the first time, I see something close to fear. "I think we need to understand why you've manifested these abilities and maybe find the woman who made the original prophecy."

"Do you know where she is?" I whisper.

"She was born in Varethos. Likely a seer from there. If she's still alive, that's where we'll find her. I'll need to request time off, but perhaps after the Veilfall Festival, we can go."

"And how do we even begin figuring out why I have these powers?" I ask, pushing my food around the plate.

Rina leans back, candlelight flickering against her thoughtful face. "I still have a handful of old documents, records salvaged from Elarindor before it fell. We'll start there. But anything about your father's past would be in the Royal Library. And gaining access to that will be... difficult."

"But it's possible?" I ask, a spark of hope lighting inside me.

She sighs. "No one is permitted inside the Royal Library."

The spark fades. "Okay. Then we'll start with what we can. Elarindor. The Nareth Peaks. Why it fell. Why no one took it back. And figure out how to find the other two."

"It was thirty years ago, when my father sent us away," she says softly. "Maybe he trusted the wrong person. They were searching for something powerful but we still don't know what, or who. Somehow, it's all tied to the three."

My stomach twists. "If that's true, why would killing us hurt Elarindor? Or destroy the realms?"

"We don't know," she admits. "Only that you three are the key. That's what I need to uncover. For now, we start with the documents and prepare for Varethos. Their archives are vast, second only to their prophecies."

Silence settles between us. Not uncomfortable, but heavy. Dense with too many unanswered questions. Rina stands and gathers the plates. I follow her automatically, the simple rhythm of washing dishes grounding me.

"I hate this," I say finally, scrubbing harder than I need to. "Not you, I trust you. But everything else. The lies. The secrecy. Now I find out I'm part of some hidden line of fae, that there's a prophecy about my death and if I die, the kingdom dies too. It's insane. What more could there possibly be?"

She hands me a towel, her gaze filled with sorrow. "I know. I wish I could change that for you. I hope we don't find anything else but with your Veilfall Festival coming up..." She hesitates. "I think more is coming."

My throat tightens. "It just feels like every answer leads to ten more questions. We don't even know if my parents had a plan. Or what they found before they died."

She places a steady hand on my shoulder. "Then we'll find the truth together. Piece by piece."

Tomorrow, we'd start digging through her old documents. Add that to my academy work, my Order training, and now this. Training my powers, researching a fallen land, planning a trip to a place of prophecy, and finding two other girls who share my fate.

I dry the last plate and place it on the rack. The kitchen hums quietly around us, the faint drip of water, the crackle of candlelight. My thoughts won't stop spinning. But at least, for now, I'm not alone in them.

Chapter 22: At Least I'll Have Backup

Cae

I spent the rest of the afternoon hiding out in the library with El. Pretending to study and get homework done but my thoughts are lost on Vera. I don't know what happened in the library, one minute she was fine then the next she closed her eyes and her aura glowed.

I didn't even touch her this time and I was able to see her full aura and her life thread. I don't know what she was doing, but our threads connected a little more. I could feel it like a warm current flowing through me as it connected with my own and then her eyes snapped open and she was panicking.

I watched her run into the bathroom, so I went to our next class waiting for her. She came in at the last second and didn't sit by me. It would be too obvious if I got up during class and made someone move, so I sat. Not listening to what was being taught, gritting my teeth wanting to go to her.

Then in battlecraft she was starting to look better, to other people she looked fine but I could feel the panic, through our growing bond. I could see her aura pulsing and our thread that keeps us connected was pulsing with it. For some reason after the library I could see her aura a lot better. I still don't understand why and I don't know why it was being veiled in the first place. I could sense she needed something, I wish I could wrap her in my arms.

Because I am now certain that she is my fated, but we weren't meant to figure it out until the night of the Veilfall. At this time I still can't make it known that we are fated. I think she can sense me too but she's trying to deny it. She's protecting herself that much is clear.

As much as I wanted to storm in and take over and make her understand that we were fated, I had to wait. I couldn't force her into the limelight with me. Not with this mess with Cassia and her parents. I *really* need to get this figured out with my dad and fast.

"Okay, what's up?" I look up to see El looking at me curiously. I look at her jade green eyes that are so similar to my own, where mine are sharper hers are light, with the matching gold specks. She is my best friend but also my twin. While I am usually forced into crowds and having to work with various groups as the next heir, she only has to do it sometimes. She certainly helps me, but she mostly loves burying her face in books and learning to manipulate and control her gifts.

"Nothing. I am just studying." I say waving a hand towards my open books in front of me.

"Oh stop, I can sense lies just like you. You have been distracted this whole time. Usually if you are trying not to study, you play on your phone."

Looking around I make sure the door to the library is closed.

"It must be about Vera." El looks at me wryly.

I just look at her, wondering how she could possibly know.

"Why, is it because she won't sleep with you?" I looked at her in shock.

"Don't look at me like that. All the girls like to talk in the bathroom, the hallways, even in class and it's disgusting." She says, rolling her eyes.

"I'm not even going to answer that. But no, I can't even get her to really talk to me. Whenever she does, something happens and she freezes then pushes me away again. I don't know. I can barely get her to talk to me and nothing real. She hasn't said where she is from. Only that her parents died, and she lives with her aunt. The other night when I left during dinner I was able to find her through our thread. She lives with that recruiting guard, Rina."

"Yeah, thanks for leaving me with those people by the way."

"Sorry, I just can't deal with it anymore."

"Have you told, dad?" There's a lot I haven't told him.

"No, you know how he's been lately. He's so checked out and is going along with this stuff to marry me off to Cassia, I don't get it."

"How did you find Vera?"

"You know how I am able to see people's life threads?" She nods her head. "When I first touched Vera our threads glowed and connected. I thought I would do what you said and use it to find her and it worked."

"Does dad know about the threads?" I shake my head and she looks sad.

"Hey, don't be sad."

"I just miss mom but I also miss the way dad used to be." With that we went back to studying. There's nothing more I could say, we've had this conversation a lot and I miss her too. Little did we know our father heard the last part where El said she missed the way he used to be.

At dinner, at least it was just us tonight. Calindra was chatting nonstop about her day and the upcoming festival. She droned on about lunch with Cassia's mom, and I wanted to roll my eyes, but I didn't. My mind was lost on *my Lilac*, wondering how she was doing. Wondering if it would be weird if I just showed up at her house. Remembering the way she looked when she was sparring. And running the practice course. And stretching. Shit. I need to think of something else.

Both my father and El look at me questioningly but neither says something. Did they see something in my aura? I take a deep breath and make sure I am concealing it. Calindra kept talking, this time about her best friend and her perfect daughter, about how perfect it would be when we got married in the spring. No one responded.

She frowned, finally catching on. "What's going on with you guys?"

"Just worried about my test," El said smoothly.

"You're too obsessed with that school stuff. We should get our hair done this weekend."

"Sorry, I have a test to study for." I barely held back a smile.

"Lucan, your children need to relax and have some fun," she whined, her voice grating like a dull blade.

"My children are just fine," he said, his voice firm.

El and I both looked up, surprised. He hasn't defended us in a long time, even though we're good kids. We study hard, get all A's, and we're not out partying like everyone else. Well—okay, I do sneak out sometimes, but they don't know that.

Calindra blinked, clearly thrown off. Her eyes, the color of storm-swept skies, studied everything with cool precision, as if she were forever calculating, measuring, weighing the world against her own ambition. Even now, when she smiled, it didn't quite reach them. It never did.

"I just meant they should have fun sometimes," she said lightly, her tone too smooth, too rehearsed.

No one replied. The rest of the meal passed in tense silence, and when we finished, I tried to slip away quietly.

"Cae, can you meet me in my office?" Sighing, I rise from the table as El helps Thalina clear our dishes. I follow him up the stairs to his private office, the quiet between us heavier than usual.

"Close the door."

I do as he asks and freeze a little when he pours himself, his favorite whiskey drink from the decanter. I don't see him drink much anymore, although most nights El and I stick to ourselves. Without a word, he sits on the leather couch. I lower into one of the chairs across from him, unsure what this is about.

"I'm sorry." The words hit like a stone. I blink, shocked, watching him carefully as he exhales.

"I went to check on you and your sister. I heard her say she missed your mom... and me. I didn't realize how far I've drifted. How much I've failed you both."

I just stare. He *has* been absent, checked out since marrying Calindra. Not once has he asked about our lives unless it benefited the crown or her. I don't say anything, waiting to see where he is going with this.

"Your mother would've killed me if she knew I let it get like this. I promise, I'll do better." I want to believe him. I *do*. But hope feels dangerous. Still, I say nothing.

"Can you say something?" he asks quietly.

"I don't know what to say," I answer. "You've been gone. Not physically but you haven't *seen* us. Not me, not El. It's always been about the kingdom... or her. Appeasing her every wish, letting her belittle us especially El."

He slumps, the weight of the truth finally sinking in.

"I know. I'll do better," He says quietly, his eyes searching mine. "Tomorrow, after school... maybe we could do something. Like we used to."

"Call off the arranged marriage." I demand.

He blinks, caught off guard. Then, the weariness seeps in, his shoulders sink, eyes dim. "Caelum..." he starts, voice low. "I just want you to be happy. But it's getting harder for our kind to find their fated. If you haven't by now—"

"I *will* find her," I cut in. "I just need time. I don't want to be forced into something that feels like a lie." Forced into something like he allowed himself to be.

His gaze sharpens. I press on before he can redirect.

"I'm ready, Father. Ready to lead. I want happiness too but not with *her*. I can't even stand being in the same room with Cassia, yet you and Calindra keep making plans with her family like I'm some piece to be moved on a board. You won't even give me time for my Veilfall to find my fated." He winces at that, like I've struck too close to the truth.

"There's already an agreement," he says finally, the weight of it thick in his tone. "It's not something we can just dissolve overnight. There are political ramifications."

"Then find a way," I say, standing. My voice is calm, but firm. "I've been patient. I've played the role. But I won't do it anymore. I'm not a child, and I'm not a pawn. This is *my* life. I'll carry the crown, but I won't if it means giving up who I am."

He stares up at me, jaw clenched, like he's seeing me clearly for the first time in years. And I mean it. Every word. I turn to go.

"Son?" His voice softens behind me. "Have you found someone?" I glance back, shake my head, and leave. I don't know why yet, but I do know I need to protect her and I hate that I have to protect her from my own dad.

I decided to go for a jog. At least, that's what I told myself. Truth is, I need to see her. I find her sitting in the living room with her aunt. I stay hidden beyond the trees, cloaked in the darkness. It's hard to make out every detail, but it looks like they're pouring over books together. Serious ones.

She looks worried. Sad. But still so breathtaking it hurts. I've been reduced to stalking her and I can't even bring myself to care.

Fresh from a shower, her long dark hair tumbles down over her shoulders, damp waves just brushing where her breasts rise beneath a thin forest green tank top, the color makes her eyes glow even from this distance. I wish I could hold her, pull her into my arms and promise her she's safe.

Then her eyes snap up, startled, locking on the exact spot where I'm standing. Can she see me? My breath catches. Slowly, I start to step back. But she smirks. A soft, knowing curve of her lips before she glances back down at the page in front of her like nothing happened. How the Veil did she know I was here? I'll have to ask her. *If* she'll tell me. That would mean she would have to admit she senses me. *Or* I would have to admit that I have been basically stalking her by standing outside her house.

Later, when I'm lying in bed, all I can think about is her. My fingers absentmindedly toy with the thread I feel pulling between us. That invisible cord tying me to her, subtle but constant. She had known I was there. Does that mean she can sense me when I am close by? Does she know what our connection means?

I close my eyes and let my mind drift—on her. Always her.

That invisible thread between us hums in my chest, and I pull on it, wrapping my thoughts around her like a lifeline. The faint glow sharpens into heat, and suddenly I can almost feel her, close, tangible, just out of reach.

My hand curls around my cock, stroking slow, deliberate, as if she's the one guiding me. The thought makes my breath catch. I picture her moving against me, the strength in her thighs, the way her body would ride mine with that fierce determination she carries into everything. Her ass grinding down, her legs tightening around me, her breasts bouncing in time with every thrust, every inch of her made to undo me.

The ache builds too fast. I try to hold it off, savoring the image of her mouth, her sounds, the look in her eyes if I were buried inside her. But the pressure crests sharp and hot, and with a low groan, I spill across my stomach, shuddering with the release.

I lie there in the aftermath, chest heaving, the thread still glowing faintly inside me. And gods, I wish it had been her. I wish I'd come undone inside her, marking her as surely as she's marked me. Soon, I hope she'll let me in. I tug on her thread once more before sleep takes me, comforted by the faint pull that reminds me she's never too far.

I eat breakfast with El in the small breakfast nook. She is barely eating. I know Calindra won't be up for several hours, but my dad should be down here soon.

"What's up, El?" I ask her.

"Did dad apologize last night?" She looks hopeful, almost happy.

"Yeah, in the office. He said he hadn't realized he had been so distant."

"Yeah he said the same to me. Did you tell him about Vera?"

"He knows there is someone, I am not ready to share who she is yet."

"Good, do you think he meant it? That he will start being our dad again?" She whispers. I wrap my arm around her and pull her closer.

"I mean it." We hear and both look up to see him standing in the doorway. Watching us with a sad smile. How much of that did he hear?

"So, tell me about Vera." He says when he sits down with us. I guess he heard all of it. El and I just look at each other. I don't know why, but I feel the need to protect her.

"She's just someone I have been talking to. She is incredibly smart, strong, and stubborn. She won't let me talk to her." I say with a laugh. I hadn't intended to tell him so much but it just flowed right out of me.

"That sounds like your mom. She hated that I was a prince and how popular I was especially with the ladies. I was never around her much growing up but when I first laid eyes on her at Auravale, I knew. I knew she was my fated. And Veils did she make me work for it." he says with a laugh. He looks happy and sad, remembering his fated. I don't know what I would do if I ever lost Vera.

"She doesn't know I am the prince. She is just really guarded."

"How does she not know who you are? Everyone in the kingdom has met you."

"She just moved here." I say shrugging.

"I would like to meet her."

"I won't bring her here, not with you and Calindra plotting my marriage to Cassia, who has been tormenting Vera."

"I will talk to Calindra today. I promise, I will help figure this out." When I start clearing my plate to bring it into the kitchen, he stops me again.

"Cae? Is she your fated?"

My shoulders tense and I say "I don't know." I have never really lied to my father. But at this time I shouldn't have told him as much as I did. Valerian told me to tell no one I can trust with her life. Unfortunately, I don't know if I can trust him and I certainly don't trust Calindra.

Again, I wait in my car for her. I watch the school doors, tapping the steering wheel, hoping to catch even the smallest glimpse of purple eyes or the wild sway of her dark curls. But the minutes pass, and the warning bell rings. Still no sign of her.

Maybe she slipped by. Maybe she's already in class, tucked into her usual seat with her head down. I make my way to first period, trying not to sprint. But when I slide into my chair and scan the room, it's empty in the way that only matters to me, no Vera. I feel the fear start to crawl up my spine, I prepare to start looking for her.

Before I even get a chance to focus on our thread, she slides smoothly into a seat but not by me. So we're back to her avoiding me, again? I smile, knowing she can keep trying to push me away but I won't let her get too far. I know I let my anger get the better of me yesterday, frustrated with her pushing me away. But I won't let her, I will do whatever it takes to earn her trust.

The day crawls by. In every class, I keep pulling on that invisible tether. Checking for signs of fear, of pain, of anything that could explain why she was late today. But it remains unchanged. Calm. Distant. The more I pull on it the more I can feel her. I know in this moment that she needs space and as much as I crave to be around her, to feel her. If I keep pushing the way I am, it could make it worst. She's guarding herself for a reason.

At lunch, I sit with El, who's trying to act normal while I push food around my tray. I wanted to go to her but I can sense that she needs space. I won't give it to her for long, maybe if I am not her constant shadow she will miss me. Yeah. I don't really believe that, but there is something that is really bothering her. I plan to find out. I do know that if I keep pushing her she will continue to stay away from me. I need to show her she can trust me.

She's midway through a story about how two students nearly blew up the alchemy lab when the atmosphere shifts, cold and sharp. Cassia. She appears in a whirl of expensive perfume and frosted arrogance, practically throwing herself into the seat beside me after making Sylas and Nero shuffle down. Her posse forms like vultures behind El.

I raise an eyebrow at my sister. She gives me a look—*abort mission*—and nods subtly. We rise together, trays in hand, and leave without a word. But Cassia's not letting go that easy. Her hand clamps down on my bicep.

"Where are you going?" Her voice is honeyed poison. "I've missed you so much at lunch these past few days."

El snorts behind me. Cassia's smile drops into a venomous glare. I step between them.

"Don't touch me," I say, keeping my voice level. "And don't look at my sister like that." Her eyes flare, ice-blue and full of spite.

"There is nothing between us. There never was. And there never will be." I enunciate every word. Loud enough for everyone at our table and a few nearby tables to hear.

Her face twists. "Is it because of that little bitch?"

My blood flashes hot. "You don't talk about her like that." My voice drops, hard as steel. "What Vera and I have, whatever it becomes, it's *real*. Something you wouldn't understand." She recoils like I slapped her. I don't wait for her reply. Wrapping my arm around El's shoulder, we walk away. I wonder if that was the wrong thing to say, especially out loud. But there is no denying my obsession with her, my intentions need to be known. To keep any guys away from her and hopefully the girls get the message to stay away from me.

"Wait until your parents hear about this!" she shrieks after me.

"Looking forward to it," I mutter under my breath.

El chuckles. "Well, this is going to be *fun* tonight."

"At least I'll have backup," I say, squeezing her shoulder.

A beat of silence passes. Then she asks, quieter, "Hopefully *I* will have backup." She's says sarcastically. "How come you sat with us today?"

I glance at her. "Just giving her some space."

"You're going to check on her, aren't you?"

"Yeah. I was thinking about asking if she would want to hang out this weekend. I want you to meet her."

She grins. "Sure, if she doesn't ditch you."

I laugh despite myself. "Not funny."

"She will, though," she teases, making me shake my head.

Our last two classes I am surprised she allows me to sit next to her. My theory of giving her space must be working. We don't talk but I scoot my seat as close as possible.

After school I head right home, keeping a mental tug on her thread the whole time. I think that's the only thing keeping me sane right now. I head inside, drop my bag in my room, and make my way toward my dad's office down the hall, and I knock before stepping in. He's inside, speaking with Calindra. Her shrill voice grates my nerves before she even sees me.

"Oh, look who finally showed up," she says with saccharine disgust.

"I came right here after school," I replied, deadpan. Although, I wish I could have spent more time training with Vera. I will take any alone time I can with her.

Calindra has no real magic, just a bit of wind, and a lot of noise. But my dad can read me. I keep my aura neutral, bored, indifferent.

"Well, *Cassia* was upset. Her parents called. We won't stand for this." She squares her shoulders like she's royalty. "We *agreed* once you take the crown, you'll marry her." She's waving her arms around and the long sleeves of her black dress flaps around with her. The charm on her bracelet swinging with her movement.

"No. *You* agreed." I stare directly at her. "I never did."

"Oh yes you will! Your father and I—"

"He will not marry Cassia." My dad's voice cuts through the room like a blade.

Calindra gapes at him. "Lucan! You *agreed*!"

"I can't force my son into a sham of a marriage like my own. I want to take a look at the contract."

"Sham of a marriage? Lucan!" Her voice breaks into a high, wounded cry. She clutches at her chest like she's just been struck. "I—I thought this is what you wanted. We had dates, dinners, I even spent time with your children." Her eyes glisten as if she's trying to summon tears.

My dad's stare is unyielding. "They were meetings, Calindra. Council obligations. And you haven't helped—you've only pushed. This arrangement with the Corvinas is over."

For a heartbeat, her expression falters, lips trembling as if she might plead. Then the mask shatters. Her face hardens, the false sadness draining away in an instant. Red blotches rise on her cheeks. I guess she is tired of acting.

"What am I supposed to tell the Corvinas?" she spits, voice sharp now, venom in every word. "They were *counting* on this union. As soon as Caelum and Cassia got together. They paraded Cassia around like she was already a princess, and now you want me to tell them it was all for nothing?"

"I was never with her," I say flatly. Calindra glares. My dad stands, suddenly older than he looked a moment ago.

"Do not speak or look at my son and your future king that way," he snaps. "Maybe you should have realized sooner, then. The only Princess here is Elowen. We're done here." She huffs and storms past me with all the grace of a flapping goose. I shoot a text to El.

Me: *Heads up. Storm squawking your way.*

El: *Great.*

Dad gestures for me to sit. I do.

"I think I'll be contacting our lawyer," he mutters. "How was school?" he adds.

I shrug. "Same. Training for the Veilbound Order. But no one's talking about phase three."

He nods. "They should. Facing your greatest fears isn't something you spring on kids."

"Not everyone has a council of trained advisors and warrior parents prepping them," I mutter, thinking of Vera's wide eyes and quiet awe.

"This have something to do with the girl?" he asks, eyes twinkling. Shit. Caught.

"Yes," I admit. "But there might be others like her."

He smiles. "Then help her. Teach her. That's what a real king and mate would do."

Tomorrow. I will find a way to ask her to do more training. She allowed it once, I want to find a way for her to let me in.

Chapter 22: At Least I'll Have Backup

Chapter 23: You Must Be Slow

Vera

I stepped into the classroom, heart already unsettled. I wasn't sure if I should've come early but I needed space, air, time to think without running into *him*. Caelum.

I'd managed to avoid Nero yesterday and again this morning, and thankfully, Cassia and her shadows hadn't surfaced either. But Caelum… he wasn't here yet, and that didn't mean he was far. Since I'd tried to feel him the other day with my gifts, there'd been this hum. Faint, constant. Like a thread tugging at the edge of my awareness, always there. I didn't know what it meant, and I wasn't sure I wanted to.

I took a seat near the window. The room was empty, still early. The quiet should've felt Calming. Instead, it amplified every thought swirling in my mind.

The door creaked open behind me. I looked up instinctively. Mr. Valeis walks in. He entered with the same silent grace he always carried, his long charcoal coat shifting as he moved. He set his things down at the desk, then turned his head slightly, those pale silver-flecked eyes settling on me. A flicker passed through them. Curiosity? Recognition? It vanished too quickly to name.

"Vera," he said softly, his voice like velvet against glass. "How was your night?"

There was no accusation in his tone. But something about the way he asked made me feel like he already knew the answer. Or was trying to see past the one I might give.

"Great," I replied carefully. "How about yours?"

"Quiet," he said. "I was home alone. Nothing to do but read."

I nodded, trying to seem casual. "What are you reading?"

"A recent history on Elarindor," he replied, his gaze never quite leaving me. My fingers curled slightly around the edge of my sleeve.

"Just preparing for next week's lesson," he continued. "Their magic has always fascinated me. Especially how it flowed through their land so naturally."

"What kind of magic?" I asked, keeping my voice light, even as my heartbeat ticked up. I didn't know why I was asking. Maybe I needed to know what he knew.

"They had a deep affinity to the earth, something instinctive. And like all royal lines, they could command all the elements. But there were rumors of healers in the bloodline." He paused. "Of course, that's mostly considered myth. Heresy, even. Never proven."

He smiled slightly, though it didn't quite reach his eyes. "Still, it will be interesting, diving into their lost land next week."

"Why is it considered lost?" I asked, feigning only mild curiosity. Careful not to sound too interested. Careful not to care too much about something that already felt too close.

Professor Valeis didn't look up at first. His fingers traced the edge of an open book as if considering how much to say. "Some say the family was targeted," he said finally, voice firm and deliberate. "There was talk of a prophecy, a girl, rare and uncommonly powerful, connected to others. Others claim Sylvaeris dismantled the region itself, burned the roots before they could grow."

He paused, eyes meeting mine.

"Their bloodline was tied to the Nareth Peaks, its wild magic, its ancient nature. If the prophecy came true, it was said the crown would fall. But of course something seems to be missing, the land was never taken over but what happened to al those people?" Am I the threat too the crown? No, that can't be right because the prophecy said if I die the crown will fall. Could it be possible they are still there? Hidden in the Nareth Peaks.

Before I could respond, the door opened again. Caelum stepped into the room. He froze. His sharp green eyes flicked between me and Mr. Valeis, his jaw tense. I felt his concern before I saw it, waves of emotion crashing into me, raw and overwhelming. My own shields weren't ready for it, and I hated that. Hated how easily his presence affected me. I need to work on shielding myself if that was even possible.

"What's going on?" Caelum asked, voice low but clipped. I didn't move. Didn't speak. I wasn't sure what answer he was looking for.

"Just talking about some history of the lands. Preparing for next weeks lesson. Vera, here was wondering what happened to Elarindor. I was telling her some of the theories."

"The official statement is that the family died. No one knows what happened. The old palace burned down and the Qaresar and his daughters were in it." He says it so matter of factly. Like the disappearance of this family didn't mean anything. He doesn't know that it's my family. Just another thing he can't know about.

He takes the seat next to me, his easy sexy smirk. "How was the rest of your night?"

"It was good thanks." I give him my brief answer and turn back to to the front.

"Mine was also good, thanks for asking Lilac." When I don't respond, he chuckles. Soon people start filing in. So much for avoiding him, why does he make it so hard.

The rest of the day passes the same. When it's time for lunch I find a secluded spot in the library. I tell myself I am not disappointed when he doesn't show up.

I quietly eat my lunch and contemplate what Mr. Valeis said. Did the kingdom of Sylvaeris have something to do with it? I don't know the royal family so it's hard to know. Maybe when I meet them I could sense any intentions.

Could they be who is after me? Maybe they know that the daughters didn't die. Rina said the former king helped hide them, so that doesn't make much sense either. If they wanted them dead they could have gone after them sooner, not well after thirty years. Something new to discuss with Rina.

As I step out of the locker room, the sharp scent of sweat and stone hits me but that's not what makes me freeze. Cassia is standing there, waiting. She straightens the moment she sees me, moving with that calculating grace that always puts me on edge. She's still favoring her side and some bruises still litter her arms. Her platinum blonde hair lies perfectly down her back, not a strand out of place, as if even her hair is too proud to misbehave. She's wearing a fitted, pale-gray sweater over her training gear, probably still hiding bruises. Bruises from when I knocked her down.

I used to assume everyone healed as fast as I did. I never paid attention to how long my dad took to recover after sparring, or if my mom did too. But now I wonder if they had that ability. Were they like me? Cassia steps in front of me, blocking my path.

"I want to know how you showed up out of nowhere," she says, voice low and sharp. "How you're able to fight the way you do. How you healed so fast. And most of all, how you managed to get Cae's attention."

She crosses her arms, eyes narrowing. "Not that it's hard. He chases girls all the time. He just usually doesn't work for it. You're different. I want to know why."

I blink, trying to keep my voice calm. "I don't know what to tell you. Sorry he's not giving you the attention you're desperate for?"

Her jaw tightens, and for a second, I swear I see red flicker around her. I blink rapidly wondering what that was. "I'm not desperate. He *will* be mine. You're just something new. Temporary."

I sigh, exasperated. "You must be slow. I've told you multiple times, you can have him. I don't control what he does."

But Cassia isn't listening anymore. She's not here to hear logic. She's here to draw blood. Before she can throw another accusation, a low growl cuts through the tension.

"What the veils is going on here?" The sound slides over my skin like velvet laced with thorns. I stiffen from the warmth of him directly behind me.

I can feel his breath at the back of my neck before I even turn. It's warm and close, and it sends an involuntary shiver down my spine. I try to step aside to put space between us, to keep Cassia in my line of sight and to breathe but before I get far, his hand snakes around my waist. He pulls me back into him like it's nothing. Like he's done it a thousand times.

Like he owns me. Cassia's sharp blue eyes drop to where his hand grips me. I forcefully push away from him and glare at him.

Her nostrils flare as her arms fold tighter across her chest. She's seething. He's not helping my case. At all.

"Listen, Cae," she starts, venom thick in her tone. "Sleep with whoever you want. But we both know how this ends. You and I will be married. That girl—" she tosses a hand toward me like I'm some kind of stain, "—she's just a phase. Once you're done using her, you'll come back to me."

The possessive fury that pulses through him surprises me.

"You're delusional," Caelum snaps, voice low and deadly. "You were the temporary one, Cassia. You're *nothing* to me. Not then and certainly not now. Vera…" He pauses, and his next words wrap around me like a net I don't want and can't escape. "Vera is everything." My heart lurches. My stomach drops.

No, no, no. He just made it worse. Yet again. Caelum moves forward and his arm tightens around my waist. Before I can protest, he's steering me away like we're a team, like we belong together. My legs move without thinking, dazed and buzzing. I don't even look back, but I feel Cassia's glare burning into the back of my head. For a moment I almost feel bad for her. Almost.

Inside the Echoforge, I jerk out of his grasp again the moment the door swings shut and storm off, fury sparking beneath my skin. I came here trying to fly under the radar. I didn't ask for attention. I didn't ask for this. And now? Now I'm the center of a war I want no part in. Because of him.

Nero's talking to Halric near the entrance to the Rite of Steel, but I march past them and claim a quiet corner. I sit, stretch, trying to bury the wildfire in my chest. Of course, he follows.

"I'm sorry, Lilac," he says gently, crouching beside me.

I don't look at him. "For what exactly?"

"I'm not sure," he says with a faint smile. "But I know you're mad."

"Brilliant deductive work." I glance sideways at him. "Let me make something clear. You *don't* get to claim me. I've said it already, I'm not interested. I don't even want to be friends right now. I'm just trying to survive this academy."

His expression shifts, less playful, more pained. "You're right," he says after a moment. "But I *want* to claim you. And I know you feel something too. I can see it. I can *feel* it. I don't know why you're fighting it, but I'm asking. Just give me a chance."

I shake my head. "I'm not here for romance. I'm not here for anything. Plus, according to her you're going to marry her, so that makes us nothing." My voice is quieter than I intended. Raw. I point between him and I and his hand catches mine. The moment our skin touches, that warmth flows through me again, dangerous, and addicting.

"I won't push for anything more," he whispers. "But can we train together after school today? Just for an hour." It could help getting practice sparring with someone bigger and stronger.

I want to say no. But I need the training. I need the edge. I need to work off this pent up stress and fear. Especially after what Mr. Valeis said. If there's even a chance I'm connected to this Elarindor prophecy, or if its the same prophecy, I need to be ready. And maybe I can find more books on Elarindor myself. Try to figure out what the academy doesn't want me to know. Find out if there are people still there.

Yeah, it would help to work off some of this anger.

"One hour," I say finally. He thinks he is stronger than me, when I have been fighting my dad my whole life. I won't go easy on him.

He grins. "What's so funny?" I smirk. Before he can ask more, Halric claps his hands and bellows that we'll be running the course again. Saved by the training bell.

"Come on. Let's join the group."

Caelum holds out his hand, and like a fool, I take it. His palm is warm, his grip firm, and the second our skin connects, that now-familiar tingle rushes up my arm. It's like the world softens for a heartbeat. I hate how much I like it. Not that I'd ever admit that out loud.

He tries to hold on a little longer, fingers lingering, but I slip my hand from his and tuck it into the hem of my shirt like it burned. I glance over just in time to see Nero approaching. His eyes drop to where our hands were joined, then lift to mine with a knowing smirk that earns a low, guttural grumble from Cae.

Chapter 24: You're Alive, You're Capable, You're Strong.

Vera

Halric's voice cuts through the murmurs around us, commanding attention.

"Alright, listen up. Today I want to see you all run the Gauntlet again. Monday, Tuesday, and Wednesday, our Head Guard will be here watching. You'll be doing it all again. And by Thursday, those who are getting cut from the program will know." A collective inhale echoes across the group. Even the cocky ones straighten up. Ryven looks like he's bored.

"I'd rest up this weekend if I were you, because next week we will push you harder than you've ever gone before. Today, you'll each run the course individually. When you're not on it, you'll be sparring in pairs. Same teams as yesterday." He glances at Caelum and Nero. "These two will be observing. Helping out. Those enlisted for Head Guard training will be switching out every two weeks. I don't want any more incidents today. Got it?" I glance back over at Ryven and he is glaring at Nero.

I sense he has bad intentions, but since it's not directed at me I can't tell what. Suddenly his dark eyes scan the crowd and he locks his eyes onto me. He gives me a slow smirk, his eyes scanning over me. Assessing me. I hope I don't get paired with him, something tells me he wouldn't hold back. I need to ask Nero about him. He's in my truthsense class so maybe he know's that Ryven is planning something.

There's a chorus of "yes sir," followed by Halric's grin.

"First up—drumroll…" A few students slap their thighs in an uneven rhythm. "Better. Sylas! Let's go." Across the field, Sylas looks up from whispering to one of Cassia's ever-present shadows. He flashes the girl a lazy grin and jogs toward Halric. Typical.

I turn to the girl I sparred with yesterday. She offers me a shy smile, brushing her curly brown hair behind her ear. Her eyes dart nervously to mine. Did I hit too hard yesterday?

I force a smile. "Hi. I'm Vera." Maybe I should've started with that yesterday after she apologized. I'm just too frazzled to even think of proper manners.

She lets out a soft laugh. "I'm Lyra. You're a good fighter… even when you're holding back." She could tell?

I blink. "Thanks. You were good too."

She giggles again, shaking her head. "I'm not. I don't even know if it was a good idea to be in this program. But maybe you could show me a few things? Help me survive it?"

"Absolutely." Maybe she could be a friend.

We dive into the basics. Her footwork's hesitant at first, but once I break it down for her, she finds a rhythm. She quickly picks up the movements. When she nails a proper jab-kick combo, I cheer her on, and she beams with pride. It feels…nice. Not something I'm used to. Teaching. Encouraging. Being seen as someone capable.

Eventually, her name is called for the course. She gives me a hopeful look before jogging off. I straighten up, wiping sweat from my brow. My eyes drift to the far side of the field where I spot Cae—

unfortunately—talking to Cassia. Her laughter carries across the open space, high-pitched and fake. Her hair swishes like she's in a performance. Of course.

I bristle. He's demonstrating a move, an overhand punch, I think but she leans in way too close, giggling like he just told her the funniest joke in the realm. My gut clenches even though I know better. Just as Caelum turns, eyes scanning for me, I look away and start walking in the opposite direction.

"Don't let her get to you," a low voice says at my side. I jump slightly—I hadn't even noticed Nero's approach. "She's trying to upset you. Drive a wedge between you and Caelum."

"I'm not upset." I say the words calmly, evenly, like they aren't a blatant lie. "And there's nothing between me and Caelum to drive a wedge into." He watches me for a beat, maybe waiting for me to contradict myself. I don't. Thankfully, my name is called next, sparing me more analysis.

I step forward, muscles buzzing, the last one left to run. Most of the group has already drifted toward the locker room, but enough linger to form a small audience, including the very reason I keep trying to stay invisible. Screw it. Cassia's gone. Hopefully no one else is watching too closely.

The Gauntlet looms before me, stretching impossibly high, shadows swallowing the top. Platforms shift with the slow, deliberate pulse of old magic, rearranging themselves like they've been waiting just for me. My stomach twists. I've trained on obstacle courses before, but never one that felt alive. I want to see what I can do.

I launch onto the first platform, wood shuddering beneath my palms. The rope spirals upward into blinding light, and for a second, I falter, my hand slipping as the fibers thin to near nothing. My chest lurches, but I catch, fingers burning as I drag myself higher. One mistake. I won't give it another.

The poles ahead sway in phantom winds, bending like reeds, but I flow with them, using their rhythm to propel me across. The illusions rise at the edge of my vision, rivers roaring below, cliffs yawning open, the sky tilting as though gravity itself wants me to fall but I push them aside. Fire hums in my veins, steady and sharp. The cool rush of air fills my lungs. The quiet strength of earth steadies my footing. Water moves in my muscles, fluid and precise.

Every gift thrums through me, threading into the climb. My body remembers what my father drilled into me, but now it's more. More than memory. More than muscle. The elements answer me.

By the time I hit the final wall, slick with conjured mist, shifting from stone to glass to steel, my arms burn and my legs scream. I grit my teeth, hauling myself upward. The wall changes beneath me, cruel in its rhythm, but I match it, refusing to break.

I heave over the top and land hard on the last platform. My lungs are on fire, sweat stings my eyes, and yet—this is the kind of ache that means something. Alive. Capable. Strong.

A hush lingers, thicker than before. Halric's arms are crossed, a knowing smirk pulling at his mouth like he's just had something confirmed. Lyra and Sylas stare like they've seen a ghost. Cae and Nero both watch with the same pride, though Caelum's gaze has that sharp, hungry edge of something more. Behind him, Ryven's jaw tightens, fury barely contained.

I hop down, heading for my water bottle, ignoring them all. I don't want praise. I just needed this moment for me.

Footsteps approach. I turn to see Lyra approaching. "Wow, that was amazing," Lyra says, a little breathless. "I have to get home, but I'll see you Monday?"

"Yeah, of course. Have a good weekend."

She jogs off, and Nero nods toward me with a grin. "Impressive. I heard you're staying after for more training. Guess I'll see you Monday." So he's just friends with Caelum now? After they were really trying to hurt each other just the other day. I wonder what they said to each other up there.

And then he's gone too, leaving me alone, until I hear slow, steady footsteps. More saunter than walk. Caelum. He has no right to look that good after what he did earlier. I'm still mad that he thinks he can just claim me. Still flushed from exertion, his hair damp and messy, he stops in front of me with that half-smile that should be illegal.

"You did good, Brightstep." My pulse stutters at the new nickname. I roll my eyes to mask the flutter in my chest, but my voice comes out softer than I'd like.

"Vera." I say calmly like my heart isn't fluttering.

"What?"

"My name is Vera. Not Lilac. Not *Brightstep.*" His smirk only serves to upset me further. He's just staring at me like I am just cute, like what I just said doesn't matter.

"Okay, *Vera.* Let's get started on the sparring. Let's head up to the platform." As I follow him, I wonder if I should just beat him quickly then just leave. It would serve him right for being so arrogant. I know what Cassia has said was true. He's probably had lots of girls and can get any girl he wants. So what he wants with me is anyone's guess, unless it's just the challenge he likes.

He walks to the middle and turns to wait for me to step up to him. I get into my stance and wait to see what he's going to do.

"Okay, *Vera.* Let's see what you got."

For the first twenty minutes, I went light. Like I was doing with Lyra. He kept pointing out different things I can do to improve.

"No, put your weight into your center. You're power comes from your legs, so when you go to throw your jab your starting at your leg. Like this." He does a slow punch forward showing me every movement. I'm mostly watching because I love the way the muscles move over his leg and then ripple through his arm. I'm too distracted to laugh.

Again I pretend to throw a lopsided punch. I don't know how much longer I will be able to keep pretending.

"No, watch again." There is a slight frustration in his voice but again I am too busy watching the muscles in his legs and arms. My eyes land on his chest where I can see every muscle through his shirt. Wondering if I could get him to take his shirt off.

My cheeks start to warm and he stops and looks at me. "Are you paying attention or just admiring my body?" He asks teasingly.

"I'm paying attention. Let's do it again, I am certain I can do it now."

"Okay. Let's see it, Lilac." I glare at him. It took like two minutes of our training for him to go back to using my nickname.

He just chuckles but we get into the stance. This time I let myself really fight. I bounce up on my toes and throw out my favorite combo. Starting with my jab, I quickly move to the cross then left hook before spinning and grabbing him easily and throwing him over my shoulder and onto his back.

Before he has a moment to figure out what happened, I am walking away. The shock on his face was hilarious and I can't help the giggle that escapes.

Suddenly I feel arms around my waist and I am being lifted and thrown into the air. He spins us around and we land onto the platform, he still takes the brunt of the fall, but I am winded and surprised. Hell —I mean Veils. I really need to get this lingo down. I should have kept paying attention. I assumed he would be down for a minute. He quickly spins us so he is straddling my waist.

When I open my eyes he is over me staring down at me. "You've been faking it this whole time? I should have known. You excel at everything in battlecraft, Brightstep."

"Vera." I say and try to buck him off of me but he is too heavy. He is putting most of his weight over my legs so I can't use them for leverage and his hands are holding my arms above my head.

"Which means." He keeps going like he didn't hear me. "My, Brightstep. You were just admiring my body. Don't worry. I won't tell anyone. I have been admiring yours too. The way you move, every step is with purpose, agility and brightness. Even when you're pretending." He whispers the last part with his lips a breath away from mine. I can feel the puff of breath. My lips part instinctively waiting for more.

A shudder runs through me. And he smiles.

"You can't keep denying us. Stop pushing me away."

That did it, I remembered I can't let him get too close. "There is no us. Get off of me. I have to get home." I try keep my voice even but I hear the shakiness.

"Make me. I want to see what you can really do. If I can keep my hold on you then I get to see you Sunday, for more training, of course. I will pick you up from your house. If you can get me off, well then I will have to wait until Monday to see your beautiful face."

"Okay, deal." I take a moment to relax, ground myself. Closing my eyes, I feel where all of our body parts are touching. Wait, nope. Don't think about that. I can feel the pressure over my stomach but it's light enough I know he's holding back. His hands are holding my wrists firmly but not holding them down. I open my eyes and smile sweetly at him.

He narrows his eyes at me but his eyes slowly lower to my mouth. Then lower yet to where the top of my breasts are pushing out of my sports bra and against my top. My breath hitches, then speeds up when I feel something pressing harder against my stomach. His eyes remain on me. Scanning from my mouth to my neck to my breasts and back again. I know when I go to move my left leg I will feel him even more. Just as his eyes reach mine, I throw my left leg over, twist my body and use my wrists to throw him over. I land straddling him, his long thick shaft resting against my core.

I look into his surprised green eyes. "Veils, Brightstep. I'm starting to think you don't need extra training."

"Like you said. I need to learn to fight against someone stronger. I guess I will have to ask Nero. See you Monday. Oh, and I'm not interested in being with anyone right now. When I am ready I want to be with someone who only wants to be with me." I quickly hop off him and run out of the echoforge before he has a chance to catch me. I can hear him shout my name, but I keep going.

Chapter 25: It's Not Final

Cae

Shutting down the echoforge, I head toward the locker room and find Halric packing up his things.

"Surprised, you held yourself back. I had to stop watching, when you had her pinned under you." He laughs. Veils, I didn't even realize he had been watching. My attention was only on her. The feel of her body under mine.

"She's really good," he says, slinging his bag over his shoulder. "I can tell she's holding back. Except at the end when she flipped you over onto your back. Is she from around here?"

I nod, then shake my head. "No idea where she's from, actually."

"Whoever trained her is damn good. If we can get her to go full force, I bet she could challenge the Head Guard. Hell, maybe even Lucien. No one has beaten his record on the Gauntlet, and it's been 18 years." Lucien. The name of the former Head of the Guard who disappeared not long after I was born. No one knows why he vanished, but I'd heard plenty of speculation during my training. The members of the Guard sure like to gossip. I know they were probably hoping I would get some information for them, but I was more focused on getting better than all the members. I was raised knowing I needed to fight as well as them if not better.

My father would tell El and I constantly about his stories of battles in The Shattering. He said he fought side by side with his best friend and together they were able to beat back the rogues of vampires and werewolves that had got past the borders and made their way to the Grove.

El and I were a few months old at the time. My mom kept us safe and hidden deep inside the Grove so we couldn't be found. He was by his father when he got killed by a rogue shifter. He always chokes up a little, when he tells the story. I never understood the gravity of what he went through.

Then ten years later we lose mom. It was hard on all of us, but I never could have imagined what it was like for my father. Now it feels like for the first time I could. I can't imagine since I met Vera. Already knowing she is in some kind of danger is enough to push me over the edge. Yet, I have to keep pretending like she's not my fated mate because she keeps pushing me away, the harder I pull the harder she pushes. I don't even know if she feels me like I can feel her.

"Yeah, probably," I reply with a laugh. Veil, she could definitely take me out. Maybe I should let her train with Nero, but I am too selfish and I need all the time I can get with her. Plus, I want to make sure that I am the only one touching her body.

Halric's been around my whole life. He's been a guard for ten years now, following in his father's footsteps, just like a lot of fae families do. His father before him was the training guard.

"See ya, kid." He waves as he heads out.

I trail after him, slipping into my car. On the way home, I take the long route through her neighborhood. Just for a glimpse. It's ridiculous, but I can't help myself.

No time to relax. I've got a meeting with my dad and the council. I leave my bag in the car and head straight to the library. El's curled up on the large sofa with a book in her lap. I decide to leave her be and head up to get ready for the meeting. Eventually I will need to talk to her about all the things I have been learning, she's always clear headed and able to help me.

As I start up the staircase, shouting echoes down from my father's personal office.

"You can't do this, Lucan! I love you! I was only trying to help with your kids!" Calindra screeches.

"I'm sorry, Cal," my father replies, his voice quieter. "It's not going to work anymore. It's time I focus on my children. I don't need your help."

"They needed a mother, so I filled that role!" I scoff quietly. She did nothing of the sort, just spent my father's money on parties, lunches and luxuries.

"He needs to marry Cassia. It's what's best for him and the crown. If he hasn't found his fated, he never will."

"You're overstepping again, Calindra," he says sharply. "I'm their father. We will see how the Veilfall Festival goes. Now it's time for you to leave. We'll discuss this later, I have a meeting." I check my watch. Five minutes late. I step forward and knock.

The door swings open, and Calindra storms out. When she sees me, she scowls, then leans in and hisses, "You will marry Cassia, whatever it takes." My dad sighs, having heard her perfectly despite her trying to be quiet. I don't think she's ever been quiet in her life.

I ignore her and enter the office. She has no power, not magical, not political. But it's time I started watching her. And Cassia.

"Hey, you're late," my dad says. He looks tired, worn down.

"Sorry. Stayed after school for some extra training."

"Good. I want you ready for the Order. Did you train with your Vera?" My Vera. He's not wrong. Even if she keeps fighting it.

"Yeah. Got her to agree to train more with me after school. I'll make sure I'm back before the council meetings."

"Good. You seem... lighter. Happier." He's not wrong there either. I now realize, I was living an empty existence. Just doing what was expected of me at home and at school. Not anymore.

Later, after the council finishes, another round of vague concerns about the Veilfall, my father and I return to the library. Torvyn's gaze follows us on the way out guarded, maybe even resentful. Probably realizing his daughter won't be getting close to the crown. *He* won't be getting any close to the crown.

El's in the same spot on the sofa, and Thalina is tidying up nearby.

"Thalina," my father greets her warmly.

"Oh, you boys are done. Dinner will be ready soon."

"Would it be alright if we ate in here tonight?" he asks, not because it's her call but because we all know she's the heart of this house. The one who held us together after Mom died. Well, maybe it is her call, if she would say no I don't think any of us would argue.

"Of course. I'll bring your food. What shall I tell Ms. Calindra?"

"Just tell her I want time with my kids tonight."

Thalina beams. She's never liked Calindra. The satisfaction on her face is clear and unsurprising to El and I. But Dad looks almost, surprised.

When the door closes behind her, he turns to us. "Does no one like her?"

El and I exchange a glance. The answer is clear without words.

"Dad," El says gently, "we just wanted you to be happy. But when you weren't around and even lately in front of you she wasn't kind." That's the nice version. Truth is, she was awful. He doesn't respond. Just looks at me.

I shrug. "We dealt with it."

I wander over to the shelves housing old records and scrolls from other kingdoms. All day I've been thinking about what Thorian said how he looked at Vera when they were talking about Elarindor. She is able to heal quickly, too quickly for even a fae, is this a gift? Like mine? I think that is a gift that originated from that region. There are several gifts that we both have, that cannot be a coincidence. I don't know what they were talking about but she looked worried when I walked in.

If she's connected to that ancient line, it could explain everything. Her powers. Why she is so guarded. The way she carries herself.

I already know she can read intentions. Truthsense too. Then with my help she was able to create sparks, I bet she could do more with the sparkstone on her own too. Which makes me wonder where she was raised, most fae parents teach their kids these things as they grow, of course most fae don't get full access to their gifts until their 18th Veilfall, but she seems to be able to use her gifts just fine.

I find the scrolls I'm looking for and pull them down.

"What are you looking for?" Dad asks, settling beside me.

"We started talking about Elarindor in one of my classes. Wanted to see what we had on why it fell."

"Ah. I wish we had more. My father was still king then. He and Eryndor were friends. He wrote that there was unrest in Elarindor, a group trying to take the crown. No real details. Just... tension. And then Eryndor sent his daughters into hiding before he was killed. There was never any real details, we never knew who was watching. It all happened too fast."

"Did your father try to help?"

"He sent a team to investigate. They found the castle burned down. No blood. No bodies. No one claiming the throne. Just silence. The town was quiet."

"Do you know where Eryndor sent his daughters?"

"He sent them here. Said they'd be safe."

"Do you know who they are?"

"Yes. But this doesn't leave this room." He gives El and I a hard look. We both nod. We've been raised to keep the Kingdom's and the Grove's secrets. "One of the daughters is the recruiting guard. Rina. The other was Viv, she is fated to my best friend, Lucien. After their daughter was born they had to go into hiding, we never got those answers either." I barely stop myself from reacting. I school my features. Smooth my aura. El catches it, but stays silent. She's the daughter of my father's best friend. The infamous Lucien who was Head Guard and no one can beat his records. It all makes sense why she is so powerful and graceful in her movements.

There's a knock, and Dad rises to let Thalina in with dinner. I tuck the scrolls away to revisit later.

So, Vera could be the heir to Elarindor. That explains a lot, her strength, her wariness, her power. I think back to the conversation with Thorian. I made it seem like it meant nothing at all that her family disappeared that they all died, fuck. It's no wonder she was upset after that, I could see the distrust in her eyes before she locked it away. Now I just need to find a way to get her to trust me. Let me in, without revealing I know everything because I can already tell that won't go over well. She is very guarded, could there be someone still after their family? I don't want to ask my father yet because I don't know who to trust, either. I need to figure out more about Vera before I approach her again, I want answers before I question her.

We eat Thalina's stew in silence, each of us lost in our own thoughts. Finally, I set my spoon down. "Dad, what's your plan with Calindra?" I try to sound casual, but I'm hoping, really hoping, he's finally done with her.

He exhales slowly and pushes his bowl away. "I'm divorcing her. Our lawyer thinks it can be finalized by the Veilfall." Next weekend?

Relief washes over me, but it's tangled with something else. Worry. Unease. "There's something about her I don't trust. I think she's planning something."

His eyes narrow. "Like what?"

"Something to do with the crown. I don't know, I just know Cassia's getting more desperate at school. And today, at the council meeting, Torvyn was watching us. Watching you. Then Calindra said the same thing Cassia did this morning: that I *will* marry her. 'Whatever it takes.' It was almost word for word."

Dad leans back, frowning. "I think I'm losing my edge."

"You've been distracted," I say gently. "Especially the last few months."

He nods slowly. "Yeah, something's been off. A few weeks ago, I got sick. Not seriously, just low energy. Cold. Weak. Calindra started taking care of me."

El sits up straighter, her expression sharpening. "Off how, exactly?" I keep my focus on him, reading his aura.

He hesitates. "It felt like my strength just dipped. Not enough to stop me, but enough to notice. I figured it was age, stress. But it was sudden."

"What was she giving you?" El asks.

"Just a tea to help with energy, she would make it every morning. I haven't had it in a few days, not since I forced her to move into the other wing of the Grove."

"Did it go away?" I ask.

"Not completely. Some days are better than others, but I've never fully bounced back." What would have caused his initial drop in energy? After dinner we help Thalina clean up. I go for a run. I need to get this excess energy and frustration out, but mostly I want to see her.

When I get to their cottage, they are looking over old scrolls. I feel for our thread and gently pull on it. Reveling in the warmth that spreads through me. I can feel her frustration and her worry. I guess I am not the only one.

She looks up and out the window towards me. It's fully dark there is no way she could see me but she must sense me. She puts her papers down and excuses herself. I watch her slowly make her way to the back door and I walk around to meet her.

"What are you doing here?" She whispers.

"I just wanted to see you."

"I felt you the other night too, how is that possible?"

"I don't know, but I need to see you." I do know, but I also know she is not ready for the truth yet. Any time I say anything remotely intimate she goes running.

"Why? Are you having a bad night?"

"I just found out my dad has been having some health issues." I don't want to bring up Calindra yet and her scheming with Cassia's parents.

"Oh no, will he be okay? Is it what your mom had?" Like my mom had? I never told her how my mom died, but she was sick at the end. My mind is reeling and she is patting my chest, I feel the warmth spread between us grounding me back in this moment.

I take a step closer, I want to reach for her but I wait.

"Yes, he will be okay. I just needed to see you. I don't know if I can make it the whole weekend without seeing you." I take a chance by pulling her into my arms much like she was earlier. Where she is meant to be.

After a few heartbeats she relaxes and rests her head against my chest. Every time we touch the bond between us strengthens. I don't know if this is normal for all fae, we still need to complete the fated ceremony. It's getting easier to see through her veiled aura. I can feel her presence and I hope eventually I can feel her emotions, fully. Right now I only get glimpses when she is feeling something strongly enough. It must be rare among fated fae, but her and I already seem to have a strong connection.

"A deal is a deal." She whispers when she lifts her head up. The moonlight is shining through the trees just enough for me to see the teasing smile on her face. I desperately want to kiss her, but I don't think she is ready for that, either. Even when I had her underneath me in the Echoforge earlier. My body reacted instantly to the feel of her body against mine. That was it for me. My dick was already semi hard watching her, when I realized she wasn't paying attention to the training, just checking me out. She keeps denying us, keeps pushing me away but I am not going anywhere.

"What can I do to convince you?" I keep her close to me, wrapping my arms around her, resting on the small of her back.

"Nothing. I'm sorry, I need to focus on my own things. I think it's time you move onto someone else, there will never be anything between us. I'm not interested." I don't point out that her body is relaxed against mine as she rests her head against my shoulder. Our thread buzzing with the energy of them coming trying to come together.

"It's just you. I'm not with anyone else, there will only ever be you. I can't move on." My voice cracks, the truth raw and pleading between us.

She gives me a small, sad smile and starts backing away.

"Thanks for the training, Cae. I don't think I'll need any more help. From now on, we're just classmates. Nothing more. Please respect that."

"I can't stay away from you," I breathe. "Let me show you why."

Before she can turn, I catch her hand and pull her against my chest. The air between us snaps, electric. Her breath catches and then my mouth finds hers. For a heartbeat, everything goes still and silent. And then she ignites.

It's like touching a live current, heat flaring beneath her skin, rushing through me until my veins hum with it. Her fingers clutch at my shirt, her lips part in surprise, and the world blurs around us. She tastes like something bright and wild, the faint sweetness of the forest air clinging to her.

She melts into me, her body aligning with mine until there's nothing but heat and breath and the ragged sound of wanting. My hand slides up the curve of her spine, memorizing the tremor that runs through her when I touch her.

Her gasp turns into a quiet, helpless sound that unravels what little control I have left. I press her closer, feeling her heartbeat thrum against mine, a rhythm that feels like it's been waiting for this moment all along. I slide my finger back down the curve of her spine, loving the shiver, I can feel her nipples harden through her shirt where it's pressed firmly against my chest.

My hands reach her ass I grip them both firmly before I haul her up and her legs go around my waist. Her hands grip the tops of my shoulders. I tremble as her hands go down and squeeze my biceps before sliding back up and gripping my hair. Holding my head to hers. I groan out when my cock finds her warm core. Wishing there were no clothes between us. I take the kiss deeper again and our tongues dance together as I keep pressing my cock to her hot pussy. I could come from this alone, she grips my shoulders roughly digging her nails into me.

When I finally tear my mouth from hers, her lips are flushed, her eyes dazed—like she's seeing the world for the first time. I give her one more gentle kiss to her lips before I lower her gently to her feet.

"Umm." It's all she manages, her breath catching in the dark between us.

"You came alive for me," I whisper, still tasting her on my lips. "Just give me a chance."

"Cae…" Her voice wavers, torn. "I can't. It's not a good time."

"Things will always get in the way if you let them." My thumb brushes her cheek, tracing the heat still blooming there. "I'll let you think about it. I'll find you again soon."

Before she can argue, I steal one last quick kiss, but enough to feel that spark again, that pulse of something wild and real flickering between us. Then I force myself to turn away, slipping into the shadows before she can stop me or give me anymore protests.

The night air feels cooler against my skin, but there's a buzz under it, an echo of her, humming through my veins. Every step through the trees feels unsteady, like I'm walking through the aftermath of a storm I didn't see coming. A smile splitting my face, I finally get to feel her and kiss her like I want.

Then her words return, soft and sharp as a blade: *Your dad… he's sick, like your mom was.* The world stills. That buzzing turns to ice. I really need to talk with El.

Chapter 26: I Lost All Sense of Reason

Vera

Walking into the Sylvaeris library feels like stepping into a dream stitched together from quiet magic and old stories. The air is thick with the scent of parchment, lavender polish, and the warm dust of centuries-old pages. High vaulted ceilings stretch above me like the inside of a cathedral, all steep beams and carved arches that seem far too dramatic for a school library, until I see the shimmering gold sign above the arched doorway: *The Enchanted Library.*

Is it truly enchanted, or just charmingly named? With this place, I honestly can't tell.

Inside, the space hums with a quiet kind of life. Lanterns float gently above each aisle, casting a soft glow over the towering shelves. The spines of the books gleam with handwritten titles, some in languages I can't yet read. Vines, real or enchanted, who knows, crawl up the far corners, their leaves glossy and deep green. There's a velvet hush to the air, like the library is listening.

At the front counter stands a girl who looks about my age. She glances up from a large open ledger and beams at me. She's a little shorter than I am, with long honey-blonde hair braided over one shoulder and big hazel eyes full of sunlight. Tiny piercings glint along the edges of her pointed ears, a golden stud set right at the tip and delicate tulip charms hanging from a fine chain below. I can't help admiring the stud at the top; it catches the light just right.

She's wearing a sunny yellow sundress dotted with white tulips, and her heels match, bright and cheerful. It's such a contrast to the solemn space, like a streak of sunshine in a forest.

"Welcome to the Enchanted Library!" she says in a lilting, musical voice. "I'm Elyria. Is there anything I can help you find?"

I can't help smiling back. "Thanks! I love your dress."

Her face lights up even more. "Thank you! I love it too. I found it at *Lily & Laurel*, it was on sale, but I still kind of splurged." She does a playful little twirl, making the skirt flare out like a buttercup in bloom. I decide right then and there that I love her. Anyone who works in a library and loves a tulip-print sundress is destined to be my best friend.

"It was definitely worth it. You look amazing. Actually, I could use your help I'm working on a school project."

"Ooh, fun! What are you researching?"

"Some history about Sylvaeris… and maybe the land of Elarindor?" I try to sound casual, like I haven't already run several scenarios in my head.

"Got it. Come with me!"

She lifts a panel off the counter and steps out, heels clicking cheerfully against the wooden floor. I walk beside her, momentarily distracted by how perfectly her shoes match her dress. It's the kind of coordination that says she put thought into today. I wish I had the energy to dress up like that every day.

"It's not a huge place," she says over her shoulder. "But we've packed in a lot. This way." We round a curved corner, and she gestures toward a cozy alcove with soft reading benches and skylight windows.

There's something gentle and timeless about the space.

"How long have you worked here?" I ask.

"Just the last six months," she says with a hint of pride. "I started right after I graduated. I've always loved books and honestly, this place feels like it chose me." I believe her. She stops in front of a tall shelf labeled *Historical Records* in scrolling silver script.

"This is the Sylvaeris history section. Older records are further back, and the more recent stuff is up front." She points toward a shorter shelf beneath a window, sunlight streaming through like a spotlight. "And over there we've got regional histories; Duskmere, Varethos, and Elarindor."

I nod, trying to soak it all in. "Thanks! Um, how many books can I check out at once?"

She's halfway turned around but pauses with another brilliant smile. "Five at a time. Two-week period."

"Perfect." There's a pause between us. She tilts her head, studying me for a beat.

"You're not from here, are you?"

I smile, but it's guarded. "Just getting my bearings."

Her grin softens into something kinder. "Well, I hope you find what you're looking for whether it's in a book or not."

I begin with the historical section on Sylvaeris, trailing my fingers over the spines of ancient books that smell of cedarwood, pressed flowers, and time. The shelves creak faintly under the weight of their knowledge, and faint motes of dust spiral in the sunlight pouring through the window above.

I'm looking for older documents, anything that traces the royal bloodlines, alliances, and relationships with the other provinces. Anything beyond 30 years ago. Eventually, I'll move toward the more recent volumes. I need to know what was recorded about the disappearance of Elarindor.

I collect a few titles that seem promising and cradle them against my chest. Then I sink down to the floor in front of the smaller shelf labeled *Regional Histories*. The rug beneath me is thick, moss-green, and worn in the corners from decades of quiet study. I start with the section on Varethos.

Maybe—just maybe—I'll find something about the woman who told my father the prophecy. But the deeper I go, the more I realize how difficult that may be. According to Rina, the seer told him here, in Sylvaeris. But does that mean seers from Varethos travel often? Or was it someone of importance? A leader? A High Seer? Is that what they're called? I think back to all the fantasy books I used to read. It could be that maybe it was something important so they came just for that.

I flip through the books slowly, careful with the delicate pages. There aren't many. Just a few thin volumes with fading covers and cracked spines. Same with Duskmere. Not much to go on. Still, I decide to focus on the last thirty years of history from both provinces. I'm not sure why I include Duskmere, I just don't want those books to feel left out.

Scooting closer to the far end of the shelf, I brush off a thicker layer of dust clinging to the books on Elarindor. My breath catches. There's more dust here than anywhere else, like these poor books haven't been touched in years. Maybe decades. My fingers tremble slightly as I pull one out.

The cover is deep green, its edges gilded in gold leaf worn smooth with time. Embossed in the center is a symbol I don't recognize. A crescent moon cradling a sun, ivy leaves curling around them in a delicate wreath. The design glimmers faintly when I tilt the book. When I open it, the first page is a photograph.

A family. Two small girls holding hands, one with purple eyes like dew-laced lilacs, and the other with eyes that look exactly like mine. A man stands stoic behind them a hand on each of their shoulders.

My breath catches. My mom. And Rina. And, I blink. My grandfather. It's the first time I've ever seen a picture of one of my grandparents. The thought hits me like a wave. My throat tightens. What about my dad's parents, are they still alive, hidden away somewhere?

I brush my fingertips gently over the glossy photograph, and then flip it over. On the back is a caption, written in fine script:

The history of Elarindor is one cloaked in beauty, sorrow, and silence. Hidden in the Nareth Peaks, the Elarindorians thrived for millennia with a natural affinity for the land and its lifeblood. But in the years before the Shattering, tragedy struck. The Qaresar, once vibrant and wise, began to wither after his mate died in childbirth. He spoke of shadows that clouded his mind, a sickness of the heart that no healer could mend. When the Palace mysteriously burned to the ground, the King and his daughters vanished, never seen again. What remained was ash, rumor, and a land lost to time.

Tears sting the corners of my eyes, but I don't let them fall. Instead, I press the book gently into my lap and run my hand along the shelf for another.

That's when I feel it, something odd. A smooth carving on the inner rim of the shelf. I lean closer. There's a small wooden protrusion tucked just under the edge, camouflaged perfectly with the rest of the wood. Curious, I trace it with my fingertip, then push. With a soft *click*, a hidden compartment pops open, the sound barely audible. Inside is a single, folded piece of paper, that flutters down into my hand.

I reach for the slip of paper and quietly shut the hidden compartment. The wooden latch clicks back into place with a soft *snick*. I should've checked for cameras when I walked over here, but it's too late now. Sliding the folded paper into my pocket, I make a mental note to look at it later, when I'm alone.

Just as I turn back to the books, sifting through titles and stacking the ones I want to check out, a hand suddenly glides over my shoulder.

"Ahh!" I yelp, heart jumping into my throat as I scramble to my feet, nearly knocking over a stack of books.

"Whoa, sorry, Lilac," comes a warm voice behind me, and I immediately know who it is. "I didn't mean to scare you. Are you okay?"

Caelum stands just a breath away, eyes wide with concern but then they drift lower. First to the books scattered at my feet, then slowly up my legs, taking their time. I realize my shirt has shifted askew, the neckline tugged lower than it should be, revealing just the hint of cleavage. His gaze catches there for a heartbeat too long before finally meeting my eyes, and there's no mistaking the glint of amusement or interest lurking behind the concern. I quickly tug the fabric back into place, my cheeks heating. I can still feel that kiss from last night, I swear my lips still tingle and I want to touch my fingers to them to see. It took me forever to fall asleep last night, my entire body was on fire the whole night.

Mortification floods my cheeks. My whole body seems to flush under his stare, warmth rising from my neck to the tips of my ears. From his gaze on me now and remembering how I reacted when he kissed me. I lost all sense of reason the second he kissed me—every ounce of restraint just gone.

"I'm fine. I just wasn't expecting anyone," I mumble, kneeling quickly to gather the books, pretending I didn't see his not-so-subtle glance.

I pick up the ones I want and slide the others back onto the shelf, willing my heartbeat to return to normal. When I straighten, he's still watching me. With that infuriating smirk that makes my knees a little wobbly and my brain uncooperative.

"What books are you getting?" he asks, casually taking the stack from my arms. He doesn't even glance at the covers. Just holds the large hardcover books like they weigh nothing.

"I want to learn more about the different provinces of Sylvaeris," I say simply, trying to sound distant. Detached. Like I haven't been picturing him in one of my favorite fantasy book scenes lately.

He grins. "Anything you want to know, I could help you. I know a lot about the history."

"That's okay," I reply quickly. "I'm not looking for anything in particular. Just curious."

"So reading history books is something you do for fun?" he asks, raising a brow.

I nod. "Sometimes. Sometimes I like to read other books too."

He tilts his head. "What other kinds?"

"Romance," I say before I can stop myself, then immediately regret it.

He takes a subtle step closer, lowering his voice to a near-whisper. "What kind of romance, *Lilac*?" His voice brushes against my skin like silk. My pulse trips over itself.

"Supernatural," I say, my voice barely above a whisper. "Fantasy. Mostly young adult." The embarrassment is instant. My cheeks blaze. Why am I telling *him* this? I haven't even had time to read lately, but now all I can imagine is him in any steamy scene I've ever read. I wish not for the first time that I had some of my old books.

His hand, warm and deliberate rises, and the backs of his knuckles gently graze my cheek.

"Yeah?" he murmurs. "How come your pretty cheeks are blushing then? What happens in those books?" Gods, I hate how I lean into his touch. How my body betrays me when I've told myself to keep my distance.

I step back, creating a breath of space. "None of your business," I snap softly, wrapping my arms around myself. "Now I need to get going. I told my aunt I'd run a few errands and then head back home." His expression falls for a moment, and then he tries again.

"Can I take you to lunch?"

I blink. "Why are you even here? You were supposed to wait until Monday at school to see me."

"I was just walking by the window and saw you," he says, almost sheepishly. "I don't want to stay away. Come have lunch with me. Just lunch."

I sigh, turning to walk toward the front desk. "I don't know. I need to stop by a couple other stores too." Like finding out how much that dress costs. He follows quietly behind me, not pushing, just present. And I hate how much I like it. As we approach the desk, Elyria is sitting behind the counter, scrolling on her phone. She looks up with a sunny smile as we arrive.

"Oh! You found what you were looking for. Do you have a library card?" she asks, standing up and brushing her sundress flat.

"No, can I sign up for one?" I ask, already dreading the answer.

"Sure, I just need to see your ID." Shit. I freeze. My mind goes blank. I never had an official ID in the human realm, and I definitely don't have one here. My parents didn't want me to drive and now I know why they were so adamant. Before I can say anything, Caelum steps up from behind me and places a hand on the small of my back for a just a moment and it's gone too soon. Smooth. Effortless. He pulls out his wallet and slides a sleek card across the counter. *The Enchanted Library*, etched in swirling gold script.

"Just put it on mine," he says, placing on top of my books on the desk.

"You don't have to do that," I whisper, caught between gratitude and guilt.

He glances down at me, all warmth and quiet assurance. "I trust you." And the worst part? I think I'm starting to trust him too.

"Oh, Cae! I didn't realize you were here," Elyria exclaims brightly, her eyes lighting up the moment she spots him.

"Yeah. I'm here with Vera." His reply is clipped, his posture stiffening as he steps closer to me. One of his hands comes to rest on my waist, as if worried I might bolt. Again with the grabbing me, why does he do this when another girl is around? He's using me as a shield I realize. Trying to keep other girls away, but that doesn't make sense either. I know he can get any girl so why is he clinging to me. I assume he can handle himself just fine with girls.

Her eyes scan down to where his hand has landed.

"I missed you," she continues, twirling a strand of her honey-blonde hair around one finger. "I tried texting you. I was hoping we could spend more time together." *More time.* Right. So this is one of his many girlfriends Cassia was warning me about.

"I'm not interested," Caelum says bluntly. His voice is cool and dismissive, and I catch the flicker of disappointment in Elyria's eyes. A pang of guilt flutters in my chest, but I quickly squash it down. So, no, Elyria won't be someone I'll be friends with. Not now. Maybe not ever.

But it doesn't matter. It shouldn't matter. I won't be another one of his many. I won't let myself fall into that trap. She's so beautiful and well put together, I can't compete with someone like that. I take a step away from him, putting space between us. "You know what? I actually need to go. Sorry, I don't need the books." I turn on my heel and leave them on the counter before either of them has a chance to say anything else.

"Veils," I hear Caelum curse behind me.

Chapter 27: Guess That's Karma

Vera

I'd planned to check out a few shops, but the rush of emotions crashing through me is too much. I head straight for the herb shop—*The Verdant Nook*—to get the supplies Rina wanted. Maybe afterward I'll look for a bookstore. I don't want to spend a lot of money on books, but if I have to, I will. Especially if it means avoiding Caelum and my own spiraling thoughts.

I practically run toward the shops tucked around the corner, like I can outrun the twisting in my chest. I try to remind myself that Caelum isn't mine. But even as the words echo in my mind, my heart stutters. I can't even convince myself. Not really. A hand snakes around my waist and pulls me to a stop.

"Ahhh!" I yelp, stumbling into a firm chest as I'm spun around. The books in Caelum's arm tumble to the ground and land squarely on his foot.

"Veils!" He hops on one foot for a moment. "Brightstep, you're too fast." His voice is half-laugh, half-breathless. His arms circle me and hold me close, grounding me. I squirm, trying to back away. As stupid as it is, I was hoping I could escape these feelings. But I can't do that, not if I'm in his arms.

"Stop doing that!" I shout.

"Stop running from me." He says softly.

"Let me go," I whisper, voice cracking. "I told you to stay away. Whatever you're doing, it's not going to work. You clearly have plenty of others who would be more willing." It hurts to say. But I need to say it. I need to protect myself.

"I don't know what's going on with you, but I'm not going anywhere," he says, his eyes intense on mine. "There were other girls before I met you, yeah. But they mean nothing to me. It was just something to do, something that felt expected." His voice softens. "But you? You mean *everything* to me. You're not like them. This..." He gestures between us. "This is forever. I'm not asking for anything from you. Just your time. Stop running. Let me help with whatever it is you're hiding from. You can trust me." Forever?!

"I'm not hiding," I lie, weakly.

He arches a brow. "Like you, I have truthsense. I know when you're lying. Or giving me half-truths." Damn. I should've known.

He bends down to gather the fallen books, then slings his arm back around my waist, guiding me forward again. "Now let me help you with your shopping. I'll take you to lunch and drive you home."

I don't say anything. I just let him lead me. I hate how obvious it is that I'm hiding things. Nero knows something too. I just don't know what or how much. Or who I can trust. I'm stuck in this strange, dazzling world, trying to find my footing.

Even if Caelum wants more than friendship, even if I could trust him, I might not have long. Someone is still out there. Watching. Hunting. I can't let anyone get too close, not until I understand what's happening with the kingdom, the other two girls, and with me.

"This is happening," he says suddenly.

I glance up at him. *Can he read minds too?* Or can he feel my emotions like I can feel his. I stay silent and push open the door to *The Verdant*

Nook. The familiar bell chimes above us, and the warm, herbal scent envelops me like a hug. Earthy, sweet, and a little wild. The air hums faintly with enchantments; leaves in jars rustle as if whispering secrets.

I pull out the list Rina gave me and start walking the aisles. Caelum follows, wordlessly, carrying the basket with one hand, the other tucked into his pocket like he owns the place. Not a care in the world.

"Okay," I murmur, squinting at the first item. "Moonleaf powder. That's… a leaf, right?"

Caelum leans closer to read over my shoulder. "Technically, yes. But if you grab the wrong kind, it can make your tea explode."

I shoot him a glare. "Explode?"

He grins. "Only a little."

I shove his arm lightly, trying not to smile. "You're terrible at helping."

He laughs under his breath and plucks a small jar from the shelf. The label glows faintly when he turns it. "Moonleaf. Non-explosive variety."

"Noted." I cross it off my list with exaggerated focus, pretending not to notice the way his shoulder brushes mine when he sets the jar in the basket.

Next up: *Silver root.* I stare at the shelves, completely lost. "How do you even tell root from twig in here?"

"Experience," he says, voice low and teasing. "And better eyesight than yours, apparently." I look up into his eyes and they are shining in mischief.

"Oh, you're so helpful."

He smirks, picking out a bundle of shimmering roots and holding them up. "See? Easy. You just have to—" A puff of silvery dust bursts out, coating his fingers.

I can't help it, I laugh. "Guess that's karma for making fun of my eyesight."

He shakes the glittering powder off, eyes dancing. "You planning to survive this errand, Brightstep, or are you hoping to get me hexed first?"

"Depends how long the list is."

We move through the aisles like that, herb by herb, teasing and brushing shoulders, the world shrinking to the quiet, green-scented hum between us. I commit this moment to memory, even I don't ever be with him I will remember this afternoon with him.

The shopkeeper, a plump woman with a wide smile and silver-streaked hair pinned back in a neat bun, looks up as we approach the counter.

"Hello there—oh!" Her eyes widen. "Mr. Thornevale! I'm excited to see you in my shop." She gives a slight bow, flustered. Why is she acting like she's in the presence of royalty?

"Nice to see you," Caelum replies with a polite nod. "I'm just helping out today. I hope things are well." She beams and quickly starts ringing up the items, hands working faster now. She reads out the total, and before I can reach for the money stuffed into my pocket that Rina gave me, Caelum pulls out his card.

"No, I got it," I say, placing my hand over his. The moment our skin touches, a zip of energy pulses through my hand and up my arm. I snatch it back.

Smiling down at me, he presses the card into the woman's hand. "I've got it. Don't worry."

"It's not even for me," I argue. "It's for my aunt. She gave me money for it—"

The shopkeeper, *I think her name was Maeve?* Is looking between us, uncertain.

"I told you, it's not a problem. Maeve, you can run the card." She hesitates for half a second, then swipes it and hands him the receipt.

"Thank you, Mr. Thornevale," she says warmly. "I hope you two come back soon!" I force a polite smile, grab the bag, and stomp out the door. I hear his low chuckle behind me as he follows me out.

"Don't be mad. I want to take care of you, it's my job." I stop in my tracks, heat flaring in my chest. I spin around so fast my hair whips over my shoulder. I jab my pointer finger into his chest, ignoring the hard muscle. My voice sharp with emotion. Trying to regain some semblance of control I lost last night when he kissed me.

"It's not your job, because we're not anything. Stop trying to force yourself into my life. *We*—" I mimic the gesture he used earlier, slicing my hand between us. I try to sound strong like I am in control, but my voice wavers. "—are not happening." His eyes darken, his jaw tightening, and then before I can blink, he's grabbing me.

I'm yanked against him, our bodies flush from shoulder to thigh. My breath catches as his hand slides into my hair and his other arm wraps tight around my waist, pulling me in even closer. His lips crash onto mine, firm and demanding. I don't have time to react before his tongue brushes my lips, seeking entrance. Against every shred of logic screaming at me, I part them for him.

I should back away. I need to. I need to protect him and myself. This will only end in heartbreak, for both of us. But I don't. Because something about being in his arms feels *right*. Like I've stepped into a place I was meant to be all along. There's a spark, no, an entire storm raging between us. This thing, this pull, it's not just attraction. It's *electric*. Then I feel it, something hard presses against my stomach, and a slow heat unfurls inside me, curling low and deep. My body hums with awareness, the kiss deepening as his fingers tangle tighter in my hair.

I slowly move my hands down and grip his shoulders. Holding onto him like he's the only thing keeping me tethered to this world. My eyes snap open in shock, but he's still kissing me like he never wants to stop. Like I'm his oxygen. I drag my hands from his shoulders and down the planes of his chest. His muscles are hard and warm beneath my palms, and I hate how much I love the way they feel. But I have to. I press my hands firmly against his chest and shove him back. Not hard, but enough.

I stumble a step away, breath ragged. My heart is thundering like I've just sprinted miles. His chest rises and falls rapidly, eyes heavy-lidded and lips still parted from the kiss. At least I'm not the only one wrecked by this.

"Do you feel that?" He growls. "I am not going anywhere. I will keep kissing you every time you try to tell me that."

I feel the tears prick at my eyes but I hold them back. I look up at him and nod. Then I shake my head.

"We are happening," he says with finality. "It doesn't matter what you do or say, I'm not going anywhere." Then, without waiting for a response, he stoops to grab the supplies we'd both dropped in the chaos. His arm slips around my waist like it belongs there, guiding me forward again.

I don't resist. I can't. I'm still in a daze, barely processing. My brain has shut down and left my body to float in the aftermath of that kiss. I glance down, trying to hide my face. I catch sight of the way his muscles shift beneath his shirt as he carries the books. Thick forearms, roped with veins and tension, flexing with every step. Damn him. Like the kiss last night, I will remember those kisses too. For a first kiss they were amazing, I never knew what I was missing.

He opens the door to the same diner I went to with Rina. The second it swings open, the room goes silent. All heads turn. Eyes land on *us*. I freeze, my already flushed cheeks going up in flames. I instinctively take a step back, my body screaming for an exit. But Caelum tightens his grip on my hip, anchoring me in place.

"You're staying with me. Come on," he murmurs, voice low and commanding as he guides us farther into the room.

Then someone calls out. "Cae!" We both turn.

A large group of familiar students is gathered at a table near the back, loud and vibrant. Laughter buzzes around them until it doesn't. A few of them wave him over. At the end of the table, I see Cassia, all perfect hair and perfect posture, sitting like she owns the place.

"It's about time you showed up. We were expecting you thirty minutes ago. Come sit down, we ordered a bunch of appetizers," Sylas calls, flashing an easy grin. I stare at the only empty seats, right next to *Cassia.* I don't know these people. Not really. Not enough to feel anything but exposed.

I thought this was just going to be *us.* I thought maybe he meant it when he said lunch. Like a date. Stupid me for thinking that.

"Yeah, sorry," Caelum replies smoothly. "I took a detour. But we're here now." *We're here now.* So I guess he never intended for it to be just us. I feel like an idiot. As he starts walking toward the group, his hand slips from my waist.

That's all I need.

I seize the moment and pivot, bolting for the door. I slip out and duck around the corner, chest pounding. I risk a glance back, just in time to see the diner door open again.

Caelum steps out, scanning the street, his expression frustrated, *panicked, devastated* even. I don't wait to see if he spots me. I run. I run like hell, I mean Veil, hoping he didn't see which way I went. Hoping he doesn't come after me. I know I can outrun him so I don't bother slowing down until I get home.

Chapter 28: Faded Memories and Warm Candlelight

Vera

I spent the rest of the weekend hiding in Rina's cottage, tucked away like a secret I didn't want the world to see. Trying to ignore the hurt. Pretending that moment in the shop didn't happen. Ignoring the way I can still feel the tingling on my lips from that kiss, it felt like something was connecting between us. The trees outside rustled with autumn wind, brushing against the windows like they, too, were trying to understand what was happening to me.

Luckily, I managed a decent excuse. Rina didn't press too hard. I told her I hadn't been able to get books from the school's library because I didn't have any identification. That led to a whole debate about whether I should try to get some or just leave it alone. Obviously, leaving it alone won.

I can't exactly walk into the administration office and say, "Hi, I might be one of the last living bloodline of a lost province, and I don't have a birth certificate. Can you help me?"

We decided to wait and try the bookstore in town next weekend during the Veilfall Festival. I agreed, not because I felt ready, but because it gave me something to plan for. Something that wasn't unraveling in my chest like a frayed thread.

I felt him. His presence outside was like static in the air, soft at first, then louder, sharper. Taut like a string pulled too tight. I didn't look out the window. I didn't move. Just kept my eyes glued to the page I wasn't reading and pretended the sudden heat in my chest didn't exist. Even though a large part of me really wanted to go out there and let him kiss me like he did the night before.

Eventually, I felt him leave. The air loosened.

Only when night had settled and Rina had gone to bed did I sneak outside to check. The stars blinked in quiet rhythm above, the too-close moon spilling silver light as I tiptoed barefoot across the cold wooden porch. Hoping he wasn't out here somewhere lurking. On the large stump by the edge of the clearing, just where the moonlight touched it, sat the things I had left with him. My books. The bag of herbs.

I clutched them against my chest and hurried back inside. I never sensed him, I try not to let that disappoint me.

I set the herbs on the kitchen counter, trying to think of a new excuse for them. Something believable. Something that didn't scream *a cute boy I'm trying not to like returned my enchanted plants like a romantic apology.* Then I carried the books to my room, heart pounding for reasons I couldn't untangle.

The one on top was the book about Elarindor. My fingers trembled as I opened it, as if something in me already knew. Between the pages, tucked carefully into a center fold, was a piece of parchment.

Not old or cracked like the others I'd seen. This was fresh. Recent. Written in handwriting I was starting to recognize.

My Dearest Vera,
I am so sorry. I would love to explain more in person.
Please give me a chance. I know you're angry.
I should have never assumed you would want to eat around others.

I was meeting them for lunch when I saw you.
But I would have rather been with you.
Please, give me a chance. I will see you Monday.
Yours,

Cae

He should've never assumed, the thought cutting cold through my mind.

I really don't want to be around anyone, especially not the golden circle of the Academy's elite. Especially not when one of them has made it her mission to torment me. And yet, here I am. The girl he keeps chasing. Then he brought me in there to parade in front of all of them like a prize he won.

I told myself I was strong enough to say no. I told myself I wouldn't let him get too close. But every time his hand brushes mine, every time his voice finds me in a crowd, I forget what I'm supposed to be afraid of.

It's like he speaks to some part of me that's always been waiting.

I sit cross-legged on my bed, books spread like a broken spell around me. Scrolls spill off the edge, pages fluttering from the breeze through the cracked window. But I can't focus. My eyes don't register the words anymore.

Finally, I reach for the folded note I hid in my pocket at the library. I don't know why I kept it a secret. Maybe I was afraid someone would take it. Maybe I just needed proof it existed.

The parchment crackles softly as I open it.

To the One Who Finds This—
If you are reading this, then you've seen the fractures.
In memory. In magic. In the land once called Elarindor.
They will not speak of what happened here.
Not in the libraries. Not in the halls of the Order.
They have buried it under a dozen rewritten truths and broken names.
But remember this: power sealed is not power gone.
Elarindor did not fall, it was silenced.
Look for the broken crown.
The one that does not lie in a vault, but beneath the roots of the oldest tree.
There, you will begin to understand what was taken.
And who waits beneath the veil.
She remembers.

—A Watcher of the Hollow Flame

My breath catches. My hands tremble. The words carve into me like they've been waiting to find me. My blood hums with something ancient, something I don't understand. Just like everything else.

The rest of the weekend passed in a fog of tea-stained mugs, cluttered counters, and whispered questions Rina couldn't answer either. No matter how much she wanted to.

Why didn't my parents tell me any of this? Why leave me powerless in a world where knowledge *is* power? Why make me fight in the dark when a single truth could've been a torch?

Rina tries to help. She apologized, again and again. For my parents. For the silence. For not being able to protect me from the weight of everything I didn't know. I told her it wasn't her fault and it wasn't. But that didn't stop the crack widening in my chest.

We searched for more about Elarindor, but came up empty. There were no clean answers. No mentions of bloodlines or gifts. Just gaps in the histories, erased names, shadows in the margins of maps.

I never showed her the note. She already has too much to worry about. And what if someone finds out I have it? What if *they* know I know?

"So I was thinking." Rina began. "The prophecy started on the last day of the Shattering. I think we need to focus on that. Why did it start and why did it end?"

"What's the Shattering?"

"It's a war that started a year before you were born. It started with the vampires attacking the borders of Duskmere. The shifters joined in and they mostly attacked the borders of Sylvaeris. There are so many unknowns about the whole thing though. If we could meet with the King and find out what he knows, that could help."

"Can we visit the other provinces like Duskmere and Elarindor?" I asked, my voice quiet in the candlelit living room.

Rina set down her cup. "Maybe, not a lot of fae travel to the other provinces, not unless it's for business. But also not yet. Not while you're still at the Academy. It's not safe and I would rather you focus on finishing that."

"What about Varethos?"

She hesitated. "We'll wait. Maybe after you pass the Order. We can go visit all three. We'll tell people it's a beach trip." Her smile didn't quite reach her eyes. A beach trip. Sure.

"How do we talk to the king?"

"I'll keep trying to get a message to him. The thing is, it's hard to get him alone. He only attends his council meetings, and if I request a formal meeting for the guards then his Head Guard will be in attendance."

Except instead of sun and sand, I've got ancient magic coiled beneath my skin, enemies I can't name, and a boy who sees too much of me. And somehow, even with all that, I still find myself wanting him.

Even when I know I shouldn't.

We laughed once this weekend, really laughed. I told Rina when I first got here, I thought she was just really into crystals and herbal tea. Not an actual, literal fae. She laughed until her eyes sparkled and her shoulders shook, collapsing back onto the couch like the weight of it all lifted for just a second. I think we both needed that moment.

"You thought I was one of those moon-goddess Instagram witches," she said between giggles. "Didn't you?"

"I *definitely* did," I grinned. "With the dried oranges hanging from the windows and the sage bundles in every room, I was sure you were going to tell me Mercury was in retrograde and that's why I had cramps."

She snorted. "First of all, Mercury *was* in retrograde that week. And second of all, I *did* try to tell you that, but you rolled your eyes and made popcorn instead."

We both broke into laughter again, the kind that left our sides sore and our cheeks aching. It reminded me of being young and safe before everything cracked.

"I can't believe you know about Instagram!"

"Of course, we may be in a different realm but we're still connected. Humans may be weak but they sure are smart about making tools for themselves." We laugh some more.

That night, she told me more about fae life. About the Wheel of the Year and the seasonal rituals. Turns out all my mom's strange habits, moon water on the windowsill, the lavender under my pillow, the way she'd whisper to the rosemary before harvesting it, weren't strange at all.

They were ancient. Sacred.

"We used to do seed blessings in the spring," Rina said, eyes distant like she could still smell the fresh soil. "Your mom would drag me out barefoot into the garden and we'd bury tiny charms with the roots. She swore the plants tasted sweeter that way."

"Wait, like actual metal charms?" I asked, propped on my elbow, intrigued.

"She had these little carved stones," Rina said. "One year I swallowed one by accident. She didn't even panic. Just made me fennel tea and said, *'Well, now the blessing's internal.'"*

I laughed so hard I nearly dropped the tea in my hand.

Later that night, we ended up curled up on the rug with a pile of old photographs and spell journals. She pointed out younger versions of herself and my mom, covered in mud, faces smudged with ash from candle rituals, their arms looped around each other like sisters.

"You were there?" I whispered, tracing the edge of a photo where they sat laughing on a hill under a full moon, jars glowing with firefly light.

"I was always there," she said. "I was there when you got your first fever and your mom made a tea blend that knocked it out in hours. I was there the first time she let you stir the protection brew on your own, even though you spilled half of it on the floor and we had to mop it up with salt. I was there when you cut your hair with kitchen scissors and we had to do a glamour to fix it before school pictures."

I blinked, emotions tangling in my throat. "Why don't I remember all that?"

"You were so young," she said gently. "And they had to make sure it stayed buried. I couldn't keep coming around for your protection. I had to be extra careful because I didn't know who was watching and we needed to keep you safe. Everything fae, everything magic. Your mom didn't want to risk it. But it was always around you. The magic was always in you." Was that why she felt familiar?

And somehow, that was the most comforting part. That even when I didn't know who I was, someone else did. Someone like Rina.

We fell asleep like that, half-laughing, half-crying, surrounded by faded memories and warm candlelight. It didn't make everything okay. But it helped.

It reminded me that I'm not alone in this. Not entirely.

And Veilfall? That's not just a festival. It's a rite of passage. The most powerful point in the year when the veil between worlds thins. A time to honor the dead, to connect with magic, to become something more.

It starts November 1st. My birthday. Because of course it does.

Chapter 29: Too Many Shadows. Too Many Thoughts

Vera

Just stay away from Caelum. Just stay away from everyone.

I repeat the words like a mantra as I walk up the winding path to Auravale Academy, boots crunching over fallen leaves. After a moment, Nero joins me but he stays silent. I need to find a way to avoid him, too. Maybe I will have to get to school early. The clouds hang low today, casting everything in a soft gray haze. Even the stained glass windows of the school seem darker than usual, the old stone building looming like it knows exactly how out of place I feel here.

If I can just keep my head down, stay under the radar, maybe I'll get through this day in one piece.

The wind picks up as I push through the tall wooden doors of the school, and the gloom inside swallows me whole. The stone halls feel colder, heavier. Too many shadows. Too many thoughts.

Ahead, I spot a cluster of students, Caelum at the center, of course. I duck my head and hope he doesn't notice me. The pressure builds in my chest like a cartoon bomb, one of those ridiculous ones that swells and swells before exploding. The image makes me snort softly, a sound far too close to hysteria for my liking.

I don't look at him. But I feel his gaze. When I reach my locker, I freeze. Cassia is there, arms crossed, lips pressed into a scowl that looks carved in stone. Of course. Because today just can't go smoothly.

"I thought I told you to stay away from him."

"Who?" I play dumb, knowing full well it'll get under her skin.

"Caelum. He is mine. We're meant to be, and on the night of the Veilfall, everyone will know it."

I keep my face carefully blank, but inside, I'm reeling. What does the festival have to do with them being together?

A voice cuts in before I can respond. "We are not meant to be. Stay away from Vera. I will not keep telling you."

My hand freezes inside my locker. Caelum. His voice is sharp, firm. Great, more drama I didn't ask to be part of. As if I don't have enough on my plate. If it wouldn't be too dramatic I would consider banging my head against the locker. Neither of them will leave me alone.

Cassia's reply is ice. "We will be together. Whatever it takes."

"Can you two just please keep your lovers quarrel to yourself and leave me out of it?" I slam my locker shut and walk away.

I don't need this soap opera. I've got my own storyline spinning out of control. In class, I wedge myself between two occupied seats, hoping it'll keep him away. It doesn't.

"Can you move a seat over, please?" Caelum's voice is polite, for once. I don't look at him. I focus on blocking his emotions, pretending I don't feel the way his gaze hits the side of my face.

"Hey, I'm sorry about that. Are you okay?" he whispers.

"I'm fine," I mutter, still not looking at him. "Now shh, class is starting." Mr. Valeis moves to the center of the room, and I glue my eyes to him, determined to ignore him completely.

"This week," Mr. Valeis announces, "we'll be discussing the fallen land of Elarindor."

I sit up straighter. Finally, something useful. I hope. I am looking for more outside perspective, Rina and I seem to be spinning in circles.

"The royal family of Elowen was the last to rule Elarindor," he begins. "The kingdom was hidden deep within ancient forests, its people known for their profound connection to nature and spirit. Fae raised there were said to be attuned not only to the elements, but to the very intentions of others." That part makes me pause. Intentions?

"What happened to the province?" a student asks.

Mr. Valeis nods as though he's been waiting for the question. "No one knows for certain. The Qaresar was killed roughly thirty years ago under mysterious circumstances. Some say he had two daughters, hidden away to protect them from the same fate. If it's true, no one's ever found them."

A buzz of interest ripples through the room.

"As for his death," he continues, "there are theories. Some believe Sylvaeris orchestrated the assassination to seize more land, but they never expanded beyond their borders, so that's unlikely. Others suggest a secret sect was working to infiltrate the royal lines, people who didn't just want power, but control over the bloodlines themselves." His eyes flick toward me. My breath catches. This is all similar things we had talked about on Friday, but someone after the bloodlines, that's new. I write it down.

I feel Caelum's attention shift too, following the teacher's glance. What was that supposed to mean? A secret sect? Royal bloodlines? What could that possibly have to do with me?

I shove the thought aside as Mr. Valeis claps his hands. "Alright, we've wandered from the lesson. We'll come back to the fall of Elarindor later this week. For now, let's focus on their origins."

He dives into tales of ancient gifts, how the Elowen line could coax plants to bloom with a whisper, how they were born with the rare ability to sense truth and deceit, reading people with unsettling clarity.

"They were said to be deeply bound to the land itself, their power drawn from the roots of Elarindor and the winds that crowned the Nareth Peaks. Some claimed that the first wings ever seen among the fae came from their bloodline, born of their connection to sky and earth alike. The last known to bear them", he says, "was the Qaresar."

I try to take notes, but my mind keeps circling back.

Two hidden daughters. A Qaresar. A secret sect. Wings. And the way they both looked at me, like I was somehow part of the story. Like they both somehow knew. Do other people know? Am I safe, here?

Next period, I make sure to arrive late enough to dodge Caelum again. He's already sitting with a space beside him, empty and expectant. I veer the other way, and Cassia swoops in to claim the spot, flashing him a sugary smile. I try not to feel jealous. After all, I am the one that chose to sit away from him. His frustration leaks through the emotional barrier I tried to build. I giggle before I can stop myself. He turns, glaring. I look away.

A moment Nero comes walking in and claims the seat beside me. Earning another annoyed look from Cae.

"What did you do to make him mad?" a soft voice beside me asks.

I glance over. A girl with oversized blue eyes behind black glasses smiles curiously.

"I think he wanted me to sit by him," I say, shrugging like it doesn't matter.

"I can't believe you don't want to. Every girl here wants his attention."

"That's exactly why I'm not interested." In front of us, Caelum's shoulders tense.

The girl snickers. "Glad I'm not the only one. He's worked his way through most of the girls here."

Now, it's my turn to tense. I had suspected he was a player. Was told he was. It's confirmed, yet again. Just another reason to steer clear, like I needed more reasons. It shouldn't hurt. But it does. Because for a moment, I thought I was different. A challenge, maybe. But not enough.

Turning back towards her. "What's your name?"

"Thalia"

"That's a pretty name. My name is Vera, this is my friend Nero." I nod my head towards him and he gives us both a short nod of his head. I see her glance at him, but he looks straight ahead. Maybe this girl could be a friend. I think I will be hard pressed to find a girl to be friends with that hasn't slept with Cae. Not that it matters, because I will never be with him.

Today we're working with the water element. Each of us is given a small cup, barely half full. I stare at mine, uncertain. Maybe I shouldn't even try. I remember how it went testing the sparkstone, I still don't think I did that myself.

Around the room, some students are already focused, hands hovering over their cups, brows furrowed in concentration. A few seem to have an affinity for water, it moves easily under their command, swirling or rising in delicate arcs.

And then there's Caelum. He's effortlessly shaping his water into a perfect sphere, letting it hover midair before allowing it to fall in a soft drizzle back into the cup. Show-off. Of course he'd make it look poetic. His water lifts up again and shapes into a heart before falling back into the cup. He glances my way and winks. Seriously?

Next to him, Cassia scowls. She doesn't appear to be having any luck with her water. Her eyes follow Caelum's, then flick to me. The edge in her expression makes it clear that she noticed the heart and the wink. Great.

Still, with everyone focused on their own attempts, I decide to try. I exhale slowly, running my fingers just above the rim of the cup. I don't force anything. I just breathe. Feel. Let my mind quiet. I picture the water not as a task, but as something alive. Fluid, ancient, aware. Just like Rina has been teaching me.

It jumps. Just a tiny splash, barely noticeable. But it moved. I don't try again after that, too afraid someone will notice, am I even supposed to be able to command all the elements? I don't dare look at Caelum for fear he noticed. I really can't let people know that I have multiple gifts. Right? I look over to Nero and see he is able to make a few drops move but that's as far as it goes. Maybe it would be okay, he seems to have multiple gifts.

Maybe another question to write down. Rina said my dad had multiple gifts, he wasn't royal but he was a Head Guard. Like Nero is trying to be.

I avoid Cae the next period too, tuning out the waves of irritation rolling off him. At lunch, I detour from the library to the computer lab. Maybe the school servers can help me dig up more about the Fae, something beyond human myths and legends.

"Is this seat taken?" I groan. Caelum again. He slides into the chair beside me, pulling out his phone and firing off a text before turning to me with a grin that's more challenge than charm. I click out of my search screen and focus on my untouched lunch. Why does he keep finding me?

"You did good today, Lilac. I'll give you that," he says, voice low. "I'll have to step up my game. Now, before El gets here, two things: One, I will always find you." Heat rushes to my cheeks. "Two, I may have been with other girls, but that's not what this is. You and I— we're different. They meant nothing. You mean everything. I will keep saying this until you believe me."

"Did you sleep with Cassia?"

"Yes. Once. It was never more than that. I don't want her. I never have." I was not expecting his complete honesty.

"How many have you been with? You know what? Don't answer that I don't care. Thanks for bringing my things, but I won't need anymore help. I don't need any further explanation, I want you to leave me alone."

"Am I interrupting?"

A girl stands in the doorway. She is my height, but dazzling. Jade-green eyes, long waves of honey-blonde hair. Another fangirl, no doubt. He says he doesn't want Cassia, but girls like this line up to take her place. I can't compete with that. I shouldn't even try. I won't try.

"No, you're not interrupting," I say, standing quickly. "In fact, he's all yours." I grab my tray and rush out before he can stop me, catching a frustrated "Veils" muttered under his breath. I dump my food in the trash and escape to the bathroom. Hiding, like a coward. But I need space. I need to breathe. He can't be part of my world. Not when mine might end before it even begins.

The stall door creaks as I step out minutes later and the bathroom door bursts open. Caelum. I freeze as the sink sputters, spraying water up and soaking the front of my shirt. Of course. I shut it off quickly, praying he didn't notice. He leans against the door, blocking my exit.

Panic flares. Did I misread him? Is he dangerous? I scan the room. There's nothing I could use to defend myself.

But then he speaks. Soft. Sincere. "Lilac, I can't change my past. But you are my future. Please, give me a chance. I don't know why you're so guarded, but I want to be with you. Only you. I am sorry about Saturday, I finally got a chance with you and I messed it up. I will explain more but I want to do it in private." His green eyes lock onto mine, and I hesitate.

"You really don't need to explain. All is forgiven, but I am asking you to please leave me alone. Nothing can happen between us. For both of our sakes. Please. I am just here for the training, not to make any friends or anything else. I can't keep having this conversation with you, I am asking you to respect my wishes." I feel the tears in my eyes, but I refuse to let them slip. Not in front of him.

He walks closer and wraps his arms around me. I hate how heart broken he looks. So defeated. "Okay, I will give you space. But I am not going anywhere and I won't be with anyone else. I don't want to push you, I am sorry, I will wait until you are ready." With that he turns and leaves the restroom, his face looks gutted. I hate all of this back and forth. I hate that I hurt him.

Alone, I let the tears slip, just a little. I wish that I wasn't in this situation and I could be some girl giddy and nervous about her first boyfriend.

In Battlecraft, the air practically crackled with anticipation. Voices buzzed across the open field—nervous, excited, speculative. Even the wind seemed to hum with unease, carrying the scent of dewy grass and sun-warmed earth. Students adjusted their clothes, boots thudding softly against the packed earth, all waiting for the same thing: the arrival of the Head Guard.

He would be here the next few days, watching, judging, deciding who would advance in the program. My stomach twisted tighter with every passing minute. I couldn't shake the feeling that something wasn't right. It wasn't just nerves, it was something deeper, like a thread tugging at my core.

I moved away from the crowd and dropped into a low stretch, trying to focus on my breathing. One beat at a time. Lyra came and sat next to me doing the same. That's when I noticed Nero silently walking over. He didn't speak, just dropped down next to me and began stretching in perfect sync. The air around him was taut, as if he were holding something back.

Then I heard them before I saw them. Deep voices, the easy rhythm of laughter. Caelum walked in with Halric at his side, followed by a towering figure whose very presence made the air feel heavier, like the moment before a storm breaks.

The Head Guard was cloaked in darkness, not just in color, but in presence. His armor was a deep forest green so dark it looked black until the light caught it, each plate reinforced yet fluid enough for movement. Etched across the surface were ancient silver runes, catching faint glimmers like starlight with every step. Over it all, he wore the ceremonial mask of his order, forged in the solemn style of the old Sylvaerin guard, a relic of the empire's forgotten past. It revealed nothing. Not his expression. Not his intent. Only the immovable weight of his power.

Power clung to him like a second skin.

The group's laughter faded as their boots crunched across the gravel path. Caelum's eyes found mine immediately, his gaze like a spark through my chest and I hate the way my pulse jumps. He looks relieved. Like he needed to see me. I forced myself to look away and blamed the flutter in my belly on nerves. Not on the way his brilliant emerald eyes always, *always* found me. Or how mine always found his.

"All right, listen up!" Halric's voice boomed across the field like a crack of thunder, snapping everyone to attention. "As you all know, the Head Guard will be spending the week with us. Assessing, advising, and ultimately helping determine who advances. So allow me to introduce the great and powerful, yes, I said powerful and I'm not just saying that because he's my boss. He's served as Head Guard for eighteen years. Tasked with the protection of our current king."

A handful of claps follow. Halric wasn't wrong, our group was awkward, too tense to pretend enthusiasm. I glanced over at Nero as he stood from his stretch. But something in his posture shifted instantly. He stiffened. His shoulders locked. His chest barely moved with breath.

I followed his gaze toward the front, where the masked figure stood, still and silent beside Halric and Caelum.

"Nero?" I whispered, my voice barely more than a breath. He didn't look at me, didn't blink. His jaw clenched, and the muscle near his temple twitched.

"Are you okay?" I asked again, softer. He gave me his usual silent nod, but it was different this time, too rigid, too rehearsed. Like he needed to keep from falling apart.

"Alright," Halric barked, clipboard in hand. "Like last Monday, we're starting with track drills. And before anyone asks, yes, I've already assigned the teams. No last-minute switch-ups." His eyes lingered pointedly on Cassia, whose narrowed eyes and tightly crossed arms spoke volumes.

When he called out the names, I heard mine paired with Nero's and another boy I didn't recognize. I moved to join them silently, my limbs suddenly feeling heavier. I should probably learn some of the other students names.

We walked a few paces away from the crowd. I waited until we were out of earshot before leaning slightly toward Nero.

"Nero, what happened back there?" He didn't answer right away. His eyes were still fixed ahead, unreadable. But then, quietly, he spoke.

"That man… There's something about him." My breath caught.

"I—I don't understand," I managed.

"I don't understand it either." He said.

Chapter 30: Untouched, Unbothered, Unreachable

Vera

The midday sun beat down on the training fields of Auravale Academy, heat shimmering off the red clay track that circled the grass. The stands sat empty, silent sentinels around the field. At the far end, the recruits gathered in a loose line before Coach Halric, tension thrumming in the still air. A short distance behind him stood the Head Guard, a towering figure in deep forest-green armor traced with silver runes, his ceremonial mask hiding every trace of expression, unreadable and immovable as stone.

"Do you know him?" I ask.

Nero's gaze flicked over to me, something unreadable in the golden hue of his eyes. "I don't know, I will have to try and figure it out." he said, voice low but firm. There was weight behind his words, urgency.

Now was not the time for questions. Now was the time to prove myself. The groups were being called onto the field. One by one, names echoed from a magically amplified voice overhead. Or Halric is just that loud. My stomach twisted as we walked to line up with the others, the nerves thrumming beneath my skin like a live current.

Cassia stood on the team next to mine, flanked by her two ever-present shadows, all impossibly perfect in their matching silver uniforms. She looked over, caught my eye, and smirked. Not friendly. Not even smug. *Territorial.*

That was all it took. I don't know what came over me, but suddenly, it was all I could think about. I *had* to beat her. Not just for myself. Not just for Caelum, or even for the Veilbound assessors watching from the edge of the field.

But because I wanted her to know, that I was not the girl she thought I was. That no matter how polished or powerful she appeared, she didn't scare me. I had fought too hard to become who I was. I wasn't going to be pushed aside, underestimated, or overlooked. Not again.

The whistle blew once, sharp and shrill, calling our attention. The first event was about to begin. I crouched at the starting line, fingers sinking into the dirt, heart hammering like a war drum. Every breath I drew burned with determination.

Cassia settled beside me, her ponytail swishing as she rolled her neck. She didn't look at me, but I felt her presence like a blade at my back.

The Head Guard raised his hand. Silence fell like a blanket. I narrowed my eyes on the path ahead, blocking out everything else. *This is it. Let her come.* I was ready.

His hand dropped and I gave myself over to my senses. I felt the wind flowing through me, pushing me. I was seconds ahead of everyone else. Closing in on Nero, I got the baton ready to pass and it cleanly went into his hand and he was off.

He was focused, looking ahead as his feet pounded. He looked like he glided through the air, he was already halfway around by time Cassia passed off her baton to Ryven who was waiting there impatient, angry. She slowed down and was panting beside me. I kept her in my peripheral but didn't acknowledge her.

Ryven tried to catch up to Nero but it didn't matter. Nero and I are both faster. Maybe this was an unfair team.

Again, seconds ahead of everyone else, Nero surged down the track and passed off the baton to the next runner Talon, I think his name was, who took off like he'd been launched from a catapult. He wasn't as fast as Nero, not even close, but he had solid form and impressive speed. Nero had looked like he was flying.

I walk slowly back toward the rest of the group, my legs still burning, breath gradually returning to normal. The sun beat down on the field, and the scent of grass, sweat, and churned earth filled my lungs. I risked a glance at the judging line.

The Head Guard was watching me. Not just casually observing, *watching*. From behind the polished obsidian mask, his gaze swept between Nero and me, unreadable and unblinking. I couldn't see his eyes, but somehow I felt them, sharp, searching. Like he was trying to piece something together. There was a stillness to him, a weight in the silence, and though his face was hidden, I sensed the flicker of confusion before he gave a slow, deliberate nod.

Next to him stood Caelum and Halric. Both of them looked proud, though Halric had his arms crossed dramatically like a coach trying not to cry. Caelum's eyes met mine, and in an instant, the tension that had been knotting up my shoulders, eased. There was something about the way he looked at me soft, steady, proud. Like he knew what I was capable of, even when I didn't.

"Alright!" Halric's voice broke the moment, booming over the field. "Great round! Now we move on to the second heat. Whoever wins this round will go on to face Nero, Vera, and…the kid who runs like a very fit gazelle—Talon!"

There were a few light laughs from the gathered crowd. Halric added in a mock whisper, "He's the only one I don't have a nickname for yet, so please run dramatically so I can think of one."

I sat down in the sun-warmed grass, stretching my legs out in front of me. The blades tickled my skin, and the ground vibrated faintly with footfalls and distant cheers. My eyes drifted to Caelum as he stepped forward for his turn.

His body was nothing but controlled power and grace. I watched him roll his shoulders back, muscles rippling beneath his shirt as he got into position. I bit my lip, remembering the feel of those arms wrapped around me, the warmth of his breath on my skin. The way his muscles bunched as he held me up. My hand feels his stomach when he pressed me into him. My stomach fluttered at the memory of his mouth on mine.

Suddenly, his head snapped up and those brilliant emerald eyes locked onto mine. Oh no.

His lips curled into that damnable smirk. The one that made me want to punch him *and* kiss him all at once. My cheeks flushed instantly. *Seriously, can he tell what I'm thinking?* That would be unfair. Then again, I'm starting to learn that unfair might just be normal around here. He gave me a slow, knowing wink before dropping into a runner's stance.

Gods, he had a nice ass too. Pure muscle, smooth motion, like the wind had shaped itself into a person. Just before the whistle blew, he let out a loud, single laugh that sounded way too cocky for someone about to sprint at full speed.

"You know," Nero's voice pulled me out of my very inappropriate thoughts. He plopped down beside me, arms resting on his knees, "you keep pushing him away, but I actually think he'd make a great ally."

"I don't know what you mean," I said, still watching Cae. "I don't need an ally."

Nero chuckled low in his throat. "You do. And not because you're weak but because it's exhausting carrying everything alone. You don't have to." His tone was calm, not pressing. Like he wasn't trying to convince me, just remind me.

"You and I see more than most, Vera. Let us be there for you." I stayed quiet. What could I say when they clearly saw right through me? The part of me that still wanted to believe I was just fine on my own—untouched, unbothered, unreachable—was shrinking.

I watched Caelum burst forward at the sound of the whistle, his form flawless, speed unreal. Even from a distance, I could see the sheer force behind every step. He wasn't just fast, he was purposeful.

"You keep pushing him away," Nero added as he stood and brushed off his pants, "but it's obvious you want him."

A shadow falls over me and we both look up to see Ryven standing there.

"You got lucky." He sneered to Nero. "I will be demanding a rematch."

"I don't think it would have mattered who your paired with. You certainly can't run like Nero can." I said haughtily. Which made him more angry.

"I don't know where you came from but I will be coming for you too. That Head Guard position will be mine." He said before he walked away. Leaving me wondering if I have another person trying to take me out. Does he know I'm not even interested in the position? I thought you had to sign up for that.

"Just think about what I said." Nero says before he gets up and leaves me alone with my thoughts.

I'm staring off into space, the kind where your mind is a blur and the world becomes background noise until a solid thump beside me snaps me back. Caelum collapses dramatically onto the grass, arms sprawled, breath coming in short bursts.

"You're crazy fast," he gasps, shooting me a look. "Didn't even seem winded when you were done. Are you even real?"

I just smile. A small one. The kind that slips out before you can stop it. I don't answer him. Could I trust him? The question drifts through my mind like a leaf on wind.

Before I can figure out the answer, Halric's voice bellows across the field. "*Lovebirds! Line up!* Looks like it's you two head-to-head now. Try not to make it weird." A few students snicker. Cassia looks like she might explode. I cough and my face flames all the way to my ears. I can't believe he just said that. Cae laughs and jumps up reaching a hand out to help me up. Of course he doesn't care.

Cae and I step up to the starting line. He takes a big drink from his water before dumping some over his head. My mouth drops open as he runs his head through his damp hair. I think it just got hotter out here. I clear my throat and glare at him while he just smirks. He knew exactly what he was doing.

The sun is higher now, pressing warm against my back. The scent of grass and dust clings to the air. A breeze picks up, brushing sweat-damp hair from my forehead.

"Care to make a bet?" I say, stepping beside him.

His head tilts toward me, eyes sparkling like he already knows I'm about to challenge him. "What do you have in mind?"

"If I win, you keep training me after school." I wonder if this is a mistake, but part of me wonders if what Nero says could be true. Not even a whole day went by and clearly I'm not staying away from him.

His grin spreads slowly, lazily. "And if *I* win?"

"Name your price."

He hums like he's pondering something serious, then flashes that smirk that makes my stomach lurch in a very annoying way. "If I win, I get to take you on a date."

I roll my eyes so hard it nearly hurts. "That's not very original."

"Well, it's a good thing I don't plan to lose," he says, winking as he drops into his stance. "Besides, you just gave me *very* good incentive."

"Don't make me regret it," I whisper.

"I won't." It's not just words—his eyes hold the vow long after the sound fades.

The whistle blows.

I launch forward, legs driving into the earth, the wind rushing past me like it's part of me. I feel the rhythm in my blood, the thump of footfalls, the stretch of each stride, the sun warming my skin. I can hear Caelum breathing just behind me. He's close. Too close. So I dig deeper. Push harder.

He keeps up with me step for step, and when I glance sideways, I see that look, competitive and wild, like this is the only place he feels free. I grit my teeth and surge ahead, the baton clenched tight in my hand. Nero's already in place, waiting. My focus narrows. Just a few more steps, I pass the baton and stagger to a stop, chest heaving. Caelum finishes right after me, nearly folding in half as he bends over, hands braced on his knees. He's panting like he just ran from a bear.

I laugh. I can't help it.

He looks up at me with flushed cheeks and tousled hair, like I'm the only thing anchoring him to the ground. "We start today," he says between breaths. "I seriously need to get my stamina up. Because I *will* win the next bet."

"Yeah. We'll see," I say with a smirk of my own, brushing past him.

As I walk back toward the others, I catch Cassia glaring at me like I just lit her hair on fire. Arms crossed, jaw tight, practically vibrating with rage. I wonder if she has any other look.

Halric, meanwhile, looks like he's *physically restraining* himself from laughing, biting his knuckle like it might stop the sound from escaping. When I pass him, he mutters, "If looks could kill, Cassia would've turned you to ash five minutes ago."

The Head Guard is unreadable. Still. Silent. His arms are folded like stone columns.

Finally, Halric claps his hands like a schoolteacher wrangling chaos. "Alright! Stellar job today. I'll see you all tomorrow for the first run of the Gauntlet. And please—hydrate! Not all of you have magical stamina and mysterious backstories."

A bell chimes in the distance, signaling the end of the period. Just like when they arrived, the Head Guard, Caelum, and Halric head off together, Halric launching into some story with wild hand gestures. Cae glances back at me once before they disappear from view.

And just like that, I'm left with the sun on my skin, my heart racing, and a growing tangle of questions I'm not ready to face. I guess I won't be training with Caelum today. That's alright. If I'm honest, I'm more curious about what Nero meant earlier.

I spot him heading up the hill toward the building, walking like the weight of something invisible clings to his shoulders. I change quickly, dodging Cassia, she looks like she might combust but thankfully she doesn't say a word.

Just as I'm stepping out of the echoforge, a hand curls around my wrist and yanks me back inside. My back hits the wall, not hard, but enough to make my breath catch. I'm suddenly eye-level with Caelum, his face shadowed and intense. His palm is braced beside my head, and his breath fans hot across my ear.

"Where are you going, my Brightstep? We start today." A shiver dances down my spine.

"Actually," I say, trying not to sound breathless, "can we take a rain check? There's something I need to check on at home." He leans back slightly, just enough so I can see his face. The disappointment there so raw and real, makes my chest ache. Another reason I shouldn't be letting him get this close.

His brow creases. "What does *rain check* mean?" He says it like he's testing the shape of the words in his mouth.

"It means to do it later. I won't renege on our bet, I just, I need to handle something first."

I try to press honesty into every syllable. I want him to know I'm not lying to him.

His expression shifts, softened by something unspoken. "Is everything okay?" he asks, voice low and laced with concern. I can feel it. His urge to reach for me, to hold me, he's holding himself back.

"Yes. Everything's fine." It's not. Not really. But it's the only answer I can give. I step away, needing the space. From the moment. Him.

"Okay," he says gently. "I'm here if you need any help." He places a kiss on my forehead again and I fight not to completely melt into him.

I nod, not trusting my voice, and head back into the school. The halls are mostly empty, only a few students hanging around talking while the teachers are gathering their things. I grab my things quickly, from my lockers, shoulders tense with everything I'm trying to ignore.

Outside, I spot Nero just reaching the start of the trail. He walks like he's on autopilot, stiff and preoccupied. I jog to catch up.

"Nero! Wait up!" I yell.

He keeps walking, but his head turns slightly, pace slowing. "I thought we didn't talk," he mutters over his shoulder, dry and guarded. I deserved that.

"I know," I say, catching up. "We don't. But you dropped that bomb, and now I want to know more. I want to help."

He snorts. "You never want my help." I let out a frustrated sigh. Of course he's right. I've refused every hand extended my way. If he knew why, maybe he wouldn't blame me. But I haven't told anyone. Not really. Not even Rina, not everything.

"I don't know who to trust," I admit, voice quieter now. "It's complicated."

He's quiet for a moment. Then, a slow exhale. "Yeah. I get that."

We walk in silence for a few steps, just the crunch of dirt beneath our shoes and the chirp of birds in the trees. The school is no longer visible behind us, but we haven't yet reached the stretch where the homes peek through.

"You can trust me," he says. "I know it'll take time, but what I'm about to tell you, you can't repeat it. I need to figure this out. I need to get in touch with my mom. When he walked in, the head guard, he felt familiar to me somehow. But I've never met him before." I nod, giving him the space to continue.

"Do you think you might know who he is?"

He stares ahead, eyes fixed on the woods like he's trying to see the past. "Do you know about the Shattering?"

I shake my head. "A little, not much."

"It was the last war. Eighteen years ago. Something sparked it, something bad. The realms were still united then, hidden from the humans. But the vampires went rogue first. Attacked our borders. Then the shifters joined in."

Maybe this is my chance to try and get some answers. "How could no one know why? Shouldn't the royal families have answers? Do shifters and vampires even have kings?"

"Yeah, they do. And it started with the royal families. According to the shifters and the vampires, they didn't even know their own people were attacking us. They accused King Caedor—King Lucan's father— of starting something. None of them believed the other. Chaos broke out. Vampires hit Duskmere hard, and the shifters pushed deep into

Sylvaeris. The king was killed in the fighting. That's when Lucan took the crown." I swallow hard. "So they split the realms," he says, "and as far as we know, they don't talk to each other."

"My mom was pregnant with me then," he adds. "She couldn't fight, so she worked the control rooms. My father, he was the head Solenar for Duskmere. He advised the Caezar, helped train future members of the guard. For both those who wanted to come to Sylvaeris and who wanted to stay in Duskmere. He was on the border when the vampires hit."

His voice lowers. "She felt it when his life force vanished. Said it was the hardest thing she's ever experienced. But she had to stay strong for everyone else, for me. They never found his body. Assumed the vampires drained him and left nothing behind." We stop walking. The wind whispers through the trees, brushing the leaves like fingertips on silk.

"She became the Solenar after that. Raised me with stories about him. Called him a hero. Her office? A shrine. Pictures everywhere. Said he was her fated. That it *physically* hurts to lose a mate like that." I stay quiet, sensing what's coming.

"Do you think that man was your father?"

"I don't think so. I mean, that would be impossible. My mom *felt* him die. But there was definitely something. A bond. Familial."

"Maybe an uncle you never knew about?"

"Could be. I guess I'd have to ask my mom. I don't want to worry her. I want to figure it out first."

"Isn't there a record we could check? Something that says who he is?"

"No. Only the royal family knows his true identity and they don't reveal it. Its meant to be sacred, a vow between the Head Guard and the king he protects."

"Oh. Well, Cae and Halric seemed kind of familiar with him when they walked in. Maybe you could ask Cae." He gives me a side-eyed look but keeps walking.

"No. Let's keep it between you and me for now," he says gruffly.

Chapter 31: Do You Feel It? Something's Weird.

Vera

Sleep had been a distant thing last night, fleeting and fragile, always just out of reach. My mind refused to rest, circling over everything Nero told me on the trail. Every word clung to me like mist, especially the part about his father. About whether or not we should tell *him.* Caelum.

I remembered Nero's voice steady but careful, as he said Caelum would be a great ally. I didn't even argue, because he was right. But both of them clearly knew I was hiding something. They didn't push, but it lingered between us, unsaid but known.

And the truth I was afraid to admit? I was getting closer to Caelum. Too close. Not because I was trying. In fact, I *wasn't* trying. That's what scared me most.

Every time our paths crossed, an invisible tether between us pulled tighter. I felt more of him, not just his presence, but his intentions. His emotions. Like they were brushing against my skin. Something in the air changed when he was near, and I wasn't sure how long I could keep resisting it.

I wanted to give in. Stars, I wanted to. But what if this connection was a trick? A carefully spun illusion to disarm me? I had no experience with boys back in the human world, especially not ones with eyes like his and smiles that slipped past my defenses. I didn't know how to tell the difference between real and rehearsed.

And the prophecy loomed over it all like a shadow I couldn't escape.

Now, walking to school, the leaves whisper around my ankles with every step. The morning air clings to my skin, cool and sharp with the scent of wet stone and fading flowers. Nero walks beside me, unusually silent. No sarcastic remarks. No awkward attempts to ease the mood. Just tension.

Thick. Heavy. Suffocating. It's like we're both still caught in the web of yesterday's conversation, spun tight with memories, questions, and truths that came too fast.

As we near the academy, my skin prickles. A faint pulse beneath it. Something is wrong.

I pause, subtly scanning the path ahead. The towering trees creak in the wind like they're warning us, and the overcast sky churns with heavy clouds. The wind wraps around me, whispering in my ears, and I feel it in my bones something is off. Wrong. Unsettled.

I glance at Nero. "Do you feel it? Something's weird."

He shakes his head. "No. Everything seems the same to me." That makes it worse. What can I feel, that he can't? Or is all the stress getting to me. I bite my lip and follow him the rest of the way, eyes sweeping the building as it comes into view. There's no sign of Caelum. The absence hits harder than it should, but it's there, a space unfilled. Like anti-matter, I don't know what this is that I am feeling but I know it's not good.

Inside, the foyer buzzes with chatter. Excitement hums like static, loud and chaotic. Students group together in little clusters, all talking at once. The sound of it makes my pulse stutter. Something *happened.*

Nero disappears down the hall and I veer toward my locker. I just want to keep my head down, but as I open the door, two girls pass behind me in a flurry of perfume and silk.

"Did you hear the prince is getting *married*?" one whispers.

"I know! It's so exciting! Do you think we'll be invited?"

"They'll probably hold a big public ceremony once he takes the crown. Oh, can you imagine?" I freeze. *Married?* The words echo inside me like a dropped stone in a still lake. I don't even know the royal family. I blink and shake it off, stuffing books into my bag. Maybe it's normal here. Maybe royal weddings are announced like school dances. Maybe it's just gossip. But still, something inside me curls tight.

By the time I make it to class, I feel like I'm carrying a stone in my chest. Mr. Valeis isn't here yet, and the other students are still buzzing. Whispers. Laughter. Rumors like wildfire. I sink into my seat and try to disappear, scribbling absentminded trees into the margins of my notes. Each stroke feels like a breath, something to ground me.

Then the air shifts. The room falls silent, like someone flipped a switch. I look up to see Caelum walk in. He's a storm made of flesh. Shoulders tense. Jaw tight. His expression is carved from stone, until his eyes find mine. And then softness. Just for me. The storm calms, briefly.

Behind him, Mr. Valeis enters, his usual unreadable expression in place.

"Hey, Lilac," Caelum murmurs as he passes, but it's not the playful tone I've grown used to. It's quiet. Strained. There's something *broken* under the surface. His eyes that are usually glowing only show regret.

"Are you okay?" I whisper, not even sure he can hear me.

He nods. "Better now that I got to see your beautiful face." I scoff, but my cheeks betray me, going warm anyway.

Class begins, and the lesson drifts into the history of Elarindor. The words feel familiar, pieces from the book I found in the library but I can't focus. Because next to me, Caelum is burning.

Not outwardly. But I can *feel* it. Rage curled like smoke beneath his skin, suffocating and silent. I don't know what happened before he walked in but I know this much: Something is wrong. And whatever it is, it's only just beginning. When class ended I started gathering my things and Cae lingered beside me. His hands curl into fists, then release, like he's fighting the impulse to reach for me. I look up at him, needing to understand what's happening, but his eyes are far away. Lost in something I can't see.

We walk to our next class in silence. Not the comfortable kind, either, this one hums with the weight of things unsaid. I can feel the words sitting on the tip of Caelum's tongue like storm clouds about to break, but he says nothing. His jaw flexes as if he's biting them back, choosing silence over whatever might spill out.

The hallways buzz louder than usual, but it isn't the typical chatter of sleepy students. It's sharper. Quieter. Hushed voices behind cupped hands. And they're looking at *us*. That part isn't new, he's always been someone people notice, orbiting around him like he's some untouchable sun. But this time, the glances sting. Curious. Calculating. I don't ask him what's going on. I can't. Not yet. Not with the fury simmering under his skin and the dread curling tighter in my chest.

We slide into our seats and I feel like I'm balancing on a tightrope. The tension is so thick I could cut it with the tip of my pencil. A moment later, Nero drops into the seat on my other side. Hard.

He doesn't say anything either. Just stares straight ahead, his whole posture coiled like a spring. I turn to look at him, silently asking what's wrong. He meets my eyes just long enough for me to see the fire there and then he shifts, his glare landing squarely on Caelum.

Did they fight? *Again?* Something's unraveling. Then Cassia enters. Like she owns the air we're breathing. Her platinum hair swings behind her in a glossy wave as she struts into the room, every movement calculated to draw attention. She doesn't need to speak, her presence alone is enough to command the space.

She flicks a glance in our direction, her mouth curving into a smug, satisfied smile. It sends my stomach lurching. Something's wrong. Really wrong. *Do they know who I am? About the prophecy?*

"Lilac?" Caelum's voice slices through the noise like a blade. I turn to him, startled, there's fear in his voice, raw and unhidden.

"There's something I need to talk to you about," he says, low and urgent. "I need you to hear me out and don't run."

My heart thuds once, loud, painful. "What is it? Is everything okay?" He scrubs a hand roughly down his face. I can see the strain in every line of his body. The pain in his eyes. Before he can answer, the teacher strides in. The moment is lost, sealed under the start-of-class murmur.

"After," he says. "Just… promise me." But I don't promise. Because I already know whatever he's about to say will shatter something.

I glance at Nero again. Still silent. Still forward. I can't feel anything from him, not like I can with Caelum. Nero's always been harder to read, like a locked door with no handle. I don't know if he's just better at hiding it, or if there's something else going on.

The lesson floats past me like wind through leaves. I think the professor is talking about wind currents and elemental conduits, but I barely hear a word. Every now and then, a breeze slips through the open window and twirls strands of my hair around my face. But the wind never *touches* me. It brushes past, like even the elements are holding their breath.

When the bell finally rings, I start gathering my things, trying to hold myself together. That's when I feel the shift. A shadow falls over my desk.

Cassia. Of course. She's looking down at me with a mixture of irritation and smug satisfaction, an artist admiring her masterpiece.

"Back away, Cassia." Caelum's voice cuts in, cold and sharp. "I told you to stay away from her. And from me."

Her smile doesn't falter. It sharpens. "Stay away?" she repeats sweetly. "I can't stay away when we're *about to be married*. I just think my fiancé needs to understand I won't tolerate him touching another woman." Her eyes flick to me like knives, and she basks in the silence that follows.

Married? The word echoes like thunder in my skull. She's said that before but I just thought she was delusional. I turn to Caelum slowly, every movement stiff. His face is a battlefield, desperation and guilt warring behind his eyes. He doesn't deny it. He *can't*.

I rise, my chair scraping hard against the floor. I don't say a word, just finish gathering my things with trembling fingers.

"Lilac, please." His voice breaks. "I'm not marrying her. It's an arrangement. A stupid one. My parents were trying to force it, but my dad is helping cancel it. I won't go through with it. I don't want her. I want *you*."

And that's when it clicks. The whispers. The girls in the hallway. *The prince is getting married.* My heart stutters.

"You're the prince?" I ask, barely able to force the words out.

"Yes," he breathes. "I'm the Prince of Sylvaeris." And in that moment, the weight of it all crashes down.

The secrets. The lies. The prophecy. The growing bond between us.

He's the prince. And I'm already falling. I fell for him, for his lies. Now, I put myself into danger. Emotionally and physically.

I tear away from his reaching hand before I can change my mind. My heart pounds in my chest, thudding harder with every step as I bolt from the room. I don't know where I'm going just that I *can't* stay. Not there. Not with him.

The library's out. Too obvious. He'll look there first. I take the stairs two at a time, past the second floor, past the third. My breath comes in short bursts by the time I reach the fourth floor, a place I've never explored. For all I know, it's off-limits. But right now, I don't care.

The hallway here is different, quieter, more open, filled with a soft ambient light that trickles down from skylights above. To my surprise, there are small shops tucked into the corners of the floor. One sells elaborate notebooks and pens that glimmer faintly. Another seems to sell crystals and magical trinkets. There's even a coffee shop, cozy and warm with velvet chairs and a display of pastries behind a glowing glass case.

Why did no one tell me about this? All this time, I've been envious of all the students carrying coffee.

I skirt around the edge of the coffee shop, drawn toward something that feels *alive*. Behind it is a wide arched entryway framed with ivy. I step through and stop.

Glass walls surround the space, tall and seamless, rising high into the canopy of the forest beyond. Golden light filters through the trees outside, casting a shifting, dappled glow across the floor. At the center is a tiled pond, not large, but elegant. Its turquoise and cerulean tiles shimmer beneath the clear water. Lily pads drift lazily across the surface, dotted with delicate blooms in blush pinks and soft whites. Ferns and flowering plants spill from ceramic pots nestled in each corner, and tiny dragonflies hum through the air, their wings catching the light like shards of stained glass.

I collapse onto a wooden bench and press my hands to my face, trying to catch my breath. My chest aches. Everything's unraveling. I almost trusted him. With everything. With who I am.

I lean forward and watch a lily pad spin slowly, mindlessly, letting the stillness soothe my racing thoughts. But they come anyway.

It all makes sense now. The way he carries himself. The respect he commands from the teachers, how some even bowed their heads. He addresses them by first name. How everyone gathers around him, just trying to get close to him. Halric spoke to him like an equal. He trained with guards. He's going into politics. Not just politics, ruling. Of course he knows the Head Guard. Of course he does.

Nero told me not to go to Caelum with his stuff. Not to trust him. But then... Nero wants to be Head Guard. To protect *him*. And still, he encouraged me to be with Caelum. If Nero helped Cae win me, was he hoping to get in the top spot for Head Guard? Again and again. My head spins. None of it makes sense. And yet somehow, it *does*. And through it all, one question needles at me: If he was promised to someone else, why did he keep pursuing me?

Why did he *make me fall for him?* The tears come suddenly, slipping down my cheeks without permission. I don't bother wiping them away. Not yet. I just breathe in the earthy scent of the greenhouse-like space, of flowers and water and warm soil.

I don't hear the footsteps until a gentle voice breaks the quiet. "Oh, sorry. I didn't realize anyone was here."

I startle and turn, heart skipping. A girl stands just inside the glass door, her honey blonde hair braided over one shoulder, her eyes kind and steady. "I usually come up here before lunch and lately during lunch too. I'm Elowen." Elowen? Like my aunt and mom's family name.

I blink at her. I recognize her faintly, one of the girls I've seen near Caelum in the dining hall. She was also the one that came looking for him when I was in the computer lab. One of his many admirers, no doubt. My guard rises instinctively.

"Oh, um, sorry, I've never been up here. I was just curious," I say quickly, rising and trying to discreetly swipe at my face. "I didn't mean to intrude."

But she waves me off, walking toward the bench with a soft smile. "Please, stay. There's more than enough room for both of us. What's your name?" I hesitate but then I reach out, brushing my senses across her energy. Like Rina has been teaching me. Just trying to be gentle so she doesn't feel it. All I feel is warmth. calm. Curiosity. *No lies. No malice.* Something about it feels familiar but I don't know what.

"Vera," I say. Her smile deepens almost like she already knew. "It's nice to meet you, Vera. You've got the school buzzing, you know. Word is you're the most athletic girl anyone's ever seen, you might even break old records. I heard about your training in the Order."

I smile faintly, the compliment falling strangely on my ears after everything. "I think I've seen you around before." I hint to see if she mentions anything about Caelum.

"I'm in different courses," she says with a shrug, sitting beside me. "I never wanted to pursue the Order. I *can* fight, but I'd rather not have to. I'm more focused on the political track. Honestly? I'd rather spend my life reading books." She chuckles, brushing her fingers over the carved armrest.

That makes me smile, despite myself. "Same. Though lately I've only been reading textbooks and history books. I miss my romance novels."

Elowen's eyes light up. "Oh, I *love* romance. But I've been deep in plant studies lately. Learning how to grow the healing herbs, how to blend them properly. I want to be able to help people, really help. With my hands. My knowledge."

"That actually sounds amazing," I say softly. "I never thought about learning healing plants, but that seems like a skill worth having."

She grins. "You should come look sometime. I can show you the ones that calm the mind. Good for overthinking." She winks. I laugh, something light easing through my chest for the first time all day.

"I'll definitely take you up on that. If I ever get a moment to breathe."

"You will," she says, her tone confident and oddly certain. "Maybe not today. But soon. After we graduate, we'll have our whole lives ahead of us." Her words settle into me like sunlight. She is a breath of fresh air.

For a moment, I forget who I am. Forget that I might not have the rest of my life. Forget who she might be. We're just two girls, finding peace beside the water.

Just then, the bell rings, signaling the end of the next class. Which means it's time for lunch. I stay on the bench, unmoving. I'm not leaving this space, not yet. Not while the quiet still holds me like a fragile shield. Not while he hasn't found me yet.

"Don't you have class?" I ask Elowen after a while, breaking the silence.

She smiles brightly. "No, I had a free period. But it's time for lunch, want to join me?"

I shake my head gently. "I think I'll stay here for a bit longer. But you go ahead."

"I brought lunch from home," she says with a soft laugh, the kind that sparkles like water under sunlight. "My brother started packing one, so I decided to copy him."

I chuckle. "In that case, go ahead."

She begins to unpack her things neatly, with care and I rise to stand near the wide windows. The forest beyond moves with quiet grace, every leaf shimmering under the midday light. It feels *alive*. Like it's watching me. Like it knows.

"Hey, what are you doing here?" My entire body goes still. His voice. Rough velvet. Strained. Too close.

Elowen answers before I can turn. "Well, *I* usually hang out here. I could ask you the same, but..." she trails off knowingly. "I think I already know."

I close my eyes, inhaling deeply, steadying the crack in my chest. Trying to hold it together so it doesn't crack further. When I finally turn to face him, I clock my exits first. Old habit. He won't let me just walk away. But I won't be staying, either.

When I look up and meet his eyes, the impact nearly takes me down. His green eyes, so sharp and striking before, look *pained*. There's a vulnerability in them I've never seen. His jaw clenches slightly, his lips part like he's about to speak, but he hesitates.

I shut everything down. I seal off my heart, push it down where he can't reach it. Where it can't betray me again.

"Vera, my Lilac..." His voice catches. "You have to let me explain. You're probably sick of hearing me say that. I know you're angry. You have every right to be. But *please*—"

"I don't want to hear anything," I cut in, my voice firmer than I expected. "Like I've told you, we are not friends. We are not anything. You need to leave me alone. I'm here for my training, for the Order. Nothing else." Pain flashes across his face, and I feel it twist in my own chest like a blade. But I keep going. If I stop now, I'll fall.

"No," he says, shaking his head, stepping forward. "We are something. I should have told you I'm the Prince but gods, Vera, it was so... freeing. Being around someone who didn't care who I was. Who challenged me. You don't pretend. You're real." His voice thickens. "I wasn't going to marry Cassia before I met you, and I *sure as Veil* won't now. You have to believe me. I know you have truthsense, please, *feel me*. Everything I'm saying is true."

Elowen begins to quietly pack up her things. "I think... I think I'm going to go," she murmurs.

"No, don't go." I turn to her quickly, grateful for the distraction. "I'm leaving." I shoot Caelum a look. "And you're not going to follow me. You're not going to talk to me anymore."

"I can't agree to that." His voice drops lower. "I know I messed up, Veils, do I know but I'm not giving up. I want to be with you. I will *earn* your trust again. We're going to finish our Order training, and I'll prove myself to you. Whatever is haunting you, we'll face it together." My gaze flicks to Elowen, uneasy.

He catches it. "Don't worry about El. You can trust her too. She's my best friend. The only one I've ever been able to truly talk to until you."

I snort before I can stop myself. "Someone else you probably slept with?" *Gods*, that sounded jealous.

Elowen bursts into laughter, the sound sudden and melodic. "Oh gods, I love you. No, no. That idiot is my brother. Always has been him and me against the world." My brain stutters. His sister?

I look between them. And now I see it, really see it. The same sandy-blonde hair, though hers is lighter in the sun. Her jade green eyes are softer than his, more thoughtful, but unmistakably related. She smiles at me gently, like she's trying not to startle a bird.

"Did you know about me before?" I ask her. "Like, more than just someone athletic, from the Veilbound?"

"Yes," she says, no hesitation. "I'm sorry we haven't met. Cae's been talking about you since the day he saw you." It should warm me. Instead, it burns.

I glance at him again. His expression is devastated. Hopeful, but hanging by threads. His hands twitch like he wants to reach for me, hold me, but doesn't dare. He takes one slow step forward. Then another.

I raise my hand. "Don't." He freezes.

"We're done here," I say, and this time my voice is ice. "I'm going to class. You're going to stay away from me." He swallows hard, jaw tight. A muscle ticks in his cheek. He doesn't argue. Doesn't speak.

"*Your Highness*," I add, with an awkward little curtsey. And then I turn and walk out.

My back is straight. My chin lifted. I don't let them see the tears prickling in my eyes. I don't let them see how my chest is collapsing inward. I don't cry. Not here. Not until I'm alone. Alone in my room, with no one to hear the sound of something quietly breaking.

Chapter 32: Raging Hormones and Teen Angst

Cae

I crash down on the bench, defeated. Placing my face in my hands. How did I mess this up so much? She is my fated and she won't even come near me anymore.

"Cae? Are you okay?" El asks softly beside me. Her hand resting on my back.

"No, El. I am not okay. She's my future and I just lost it."

"You didn't lose her. You just have to give her some space."

"I can't. I don't want to, she was slowly letting me in, I worked hard all week and finally yesterday she started to trust me. I keep messing up. I should have told her the truth."

"Hey, none of that now. We will fix this."

"How?" I am desperate at this point. Desperate to keep my girl and to get rid of Cassia and her father.

"I think first we need to find out what changed. Why are the Corvina's announcing the marriage now? I know dad was going to look closer at the contract to see if there was a way out of it without any political ramifications. We need to see that contract and as much as you don't want to, you need to talk to Cassia and find out what she wants."

"What she wants is to marry me, all last week she was saying we would end up together." I shiver in disgust.

"After school we will start combing over the contract. You might need to think about telling dad you found your fated, things have changed maybe he will help."

"I don't trust that he will help. Vera is hiding for a reason, I don't know why fully but I want to keep attention off of her for as long as possible. Plus, just other fae's knowing she is with me they will start watching her more, trying to find out who she is."

"News flash, brother. Everyone in school knows your into her. I am sure word will be getting out soon enough."

I smirk at her. "Okay, now what do I do about Vera?"

El sighs, her expression gentling. "That part... I don't know. She was really hurt, and I think a little scared too. I can't pretend to be an expert in relationships. You're not either, you've never really let things get past the surface. This is different, though. If she matters to you, you'll have to show her that."

I gave her a dry look. "Wow. That was incredibly helpful."

She just laughed softly. "You're the one who knows her best, Cae. But for what it's worth, I like her too. I think she and I could be close, maybe even best friends someday. Whether or not you manage to fix things with her, I want her in our lives. She's... different. Refreshing. And I think she might be exactly what you need, even if you don't see it yet."

"I *do* see it. But thanks for helping me, for always helping."

"You're welcome. Now go start fixing your problems. I am going to finish my lunch. Maybe give her some space though, don't go straight to her. Or at least don't talk to her." She laughs.

"There's something else I need to tell you. I've been thinking about it for a couple of days," I say.

Elowen tilts her head, curiosity flickering in her eyes. I tell her about what Vera and I talked about outside her cottage. That Mom had been sick before she died, that if there was a real reason, no one ever told us. And now Dad's ill too. Maybe it's connected.

She nods slowly, concern tightening her features. We start talking through ideas, quietly forming a plan to dig deeper.

"There's more," I add, standing from the bench. "But I need to say it in private. Meet me in the greenhouse after dinner?"

"Sounds serious," she says, rising with a faint smile. "But yes, I'll be there."

I give her a wave and walk off. I think my first step is finding Nero. I skip lunch altogether and go sit in my car. As much as I want to go find her, I know I need to give her some space. At least for the rest of today, I don't think I could stay away any longer. I could easily find her when she ran off before but I wanted to give her a moment to calm down. I instinctively keep a pulse on her thread, our joined thread. Our thread that seems frayed a little, I don't know if it's because she is so angry or if it's my imagination.

When the bell rings, I know it's time for class. I head toward Runes and Relics, my last class with Vera before Battlecraft, dreading the inevitable tension waiting for me. Students pass by in small groups, whispering behind cupped hands or failing to hide their curious stares. I ignore them. I've gotten used to it.

The halls are lined with festive Veilfall decorations, silver lettering spelling out the festival name, bright garlands in deep reds, golds, and burnt orange strung along the archways. Autumn leaves drift in lazy spirals under the charm-cast breeze.

I don't take any of it in. None of it matters right now. Not the celebration. Not the rumors. Not even the upcoming trials. Not when everything feels like it's unraveling with Vera. I push into the classroom. Thorian is already there, leaning against the far wall, his usual unreadable expression in place. No one else has arrived yet. Good. I need a moment to pull myself together before she walks in.

Without even looking up he says, "There will be hard times coming. With you, the crown, and Vera. United you will succeed, divided everything will fall." He looks up and I see his eyes go from white to his usual grey. It's very unsettling when seers do that. He looks up at me and smiles.

"I can feel your inner turmoil, and hers. When you're together you two are powerful. Apart she will still be powerful and she has a slim chance of succeeding." He adds.

"What does that mean? I want to be united, I will help her in all things. What is she fighting?"

"We can't see yet, but it threatens the crown."

"What is threatening the crown?" I demand. Students start walking in and I take two steps back from his desk.

"We don't know, I see a lot of blood and death coming." Veils.

Vera comes walking in but she avoids eye contact with everyone just sits down in the back row. I follow and sit next to her, her body stiffens but she doesn't move. I don't say anything, just glad she's allowing the proximity. I know I can't push her.

When class ends she darts out of there. I lock eyes with Thorian and catch him assessing her, again. I can tell he is withholding information at this time, but speaking in front of others isn't an option right now. Maybe I can find him after school or tomorrow. I change quickly into my workout clothes and wait for Halric to come out of his office.

Ro steps into the doorway of the locker room, all 6'8" of him cutting a solid silhouette that seems to blot out the light behind him. He's easily one of the tallest fae I've ever met, less fae, more shadow carved from mountain and metal.

He nods to me and turns as Halric and I approach.

Ro never speaks in public. It's part of the ancient Head Guard tradition, duty over voice, presence over command but that never stops Halric from trying.

"I hope you're ready for another fun-filled day of raging hormones and teen angst," Halric says with a smirk. "Truly, we live the dream." Ro only gives his signature grunt in response.

Halric squints. "Wow. Tough room. I guess you two are in a mood today. Here's hoping the whole class isn't like this." I don't answer either. I too am in my head. Too focused on *her*.

When we step into the Echoforge, it greets us with its usual hush of reverence, half cathedral, half crucible. The vast platform looms like a stage for gods and monsters, and the obstacle course stretches beside it like a beast waiting to be tamed.

My eyes find her instantly. Vera.

She's stretching alone, face unreadable, blank like she's locked everything behind stone walls. I feel that wall between us like a punch to the chest. Nero approaches her slowly, cautiously, like he's nearing a wounded creature, and she whips a glare at him that could crack glass. He freezes.

Then he looks at me. And if glares could kill, I'd be a pile of ash. So yeah. He's mad at me too. I deserve it. He doesn't speak to her. Just stays near, like proximity might be enough to protect her. Or like he doesn't quite know what to do with the space between them either.

"Alright, listen up," Halric calls, clapping his hands. "We're doing things differently today. One at a time on the course. Quick rotations. After your run, partner up for sparring but we're only assessing the obstacle course today. Sparring starts tomorrow."

Students start to line up. As planned, Halric sends Vera, Nero, and me to the back, best performers last. Standard strategy, not that any of the students know that. The others chatter among themselves. Vera doesn't say a word. Doesn't even glance my way. Nero throws me a look, *What the veils did you do?*

Fair. I don't even know how to explain it to myself. But I *do* know I have to fix it. I just don't know where to start. With her. And with everything spiraling at home.

The first few runs go by fast. I watch with half my attention. Cassia stumbles twice but finishes just under the cutoff time. Sylas breezes through it like he's flying, he's trained with me for years. Vera's new friend, Lyra, struggles near the end. I make a mental note to ask Halric about her placement later. She might not make it.

Then it's Vera's turn. She doesn't look back. Doesn't hesitate. She just *moves*. Glides through the course like she's part of it, fluid and relentless, every limb precise. She moves like wind over water, like a blade remembering it was forged to cut.

Nero's called right after and tries to keep up. He's fast, always is but Vera moves like she's trying to outrun something. Today, she just might be. I think she is damn close to taking over her father's record.

Ro turns fully toward them. His body goes rigid, not the usual stillness of a guard, but something alert. Focused. Like a predator watching prey. I can't see his eyes behind the mask, but his energy hums with something strange. Something I *can't* read, and that unsettles me more than I want to admit.

I glance at him again. Still nothing from his aura. But something's beneath the surface. Tense. Electric. I need to talk to my father. See if he senses it too. Tonight's council meeting might be my only chance.

When Halric calls my name, I push off the wall and dive into the course. I don't think, just move. Let my body carry me through each motion. All the anger and frustration from today fueling me. But my mind still clings to her. To the look in her eyes this morning. That mix of sorrow and fear that she tried to hide and I can't unsee. I hate that I put it there.

After Battlecraft, it takes everything in me not to go after her. Not to chase her down the hall and say *something*. Anything. But I have a meeting with Ro and Halric before the council meets. And I need to be sharp. I need to be ready. Because something is shifting beneath all of this. Beneath her silence. Nero's tension. Ro's aura.

And I can't shake the feeling that if I don't figure it out soon, I'm going to lose more than just her.

When I get home, I manage to avoid Thalina. She'd see through any mask I wore today, and I'm not ready to answer the questions in her eyes.

I retreat to my room, change into the required formalwear, black slacks, a crisp button-down and barely finish fastening the cuffs before there's a knock at my door. I open it to find my father standing there, wearing the kind of careful, measured smile that sets my nerves on edge.

"You ready?" he asks.

"Yes. Is everything okay?"

He doesn't answer right away. Just turns and starts down the stairs. I follow, each step heavier than the last. At the bottom, he finally speaks. "Before we go in, I heard it was announced today. The marriage contract with Cassia. Calindra and the Corvinas pushed it through." My breath tightens. My jaw locks.

"I've reviewed it," he continues. "The only way out is if both parties agree to void it, or if one or both of you finds your fated mate." I stop just outside the conference room doors. My heart pounds in my ears. *I did find my fated.* But I'm not ready to say it out loud. Not until she knows. Not until she chooses me back.

"Can I see the contract?"

"Yes. We'll go through it after the meeting. I just wanted you to be prepared." He lowers his voice. "I don't know what Torvyn's up to. I can't remove him without due process, not until you wear the crown and Sylas takes Solenar. For now, he's protected."

"So you don't trust him anymore?" I ask sharply. "That's new. You've spent the past year bending over backwards for the Corvinas and Calindra."

He flinches, just barely. "Things change. I'm not happy about all of this either but I'm going to fix it." I don't answer. I just push the doors open.

The room is already full, council members chatting over wine and papers, the soft clink of ice in glasses filling the silence. I shake hands with each one, my smile practiced. Controlled.

When I reach Torvyn, I hold his hand a beat too long and squeeze just a little too hard. He startles, caught off guard by the pressure. I let my aura slip, just enough to brush against his. Red. Burning. Calculating. Scheming. I meet his eyes and let mine go cold. *You're not the only one playing games.*

We take our seats, my father at the head, me to his right, Sylas beside me for the first time. He looks excited, but also like he knows he should keep his mouth shut.

The meeting rolls on, mostly standard. Reports. Budget updates. Trade route discussions. New construction proposals. Nothing that would give anyone a reason to notice how badly I want to tear Torvyn's smile off his face. Until the end.

"Anything else to address?" my father asks, eyes scanning the table.

Torvyn clears his throat and rises, smoothing his jacket with far too much ceremony. "Yes. I'd like to propose we begin planning the Prince's coronation. And, of course, his upcoming nuptials to my daughter, Cassia."

The room stills.

My father nods slowly. "Yes, the coronation will be planned soon. It'll be fairly standard unless Caelum requests otherwise."

Torvyn beams. "Wonderful. I'm sure Cassia would love to assist in the planning."

"That won't be necessary," I say, voice even but iron-edged. "My father, my sister, and I will handle the details. You'll receive an invitation like everyone else."

Across the room, I see Ro shift slightly, just a flicker of movement, but enough to catch my eye. Sylas stares between Torvyn and me like he's watching a duel.

Torvyn's smile twitches, falters for a fraction of a second before he catches it. His aura flares, hot, impatient, angry but he tries to hide it. Tries being the operative word. He's not good at masking. Not like I've been trained to be. I let a ghost of a smirk slip onto my lips. Just enough to let him know I saw it.

He clenches his jaw, recovers. "Well," he says brightly, clapping once, "Cassia, Sera and Calindra have already started planning the ceremony. It'll be the grandest wedding the realm has ever seen." Silence. Not a single council member responds.

Inside, I'm burning. But I keep it all locked away. Buried. I'll give him his silence. For now. Because tonight? Tonight El and I start planning.

I'm done letting others make moves while I sit on the sidelines. I'm going to find out what he's hiding, why the kingdom feels like it's teetering, and how the hell I'm going to protect Vera from all of it.

My father closes the meeting. "Torvyn, can you stay for another meeting? I would like to discuss something in my office." He nods his head and walks out, knowing where my fathers office is.

As people begin to file out, Sylas lingers with me, hands in his pockets, grinning like he just survived a battlefield.

"Damn," he says. "That was intense. Are all the meetings like this?" My father and I both laugh, quick, sharp, shared relief.

"No," my father says, shaking his head. "They're usually boring."

"It's true," I add with a crooked smile.

Sylas raises an eyebrow. "So, what's the deal with the wedding?" His voice takes on a weird edge, but I'm too angry to really pay attention.

"It's just a contract," I say, letting the smile fade. "One I don't intend to follow." And I mean it.

My father walked out first, and I lingered with Sylas.

"So, what happened today at the academy? That Vera girl seemed pissed," he asked.

I studied him, trying to decide why he wanted to know. He'd always been someone I trusted, but right now everything felt uncertain. Unknown. And all I could think about was protecting Vera.

"Yeah, she wasn't happy," I admitted. "I really like her, Sylas. You know Cassia, she won't leave me alone, and she's not making it easy."

He snorted. "She's always been itchy to get to you. You know their family's power hungry."

"Yeah, I know." I exhaled. "Come on, let's go see if Thalina has any snacks."

We started down the hallway when a sharp sound cut through the air. My father's voice, raised. Yelling. He never yelled. Sylas and I froze.

"I don't know what you think you're doing, Torvyn, but you have overstepped," my father's voice thundered through the heavy oak doors. "This deal is over. You do not make decisions for this kingdom, not without going through me first, and especially not when it concerns my children. I expect you to recant your statement about their marriage."

"The contract was already signed. You agreed before." Torvyn's tone was smug, slick.

"That's bullshit and you know it," my father roared. "I read every line of that contract. If they meet their fated mates, it is void. You announced this farce before their Veilfall, your pathetic power play. You would rob your own daughter of her fated, for your ambition? This ends now. I want that contract dissolved."

"It was signed. We can get lawyers involved."

"Please, do," Lucan spat. "Now get out of my sight. And Torvyn—" his voice dropped low, dangerous, "I'll be watching your every move from now on."

A pause. Then Torvyn, sharp as broken glass: "Is that a threat?"

"Make of it what you will. Now leave."

Sylas and I jumped back as the door swung open. Torvyn's face was a furious shade of red. He stopped short when his eyes landed on us. For a long, charged second, he glared at me, his gaze cutting like a blade. Then, with a curl of his lip, he stormed down the hall.

My stomach knotted. This wasn't over. Not by a long shot.

Chapter 33: Where Time Slows

Vera

"Rina?" My voice comes out softer than I expect. It's been a mostly silent meal, filled with the quiet clink of silverware and the low hum of the fire crackling in the hearth. The scent of roasted root vegetables lingers in the air, but my appetite's been gone all day.

When we got home earlier, we sparred. I welcomed the distraction, the feel of my feet against the grass and the echoes of our hits bouncing off the trees. Afterward, we worked on my magic again. I can feel it right there beneath my skin, like a spark I can't quite catch. It hums under the surface, agitated, restless. Or maybe that's just me.

Anger is easier. Cleaner. It builds a wall between me and everything else. Between the ache and the fear. Between what I lost and what I'm too scared to want again.

"Yeah?" Rina looks up from her plate. Her eyes are steady, gentle, waiting.

I keep pushing my food around with my fork, tracing meaningless patterns through the sauce. "Can we go see my parents tonight? That hall place you talked about?"

"Reverence Hall?"

"Yeah. I think…" I hesitate, swallowing the tightness in my throat. "I think it would really help. Just to… see them. Or talk to them."

Rina's expression softens. "Of course. We'll go as soon as we're done eating. I should've taken you sooner. I can't imagine how hard this must be."

"It's just, there's so much happening." My voice cracks, and I stare down at my plate so I don't have to see the pity in her eyes. "I don't know what to do with all these feelings. I'm angry, and sad, and confused, and I feel like I'm going to burst from the inside out. I wish I could actually talk to them. Ask them what the hell I'm supposed to do."

"I get that." Her voice drops into something quiet, aching. "There were so many times I wished I could talk to my dad. Ask him what he knew. Why he sent us away."

I glance up. "Yeah, I guess you lost both your parents too."

"And a sister." She whispers it, like the words might shatter if she says them any louder. We sit there in the hush, both blinking back tears, then share a wobbly smile.

"Rina, as horrible as all this is, I'm glad I'm not going through it alone."

She reaches across the table, her fingers curling around mine. Her grip is warm and steady, anchoring me. "You're never alone. I'll always be here, okay?"

I nod, wiping at my cheeks with the edge of my sleeve. The tears come and go like waves lately. I stand, clearing my plate. "I'll get ready."

The drive is quiet. The trees blur past the window, silver and black against the dusky sky. The car smells faintly of cedar and the mint tea Rina always keeps in the console. When we pass the Grove's two-miles-away sign, my heart skips a beat. I straighten up, watching the shadows shift between the trees.

What if the hall is part of the palace? What if I see him?

"Is the Reverence Hall attached to the Grove of Stars?" I try for casual, but my voice wavers.

Rina glances over. "No. It's near it, though. Built close to honor the royal family and fallen guards. To keep them protected. Revered. If a guard dies and doesn't have family, the royal family arranges the funeral."

I stare out the window again. "Are there many guards without families?"

"A few. Some give everything to the Order. Most pass of old age now. There are still occasional rogue attacks on the borders." She pauses. "But thankfully no war. Not for quite some time."

"Since the Shattering?"

"Yeah. It was bad. Your dad fought hard. It didn't last long and ended the night you were born. That night, the peace talks finally happened. But the king at the time, he died in that final battle. So King Lucan took over. It was also the night of the Veilfall, which is a special night for all Veyari."

"And that's when my parents disappeared?"

Rina nods as we pass the distant silhouette of the palace, cloaked by towering trees. "Yes. The new king lost his father *and* his Head Guard that night. Everything changed. The Pontivar from Varethos came to preform the ceremonies. She is the one that does the ceremony for the royal coronations, fated mates, and the Head Guard ceremony."

"Is it bad to lose the Head Guard?"

Her fingers tighten slightly on the wheel. "Yes. When someone is chosen to become Head Guard, at the ceremony they drink a special tea. The Pontivar chants a rite in the old Varethos tongue. After that they're bound. The king and the guard. It's not just symbolic. If one dies, the other feels it. It weakens them. Breaks something."

I stare at the road ahead, then murmur, "Do you think it weakens them if they leave?"

She doesn't answer right away. Just lets the silence stretch between us, heavy and thoughtful.

Finally, she says, "I think it depends on why they left. And if they ever meant to come back. But I don't know… I don't think it's ever been done before. Your dad chose *you* over his King and his kingdom," Rina says softly as she pulls into the parking lot.

I can't help the thought that maybe if he hadn't chose me he would still be alive.

The car slows to a stop in front of a sleek, obsidian building with clean lines and silver accents that shimmer beneath the soft glow of enchanted lanterns. It's surprisingly modern, minimalist, even yet regal in its simplicity. The structure rises from the earth like something sacred, quiet, and resolute.

Above the grand entrance, etched in elegant silver script, one word gleams against the dark stone: *Reverence.*

I stare up at it, my throat tight. "Wow, this building is incredible. I never would've guessed it was a place to honor the dead."

"It's beautiful, isn't it?" Rina smiles faintly. "Wait until you see the inside. I'm going to have you go in alone. The guards here know me, and if I bring someone in, they'll ask questions. They won't bother you, though."

I glance at the door, nerves fluttering in my stomach. "How will I know where to go?"

"There usually aren't many visitors this time of night. Just follow your instincts. You'll be fine."

I nod slowly, then inhale a shaky breath and step out of the car. The air is cool and still, filled with the soft scent of pine and something faintly floral, like night-blooming jasmine.

The tall black doors are polished to a mirror finish, their silver handles shaped like entwined branches. I push one open and step inside and stop cold. I expected darkness. Shadows. Silence.

But inside, it's glowing.

To the right there is a small office where a guard sits, keeping an eye on everything. He smiles kindly and gives me a head nod.

Light pours through a massive enchanted skylight above, filtering down in soft golden shafts, as if the sun itself had been caught in glass. The air is warm, not in temperature, but in presence. Sacred. Hushed. Alive.

The interior is designed to feel like a forest, tall, living trees stretch up toward the domed ceiling, their roots woven into marble-tiled floors. Moss and ivy spill gently over stone walkways, and delicate lanterns hang from low branches, flickering like fireflies.

Scattered between the trees are glass caskets, each nestled into its own alcove of greenery and glowing crystal. Each one is unique, some encircled by carved runes, others surrounded by softly blooming flowers or flickering candles. It doesn't feel like a tomb.

It feels like a grove of remembrance. A sanctuary.

My footsteps are silent as I move forward, the air hushed and sacred around me. I feel like I've stepped into another world. One where time slows. One where the veil between life and death is thinner, more tender.

I have no idea where I'm going, but somehow, I know I'll find them.

The path beneath my feet is smooth stone laced with moss, soft beneath each hesitant step. Pale light from the enchanted canopy above dapples the ground, shifting like sunlight through water. I move quietly, reverently, the air thick with the hush of unspoken stories.

Most of the glass caskets I pass are empty, waiting. Silent vessels surrounded by small offerings: a sword leaning against one, a pressed flower tucked into another. One is occupied by an elderly man with deep lines etched into his face, hands folded neatly over his chest. He looks peaceful. But the sight is still so unbearably sad it hollows something in my chest.

I don't know if I can do this. I stop walking, my breath caught somewhere between inhale and sob. And then I see them.

Nestled beneath the arch of two slender silverleaf trees are twin glass caskets, side by side. There's no name etched above them, no grand display. Just the quiet reverence of the space around them, as if the forest itself knew to guard this sacred spot.

I step closer, and my knees buckle. I fall to them hard enough to feel it in my bones. They look exactly as I remember.

My mom's dark brown hair spills across her pillow like silk. Her lips are curved in the faintest smile, so serene it steals the breath from my lungs. My dad lies beside her, his lighter brown hair tousled just as it always was, his expression calm, like he's just dozed off.

Their eyes are closed. Their chests still. It's like I've stumbled into a moment frozen in time. Like they're just napping. A sob rips from my throat before I can stop it.

"I can't believe this," I whisper, my voice cracking, breaking. "Why?"

Just one word but it carries everything: the pain, the betrayal, the aching emptiness of growing up without them. Of never really knowing the truth. I wait.

Of course, I get no answer. Only silence and the soft rustle of leaves high above.

I glance around, desperate for something, *anything*, to explain this. A letter. A clue. A reason. But there's nothing. I turn back to them.

"I could see why you wouldn't tell me when I was little," I say, voice thick and trembling. "But what about when I got older? When I had no friends? When no one would talk to me because I was different? I was alone. Isolated. I didn't understand why." I wipe my face angrily, but the tears keep coming.

"And now I'm in this whole new place… and I have to *keep* isolating myself. Because you were cowards. You could have told me, shared what you have learned." The words spill out, choked and bitter.

I look around one last time. The silence feels heavier now. And when I turn away, it's with lead in my limbs. I wipe my tears and walk back out the way I came.

Rina's waiting for me in the car. She doesn't say a word. Just gives me a soft, understanding smile and puts the car in gear. The ride back is quiet. The forest outside blurs by in silver and shadow. It's late. I still have school tomorrow. Another thrilling day of trying to survive a program I'm not even sure I belong in.

As we pull up to the house, a whisper brushes through me like wind in the trees.

"It's okay to feel. Just don't drown in it." My mom's voice. Not a memory, something deeper. I close my eyes. I know she's still with me. Somehow.

That's what I'll do. I'll wallow tonight. I'll let myself feel the grief and the anger and the ache. But tomorrow? Tomorrow, I'll get back up. I'll find the answers they never gave me. Or die trying.

Well, I think, a small, dry laugh catching in my throat, *that was darker than I meant it to be.*

The soft clink of porcelain meets wood as she sets her cup down in the kitchen. Rina's morning tea. It's earthy and bright, always the same. A kettle hisses quietly. Outside, morning light spills through the curtain in fractured gold, dust motes dancing lazily across the air. Everything feels still. The kind of quiet that settles over grief before the world forces you to move again.

I can do this, I think. My chest aches with doubt, but I whisper it anyway. "I can do this." Maybe if I say it enough, it'll become true. I don't move for a long while, just stare at the ceiling, my breath rising and falling in slow waves.

I swing my legs out of bed and tug on my workout gear, black leggings, a deep green tank, the one that clings just right. It also helps my eyes pop more, which I love. I pull my hair back into a braid, letting the rhythm of the motions settle my nerves.

When I pad into the kitchen, Rina's already moving with her usual calm precision. The warmth of the kettle fills the space, and sunlight filters in through the wide window, painting streaks of honey across the counter. The air smells like bergamot, sage, and a hint of vanilla.

I slump into a chair, stifling a yawn with one hand. She sets a warm mug in front of me, the steam curling up in soft spirals. I cradle it, letting the heat seep into my palms.

"How are you doing today?" she asks gently, her voice like a balm, soft and familiar.

"I'm… okay," I murmur. "I didn't get any answers, but I think it helped. I've just been feeling so lost. Like I'm stuck in this losing battle because there's nothing to fight *with*. No answers, just this endless not knowing."

"It does feel that way, doesn't it?" she says with a small sigh. "Like there are too many questions and no one left to ask. I was thinking about you a lot last night too."

She pauses, then sits across from me, her own mug held in both hands. "Maybe what you need isn't just answers. Maybe it's closure. We could plan their funeral. It might not be the traditional guards' ceremony they deserve, but it could be something. Just for the two of us."

My throat tightens and tears gather in my eyes again, uninvited but familiar now. "I think that would be nice. And if someday, in the future, we do figure everything out, could we give them a proper ceremony? The one they were owed?"

"Yes." She reaches across the table and squeezes my hand. "I think we could do that."

I nod, blinking away the tears. "Okay. Enough sad talk. Today's a new day. I need to focus on guard training, passing the Order, and figuring out this prophecy business."

And definitely not on a certain green-eyed prince who makes my head spin with just a glance.

After our training, I take a long, hot shower, letting the water pour over me like a spell I don't fully believe in. I draw it out on purpose, because I don't want be late to school, and definitely not early. My fingers trail slowly through my hair, through steam. When I get dressed, I keep it simple and armor-like nothing too pretty, nothing that says I want to be noticed.

The walk to school is quiet. A low fog clings to the ground, catching the early sun in silver threads. The birds are louder here, brighter, too. It's almost beautiful enough to make me forget. Almost.

The school day moves like water over stone cool and distant. Cae sits beside me in every class, close enough to share breath, but he never speaks. Not once. I think I give off the kind of energy that says *don't ask* and it seems to work. Even Nero stays quiet in our shared class. The silence suits me. Because I am mad at him too.

Until battlecraft. I enter the Echoforge and freeze.

Caelum is already inside, talking to *her*. Cassia. Her platinum hair gleams under the high lights of the chamber, and she's laughing, full, flirtatious, practiced. She leans toward him like she's made of silk, brushing invisible lint from his shoulder. His posture doesn't shift. But still, something twists in my gut.

I look away and head for the mats, keeping my expression neutral as I start to stretch. My muscles pull tight, tense, jumpy, unsettled. My fake smile is already on when Lyra walks up beside me.

"What's going on?" she asks, laughing gently. "That smile was obviously fake."

I let out a breath. "Just too much. But mostly I'm dreading today. I'll be happy when this part is over."

"You're *nervous*?" she whispers in disbelief. "You're amazing at *everything*. If you're nervous, then I'm officially terrified."

I huff a dry laugh. "It's not the sparring, it's being watched. I don't know how to explain it, but something about that Head Guard creeps me out."

She shudders beside me. "You're telling me. I swear, his eyes follow you, even though we can't see his eyes."

"Yeah I don't get it," I mutter.

Lyra sighs. "I'm okay with the course, but sparring? Ugh. I'm going to fail. I'm going to be kicked out and they'll never even remember my name." I hear the panic creeping into her voice and reach out, giving her arm a reassuring squeeze.

"You're not going to get booted. I'm sure we'll be partnered together. I'll help you. Just breathe. We've got this."

She nods slowly. "Okay. Yeah. You're right." Sure enough, we're paired up.

Cae and Nero are partnered again too, probably not by coincidence. The Head Guard, stiff and silent, watches from the edge of the sparring pit, his arms crossed, eyes shadowed beneath the dark slant of his helmet.

The first match begins. A blur of motion: grunts, sharp exhales, skin against skin, the crack of contact as boots meet bone. The sounds of sparring echo through the chamber, rhythmic and raw. The air smells like sweat, leather, and magic, the iron tang of effort sharpening the tension.

I shift into position, eyes narrowing. Let them watch. I'm not afraid to be seen anymore.

I watch Nero and Cae for a moment. Their sparring doesn't look like practice, it looks real. Brutal. Furious. Every move is sharp, every step purposeful. There's heat in the way they move, too precise to be casual. They're saying something to each other, their mouths moving through clenched jaws, but I can't hear them over the grunts and pounding steps echoing off the Echoforge walls.

Then Nero lands a hit, a solid, sickening blow right to Cae's nose. I swear I hear the crunch of bone. Blood already pouring out.

Cae reels back, stunned for only a breath before he surges forward and slams a fist straight into Nero's face. A sharp gasp escapes my mouth as I spot the blood blooming from Nero's cheek, already starting to swell. Both of them are bleeding now.

And no one is stopping it. Halric and the Head Guard just watch from the sideline, unmoving. Why aren't they stopping it? The whistle blares. Everyone halts. Everyone except them.

"Boys, quit your pissing contest. Don't make me come up there," Halric barks.

Still, they keep going, fists flying, eyes wild. Then finally, Halric and the Head Guard jump into the ring. The guard presses a firm hand against Cae's chest, holding him back. Cae's shoulders rise and fall with deep, ragged breaths, eyes still locked on Nero like he wants another round.

I want to run to them. I want to ask what the veils is going on and if they're okay. But I don't. I root my feet to the floor and hold my ground. This is the new me. I'm not going to get swept up in anyone else's drama, not even his. Not anymore.

My name is called. I draw in a breath and step forward to meet Lyra.

"Just do as I do, and I promise I won't hit hard," I whisper, giving her a reassuring smile. She nods quickly, nerves buzzing off her like static. When the whistle blows, we begin.

She mirrors me well, keeping her balance, moving with cautious focus. There's something about sparring with her that feels easy. Honest. And for a moment, I let myself just be in it. In this space where strength and trust intertwine.

Then she surprises me by landing a clean kick to my thigh that makes me grunt in shock.

Lyra gasps and starts apologizing immediately. "Oh my gods, I'm sorry—"

"Don't apologize!" I laugh. "That was awesome. Keep going!"

We keep at it, and when the whistle blows again, we stop. Lyra's panting, hair sticking to her face, but she's beaming like she just won the crown. I laugh again, genuinely this time. That's when I feel it. A warm, electric zing across my skin. I look up.

Caelum is watching me. And the look on his face, gods. It nearly buckles my knees. There's something tender there, something deep. Something that scares me a little, if I'm honest.

Cassia stands beside him, talking, but he's not even listening. Our gaze breaks as Nero walks up beside him. My breath catches, heart clenching as I brace for another explosion. But instead, they shake hands.

They smile at each other. What was all that about?

Halric claps his hands and draws our attention. "Alright, great job everyone. Except Cae and Nero, I guess." A few chuckles ripple through the crowd.

"We've got one more day of assessments. Tomorrow, we do all three. Then Friday you'll find out who made the cut." He pauses, his tone lightening. "Oh, and an early day on Friday. In celebration of the Veilfall Festival." That gets more of a reaction, some cheers, a few excited murmurs.

"Oh, now you guys show me some kind of reaction," Halric mutters, rolling his eyes as he turns away.

I don't wait around. I jog toward the locker room, eager to change and avoid any run-ins. My pulse is still high, not just from the match, but everything. The fighting. The looks. The way I felt seen for a moment and then pulled back into myself just as quickly.

But as I zip up my bag and sling it over my shoulder, I remind myself of the truth: Today *was* a good day. I kept my focus. I helped a friend. I didn't let the chaos suck me in. And tonight, I'll keep digging into the kingdom. The provinces. The Order. The prophecy. Anything that might lead me to the truth. Because someone has to find it. And maybe, just maybe, it'll be me.

Chapter 34: It's Overwhelming. But it's Not Enough.

Vera

I didn't find much in the textbooks. Still, I've started mapping it all out anyway. A timeline. A trail of smoke and shattered glass.

First, thirty years ago: Elarindor. The name alone carries weight, like it still echoes through the ruins. That's when my mother and my aunt were sent away. My grandfather, the Qaresar of that territory was killed. The palace burned to the ground, and the world was told my mother and her sister died in the fire.

But the fire wasn't about conquest. It wasn't about taking land. If someone burned it down, it meant they weren't trying to claim it. They were trying to erase something. But what?

Rina was only 10 when she was sent away. She remembers flashes, but not much else. And no one ever asks. No one even knows who she is to ask.

Then, eighteen years ago, The Shattering.

The word feels too poetic for something so violent. Something triggered the shifters and vampires to rise against the fae. It was chaos, blood, betrayal. It ended the day I was born. No one will claim who started it. A truce was called, but no one ever explained why the war started to begin with. Nor, why it ended.

Now, the realms stay separate. Fae. Vampires. Shifters. Witches. Their borders are quiet. But brittle.

Those are the last two major historical events and no one knows the real reason behind either. I scribble the last of it down in my notebook and exhale through my nose, frustration knotting in my chest. I would *love* to know what the royal family knows. But talking to the king? Not likely.

And Caelum? Absolutely not. I remind myself I'm not the only one who wants answers. Maybe that's comforting. Maybe not.

Today is much the same as yesterday. I leave late. Keep my head down. Walk alone. Anything to avoid unnecessary run-ins or aching reminders.

When I get to school, the bell hasn't rung yet. The courtyard hums with soft laughter and the scrape of boots over stone. Caelum stands with his usual circle of friends, looking infuriatingly effortless. That untouchable kind of royal charm. Now that I know he's the Prince, it's so obvious now. He looks up and his eyes lock on mine, I try to quickly look away so he didn't catch me staring. Then Cassia screeches and I instinctively look up to see the commotion. It's weird I know her scream after only being here a week.

My stomach drops as she throws herself into his arms. Her platinum hair gleams under the morning sun like a blade, and she clings to him like she belongs there. Caelum steps back slightly, enough to keep her on her feet, but his arms are still around her.

I turn away quickly. *Good.* Let him be with his future wife. Let them play their parts. At least now he's done pretending. But the sharpness in my chest betrays me. The truth is, it hurts. Like lightning cracking through my ribs. I tried to keep my heart out of it. I knew better. I *knew.*

I feel his eyes on me. But I don't flinch. I pretend not to notice.

Because it isn't my business anymore.

I move down the hall, keeping my head low as students rush past in clusters of laughter and excitement. The halls have been transformed for the upcoming Veilfall Festival, silver script glimmers across the stone archways spelling *Veilfall*, and enchanted leaves drift through the air in slow, spiraling patterns. Garlands of russet, gold, and copper wrap around the pillars, and tiny flickering lanterns hover near the ceiling, casting everything in a warm, golden glow.

It should feel magical. It doesn't. I'm too wrapped up in my thoughts, in how Cae looked at me, in the weight of secrets pressing down on my shoulders. The decorations blur at the edges of my vision, just more things I can't connect with right now.

I reach my locker, grab my things, and head toward class. Just before I reach my desk, Mr. Valeis brushes past me. I barely register his presence until suddenly, his hand closes around my wrist. My whole body stiffens. His silver eyes fade into white. My heart lurches.

"Veralyn," he whispers. His voice is distant, carried on something older. Deeper. "You cannot do it alone." I yank my wrist back like it's burned. That name. Only Rina calls me that.

His eyes blink back to grey. He stares at me, steady and relaxed, as if assessing not just me but everything I've seen, everything I *am*. I glance around. No one is watching us. Not closely, at least.

"I'm not trying to scare you," he says gently, voice low. "Sometimes I have visions. Please stay after class. I'll explain. You're safe here, I promise."

I open my intuition, let the fae magic rush in like a tide and feel the truth in his words. Try to remember what Rina has been teaching me with my gifts. Golden threads spiral around him. Warm. Honest. Steady. He means no harm. I give a slow nod, then slip into my seat just as Caelum enters the room.

Again, I feel his gaze like a brand on my skin. Again, I try to ignore it. Mr. Valeis begins the lecture, returning to the topic of Elarindor. But it's nothing new, everything he says I've already read. Already written down. I've scoured every page looking for more. Something is missing. Something someone buried.

Tomorrow, we begin a new unit. Duskmere. Maybe that's where the answers are. If nothing else it will be interesting learning more about where my father came from.

When he's done, I wait at my desk as everyone else packs up their things. Cae is slow—too slow. I know he's lingering, but I don't look at him. I keep my eyes on Mr. Valeis, watching him as the last students trickle out. I expect him to dismiss Caelum, but he doesn't.

Instead, he shuts the door. Then he looks at me.

"I'm sorry about earlier, Vera. I know you don't know much about our kind." My gaze snaps to Cae, confused and suddenly wary. Why is he saying this in front of someone else? How does he know anything at all?

"I think *Prince* Caelum should leave. I would like some privacy." I say to Mr. Valeis without looking at Cae.

There's a growl behind me. "I'm staying, Vera. I won't let you get rid of me." I turn to glare at him and he just smiles like he's the happiest person ever.

"I'm from Varethos," Mr. Valeis continues, ignoring us. "We all have the ability to see things but mine is a little different. I can sometimes glimpse into the future. And I also have the gift of communing with the dead."

My breath catches, but he doesn't stop. I guess what Nero told me was mostly true.

"I've already seen different outcomes, splintering paths. But I can't say too much, or it might ruin everything. What I *can* tell you is this: you cannot do this alone. You have to find the others." My shoulders stiffen.

"She's not alone," Cae says from behind me. "She has me."

I don't turn around. "No, I'm not," I say and then correct myself, voice flat. "No. I *don't*." Mr. Valeis smirks, not unkindly, just that he finds us amusing.

"All I'm saying is: use your gifts. And ask for help." I start gathering my things, jaw tight.

"I don't know what you're talking about. I'm just here for the Veilbound Order." I clutch my books and walk out.

My whole body is trembling. I understand that the people of Varethos can see things. That some of them, like Valeis, are born with gifts tied to visions and death. But what does he know? He said my real name. The name I never even *heard* until Rina found me. That knowledge, it rattles something in me. Deep.

I stumble to my next class in a daze. Nero's already seated beside me, and a minute later, Cae takes the other empty seat at my side. I don't look at either of them. I face the front, pointedly ignoring the tense glances they keep exchanging.

I don't hear a word the teacher says. I couldn't tell you what this lesson is even about. My mind is spinning.

What do I do? Walk away? Leave school, leave it all behind and focus only on the prophecy, the killer, finding the other two girls and the danger? Or stay? Stay in this school, surrounded by people I don't trust. Because maybe, just maybe, this is where the answers are.

But how? Maybe Mr. Valeis is right. Maybe I *do* need help. That's a terrifying thought. Asking for help when I don't even know who wants me dead. I don't know who I can trust. Or worse, who might be trying to take down the entire kingdom. A kingdom I barely understand.

Or maybe I just let it happen. Try to enjoy whatever time I have left and stop trying to solve something I was never meant to fix. There I go. Being all morbid again. I promised myself I'd stop doing that. I inhale slowly. Hold it. Release it. Square my shoulders. Whatever happens, I will figure it out.

I feel Cae and Nero glancing at each other again. Since when are *they* all buddy-buddy? They were just fighting again yesterday.

At lunch, I try to hide again. But this time, they find me. Both of them. They don't say anything to me at first, just talk to each other about mundane things. Classes. Battlecraft assessments. Techniques.

They don't ask me questions. Don't press. They just talk to each other. I glance at them, irritated. What's their goal? Forced proximity until I cave? I open my intuition and feel it, their intentions. Warmth. Good. Pure. Ugh.

So Nero wants me to trust them, but he won't even tell Cae about the connection he felt with the Head Guard. I *could* out him. Right now if I wanted to. But no. I promised I wouldn't say anything. I look up and meet Nero's gaze. I glare. He smirks.

Infuriating. I go back to ignoring them and sink into my thoughts. Again. I probably *do* need to trust someone. But Caelum? That's complicated. Still, the king must know something. About the Shattering. Why it started. They could have something to do with the fall of Elarindor, I mean was it even properly investigated or swept under the rug. Why it ended on the day I was born. But if I start asking questions, they'll ask their own. Questions I'm not ready to answer. Ones I don't even have the answers for. I could try to talk to them see what they know and not tell them everything, this way if they prove to be untrustworthy they won't know the whole truth.

Battlecraft is buzzing when I arrive. The energy in the room is electric. Everyone's excited, today is the final day of assessments. Truth be told, I'm relieved. I hate being watched by the Head Guard, even though part of me wishes he'd stay longer. Then maybe then Nero could figure out how he *knows* him.

We run through all the sections today, strength, speed, defense, endurance. The works. Again, I help Lyra during sparring. It feels familiar now. Almost comfortable. But underneath it all, I'm waiting.

For something to break open. For someone to finally say the thing we're all skirting around. For the truth to finally catch up with me. I ignore the way Cassia keeps trying to get close to Caelum, she makes sure I am watching every time. Like she won. I also hate how much I was even looking at him. Every time I looked away. I was also ignoring the way Ryven kept glaring at me, I never looked his way but I could feel his eyes on me. Nero stuck close when he could but still he didn't talk to me. Just a silent force and it was comforting. Like a big brother keeping me safe, even though I am still annoyed with him.

"Alright, great job everyone," Halric announces. "As I said, we'll post the final list tomorrow. Before you leave school, check the doors of the Echoforge." He and the Head Guard exit without fanfare.

I grab my water bottle and start walking with Lyra, but a hand closes around my bicep. I don't need to look to know who it is, the zing of electricity shooting through me tells me everything.

"Li—Vera, can I talk to you?"

"Go ahead, Lyra. I'll see you tomorrow," I say, managing a smile when she looks between Caelum and me, her brow furrowed. Everyone else files out. Cassia shoots a glare in our direction. Of course. Nero's still nearby, hovering.

"What do you want, Prince Caelum?" I ask, lacing my voice with every ounce of attitude I can summon.

"No need for the attitude," he says with a cocky grin. "I just wanted to talk about the cuts. For the Order." My stomach drops. Am I not making it?

"Not you, love. Your body is honed to perfection." His eyes sweep down my body and back to my eyes.

"You sick bastard. You're engaged to someone else. What do you want?"

"There's not a ring on your finger, so no. I'm not engaged. Yet." I scoff, sharp and dry, but he goes on. "I've noticed you've grown close to Lyra. She's improved, but I don't think she'll make the cut. Her times aren't there yet. It's only going to get harder from here."

"She has improved," I snap.

"I know. But it might not be enough."

"What if I train her? Put in extra time?"

He sighs. "I know you want to help. But you're already stretched thin just trying to figure out what's happening with you."

"You don't know anything," I say, jaw tight.

He scrubs a hand over his face. "I would be willing to put in a good word for her."

"Why would you do that?"

"I'm hoping I can convince you to go on a date with me." He says with a sly smile. I really want to punch his pretty face.

"You're kidding. So you're trying to extort me, for what reason? I know you're not desperate for female attention. Especially since you are *betrothed.* You know since she is all over you all the time. This is to help someone else, to help people that didn't have the opportunities you had." Damn, I sound jealous. I need to stop bringing her up.

He sighs, resigned. "I am not *betrothed.*" He imitates me. "I just want you. I am not going anywhere. I am getting rid of Cassia and her family and my father is helping me. Just talk to Lyra. If she agrees to more training, I'll recommend she be considered." He holds out his phone. "Here. Put your number in and text me once you talk to her." I don't take it. I glare.

"You're manipulating me. This is just a game to you. Maybe it's easy to play with other people's lives when you've always had yours handed to you. But the rest of us? We have to earn everything." My voice rises with each word, each truth that's clawed its way up from my chest. "You lied. Both of you. You kept something from me that I had every right to know. I was starting to trust you. And now? I don't think I ever can. Not just because of what you hid, but because you didn't even consider how it would hurt me. There's no happy ending here. Stop trying. Just put Lyra through. I'll handle the rest. And leave me alone. I don't need your help."

I turn to leave, but he grabs my arm again, gentle, but firmly and pushes me back against the wall. I feel every inch of him. The heat between us is unbearable. I hate the way my body responds, even now.

"Lilac" His voice is low, and gods help me, tender. "I'm sorry I didn't tell you. I should have. I can't change that. But I mean it when I say, whatever this is, whatever's coming, we're in it together. You heard Thorian this morning." He glances over his shoulder toward Nero. "Maybe you're not the only one with things to figure out. Maybe I need your help too. Maybe my future Head Guard does." So Nero must have told him something. His face inches closer. His breath is warm against my cheek. "Stop pushing me away. This is happening. Whether you want to admit it or not, we're already in this together."

"How can you trust me? You don't even know me."

"I do know you," he says. "Not everything. Not yet. But I know you're light. Truth. Warmth. You brought meaning into my life. You can trust me. Open your truthsense. Feel me. I would do anything for you. Protect you, even from my own kingdom. You come first." He leans forward placing a soft kiss against my lips and I have to fight myself to not melt into him. Into the kiss.

And I *feel* it. All of it. His truth. His conviction. It's overwhelming. But it's not enough.

"Let me go." My voice is softer now. Wounded. Determined. "You don't get your way just because your words feel good. You say you'd protect me but when it counted, you hid the truth. That's not trust. That's betrayal. You don't get to keep kissing me to try and prove something. I'm more than just something you can possess."

I shove him away and walk out, my heart pounding, my truthsense aching, and my mind screaming with things I wish weren't true.

Chapter 35: I've Been Doing This Since I Could Walk

Vera

Ugh. The nerve of that guy.

I manage to catch up to Lyra, weaving through the thinning crowd outside the Echoforge.

"Lyra!" I call. She stops and glances back with a smile that's genuine and curious, too.

"Hey, Vera. Is everything okay?" she asks gently. I can tell she's wondering what just happened with Caelum, but that's a mess I'm not unpacking right now. Even if I can't get the thought of his lips on mine out of my mind.

"Yeah, I'm fine," I say, brushing it off. "I just—" I hesitate for a beat. "I was wondering how much you actually want to join the Veilbound Order?"

Her smile fades a little. "Of course I want to. Why?" There's a flicker of worry in her eyes, and I instantly regret putting it there.

"It's just…" I exhale. "You might not make the cut. But I talked to Caelum and told him that if I trained with you, maybe he could push for you to get through. Only if you want to, of course." I rush the words, hoping I don't sound like I'm doing her a favor she didn't ask for. "I could work with you every day after school, maybe longer if you're open to it." She looks down, chewing on the inside of her cheek as she thinks. The silence stretches, just long enough for me to wonder if I've made her feel worse.

Then she looks up and nods. "I would love that," she says quietly. "I never really trained much. But I do want this. I want to prove to myself and to my parents that I can do something hard."

"Okay, you got it," I say, offering a smile. "We can start today, if you're up for it."

"Yes, please." Her answer is quick, maybe a little too quick. "My parents won't even notice I'm not home." That stings to hear. I glance at her, surprised, but she just shrugs like it's nothing, and we start walking back toward the Echoforge.

Nero and Caelum are leaving just as we approach, deep in conversation and too distracted to notice us slipping past. Good.

Inside, the training hall is quiet now, empty of the earlier crowd. Just the faint scent of chalk, steel, and worn leather lingering in the air. The silence reminds me too much of earlier, Caelum's hands, his voice, the way he looked at me but nope. Not going there.

"Okay," I say, shaking it off. "What's your time for running?"

Lyra winces. "Umm, not good. I'm in the last tier group. So, not very fast."

"That's okay. What about the Gauntlet of Ascension?"

"I can do it in just under ten minutes." She says quietly looking away from me.

"That's a solid start. You're already getting better with sparring, too. Let's focus on the Gauntlet today. Tomorrow, we'll work on speed." She nods eagerly.

I lead her to the starting point and point to a foothold on the climbing wall. "So when I run up, I plant my left foot in this hold, then reach up with my right hand here." I slap the top grip. "That gives me enough leverage to pull up onto the first platform."

I back up a few steps, take a breath, and launch forward. It takes me barely a second to scale the wall and land smoothly on the platform. Muscle memory. Lyra steps up next. She takes a moment, mimicking the moves, then climbs, less smooth, but steady. When she reaches the top, she's grinning.

"Wow. That was easier than I thought," she says, laughing.

I laugh with her. "Told you."

"Okay, ready for the next part?" I ask.

"Yes!" she says, eyes bright.

When we get to the monkey bars she starts to slip just like I did. I know those bars and it's hard with them vibrating and moving.

"Focus forward. Don't flight it, flow with it." I tell her what Nero told me that first time.

We work through each segment slowly, step by step. I show her every handhold, every pivot, every spot to push off. She listens carefully, nodding along, absorbing it all.

When we finish, we walk back to the starting line.

"Alright," I say, brushing my hands off. "Now I'll do the whole course. Watch where my hands and feet go."

I run it slower this time, exaggerating the movements so she can follow. It takes me almost 8 minutes. When I circle back to her, she's grinning.

"Okay, I *know* you went slow for me," she says, "but seriously, you make it look effortless."

I chuckle. "That's because I've been doing this since I could walk." She laughs, then takes a breath and steps up.

"Your turn," I say. "Don't worry about speed right now. Just focus on where you're placing your hands and feet." She nods, determination setting in, and launches forward. She takes her time, but there's something satisfying about watching her move through the course, more confident with each section. She's got potential. She just needs someone to believe in her. Today, that someone is me.

"She's right. You make it look effortless." I jump slightly and whip around. Caelum stands beside me, hands tucked in his pockets like he's been there the whole time. I didn't even sense him, too focused on Lyra.

"I thought you left," I say, a little too sharply.

He shrugs, stepping closer. "Not yet. But this reminds me, you still owe me that rain check." He draws the words out like he's tasting them. I try to hold back the laugh, but it slips out anyway, light and unguarded.

"There it is," he says softly, his gaze locked on me. "That beautiful smile." He winks, and I hate how easily it gets to me.

"Do you think we could use the Echoforge again tomorrow?" I ask, changing the subject. "For more training."

"Yeah," he says. "We can spend time in here after our last class."

"I meant, for Lyra. She's improving, and I think it might help to keep working with her."

His brows lift slightly. "Of course. But *we* should still train too. We can always sharpen our skills. Plus, if she watches us spar, she'll pick up techniques faster."

I glance toward Lyra. She's struggling with the rope section again, arms shaking, determination written all over her face. We're definitely going to have to work on upper body strength.

He nudges my arm. "I could help with her on the running track too, if you want."

I raise a brow, half-teasing. "Maybe I'll ask Nero. I could use someone who actually challenges me." His jaw drops in mock offense, but I can see the glint of amusement in his eyes. He leans in, grabbing my hand, lowering his voice to a husky whisper by my ear.

"Should I play hard to get? Might be the kind of challenge you're looking for." A shiver shoots down my spine. My cheeks heat. I grit my teeth.

"Not necessary."

He grins, clearly pleased with himself. "Just one session tomorrow. Let's try it. If it doesn't work, I'll back off."

"Fine. But I won't owe you anything after that."

Lyra walks over, catching sight of Caelum beside me and hesitating for just a second.

"That was great!" I say, offering her a big smile. Her entire face lights up, and something tightens in my chest. Has no one ever told her that before? Caelum gives my hand a light squeeze.

"Now it's just practice," I tell Lyra, squeezing her shoulder. "Keep at it until it feels second nature."

"Thank you, Vera! Seriously. This already feels different. Better." She bounces a little on her toes, excited and flushed. I remind myself to always make space for this: encouragement, joy, belief.

"Want to go again or take a break till tomorrow?" I ask.

"One more time!" she says with a determined grin before jogging back to the course.

As she gets started, I glance sideways. Caelum is still watching me. Softly, intently, like I'm a puzzle he doesn't want to solve too fast. Only then do I realize our hands are still entwined. I pull mine back. The loss is immediate and stupidly sharp.

"I think I could learn a few things from you," he says, his voice quieter now.

I smirk. "Yeah. Probably."

He laughs. Then leans in again, his tone dipping low, dangerously close to my lips. "And there are a few things I could teach you." For half a second, I forget where I am. Forget Lyra. Forget everything but the way his mouth moves and how badly I want to close the space between us.

"I love the way this training gear molds to your perfect body." He whispers into my ear and I shiver.

Then I remember. I snap my shoulders back and step away.

"You need to stop. You're basically engaged. Do you even care what that makes me look like? I won't be that girl. I won't be someone's *other*."

His smile stays, but there's something else behind it now, something unreadable. "I can't cheat on my fiancée," he says. "If I don't have one." He grabs my left hand and pulls it up to his mouth kissing my fingers, lingering over my ring finger. I stare at him. My pulse is too loud in my ears. That doesn't exactly make me feel better.

"Seriously. Just stop. I'm here for Lyra."

He raises his hands in surrender. "Alright. I'll go." Then, softer: "See you tomorrow… Brightstep." He winks.

He says it like a promise, and it hits somewhere deep. I wait until he's gone before I let myself breathe again, before I let my shoulders fall and admit how much I hate the effect he has on me. He's not going to give up that much is clear.

Lyra walks back over, cheeks flushed, hair damp with sweat, but a grin stretched across her face. I meet it with one of my own, genuine pride swelling in my chest but also a silent prayer that it drowns out whatever Caelum stirred up in me.

"That was great," I say. "How did it feel that time?" She eyes me, not answering right away. Her brow creases like she sees straight through me.

"It was good," she finally says, catching her breath. "I think I'm starting to figure out where to place my hands and feet. But strength is definitely a problem, it's hard to pull myself up on the rope."

"Yeah," I nod. "Maybe we start mixing in some weight training. Rotate different focuses each day, build strength, endurance, coordination. We'll build everything up over time."

Lyra brightens at that, nodding enthusiastically. "Yeah. I'm down. I already feel better, like maybe I *can* actually do this."

"Just let me know how you feel tomorrow," I say with a small laugh. "It might hurt more before it gets better."

She laughs with me. "Totally fair."

We walk in companionable silence back through the Echoforge and into the locker room. The warmth of the forge fades the second we cross the threshold, but Lyra's smile doesn't. We change in silence, and as we head out, I glance sideways. Her eyes are still glowing with pride, and it stirs something in me, something quiet and steady. I'm doing something that matters.

"You know if you ever want to talk about other things I'd be happy to listen." She says quietly.

"Thank you, Lyra. I might just take you up on that. I could use help navigating these stupid boys." We both laugh.

We part ways with a simple goodbye, and I take the path home alone. The air is crisp, the trees whispering softly overhead. The walk gives me room to breathe, room to refocus. Duskmere might be the key. Elarindor's texts are too vague, too steeped in revisionist history. Varethos doesn't offer much of anything. The library is the next step. I still don't have my own card, but maybe Rina has one. I could ask her to come with me this weekend.

Then I freeze. The note. The one I found in the library, in the hidden compartment. I stuffed it away in my pocket. I *need* to find that. Start looking for the connections, there has to be something that leads us to what is happening. I start making a mental checklist of what I need to do next.

Get to the library again.

Look into more information about Duskmere.

Definitely more about Varethos.

Mr. Valeis's vision still lingers in my mind. How he knew my real name. Rina mentioned the original prophet came from Varethos. What if she's still there? I won't know until after the Order finishes. Four more weeks. Four weeks that suddenly feels like a lifetime.

I start walking again, thoughts tangling and looping.

Then the air shifts. Colder. Still. A prickle of unease crawls up my spine. I stop mid-step and turn, scanning the woods behind me. Nothing moves. Nothing breathes. But I feel it. Eyes. Watching.

The trees loom darker now. Closer. I quicken my pace, boots hitting the dirt harder than before. The wind picks up as if urging me forward. The sense of wrongness won't leave.

By the time Rina's cottage comes into view, I'm sprinting.

It's dark, too dark. No glow in the windows, no flicker of the usual candlelight. The feeling intensifies. I stretch my senses, reaching for my intuition but it returns blank. *Empty.*

My hand reaches for the door just as headlights swing into the drive behind me. Rina. She steps out of the car, smiling brightly, oblivious to the storm still churning in my chest. I try to smile back, grounding myself in her presence.

Maybe I imagined it. Maybe I've been too wrapped up in the prophecy, in Duskmere, in Caelum and whatever *that* is.

Still, as we head inside, I can't shake the feeling that something was there, just beyond the trees. Watching. Waiting.

When we step inside, Rina immediately locks the door behind us. The quiet *click* of the bolt echoes louder than it should in the stillness.

"Did you feel that too?" I ask, my voice hushed, eyes fixed on the lock she just turned.

"Feel what?" she says, glancing over her shoulder as she shrugs off her jacket and hangs it on the hook above the closet door. Her movements are calm, but her gaze sharpens when she sees my face.

"The feeling of being watched. I felt it the whole way home. Like eyes were just… *there.*" A shiver trails down my spine at the memory.

She crosses to the window and peers out through the curtain, eyes sweeping the darkened trail behind the cottage. "No," she says slowly. "I didn't feel anything." But there's a flicker of worry in her tone now, and it makes guilt settle like a stone in my chest.

"I'm sure it's nothing," I say quickly, forcing a lightness I don't feel. "I was just overthinking, thinking about the prophecy and where else we can look for answers. It got to me."

She nods but doesn't look convinced. Still, she lets it go, and I follow her into the warm glow of the kitchen. The kettle hums as she sets it to boil, and the scent of herbs and pinewood from the fire wraps around us like a blanket.

"How come you're getting home so late?" she asks, glancing over as she gathers mugs.

"Oh, there's a girl in my battlecraft class. Lyra. I've been helping her with sparring, and today I offered to do extra training with her. She's not the strongest, but she really wants to pass the Order. She mentioned her parents, and it just sounds like they don't give her much attention."

Rina's face softens. "That's really different from your mom, huh?" she says, her voice quiet with memory. "I remember even when we were kids, she was just a couple years older than me, but she always cheered me on. Always believed in me."

I smile, heart aching a little. "Yeah. She was always watching, training with me and Dad, helping with school. She made me feel like I could do anything. I guess I never realized how rare that was."

"I bet it means the world to Lyra that you're helping her. And if she wants, she can train with us in the afternoons too."

"You'd really be okay with that?" I ask, surprised. "I just—I struggle with letting people in. Trust is hard for me. There've been others who tried talking to me, getting close, but I keep brushing them off. Or I try to."

She turns toward me, her eyes filled with compassion. "Oh, Sweet Girl. I know. It can't be easy. But I don't think whoever's after you is a student. You don't have to explain your secrets to everyone, but it's okay to have friends. You *deserve* friends." My throat tightens. I want to believe her.

"Who knows," she continues, "maybe one day you'll be able to *really* trust someone. I just hate the idea of you going through all of this alone. You shouldn't have to carry something so heavy *and* be isolated."

"Rina, how come you never found your fated? Like mom and dad?"

Her eyes turn regretful. "Because I guess mostly I was scared. Your mom was already gone before my Veilfall. I never went I stayed home by myself. Of course I got all my gifts, but I missed out on meeting my fated and I haven't come across them. If they're even out there. After you all left, I was worried. I didn't know who I could trust and instead of being brave I hid away. Never living my life."

"You know what I keep thinking, though?" My voice is barely above a whisper now.

"What's that?"

"What's the point of making friendships or getting close to someone if I'm just going to die? All I'd be doing is hurting them too." My head drops. The silence stretches, thick and raw.

She gasps softly, and when I look up, her face is stricken. "Don't say that," she breathes. "I *hate* that you feel that way. Don't think like that. I don't want you to turn out like me, hiding away."

Her voice trembles now. "I know this isn't easy. I'm struggling too. But you *have* a life to live. You've spent your whole childhood training, hiding. Now you're finally with people like you, in a place where you belong. This is your time to live, to *feel*. To laugh. To fall. To make memories that *matter*."

Tears sting my eyes and spill over before I can stop them. Her words crack something open in me.

"There's a teacher at the Academy," I whisper. "Mr. Valeis. He's from Varethos. He had a vision yesterday, he knew my real name. Said I can't do this alone." I shudder at the memory. "It really creeped me out."

She lets out a soft laugh, wiping my tears with the sleeve of her sweater. "Yeah, I've seen a vision before. It's definitely unnerving. But he's right. You can't do it alone. And I'm here. Always."

She takes a deep breath. "But like you, I've been hiding. I go to work, I come back. I don't let people in, not really. I've been terrified someone will find out who I am, who *you* are. But the truth is, whoever's after you probably already knows. We just don't know what they're waiting for."

I nod slowly. "There's a guy at school, another student. He says he's from Duskmere, he's going for Head Guard. He's kind. Says he wants to help me. I don't sense anything bad from him, and you know I always feel the truth. But I'm scared. Scared to trust the wrong person."

"Ooh, a *boy*," she teases, her smile teasing but gentle. "If he's really from Duskmere and letting you sense his truth? Then yeah, I'd say trust him. People from Duskmere are trained to hide their auras, if he's not doing that, that says something."

"Yeah. Just friends," I reply, though even I hear the hesitation in my voice.

Her brows rise slightly. "Is there anyone else?"

I look away. "There's another boy, he's been flirting with me, but I've been shutting it down. He's popular and I've been trying to stay under the radar. I don't want to be just another girl, I also found out he could be engaged to someone else. And honestly, if I only have a year left, I don't want to get involved with anyone. It would just hurt everyone."

"There you go, thinking like that again," she says, her voice choked with tears. She wipes her cheeks roughly and shakes her head. "You have to *live*, Veralyn. This prophecy doesn't define you. Right now, you're in school. You're surrounded by people your age. Enjoy it. Don't let fear steal what little time you have, whether that's a year or a century."

Her voice drops to a whisper. "Your mom was just like that. Always putting everyone else first. She kept pushing your father away, even after she knew he was her fated. She didn't want to let anyone in. But when she finally did, she got to live a beautiful life. A real one. With love and laughter and *you*. I think we could both learn from your mom."

Tears are rolling down my face now, hot and unchecked. I let them fall. I let myself feel every word.

"I just don't want you to miss out," she finishes softly. "Not because of 'what ifs.' Not because of fear. That doesn't mean that he's the right one for you, especially if he's engaged to someone else. Which seems odd if they are students, since you haven't had your Veilfall, yet." Again I wonder what that has to do with anything but my mind is reeling to much to focus on that tidbit.

And in that moment, wrapped in candlelight and memory and the scent of steeping tea, I feel something I haven't in a long time. Hope. Fragile, flickering but still burning. I don't know what the future holds but I know I will have Rina.

Chapter 35: I've Been Doing This Since I Could Walk

Chapter 36: Light, Warmth, Curiosity.

Vera

"Vera," Nero calls as I step onto the winding path that cuts through the misty woods toward school. "I'm surprised to see you. Thought you'd make me walk alone again."

His tone is teasing, but I catch the flicker of something else. Relief, maybe? I shift my bag higher on my shoulder and fall into step beside him.

"Yeah, I'm sorry I've been pushing you away." The damp leaves crinkle beneath our boots as we walk. "It's just—" I pause, searching for the right words. "I'm scared to trust. But I think, I think I can trust you. I appreciate you sharing your stuff with me."

I glance up at him. His warm brown eyes hold steady as the morning light filters through the trees.

"You *can* trust me," he says, voice low and certain. "You can trust Caelum, too. It's obvious something's got you worried, and you're hiding."

My chest tightens. "How do you even know that? And why do you care so much?"

"I told you," he says, nudging a branch out of our path. "I have a feeling we're going to be great friends. Like Caelum, I can see auras. We know you're hiding yours, veiling it. That's not easy to do, by the way. Also, based on your questions, it's clear you're not from around here. Not just Sylvaeris, I mean any fae land."

The air chills around me. How many others know? How many can see what I'm trying so hard to bury?

"I'm not judging," he adds, like he can feel my panic rising. "I just think you need help. And I want to help. Just like I know you'll help me figure out who the Head Guard is. And why I feel like I've known him my whole life."

"Speaking of…" I leap at the chance to deflect. "Did you talk to your mom about it?"

He shakes his head. "No. I didn't want to worry her. I want to figure it out myself. But, I did ask Caelum." He casts a glance at me as he says it, testing my reaction.

I groan. "What did he say?"

"Just that he only knows his nickname; Ro. Says he doesn't know much else, even though the guy's always been around. But something's off. Caelum said that over the last week, he's been acting different. He's looking into it."

"Can he find anything out? Can we get information on the familial bond?"

"He's trying. Things are complicated at home," Nero says carefully. "But I know about the bond. It only activates when you're near immediate family. Parents, siblings, grandparents, aunts, uncles, cousins."

My breath catches. That explains the feeling I got when Rina arrived. I wonder what things are complicated for Cae.

"What does it feel like?" I ask, already bracing for how obvious the question makes me.

He tilts his head, thinking. "It's like… like you've met them before,

even if you haven't. It's warmth. Familiarity. You feel safe. Cared for."
That's exactly how I felt around Rina. Like I could finally exhale.

We fall into a long silence. The kind that feels comfortable but full of thoughts. The trees begin to thin, and the stone towers of the Academy peek above the canopy ahead. I catch a glimpse of the curved walkway beyond the trees, the edges of the parking lot still hidden in the morning haze.

"So…" I say slowly, "Caelum's seen the current Head Guard without the mask?"

"Yeah," Nero nods. "But seeing someone's face doesn't mean you know them."

I squint up at him. "Still, couldn't we look at who went to school with the king? I'm sure they keep records. Maybe even lists of who made it into the Veilbound Order. Wouldn't it be someone who was here at the same time as the king?"

He stops in his tracks just before the sidewalk, eyes wide.

"Why didn't I think of that?" he breathes. "Vera, I could kiss you right now."

He beams at me, and for the first time since meeting him, he's completely unguarded. Lighthearted. Alive. I laugh, caught off guard by his sudden joy.

"Only *I* will be kissing Vera."

My entire body freezes at the voice behind me. That smooth, familiar, maddening voice. I don't even need to turn to know it's Caelum. But I do, slowly and sure enough, he stands there, as irritatingly perfect as ever. His light hair tousled just enough to look effortless, his jacket slung casually over his shoulder.

How does he keep sneaking up on me like that? Why can't I ever sense him? And worse, why do I still get that rush of heat at the idea of him kissing me?

"She's brilliant," Nero says, unfazed. "We need to get the school records from when your dad was here. If we can match names to the current Head Guard, we'll have something."

Caelum's gaze finds mine, intense as ever. I feel the pull again, like his soul is trying to reach mine. He clenches his fists, like it's taking everything in him not to touch me.

"My brilliant girl," he says softly. My chest tightens.

"I'll ask Senara for the archives. We'll go over them at lunch. Meet in the library."

I nod, but it's automatic. Because I won't be there. I can't keep putting myself in his orbit. But if helping Nero means I have to deal with Caelum too, maybe I can manage it. Just long enough to help a friend. Maybe that's the key, keep it about helping Nero. Not about what Caelum makes me feel.

Maybe I can even ask him to keep Caelum away. But no, he wouldn't do that. Not if they're destined to work together. Their bond is already forming, and I can't wedge myself between that. I wonder why he seems to be working closely with Nero and not with Ryven. I don't know enough about it. And it's just one more thing I'll never get to ask my dad.

"Let's go," Caelum says, nodding to the building ahead. "I'm heading to the office. I'll meet you in class, Vera."

I roll my eyes and stomp toward my locker, hoping it hides the way my heart is pounding. He's so pretentious. So sure he'll get his way. Probably because he always does.

When I get to my locker, I grab what I need for the next few classes, already praying I can get through the rest of the day without another emotional ambush. No such luck.

A shadow falls across me. I sigh, slam the locker shut, and turn to face Cassia in all her icy glory. Yet another reminder of why staying away from Caelum might be in my best interest.

She crosses her arms like she's posing for a statue of 'Royal Entitlement.' "I don't know what you think you're doing, but you need to stay away from him. There's a signed contract, he's going to be with *me*." She says it like it's law, like the universe owes her a throne and a crown. She leans in. "Keep pushing, and I'll make sure you don't pass the Order. No job, no future, no home. You'll be crawling back to whatever moss-covered rock you dragged yourself out from."

I blink, smile sweetly, and say, "Based on the wrinkles around your eyes, I'd guess you're at least eighty-seven, so I'll say it louder in case you're hard of hearing." I raise my voice a notch. I barely withhold my laugh when her hand reaches up to touch next to her eye. "I. Told. *Him.* To stay away. Caelum doesn't listen. You should know, you two have that in common. I say something, he ignores it. You say something, he ignores *you*. Take it up with *him* if you've got issues with his social life."

People are turning now. Cassia's mouth tightens like she just bit into a lemon.

"I know you've been spending extra time in the Echoforge after Battlecraft," she hisses. "Getting cozy. *Very* cozy. Someone saw you. So don't even bother denying it. When we're married, your little fantasy ends. You'll just be another one of his whor—"

My face flames. The noise in the hallway grows louder. People are definitely gathering. Of course she'd announce something personal just loud enough to cause a scene.

But before I can respond, a voice cuts in behind me.

"You need to back away," Nero says menacingly quiet, stepping between us like this is all part of his Tuesday routine. Cassia spins on him with a scowl.

"You're a nobody, just like her," she spits. "You both need to disappear, from this school and from this kingdom. I know people. I can make it happen."

Nero snorts. Actually snorts. "Yeah, good luck with that. As Caelum's future guard, you won't get a say in anything. You don't scare me. Your daddy doesn't scare me either."

He slides his arm around my shoulders like some kind of fae bodyguard prince (I guess he will be a bodyguard to a prince) and steers me away as Cassia glares daggers. I'm too stunned to argue.

As we walk, Caelum appears, arms full of papers, eyes scanning the hallway like he already knows something's gone down. His gaze flicks between Cassia, Nero, and me, calculating, assessing.

Nero stops to fill him in, but I try to make a quiet escape. I'm over this.

"Cae!" Cassia's screech pierces through the crowd like a dying banshee. I wince. Caelum audibly sighs.

"What *now*, Cassia?" he growls, already exasperated.

She stomps up to him, hair flipping dramatically. "They may not be from around here, but *you* are. I swear, Caelum, if you don't stay away from her, I will go straight to our parents and have her exiled."

She points a perfectly manicured claw in my direction like I'm a plague. I roll my eyes and keep walking. Four more weeks of this? I need hazard pay.

I make my way to class and slide into my seat, grateful for the quiet. The room's empty, probably because everyone else is still out there replaying the Cassia drama like it's the highlight of their week.

Mr. Valeis enters moments later, his long dark coat trailing like smoke behind him. His presence stills the air.

"Good morning, Vera," he says, voice like worn parchment and gravel. "How are you today?"

"I'm good. How are you?" I keep my tone polite, but my fingers drum quietly on the desk. I've been turning this question over in my mind for days.

"I'm well." He nods, then moves toward the front of the room.

I stare down at the grain of the wood beneath my hands, chewing on whether or not I should ask. But my curiosity outweighs my caution, at least for now.

"How did you know my real name?" I ask, looking back up at him. "You called me Veralyn. No one else here knows that." I didn't even know it until recently.

He doesn't hesitate. "My visions," he says simply. "They show me not just the future but truth. The thread of who someone really is. You, Vera, you are meant for power. With help, you will be nearly unstoppable."

That word again, *nearly.*

"Nearly?" I echo, brows knitting.

A shadow flickers behind his eyes. "There are hard times ahead. You'll face choices that shift everything. And not even I can see all the outcomes."

Before I can ask anything else, the door creaks open. "Well, it's a good thing she'll have me," Caelum says, striding in with that infuriating smirk. He looks so sure of himself, it should be illegal.

I groan aloud and drop my forehead against my desk. "Do you ever *not* time your entrances for maximum drama?"

He pulls out the seat next to me like it's already his. "What can I say? I aim to impress."

"Well I'm not impressed." I snark. He just laughs. It doesn't matter what I say, he's just so sure that we will be together, having fun like he's enjoying the chase.

The next class is the same as yesterday. I end up right between the two of them, again and do my best to ignore both. We've tested all the elements this week. I still can't tell if Caelum's assisting me with them or if it's actually me. I think it's at least partly me. I've been able to move things. Shape them. Wind was the most annoying. Cassia kept blowing my hair around like she was in some petty shampoo commercial.

If that's all she's got, she doesn't stand a chance against me. Not that I'm *planning* to fight her. Much. I can only dream.

After class, I decide to meet the boys in the library. I wonder if I'll regret it, but if they're asking for my help and if they trust me, then maybe I can try.

When I step into the library, I don't spot them right away. Then I see them, sprawled across the big couch by the fire, the same one I tried (and failed) to hide from Caelum on last week. Beside them sits Elowen, Caelum's sister. Now that I know, I can see the resemblance, the same blonde hair. The same confidence in how they hold themselves. I square my shoulders and walk over. The only open seat is next to Caelum. Of course.

I plop down and angle my body away. He responds by scooting closer, spreading his legs in that obnoxious power move until our thighs touch. His arm reaching behind me resting on the back of the couch.

"Hey, Lilac," he murmurs. "Glad you made it. Thought I'd have to come find you again."

"How do you keep finding me?" I grit out under my breath.

He leans in, lips brushing my ear. "Eventually, I'll tell you all my secrets." I shove him. A light push I wish was harder. I wish I didn't remember how it felt, or worse, want to be in his arms again.

"Hi, Vera," Elowen says gently. "I'm sorry about the other day. I hope you can forgive me."

"There's nothing to forgive. I'm sorry, too." I shoot a glare at her brother. "Your brother just really irritates me."

"Hey," Caelum says, mock-offended. "If you'd just let me in, I wouldn't be irritating."

"There's nothing to give into," I mutter. But the way his fingers graze my shoulder begs to differ. My skin tingles, goosebumps erupting in his wake, and those traitorous butterflies take flight again.

I glance up at him, intending to be mad, to push him away. But when our eyes meet, his glowing green gaze catching mine, I freeze. He looks down at my lips. He wants to kiss me. I feel it in my bones. In every fiber of my being and I want him to.

A throat clears and the spell breaks. He leans back with a sigh, arm still casually draped behind me. I should move. I *should*. But I don't. Just for a moment, I let myself enjoy the warmth of him beside me.

"Alright, let's look at those papers," Nero says. I grab the yearbook on the table and start flipping through.

I go straight to the student section and then keep flipping through. I stop. My father. A younger version of him, staring back at me. *Lucien Caelith* Veilbound Order. Head Guard.

I trace my index finger over his image, willing the tears not to fall.

"Okay, here's your dad," Nero says, peering over my shoulder. I look up surprised with my heart instantly thudding against my ribs. How did he know? When I look at his face he is looking at Cae. Oh. Not mine. "It says Prince Lucan and his future Head Guard. Over here's a picture of everyone in the Order, from that year."

"That's Lucien," Elowen says softly. "My dad said they were best friends. Inseparable. They even found their fated mates at the same time." She leans in and points. "Look, this one's from their Veilfall Festival."

I see the photo over Caelum's shoulder. Four young faces full of light and promise. My father, smiling. My mother beside him.

So my dad was best friends with their dad? I mean I knew he was best friends with the king but I never put it together until just now. That's more than a coincidence. Or do they already know who I am? I open myself, gently, just enough to feel intentions. I've never tried to sense so many at once. But all I feel is light, warmth, curiosity. No deceit. No threats.

The hand Caelum had resting behind me slides down to my bicep and squeezes gently, his thumb brushing over my skin. A silent reassurance. He doesn't look at me, but I feel his quiet happiness. I let myself breathe again.

Then he whispers near my ear, "She's finally getting it."

My hand drops from the book to his thigh and I pinch, *hard*. He yelps, just a little, and grins.

"Okay, here's a list of everyone in the Order," Nero says, flipping the page. "A few names have 'Head Guard training' next to them."

"My dad's first guard was Lucien Caelith," Caelum says, serious now. "They were best friends, but he disappeared with his family after the Shattering. My dad had to choose another."

I force myself to stay still. To not react. Cae's hand is absentmindedly rubbing up and down on my arm. In the human realm, my dad went by Luke Cale. I thought that was his real name.

"Did your dad say why he left?" Nero asks.

"No. He just said Lucien had to," Elowen answers quietly.

I finally find my mother's photo. *Vivi Cale*. Her name's listed as Cale too. I thought her and Rina's last name was Elowen. I didn't realize they changed their name. It would make sense if they were hiding though. My gaze drifts to Elowen. Her name, was it a coincidence, or a reflection of my family's past?

"Oh my gods," I whisper.

"So, he's a deserter?" Nero says. "A Head Guard abandoning his king? That's the one thing we're trained never to do."

"He's not a deserter!" The words rip out of me before I can stop them. I slap a hand over my mouth too late. All three of them whip their heads toward me.

I throw the book on the table, grab my things, and bolt. I don't make it far before hands grab me and pull me into a side room. I struggle, shoving until I see Caelum's worried eyes. He closes the door behind him.

"Lilac, I'm sorry. He didn't know. For what it's worth, my dad's only ever spoken about yours with respect. We grew up knowing he had to leave, to protect his family. That's all my dad ever said." He steps forward, hands settling gently on my shoulders. They slowly slides down and he grabs my waist, squeezing before he talks again. "El and I, we say we don't know why he left because that's how we protect him. And now, how we protect you."

"You knew?" I whisper. "You know who I am?"

A soft smile tugs at his lips. "My love, I've known for about a week. I asked my dad about your aunt. That's when he told me who she was. And who you are."

My heart pounds. I should have never said who my aunt was.

"I haven't told anyone," he adds quickly. "Not even El. But, she'll figure it out now. So will Nero."

"I'm not your love," I manage to say, but the panic's rising fast.

Chapter 37: All. The. Way. Baby

Vera

"I don't think now's the time to argue semantics. Are you okay? You're safe. I promise. You're safe with me."

His hands cradle my face, thumbs brushing lightly along my jaw. His eyes lock onto mine with such sincerity I feel like melting into him. But I don't. I *can't*.

"I'm fine," I say, even though the words are a lie. Nothing about this feels fine. My life feels like a tapestry being pulled apart, string by frayed string.

"Vera," he says gently, "you might not be fine now, but you will be. Please. Let me help. I know we don't know each other well, but I'm here." I close my eyes, letting my forehead rest against his chest. His lips press softly into my hair, and the warmth of it makes something in me ache.

"I don't know if I can let you help," I mumble. "Even if you wanted to, nothing can happen between us. We shouldn't even be friends, let alone anything else." He exhales slowly, and I feel the weight of it through his chest before he gently tilts my chin up again.

"You might think I'm irritating," he says with a soft smirk, "but I call it securing my future. And I don't mean my future as king, I couldn't care less about that. If starting as friends earns your trust, then fine. I'll wait. Just, let me in." His eyes plead with me, warm and unguarded.

"I'm trying to stay under the radar," I snap quietly. "Being around you is like painting a giant red arrow on my back."

"If you mean Cassia, she's nothing. Her and her parents are desperate, but they don't matter. Her father's on the council, sure, he's my father's Solenar. Like a head advisor. But he's only one vote. When we graduate, Sylas will take that position. Cassia's power? It's borrowed, and it's temporary."

That actually makes me feel better. I knew she couldn't actually fight, at least not in a real way. And if she can't get me kicked out, maybe I can breathe.

"But what if someone finds out who I really am?" I whisper.

He meets my eyes again, serious now. "Only a few people know who your aunt really is. And by extension, who you are. And those who do know, won't say a word. Would it be so terrible if they did know? You should be proud of who you are. Of your parents. Of where your family comes from."

"I am proud," I snap, then hesitate. "It's not that. You don't understand, I don't even understand all of it. I just know that someone is trying to hurt the kingdom and somehow I'm connected to that." My eyes widen. I didn't mean to say that. Not that part. Not about the prophecy.

Caelum straightens. "What does that mean? Who's trying to hurt the kingdom? If there's a threat, shouldn't I be involved? I am going to be king." Ugh. Arrogant much? I'd love for someone else to carry this prophecy weight. But him?

"So everything's all about you?" I shoot back.

"Of course not," he says quickly. "I just meant, if something is threatening us, I want to help. I should help."

"I don't know," I mutter. "I don't understand it. That's why I'm trying to keep to myself and figure it all out." I gesture wide in frustration and accidentally smack him in the chest.

He catches my wrist, and clasps his large hands over my one small, before bringing it up to rest over his heart. I can feel it gently thudding against my palm. "Okay. Calm down. Just, let me be part of this. I care about my kingdom. And I care about you."

"*Calm down?*" I snap. "You don't understand everything that's stacked against me!" I spin on my heel and storm out of the room just as the bell rings. Time for the next class and I didn't even get to eat. I head to my locker and grab everything I need for my last class. My hands are still trembling.

By the time I slip into my seat, I'm barely holding it together. Mr. Valeis enters not long after, offering me a polite smile, but thankfully he says nothing.

I try to breathe, deep and slow. Ground myself. The last thing I need is to accidentally whip up a windstorm in the middle of class.

The truth is, I'm freaking out. I revealed who I was. Even if Caelum already knew, now it's confirmed. Now Elowen and Nero know. What if they tell the King? What if word spreads beyond the walls of this academy?

My parents worked so hard to keep me hidden, and I've just blown that to pieces. And then there's the other truth, the dark, pressing one. Someone is after me. Not that I will tell Cae about that. If what Nero said was true, and they could tell I was masking my aura…

What if someone else could see through it, too? They already found me once. That day we were leaving my childhood home, in my bedroom.

Whoever it was, they knew. They saw me. But do they know where I am now? Panic claws up my throat. The air starts to shift. I can feel it, faint tendrils of wind curling around my desk. My hair lifts slightly, papers flutter. No, no, no. Not now.

"Vera." I jolt at the sound of my name. Caelum is suddenly in front of me, gripping my hands. His palms are warm, grounding. I look up into his eyes. He's not smiling. Just relaxed. Serious. Focused.

"Vera," he repeats gently. "It's okay. You're safe." And somehow, I feel it. Not just because he said it, but because something shifts inside me. Like I'm being wrapped in a warm, weighted blanket.

The storm dies down. I nod, not trusting myself to speak. Behind him, more students are filtering into the room. A few glance our way. And Mr. Valeis is watching us closely. Too closely.

Great. Just what I need. Caelum takes the seat beside mine. Beneath the table, his hand slides over mine. I know I should pull away. But I don't. Right now, I accept the comfort.

Today, Mr. Valeis is teaching us about protection symbols, sigils. Runes drawn onto objects, meant to shield or conceal. They don't last forever, but when used properly, they can offer powerful defense.

"These symbols," he begins, sketching one in the air with a finger that leaves behind a faint shimmering trail, "can be cast onto a variety of objects. Blades carried by our royal guard, relics passed down through bloodlines, items once touched by the gods." His finger drops, and he starts drawing again, this time on parchment with ink that glows briefly, then fades.

"Some choose to enchant sacred heirlooms; rings, pendants, even books. Others inscribe them into clothing or armor, or etch them into the hilts of weapons for battle. The more personal the object, the stronger the bond between sigil and bearer." I glance down at my notes, trying to keep up. My fingers are slightly trembling.

"But every so often," he continues, tone dipping low, "a sigil does not need to be drawn at all. A rare few are born with the ability to *be* the sigil. To veil their presence, bend the light and air around them without ever lifting a quill. The old texts call it *Umbrenatus.* The Shadowmarked. Those who can hide even from fate itself."

His gaze flicks up. *Directly at me.* My breath catches. Caelum's hand tightens around mine. I'd almost forgotten it was still there. I don't look at either of them. I just focus on writing. Some fae can hide themselves. I underline it. Once. Twice. A third time.

Then I start to doodle absentmindedly along the margins. Swirls. Leaves. A crescent moon. Something about the lines feels familiar. Like they're drawing me.

Mr. Valeis keeps talking, moving on to teach us the first few basic sigils, protection against harm, one for emotional steadiness, and a faintly glowing symbol meant to repel dark magic. He explains each one like a quiet invocation, less like magic and more like prayer.

And all the while, I can't shake the feeling that something inside me already knows them. Next week, Mr. Valeis said we'd begin learning different methods of traveling between realms. It's how Rina must've learned to cross into the human world. I wonder, can everyone learn to do that, or is it only a select few?

After class ends, Mr. Valeis gives me a slight nod as the rest of the students begin filing out. There's a buzzing in the air now, a growing hum of anticipation, most of us are thinking about one thing.

The roster.

"Come on, let's go check it out," Caelum says, catching up beside me. "We can start training with Lyra afterward. I told Halric we'd be using the forge, and Nero volunteered to help, too." He places a hand gently on the small of my back, steering me toward the door.

I step away, letting his hand drop. "Quit it," I whisper. He stays by my side anyway, even as I head to my locker to put things away. I can feel him watching me, just like I can feel the hum of magic still pulsing faintly beneath my skin.

Cassia is up ahead, flanked by her ever-loyal posse and surrounded by a cluster of students including Sylas. Of course.

"Go join your friends," I murmur under my breath. "Before everyone starts watching me. I don't need your help right now." Part of me hopes he won't listen. But the bigger part needs space, needs quiet, to make sure I'm not being followed. Or studied. Or targeted.

"No," he says simply. "I want to be with you. I don't care who sees. You shouldn't either."

"Hey, Cae!" someone shouts. We both glance up to see Sylas waving enthusiastically, even though he's barely twenty feet away. He looks ridiculous. I can't help the laugh that escapes me.

"Come on, dude," Sylas says. "Let's go check the roster!"

"Go," I say, nudging Caelum with my shoulder. "I'll meet you over there. I just need to find Lyra first."

He studies me for a beat, then relents. "Okay. But if you're not over there in five minutes, I will come find you. Next week I won't let you hide from me. I want to be with you." He gives my waist a tight squeeze before backing away, grinning like he owns the world. I roll my eyes, pretending not to notice the flutters in my stomach.

As I gather my things, I sneak a glance toward him. Cassia tries to slide up beside him, clearly hoping for attention, but he brushes her off without even pretending to be polite. He's talking to Sylas but from the angle of his gaze, I know he's still watching me.

I snap my locker closed and turn. Right into Nero. We fall into step together without speaking. I'm glad he's here. I owe him an apology, but for now, the silence feels like enough. We trail behind the crowd, the unmistakable "popular" group moving ahead like a current we've chosen not to join. I guess fae schools have cliques just like human ones.

"Sorry," we both say at the same time. I laugh, startled, and he cracks a small smile.

"I didn't know," he says. "I'm guessing there's still a lot I don't know. But I don't think there's anything that would ever take me from my post as Head Guard."

"You would. If it meant protecting your only child and your kingdom," I say quietly. His eyes widen, just a little, before he schools his expression.

"You're right," he admits. "If it came to that, I would."

"Please don't tell anyone."

Nero nods. "I won't. For now, but you need to tell him you're in danger. But I want you to tell me more. When you're ready." I close my eyes, take a deep breath, and nod.

When we reach the Echoforge, Lyra is already waiting. She stands off to the side, wringing her hands nervously. I brighten and walk over to her with a big smile.

"Are you ready?" I ask.

"Yes," she says, voice shaking a little. "I wanted to wait for you before checking the list." I loop my arm through hers and we wait our turn.

A few students walk away looking disappointed. Others are flushed with excitement or relief. The moment feels thick with possibility. And then, it's our turn. I scan the roster quickly, our names are there.

"Oh my god," Lyra gasps. "I can't believe I made it!" She jumps up and down, and when she grabs my hands, I laugh and jump with her.

When I glance over, Caelum and Sylas are watching us with matching amused smiles. Let them. Let everyone watch. For just one moment, I feel like I belong here. Then I look over to see Ryven and Nero in a heated conversation. Ryven starts walking away but not before looking back at me. That look alone tells me, he is pissed about something and planning something. I don't even have to open my senses to know that.

Lyra and I are walking out of the locker room and heading toward the Echoforge. When we step inside, Nero and Caelum are already there, talking. I hope it's not about me. But the second they spot us, they go silent and separate like magnets forced apart.

"All right, Brightstep," Cae calls, grinning. "Where do you want to start?"

"Brightstep?" Lyra whispers.

"Just ignore him. I do," I whisper back. Well, I try. Clearly, I am not doing a good job.

"We'll start with running," I say louder, steering us toward the side door. "I'm not worried about her being the fastest, but she needs to build stamina."

The guys trail behind as we step into the sun. It's warmer today than it's been in weeks, the light golden and soft on our skin.

"Stretch first," I say. "Always stretch, gets your muscles warm before we push them, and helps cool down after." Lyra copies my movements, her limbs a little stiff but determined.

When I walk up to the starting line, Caelum passes me and casually pulls off his shirt.

I jolt upright. "Wh—what are you doing?"

"Nothing," he says innocently. "Just getting warm. Thought this might help me cool down, especially when we're running side by side."

My eyes betray me before I can stop them—tracing the ripple of his abs, the way the sun seems to linger on him like it can't get enough. My gaze drifts lower, following the defined lines down to that impossibly sexy V, a faint trail of hair disappearing beneath his waistband. His arms look carved by gods—dangerously, unfairly perfect. Perfect for holding me and pinning me against a wall and—

"Whatever you're thinking, count me in," he says, voice low.

Veils help me. I glare at him, hoping he can't see the heat rising in my cheeks. I hate I've been caught staring at him, again.

"You won't be running next to me," I snap. "Especially now."

"What, you don't think I can keep up?" His smirk is pure mischief.

"I know you can't. I've already proved that."

"Wanna make a bet?" He's too cocky. I wonder if he's been training outside of school.

"What's the bet?" How does he get me with that every time? When did I become a gambling addict?

"If I win," he says, stepping closer, "I get to take you out on Sunday."

"And if I win?"

"Name your price."

"If I win," I say, squaring my shoulders, "you stay away from me for the next four weeks."

His smile falters. For a second, I see something real behind his eyes. I hate that look, I feel his disappointment like a sharp spear hitting my heart.

"No," he says softly. "I won't take that bet."

Fine. I pivot, stepping closer, my voice a whisper. "Then if I win... I get to choose where we go on Sunday." I hate how easily I just gave in.

His eyes widen, then sparkle with mischief. "Deal," he says before I can blink. He leans in, and I jump back like I've been zapped.

"What are you doing?" My gaze flits between him and Nero and Lyra, both frozen in confusion.

"We're fae," he says, grinning. "We seal our deals with kisses." His eyes twinkle, and I can't tell if he's serious or just messing with me.

I glance at Nero. "Is that... true?"

Nero just smirks and nods. Yep. No help there. My eyes snap back to Cae, and I give a single, reluctant nod. That's all the invitation he needs. He leans back in, and his lips meet mine in a quick, teasing kiss.

When my eyes flutter open, he's watching me, soft and unreadable.

"Let's do this," he says, stepping back.

"Wait, you never made me do that with our last bets." I tell him and he just gives me his sexy half smirk and winks at me.

I glance around. Lyra is blinking like she's seen a ghost, while Nero is leaning casually against the wall, clearly enjoying the show.

Shaking off the remnants of the kiss and my racing thoughts, I drop into a runner's stance and motion Lyra over. Time to focus or at least pretend I am.

"Here's the breakdown," I say, voice all business now. "It's about the launch. Push off strong, but pace yourself. Focus on trying to keep even breathing. Once you settle into the rhythm, then you push for speed."

"Ready?" Cae asks.

"Are we running to the next line or all the way around?" I ask, already knowing the answer.

"All. The. Way, baby." Veils. No, that definitely doesn't make me blush.

Nero starts the countdown. The second he says "Go," I'm gone. I don't think, I run. Wind whips past me. I feel the pull of magic in my limbs, the wind flowing through me and the rhythm of my steps syncing with something ancient. Cae is just behind me, but I don't dare look back.

"Veils, it's like you're glowing," he says, breathless. "So damn hot." I grunt and push harder, rounding the final bend. The finish line is in sight, I dig deep. And just as I'm about to cross it, Cae darts ahead. His foot hits the line a split second before mine.

I slow, then collapse into the grass, panting. He flops down beside me, eyes closed, chest heaving. After a beat, he reaches over and squeezes my hand.

"Are you okay?" I ask.

"Can't. Breathe," he gasps. "Worth it."

"You got lucky. I want a rematch."

"Nope." He doesn't even open his eyes. I yank my hand away and sit up. Lyra and Nero are watching us, both clearly trying not to laugh.

I roll my eyes. "Okay, while the old man over there figures out how lungs work, I'll help you get into position." I lead Lyra to the starting line and adjust her stance.

"Right foot forward, left bent behind. Push through your legs." Nero joins us, demonstrating beside her. Her eyes snap over to him and I watch her eyes flick up his legs to his torso before her sharp ears turn red and she focuses back on her feet.

He clears his throat caught up in his own spell. "Remember, this isn't about speed yet," he says gently. "Just feel the motion. The push-off. Find your rhythm. Focus on breathing."

"Don't try to kill yourself like the old man back there," I add.

"Hey!" Cae calls from the grass, still flat on his back. His breathing is steadier now, but I can't stop looking at the rise and fall of his toned stomach, the defined V disappearing into his pants. I could drown in that view. His eyes snap open and he catches me staring, again. He smirks and winks. *Shit.*

"Ahem." I spin back to Lyra, who's trying not to smile.

"Right. Do you have any questions?" I ask.

"I have lots," she teases. "But not about the running."

"Okay," I say quickly. "If you feel ready, go ahead. Take it slow. Focus on your breathing." I ignore the lots of questions part. I don't have answers anyway.

Nero lines up again, going slower to match her pace. I know he's giving her quiet tips, and part of me wonders if I should've been the one to run with her but she seems at ease with him.

I watch them for a moment, not even hearing when Caelum get up. But I feel his presence. His hand slides over the small of my back, sending a wave of heat through me.

"I can't wait for Sunday," he murmurs. He leans forward and places a gentle kiss on the back of my neck. "I'll find you at the festival tomorrow night, and we can talk more."

"I don't know if I'm going."

"You have to go. It's a rite of passage. If you're worried about people watching, we'll find a quiet spot. But don't miss it, even if it's just for the Firewatch."

"I'll think about it." Lyra and Nero are rounding the final bend. She's clearly winded, but she's smiling wide.

"Was it true about the kiss thing?" I ask him.

His smile is radiant, teasing, lips rolling as if trying to hide it.

"No, I just wanted to kiss you again."

"Seriously? That's cruel." I push him, but not hard enough. He just laughs, low and rich, his head tilting back. My eyes can't help but follow the hypnotic rise and fall of his Adam's apple. I really want to place my lips against it and I feel heat curl through me in a way I shouldn't admit.

"You did great!" I yell as she crosses the line.

"Oh gods," she pants. "I didn't but it felt good. Better. I need water, but I want to try again."

"Of course," I grin. "This time, I'll run with you." I need a minute away from these guys anyway.

Chapter 38: Reclaiming a Legacy

Vera

I walk back with Nero, mostly in silence. I did tell him I thought he was really good with Lyra. He just gave me a deadpan look and said, *"Maybe I like helping a damsel in distress."* Then nothing else.

Clearly, he was waiting for me to say something more, or maybe hoping I wouldn't say anything else. He could be just focused on his guard training or he doesn't want to talk about girls with me. Which feels unfair, honestly, because he's always pushing me to talk about Caelum. Either way, I think it was clear it wasn't something he wanted to discuss. Which strangely enough, makes me want to talk about it more.

I get home at the same time as Rina again.

"Let me get changed, then we can get started on training," Rina says, already halfway down the hall.

"Sounds good." I drop my backpack onto the couch and head to the kitchen for a glass of water. When she comes out, she's changed into her training gear and wearing a bright, eager smile.

"I'll make us some tea, and then we'll get to work."

"Could we focus more on elemental gifts tonight?"

"Yes, of course." She pauses mid-reach, swapping the starleaf she usually brews for chamomile instead. Once the tea is ready, we sit at the kitchen table, mugs steaming between us.

"So," she asks, "how was academy today?" I stir in some honey, trying to decide how much to tell her.

"It was good," I say slowly. "I talked a little with Nero, the one I mentioned yesterday. We were looking up old academy records, and we came across a photo of Dad. Someone said he left the position of Head Guard, and Nero just said he couldn't imagine deserting something he worked so hard for." I pause to breathe, the words catching in my throat. "I snapped. Said he didn't just desert it. So now Nero knows who I am."

I look down at my tea. "I kind of panicked after that. My powers flared up, I felt the wind rising around me. I managed to calm it down, but it worries me. Losing control like that." I brace for her reaction.

But Rina only smiles, calm and warm. "It happens, especially when emotions run high. That's why Auravale is important, not just for the Veilbound, but for helping all fae understand and manage their gifts."

She sips her tea, then asks gently, "Do you trust this boy? Nero?"

I nod. "Yes. I've felt his intentions, used my truthsense. He's kind. And determined. He wants to be Head Guard one day, so I think it's hard for him to understand what my dad did. But we talked again before the day ended. He apologized. Said he couldn't imagine leaving, but understood if it was to protect your child and kingdom. He said I was right."

Rina nods approvingly. "Sounds like you've found yourself a good ally."

I laugh. "He actually said that last week." Technically he said that about Cae.

"Then maybe, when he becomes Head Guard, he could help us get access to some of the records in the Grove of Stars."

"Yeah, I could ask." I don't mention Caelum. Not yet. That's something I want to keep to myself until I understand it better.

"Okay," Rina says, setting her mug aside. "Elements. Your mother and I were both gifted in all four, but I was strongest with water. Your mom was incredible with earth, I was always jealous of her green thumb." She smiles at the memory.

"You might end up gifted in all of them too, but from what I've seen, your power leans toward wind, especially in moments of distress."

"Why couldn't it be something cool, like fire?" I groan.

She just laughs. "Let's try and find out. I'll grab a candle."

We start practicing at the table. I can extinguish the flame easily, almost instinctively but lighting it proves more difficult. I manage to do it once, though. Clearly I don't need the sparkstone, and this proves it wasn't just Caelum helping me. Maybe he was just grounding me. Now that I know what the feeling is, what to reach for, I can keep working on it. I just have to stop letting my emotions control me.

The scent of seared beef fills the air, sharp and savory, as I stand at the counter, fingers tight around the handle of the knife. The rhythmic thunk of blade on cutting board steadies me. Carrots, clean and sweet-smelling, falling into neat slices beneath my focus. I force myself to stay present. Eyes on the orange roots. Don't slip. Don't bleed.

Still, my thoughts spiral. I can't stop thinking about what Nero said. That picture in the archive, my dad standing beside the King. Cae's dad. My father's best friend. All this time did Caelum know? Did he grow up with pictures of *my* parents in his home? He said he didn't realize until he asked about Rina, but I don't know. Part of me wonders if he saw me and just knew.

"Rina?"

"Yes, Sweet Girl?" she answers, her tone distracted as she stirs sizzling meat in the skillet. The rich scent curls in the air, mixing with the aroma of chamomile still lingering from earlier. I love when she called me that. It has a way of bringing me back into the moment, to enjoy what I have.

"When I was looking through the old photos with Nero, we found one of Dad with the king. You said once he had a best friend. Was it him?"

She stops stirring. When she looks at me, her expression softens into something bittersweet. "Yes. They were inseparable. It broke Lucan's heart when your father had to leave."

I blink, my throat tightening. "That's who you were trying to reach after they died, right? I should've figured that out sooner."

Rina nods slowly. "We had a code word. I sent it to him, more than once. But I haven't heard back."

"Does he usually reply?"

She shrugs, turning off the burner. The sudden silence is loud. "I don't know. I'd never had to try before. He's been absent a lot more over the past year. He still meets with the councils, but rarely leaves the Grove of Stars. Lately, guards say he's even more reclusive." I think of what Nero said. Problems with Cae. Maybe this is all connected somehow.

"How would he even help?"

"He knew the part of the prophecy that warned you would be in danger. Not about the kingdom, just you. And I know, without a doubt, that he would help keep you safe. For your father, he'd do anything."

"Can we trust him?" I ask, carefully plating the sliced carrots beside the rice as Rina dishes out the beef. "If he's barely been running his kingdom, maybe he's changed. Maybe we're putting too much faith in him."

We carry the plates to the table, steam rising in gentle curls, then sit across from each other in silence for a beat. Only after I pick up my fork does Rina finally speak again.

"I never had a reason not to trust him," she says. "But I only really knew him during that brief time after your parents got together, and a little while after they left. He and his wife Ilyra would check in on me now and then. After she died, it stopped. There was a grand funeral. I gave my condolences, and that was the last time I spoke to him."

I imagine a funeral too large for privacy, packed with fae who didn't even know her. My stomach twists.

"He had the twins to care for. And then, about a year ago, he remarried. It shocked the whole kingdom."

"Why?" I ask quietly.

"Because he was madly in love with his wife. Everyone saw it. He was a devoted husband and a good father. That kind of love doesn't fade easily."

I nod but say nothing. My throat feels thick. I can't imagine the weight of what he lost. I only know my own grief, and even that feels like too much some days.

We eat in silence, both of us chewing slower, minds drifting through memory and pain. I glance at Rina once, and she looks just as far away as I feel.

I wonder if I could ask Cae about his father. Maybe I could meet him. But I know what it would look like, to him. I'm not ready for that. Not yet. I don't know if I ever will be.

"Are we going to the festival tomorrow?" I ask finally, needing a change of subject.

"Yeah. I think we should." Rina pushes her empty plate away. "I was thinking, if anyone asks, we'll stick with our story and say I'm your host for the Order."

"That sounds like a good plan."

"Keep it vague, though. Hopefully no one looks too closely. You have your mother's eyes, and someone might notice. I want to brew another batch of the Veilbrew Elixir just to be safe. But your parents would've wanted you there. Especially for the Firewatch. It's sacred, when your gifts start to come together, sometimes they awaken more fully there."

"Could I have gifts no one's heard of before?" I ask. "Like the Virelai?"

Rina studies me, her expression unreadable. "Maybe. I don't know why you would, but it's possible. We'll find a secluded spot, just in case. And we need to find a seer, someone who can help us understand what's happening to you."

I hesitate, guilt swelling in my chest. "I don't know what to do with everything being thrown at me. So many secrets. So many questions. And I don't know who to trust. I'm terrified."

She reaches across the table and squeezes my hand. "You're right to be cautious. But I'm here. Whatever you learn, we'll add it to our very long list of mysteries. I can help you navigate at least *some* of it." I nod, comforted by her warmth, even as my heart still feels fragile.

"We could see if my teacher Mr. Valeis would be willing to help us. Maybe having you there could help me decipher some of his cryptic messages."

"I think that's a good idea, we should meet with him," she says. "If you get a chance to ask him then do it, we can make any night after school work."

"Okay." I look down at my half-eaten meal. "There's more."

She raises a brow, waiting.

"I found a note," I admit. "Hidden in the library. In a secret compartment. I forgot about it, probably because I was more scared about the fact that it was *there* than what it said."

Rina's gaze sharpens. "What else have you been keeping from me?"

"That's it," I say quickly. "And I'm not trying to hide things. Not on purpose. I just, I thought I had to figure it out alone. I didn't want to let anyone close."

"Don't shut me out," she says, voice trembling. "You're all I have left. I lost everyone. Seventeen years I waited for a sign that my sister was still out there. I finally heard her voice again, just once more. And then she was gone." Her eyes shine with unshed tears. "I won't lose you too."

My own throat tightens again. I set my fork down and lean forward. "You're right. I've been selfish. From now on, we do it together." She wipes at her eyes with her sleeve, nodding.

I was being selfish. I still don't think I'll tell Cae everything but Rina? I won't keep her in the dark again. I couldn't bear to lose her. She's the only family I have left.

"I'm going to shower," I say softly. "Then we can start going over everything I found." She nods, already moving to clear the plates.

I head down the hall with a deep breath. One step at a time. No more secrets. Not with her.

After my shower, steam still clinging faintly to my skin, I tug on my softest pajamas, worn cotton with a faded constellation pattern and dig through the hamper to find the sweater I wore last Saturday. The paper is still tucked deep in the pocket, creased but intact. A strange weight settles in my chest as I hold it in my hands.

I gather my notebook, stuffed with loose pages and scribbled timelines, and the two textbooks I've been cross-referencing, one brittle with age, the other so dense I can barely carry it.

When I settle beside Rina on the couch, I notice her trying to blink away the last of her tears. The firelight dances gently across her features, but it doesn't mask the weight in her eyes.

"I'm sorry, Rina."

She shakes her head, resting a hand lightly over mine. "I'm sorry we're even in this position. That *you're* in this position. I just want to find answers. I want you safe. And maybe, one day, I want to see Elarindor restored. Reclaimed. It was ours. What was taken should be returned."

I nod, pressing the folded parchment into her hand. It's yellowed around the edges, as if it hasn't seen light in decades.

"Let's do this," I whisper.

We place it carefully on the coffee table between us. For a moment, we both just stare at it, like we're standing on the edge of something ancient and dangerous and true.

Rina reaches out first, unfolding it slowly, carefully, as if it might crumble to dust in her hands. The paper still smells faintly of cedar and something ancient, like the whisper of a forgotten room.

At the top, there's a sigil neither of us recognizes: a crescent moon nested within a hollowed sun, both enclosed in thorns. Rina leans closer. Her brow furrows as I watch her read it.

"What does it mean?" I ask, my voice barely above a whisper.

Rina traces the sigil with her fingertips. "The Hollow Flame, I've heard that name before. But not in the context of the Order. This is older. Before even the first migration to the eastern provinces. Before the treaties."

"*She remembers*," I repeat, eyes scanning the note again. "Do you think it means someone is alive? Someone who knows what happened to Elarindor?"

"I don't know," Rina says slowly. "But whoever wrote this wanted it hidden. And if it talks about a 'broken crown,' this might not just be about reclaiming land. It could mean reclaiming a legacy. A lineage."

A shiver runs down my spine. The idea of someone—or *something*—waiting beneath a tree older than the kingdom itself feels like a tale plucked straight from the Veilbound myths.

I reach for my notebook, flipping to the back where I've been scribbling odd phrases I couldn't place.

"Wait, the oldest tree. There's a reference in one of the textbooks. A tree called Nethira, the 'Memory Root.' Supposedly, it was where the first Fae queen received her mark from the stars."

Rina looks at me, and for the first time all night, I see something shift in her expression. Hope, tangled with something sharper.

"If that's where the crown is," Rina says slowly, her eyes distant, "then that's where we go first. If the legends are true, then the Nethira Tree still stands in the Grove of Stars. I remember being obsessed with that story when we were younger. The first fae queen stood beneath its branches, and on the night she received her mark from the stars, the tree turned white."

I nod, my heartbeat quickening like a drum calling me forward.

"What about the Hollow Flame?" I ask. "Is it an actual fire? Like the Firewatch I keep hearing about?"

Rina shakes her head. "No. Everyone sees the Firewatch, it's ceremonial. The Hollow Flame is something else entirely. If it exists, it's hidden. Sacred. Maybe even alive. This note could mean it's real. That it's still burning."

Her words hang in the air like smoke. I glance down at the parchment again, its edges still curled like it had been waiting decades to be found.

"This note talks about Elarindor being *silenced,* not *fallen,*" I say, voice barely above a whisper. "Whoever wrote it, they knew something. Maybe they knew you and my mom were still alive."

"Maybe," Rina murmurs. "Or maybe they were trying to warn us. If the truth is hidden behind the Veil, then not everyone's meant to find it. Maybe the Nethira Tree is behind a veil. Which must mean not everyone can see it."

The silence that follows is different now, less like fear, more like anticipation. The kind that sparks behind your ribs before something important begins. The secrets are unraveling. And for the first time, I'm not afraid of them.

Chapter 39: I'll See You at the Firewatch

Vera

Since the moment I woke, something felt different. It shimmered in the air like heat off stone, an invisible tension, a quiet hum of magic pressing at the edge of my senses. Anticipation, yes, but more than that. It was as if the world itself was holding its breath, waiting.

I hadn't slept much. Rest was a fickle thing lately, and when it came, it brought dreams that felt more like memories.

Last night, I dreamt of a woman.

She stood in a grove bathed in starlight, her violet-black hair tumbling in loose waves to her waist. Her eyes matched the color of twilight before night fully falls, deep, ancient, knowing. She didn't speak, but her smile was radiant, like she'd been waiting an eternity just to see me. When I tried to speak, my voice didn't come. The silence between us felt reverent, not empty. I woke up with her face etched into my mind like ink beneath skin.

I can only assume she was the first fae queen, the one who stood beneath the Nethira Tree and was marked by the stars. Was that just a dream or something more? Am I connected to her?

Rina and I leave mid-morning, and even though she hums a light tune as we drive, my chest is tight with nerves. She has to park far from the center of town, there are people everywhere, weaving between stalls draped in colorful silks and lights that flicker like fireflies. The air is filled with the scent of sweetbread and spiced fruit, the sound of laughter and distant music.

But when I step out of the car, the strange feeling deepens. It coils in my stomach, not quite fear, but close. The magic in the air here is different, older, wilder. Like the land remembers something no one's spoken aloud in generations.

My feet hesitate on the pavement, the wind catching the hem of my sundress and lifting it gently around my knees. I chose this dress, my favorite green one with delicate white flowers because something about today felt like it meant something. Like it might mark a beginning. It always made my eyes shine, or so my mother used to say.

But now, standing on the edge of all this noise and color, a part of me wants to turn around. To slip back into the quiet safety of Rina's cottage. To let the past stay buried. To let my secrets stay safe. But a louder part, the one that remembers starlit eyes and whispered prophecies, knows better.

I don't want to hide anymore. Not from the world. Not from my truth. Not from the life that was meant for me, before it was stolen. From my parents. From Rina. From me. Today, I step toward it.

We step out of the car and begin walking up the winding street, my shoes crunching softly on gravel until we reach the smooth, worn cobblestone road. It curves like a ribbon through the heart of town, leading us toward the marketplace, where everything feels more alive than I've ever seen it.

Shops spill out onto the street, their windows flung open and adorned with fluttering ribbons. Booths stretch as far as I can see, hundreds of them, some shaded by colorful canopies that ripple in the breeze, others more humble, with handmade signs perched on tabletops or strung from twine overhead.

The air is saturated with scent. Roasted cinnamon, warm sugar, something sharp and herbal, and the mouthwatering aroma of grilled meat that coils into the breeze and refuses to let go. Even though we ate earlier, my stomach lets out a soft, audible growl.

"Where do we start?" I ask, eyes wide. The colors. The textures. The overwhelming life in it all. It's beautiful.

Rina checks her watch. "It's two o'clock now. Firewatch doesn't start until eight, when the sun goes down. Do you want to stay together or split up?"

"Stay together, if you don't mind," I say quickly. "This is all new to me. Clearly, I'm going to need someone to explain everything."

We both laugh. It's light. Easy.

Yesterday left a hollow spot in us, but today? Today we're filling it slowly, with color and tentative steps forward. There's a new thread between us, freshly mended and stronger than before. If nothing else these will be good memories to remember later.

We step up to the first booth, a charming display of hand-painted wooden crafts. Little signs, trinkets, carvings. Two girls dart around the table, one with a crown of daisy-chains tangled in her brown curls, the other with auburn hair that catches the sunlight like fire. Their laughter is contagious, innocent. And suddenly, I feel like I'm seeing fae children for the first time, really seeing them.

They remind me of someone. No, two someones. My mom and Rina. And I think Rina sees it too. Her eyes soften with the same bittersweet ache I feel in my chest.

"Good afternoon, ladies! Welcome!" a kind older woman says excitedly from behind the table. Her cheeks are rosy, her hair pinned up with little wooden sticks. "Let us know if you have any questions. We also have a station if you'd like to design your own board, just over there." She gestures to a table lined with paints, stencils, and small blank blocks of wood.

"Thank you," I reply, already stepping closer. "We're just looking for now."

Curiosity tugs me forward. I drift to the paint table, drawn by the stencils, letters, vines, flowers, and shapes I don't recognize. When Rina joins me, I lean in and ask quietly, "What are these symbols?"

She studies them with reverence in her eyes. "Some are sigils. Prayers, really, for safety, for love, for family. This one," she points delicately, "is the Thornevale sigil. The royal line."

I lean closer. A sword runs through its center, straight and unyielding, its hilt carved with ancient runes. Silver flames coil up the blade, twining into vines that glow faintly as if alive, their light pressing against the storm spiral encircling it. The spiral is jagged, chaotic, like a storm captured mid-turn—yet the sword and flame cut clean through, a symbol of willpower over chaos. I've seen that symbol on some of the guards uniforms and on Rina's uniform.

I trace it lightly with my finger, the lines almost warm to the touch.

"And this," she says, pointing to another. "This is the Elowen sigil. Our family's crest." She whispers that last part. "The crescent moon cradling the sun, their light twined together, circled by ivy. The moon for their bond to night, the sun for their bond to day, and the ivy for resilience, ever-growing, ever-reaching. It marks them as guardians of balance."

Her finger drifts to the next. "And here, Duskmere. The crescent moon curves like a shield, and within it, three interlocking chains form a triangle, links of iron and oath. They say each chain stands for loyalty, blood, and sacrifice. When Duskmere-born fae gather, the links pulse faintly, like a heartbeat. As if the chains remember who they belong to."

Finally, she gestures toward the last. "And Varethos. Their circle is woven mist, endless and unbroken. At its center, a silver eye of stars, the pupil carved like a crescent moon. Threads fall downward from the eye into a rippling pool, the mark of memory. Around the rim float seven runes of power, one for each seer of their council. When carved into stone, the runes shift if you stare too long, as if they're whispering truths meant only for those who can listen."

She spoke with a passion that went beyond sales. Knowledge was expected, necessary, even but this was more than that. She truly loved what she did.

I feel like something is unfolding in me. These aren't just stencils, they're pieces of a world I never got to know. A heritage I'm only beginning to remember. I spot a small block tucked in the corner and feel the pull again, like I *need* to paint something. Maybe it's silly. But I want to.

"Can I paint one?" I ask Rina, hoping I won't need to explain why.

She smiles and waves her hand. "Of course. Pick whichever you like."

I choose the smallest block and gather grey, white, and black paint, setting the Thornevale stencil down first. I try to keep my lines clean, layering shades to create a silvered effect. Then, I carefully place the Elowen stencil, using golds, greens, and soft grey to blend the ivy into the silver flame so they seem to grow into each other, unified. Balanced.

When I'm done, I don't even realize I'm holding my breath until it shudders out. It's beautiful. It looks like it belongs to me. Like it always has. Emotion stings behind my eyes. I blink it away.

"That's lovely," the woman says gently, watching me. "You have a good eye."

"Thank you," I murmur, clearing my throat, swallowing the lump that formed before I even noticed it. I offer her a smile, tuck the wooden block carefully into the pocket of my sundress, and wander toward the next booth where I spot Rina.

For the first time in a long time, it doesn't feel like I'm carrying something heavy. It feels like I'm building something new, one piece at a time.

We stroll from booth to booth, weaving through the colorful chaos. Some have fun activities clearly geared toward kids. Face painting, pin-the-tail-on-the-phoenix, and oversized bubble wands. We skip past those, but then we come across a ring toss game. The prizes include stuffed animals and a rack of glittering plastic tiaras. One catches my eye instantly: a silver one with deep purple gems that sparkle under the late afternoon sun.

I glance at the hand-painted sign beside it: *All proceeds benefit the Sylvaeris Healing Ward.*

"Do you want to try this one?" Rina asks, already fishing out some money.

"Yeah," I grin. "I want to win that tiara with the purple gems."

"You lovely ladies want to try your luck?" comes a voice from behind the table. That voice. I know it instantly. I look up to Cae looking at me with a soft smile. His eyes glowing with the gold starbursts again.

He stands behind the booth in a simple long black long sleeve shirt, sleeves pushed up to his elbows, his hair a little messy like he'd been pushing it away from his face all day. He smiles even brighter and gives me a wink. There's a warm breeze that coils around me and buries into my chest and squeezes.

Elowen sits at the table behind him. She smiles brightly at us. She is dressed in a pretty green summer dress much like my own. Her jade eyes shining. Though not like Cae's, I can see the gold flecks dancing again.

"Ah, Prince Caelum, Princess Elowen." Rina says casually. "How are you?"

"I'm good, Rina. It's nice to see you again." Cae responds politely.

"Are you in the Academy this year with Vera?" She gestures to me, carefully neutral. I can tell she's choosing her words intentionally, she doesn't reveal anything about who I am to her.

"Yes, I know Vera," he replies easily, eyes still on me. "We're both in the Veilbound Order. She sure is something special." He gives me a secretive smile. One that tells me he's thinking of something else.

"That she is," Rina says, voice gentle.

"Did you want to give it a go?" Cae asks, motioning to the game. "All proceeds go to the healing ward."

"Yeah," Rina says, handing over the money. "Vera's got her eye on the purple tiara."

He grins, already pulling out six rings. "I feel like I should make it harder for you. Maybe move the cones around or make you stand farther back."

"Fine," I say, stepping back a few paces and squaring my shoulders. "Let's see how rigged this really is."

I focus on the single yellow cone, the one I need to land a ring on to win the prize. The first toss misses, clattering off to the side. But I feel the angle now, the rhythm. The next five glide through the air and land perfectly, one after another, right over the yellow cone.

"I knew I should've made it harder," he says with a laugh, retrieving the tiara. Then he walks over to me, and the playful air shifts. He steps in close, closer than he needs to and gently places the tiara in my hair. His fingers brushing against my temple.

"This'll do," he whispers, "until I get the real crown on you." A shiver runs down my spine, and I'm frozen for a second, blinking up at him. Then he steps back with that same infuriatingly perfect smile, like nothing just happened.

"Looks good on you," he says with a wink.

"Well, hello. Fancy seeing the Thornevales here. And who do we have here?" The voice behind me is smooth. Too smooth, with just enough cockiness to raise my hackles.

I turn to find a guy about our age standing there like he owns the place. Sunlit blond hair falls in careless waves across his forehead, and sharp blue eyes glint like a sky before a storm. He wore twilight-hued tactical gear, sleek and fitted, enchanted plating layered over dark fabric that shifted with faint runes. It wasn't the bulky kind meant to hide weakness, this was forged to amplify strength. The reinforced plates curved close to his frame, leaving no doubt about the muscle beneath, the kind earned through both training and bloodline. Tall, broad-shouldered, he carried the gear like it weighed nothing, every movement sharp with precision.

At the center of his chest, etched into polished steel that glimmered with a faint pulse of magic, was the Thornevale crest—the same one I painted earlier. I grab the block in my pocket to be sure it's still there. Over his left shoulder was the Duskmere insignia: a crescent moon arched over three interlocking rings, bound into a triangle. The emblem caught the last light of the sun as though even dusk bent to him.

And of course, he knew it. His stance, his smirk, the casual arrogance in the way his gaze swept the room, all of it declared he didn't just wear the Duskmere colors. He embodied them. It matches the one inked on Nero's arm. Duskmere.

"Auren. How nice to see you," Caelum says. His tone is polite, but there's a stiffness to it, tension simmering just beneath the surface.

His arm slides more firmly around my waist, pulling me closer. It's a subtle move, but one that doesn't go unnoticed. Not by Auren. Not by Rina, either, who flicks her gaze between them, brows lifting ever so slightly. There he goes again, claiming me.

"It's nice to see you," Auren replies with a too-charming grin. His eyes flick to me, and linger. "And who's this pretty fae? I don't believe we've met. Where's Cae been hiding you?" The edge in his smile tells me he knows exactly what he's doing.

"This is Vera," Caelum answers evenly, but his fingers twitch slightly against my hip.

"A beautiful name for a beautiful girl," Auren says with a wink. "I hope I get to see more of you." I don't say anything, just try to school my expression. Auren's attention slides smoothly from me to Elowen.

"Good afternoon, El. How are you?" His voice shifts, softer now, smooth as velvet. Too smooth. Her cheeks get a little pink but her expression remains neutral.

Elowen offers a cool, polite smile. "Auren. Nice to see you. I'm doing well." Her tone mirrors Caelum's. Friendly, but clipped. Controlled.

"You look beautiful," he adds, voice lower now. "I hope I get a chance to see you again tonight."

She opens her mouth, maybe to deflect, maybe to deliver a clever retort but before she can respond, Nero walks up from behind.

"Auren? I didn't know you were coming," Nero says with a bright grin.

The two clasp hands and pull into a quick back-pat embrace. The shift in energy is palpable, Caelum's jaw tightens. Rina, still watching from the sidelines, presses her lips together like she's holding back a comment.

"Nero," Auren says, his voice shifting again, less smug now, more genuine. "How's the Academy treating you?"

"It's going great. I'll be glad when it's over," Nero replies.

"Cae said you were doing well. I hope that means you'll get Head Guard."

"You know I won't settle for anything less." Nero laughs, the sound light and rare coming from someone usually so serious.

A group of children approaches the booth, and Elowen excuses herself to greet them, her voice lifting in welcome. Auren turns to watch her, something almost reverent flickering in his expression. Caelum notices. His glare could melt stone.

"I'll catch up with you guys later," Auren says, turning away. "I'm going to find some friends."

And just like that, he walks off, every movement deliberate, too casual to be innocent. The silence he leaves behind hums with awkward tension.

Nero glances between the rest of us. "What just happened?"

"Nothing," Caelum mutters, though the word sounds strangled. He grumbles something else under his breath. I think I catch the word *douche* in there.

I stifle a laugh behind my hand.

"I should get going too," I say, tugging gently at Caelum's grip. "I'm here with Rina, I want to see more of the festival."

Caelum's hand loosens, his gaze dropping to meet mine. A faint smile tugs at his mouth, but the storm in his eyes lingers, whatever Auren stirred in him hasn't faded.

"I'll see you at the Firewatch later," he says softly, brushing his thumb against my hand in a fleeting touch before stepping back behind the booth, his voice quickly lost beneath the chatter of children crowding in.

As I turn away, the world came back into focus, the air thick with laughter and the clatter of vendors calling out their wares. I feel the weight of Rina's eyes on me—thoughtful, a little amused—and behind us, Caelum still watches, his presence pressing at my back.

I stumble a step before catching up to Rina, who's already gliding down the street with her brows arched, like she's carefully processing what just unfolded. The crowd swells around us, ribbons of music winding through the air, and once we're far enough from the booth, she leans closer, lowering her voice to a whisper.

"What *was* that?"

"What was what?" I ask, aiming for innocent, but failing at it.

"That. Him putting the tiara on your head. His arm wrapping around you. What did he *say* to you?"

I almost laugh at the disbelief in her voice. "He said it looks like I was meant to wear one." A lie. A soft one, but a lie nonetheless.

She watches me with narrowed eyes. "You know I have truthsense too, Vera." She scolds lightly. "It seemed like you two know each other. Well."

"He flirts with me," I admit, shrugging. "But I don't know. He's had a lot of girlfriends."

"He's the one you mentioned the other night," she murmurs. "The one who's been hovering. The one that could be engaged?" I nod.

"I don't know, Vera." Her voice is cautious now, thoughtful. "I could see both your auras shimmer when he got close. But I also heard that he was meant to marry Cassia Corvina."

I pause, turning to her. "What does that mean? About our auras."

She shakes her head. "I'm not sure. Maybe it just means you like each other. Maybe it means you're becoming close. Or maybe it means something more. But either way be careful." I feel like she wasn't telling me everything. So I'm not the only one worried about his past and what his true intentions are.

Chapter 40: The First Whisper of Something More

Vera

We keep wandering, weaving in and out of the festival paths as if they were spun just for tonight. The cobbled streets of the town are dressed in strands of glowing lanterns, soft orbs that hover in the air, pulsing gently with magic, casting everything in warm gold and twilight pink. The scent of roasted nuts, and herb-laced smoke curls around us like an invisible ribbon. Every corner we turn offers something new: fae artisans twisting metal into shimmering pendants, children chasing floating lights that dart like fireflies, groups clustered around musicians whose songs weave through the air like stories half-forgotten.

And still, beneath all the wonder, my stomach is a knot.

Around six, we find a booth selling burgers from that same diner we visited weeks ago. The scent hits first, grilled meat and toasted buns. And something about it makes me feel grounded. Familiar. I order without really thinking, grateful for the weight of something warm in my hands, even if my appetite's nowhere to be found.

I take a bite anyway. The tang of the sauce, the perfectly crisp edges of the bun, it should be comforting. But all I can think about is what's coming. The ceremony. The moment. Him. The way Caelum looked at me earlier, like he saw something I didn't even see in myself. Or maybe something I've been trying not to admit has been there all along.

The sky deepens as we eat, the red dwarf dipping low, streaking the clouds with molten crimson and ember-gold, as if the horizon itself were ablaze. Shadows stretch long and lazy, softening the edges of the world, making everything feel suspended, caught between day and night.

After we eat, I spot Lyra wandering on her own, slowly inspecting the booths with her arms folded tightly across her chest. She's folded in on herself as if she is trying to hide.

"Hey, Lyra!" I call. She turns, her face brightening as she sees me. She turns and starts waking towards us. "This is Rina. She's a recruiter for the guard."

"Hi," she says, a little shy, tucking a strand of hair behind her ear like she always does when she's unsure.

"Hi, Lyra. Vera's told me a lot about you," Rina says warmly. "She mentioned you've been doing great in the Order. If you ever think about joining the guard, let me know."

Lyra's eyes widen. "I… I will. I'm not sure what I want to do yet. I love books, and I'm decent with earth magic. I thought maybe I'd grow herbs, maybe work in that little apothecary off Maple Street."

"You'd be brilliant at it," I chime in. She smiles shyly, clearly not used to the praise.

Rina nods. "Well, you have time. Sometimes the path finds you when you're not even looking."

We spend the next half hour sampling snacks we probably didn't need, candied roots that taste like cinnamon and warmth, soft honey cakes, a fizzy drink that makes our tongues tingle. Lyra laughs when I nearly drop mine after it bubbles up too fast. It feels good to see her smile like that. A little unburdened. I don't know what bothers her so much but I do know I want to be there for her, like she is for me.

As twilight creeps in and the shadows lengthen, we make our way back to the car. Rina needs to grab the thick woven blanket she packed for firewatch. On the way, we run into Nero, who's somehow traded his training gear for a sleek dark tunic and a faint smudge of ash on his cheek that looks intentional. Casual and effortlessly handsome. I wave him over.

"Nero, this is Rina. She's basically my guardian-slash-boss-slash-unofficial big sister."

Rina raises an eyebrow. "Unofficial?"

He laughs and shakes her hand. "Nice to finally meet you. I've heard things."

"Only the good kind, I hope," she teases.

They fall into easy conversation about Duskmere, the Order, and the different kinds of training styles used across the provinces. They keep it light, especially with Lyra standing nearby, but I catch the glint of mutual respect in their eyes.

"I don't want you guys to feel like you have to sit with us for the firewatch," I offer, nudging Lyra gently. Who knows maybe they want to be together? They could be fated. I'm hoping.

Nero shrugs. "My mom won't be here tonight. I'll stick with you." He says it like trouble is already lurking, that familiar big-brother edge always there. Somehow, that makes me wonder—what could possibly go wrong tonight?

Lyra hesitates for a moment, then nods. "My parents won't be here either." Her voice is so soft I almost miss it, and she doesn't explain further. But I see the flicker of something in her expression, hurt, buried under practiced calm.

I thread my arm through hers and give it a gentle squeeze. She smiles up at me, grateful but silent.

"We would love to have you. We can do this together!" I say cheerily, forcing a smile even though my chest tightens thinking about my parents not being here either.

A live band starts playing just off to the edge of the wide central field, the kind of upbeat, earthy fae music that's all drums and deep strings and voices that rise like smoke. A makeshift dance floor has formed in front of them, woven mats and glowing thread marking the space. Couples and friends spin and sway, laughter ringing like bells.

All around us, the air buzzes, not just with music or conversation, but with magic. It lingers in the dirt and the sky, in the flames flickering in carved lanterns, in the marks on our skin. For fae turning eighteen this year, tonight isn't just a celebration. It's a rite of passage. A bridge between youth and power. Between potential and purpose.

I feel it in my bones.

And even though my chest is tight with nerves, even though I'm not sure what comes next, I know one thing: I'll remember this night for the rest of my life.

As we make our way toward the clearing, the narrow paths open into a wide, sloping field, and that's when I realize just how many fae are here. Hundreds, maybe more, gathered from every province. Faces I've never seen. Robes embroidered in the deep, distinct colors of each province swirl around us, each thread a quiet declaration of origin.

Duskmere's are darkest, woven from midnight black and storm-silver, echoing the land of shadows and strength. Varethos fae wear shifting robes of smoky grays and soft blues, colors like mist caught in moonlight, honoring their legacy as seers and dreamweavers.

Sylvaeris, the ruling province, glows in vibrant forest greens, shimmering golds and soft ivory. Symbols of harmony, law and the wild heart of fae power. The kingdom's influence is in every polished thread every gold trimmed edge, reminding everyone where power now resides. The only thing missing is the rich earth tones of Elarindor.

Ceremonial tattoos glinting with magic ink. Fae from all corners of the realm, standing shoulder to shoulder under the dying light of dusk.

I was told they come from far and wide for the Veilfall, especially those turning eighteen. But I didn't expect this. The air is electric, alive. Magic hums through the ground beneath my boots, sings in the branches overhead, crackles between fingertips. I can feel it in my blood, in the rush of my pulse. Like I'm standing at the edge of something ancient and sacred.

In the center of the field stands a towering wooden structure, logs stacked in a massive pyramid, arranged with such precision they seem to lean on each other like a temple. Stone markers circle the base, uneven and timeworn, like they've been here longer than the town itself. Several guards in ceremonial armor stand around the pyre, alert but relaxed.

All across the field, fae spread blankets and furs across the grass, settling in. Some recline against tree roots, others cluster in small groups, whispering excitedly. The buzz in the air grows louder with each passing minute. It feels like the land itself is holding its breath.

The band finishes their song and softens into silence.

A tall figure steps onto the raised stage beside the fire. His presence alone quiets the crowd. He moves with effortless grace, like he belongs not just here but everywhere. The forest green cape trailing from his shoulders gleams in the fading light, fastened with a silver clasp that bears the sigil I painted just hours ago, a spiraling storm pierced by a sword, encircled with silver leaves.

The king.

His hair is a dark brown, streaked with silver at the temples, and his cheekbones are cut with the same regal sharpness I've seen on Caelum. His expression is unreadable, a mask of serene power but there's something in his eyes. Depth. History. Strength honed and buried. Even from here, I feel the pull of his magic. It radiates off him like sunlight off a blade.

Near the stairs stands the Head Guard. Towering, masked, unmoving, like a statue cast in midnight bronze. He gives off a quieter menace, but no less commanding.

The king steps forward. His voice, when he speaks, its an even, low tone and somehow carries through the crowd without effort, like the air itself bends to deliver it.

"Good evening, ladies and gentlemen. Welcome to the Veilfall Festival. Tonight is one of the most sacred celebrations of our people, a night to see yourself clearly, to step forward into who you are meant to become. For some, it is also the first whisper of something more. Of destiny. Of love."

There's a collective shiver in the crowd, like his words carry more than meaning, like they carry *truth*.

"The fire will begin in ten minutes. Please find your place, get comfortable, and if you need anything, a member of the guard will assist you. May the gods beyond the Veil watch your steps and steady your hearts." He dips his head slightly, just enough to show reverence, never weakness, then turns and disappears down the steps.

My throat feels tight. There's something in my chest I can't name. Not fear. Not awe. Something in between. That was Caelum's father. I want to ask Rina about him, what he's like, what kind of king he truly is but Lyra and Nero are right beside me, and this doesn't feel like a conversation I want them to overhear. Not yet. So I stay quiet. But my mind won't stop turning.

Rina leads us toward a quieter patch nestled beneath a canopy of twisted old trees, the kind whose branches look like they've been watching over this land for centuries. The thrum of the festival fades slightly here, still audible, but distant enough to feel like we're holding our breath outside the world.

"Being by the fire is a ceremonial thing. It doesn't matter where in the world you are, on your 18th Veilfall every fae gets their true gifts. This is a rite of passage." She explains as we start to spread out our blankets.

We settle near the edge of the clearing, the soft crunch of leaves beneath our feet the only sound between us. The air is thick with tension, not the bad kind, not quite but the electric kind that zings across your skin and coils tight in your stomach. Something is coming. I don't know what, but I can feel it.

I start to pace, unable to sit still. My fingers twitch. My breath catches in my throat. The magic in the air isn't subtle anymore, it crawls across my skin like static, fizzing beneath the surface, lighting up every nerve ending.

"Are you okay?" Rina asks softly.

"Yeah, I'm just… I'm just nervous." I say quietly. My eyes flicking nervously over to Nero and Lyra. They are both watching me quietly. Neither look at me like I am something to pity or an idiot.

Then, almost on cue, the fire roared to life in the center of the field. People milled around, some laughing and chatting, others like me, pacing nervously, hearts half in hope, half in prayer for something grand.

What had been a simple pile of wood becomes a towering inferno within seconds, flames licking the sky. The blaze casts a golden-orange glow that shifts to deep crimson as the shadows thicken, swallowing the edges of the clearing. It's beautiful. Powerful. A little terrifying. The fire makes it just dark enough that faces blur in the distance. Bodies become outlines. Whispers become secrets.

I can't shake the weight in my chest. Something is coming. Something that will change everything. The fire flares again, casting a sudden, brilliant light across the clearing and two figures step into view from beyond it. Backlit by the flames, their forms are haloed in gold, shadowed at the edges like something out of a dream. At first, they're just silhouettes, blurred and surreal.

But I know him before I see his face. Cae. I can feel it, like the air shifts when he's near, charged and alive. My heart seems to recognize him before my mind catches up. His energy hits me like a jolt. Magnetic. Confident. Too much. My stomach flips as he and Elowen step into view, the fire casting flickering shadows across their faces. He looks like he was *born* to walk out of fire. And maybe he was.

"Hey," he says as they reach us, his voice low and familiar. His eyes find mine instantly, like he doesn't even have to look. "We finally found you. Not easy in this crowd."

"Prince Caelum," Rina says, rising slightly. Her tone is polite, but there's a thread of curiosity woven through it now.

"Rina." He flashes her one of those smiles I'm sure he's practiced for years, charming, a little cocky. "I thought it'd be nice to join my future Head Guard tonight. And, of course my Lilac."

He winks at me, and my heart stutters in protest. Heat rushes to my face. My stomach flips again. He glances at Rina, like daring her to challenge the nickname. She doesn't, yet. But I can feel her watching. Like she's reading the lines of a story we haven't written yet.

"Of course, I couldn't come without El," he adds. "This is a night we've been waiting for."

"How are you, Princess Elowen?" Rina asks smoothly.

"I'm great," El says brightly. "Please, call me El. I hope you don't mind us crashing. You've got a great group here. I wanted to be part of it too."

Her presence is like warm honey, sweet and soothing, balancing the tension her brother leaves in his wake. But Rina still watches. Quietly. Intently. I wonder what she sees that I don't.

I keep pacing. My hands won't stay still. My thoughts won't slow down.

"You don't want to do this with your dad?" Rina asks gently. It catches me off guard, this moment feels *important*. Sacred. Aren't parents supposed to be here?

Cae shrugs, glancing toward the fire, then back at me. "Hey, don't get sad," he murmurs under his breath, brushing his hand along my arm as I pass. It's just a touch, but it grounds me.

"He's just busy," he adds. "Giving the commencement, helping people, you know how he gets when he goes out into town. Always has to play king and savior at the same time." His words are light, but there's something under them. A shadow of frustration maybe. Or longing.

"What about your fiancé?" Rina presses, voice insistent, probing.

The word twists like a knife, and the reminder slams into me, he can't be mine. I step back, pulling free from his touch.

"There is no fiancé. Not yet." His words are steady, but his eyes cut pointedly toward me.

Before I can respond, a voice carries across the clearing, sharp and commanding: "Five more minute. It begins when the sun sets."

A ripple moves through the crowd. Whispers rise, urgent and hushed, fragments of prayers, bets, and nervous laughter. Some stand straighter, others fidget with their sleeves or blades, as if one last adjustment could change everything. The air itself seems to tighten, heavy with expectation.

I glance toward the horizon. The last sliver of sun sinks behind the hills, spilling gold that deepens into violet, then indigo. The sky holds its breath and so do we. My chest thrums with nerves, a jittery pulse beneath my skin I can't shake, like I'm a bowstring drawn too tight, waiting for release.

Another figure approaches our group, tall and unhurried. I tense immediately.

Who else could possibly be coming? This was supposed to be simple. Just Rina and me. A quiet corner on a chaotic night.

"Veils," Cae mutters under his breath, sharp and low.

Chapter 41: She Remembers

Vera

Auren. He saunters into view like he belongs here, like he's always belonged. The fire behind him catches on the twilight hue of his armor, casting fractured shadows across his face. His eyes scan the group like he's checking the perimeter, until they land on Elowen.

The air tightens. The world narrows. Even the fire feels farther away now, like it knows it's not the brightest heat in the clearing anymore.

"What are you doing here?" Cae steps forward, blocking his path with the quiet threat of someone who's had enough.

Auren lifts a brow. "No need to get worried. Just wanted to be here to support you all. Don't mind me."

He tries to sidestep, but Cae's arm shoots out, a firm hand pressing against Auren's chest. The sound of contact is soft but final. Like the first drop of rain before a storm.

Nero rises from the blanket beside Rina and Lyra, his body tense and watchful. Auren's expression doesn't change, but something around his eyes flickers. Pressure. Calculation. Old habits. Old rivalry.

"I know you have other people you could be around," Cae says, his voice no longer pretending to play nice.

"And yet," Auren replies smoothly, "this felt like the most important place to be tonight. With the most important fae."

There's something in the way he says it, something layered, like he's not just talking about the Veilfall ceremony. A dig. A warning. A dare.

Cae narrows his eyes. The space between them feels like a live wire, buzzing with unspoken history.

"No," Cae says flatly.

Auren tilts his head, unfazed. "'Fraid so."

I open myself to the shift in the air, my gift tugging at the emotional edges of the moment. Cae is unraveling. The sharp spike of rage blooms beneath his control. He's going to hit him. He wants to.

But Nero gets there first, stepping between them, a hand pressed gently but firmly to Cae's chest. A silent anchor. Cae doesn't budge at first. His eyes never leave Auren's, two storms locked in a standoff.

"No. I will not allow it."

"You don't get that say," Auren replies coolly. "Now focus on your Veilfall. I promise it will work out." And just like that, he sidesteps them both. Smooth. Effortless. Annoying.

He starts walking towards El, and she looks up at him wide eyed. She looks worried and a little sad. Who is this guy?

Nero's hand lingers a second longer before dropping. Cae exhales, sharp and short. Then he turns to me. His shoulders square, his jaw tight. But when his eyes meet mine, they soften, just slightly. Like I'm the only thing that can relax him.

I hold his gaze, but my body's already pacing again. The tension from the confrontation still buzzes under my skin. My stomach is twisting. The crowd beyond us is louder now, rising like a tide. Magic buzzes in the air, shimmering with anticipation.

What if something goes wrong?

What if I can't control whatever shows up?

What if *nothing* happens and I'm just… broken? I kind of wish there wasn't so many people here. Not that I don't like these people, it's just I was expecting it to just be Rina and I. Expecting privacy.

Back and forth, I pace in front of the blanket. My nerves feel like frayed wires. Every step feels like too much and not enough. Then two hands find me. Steady. Sure. Cae pulls me in.

One arm wraps firmly around my waist, anchoring me. The other slides up, fingers warm and rough as they gently cup my jaw. He tilts my face toward his, slow and deliberate, until our eyes lock.

And in that moment, everything else fades. The fire. The festival. The future. It's just him. And me.

"You look beautiful," he murmurs, like he's speaking a truth he's been holding back for too long. His hand grazes mine. "I love this dress on you. It makes your eyes shine."

"You can see my eyes?" Did Rina Veilbrew Elixir not work?

"Yes, but I know that only I can see it, ever since the first time I touched you. I don't know how it's veiled but it's intact."

"How do you know?"

"Because Nero can't see your aura or your eyes. Like I said it only happened after we first touched. I don't like that you have to conceal it but I love that only I get to see that vibrant starbursts."

I want to respond to tease him, to say something clever or one of my snappy comebacks. To pretend I'm not unraveling from the inside out. But all I can do is whisper, "I'm scared."

He doesn't mock me or try to brush it away. He just asks, gently, "What scares you the most?"

I swallow, the words catching like thorns in my throat. "Not knowing," I whisper. "I've felt something off all day. What if I'm a freak and I get too many gifts? Or none at all? What if this whole thing doesn't work, and I end up spending the rest of my life alone, just searching for answers I'll never find? Mostly, I wish my parents could be here."

I want to say the rest of my short life, but I don't. I'm not ready to explain that part.

His hand tightens around mine. "Vera, you could never be a freak. No matter how many gifts you have or don't, you're not broken. You're extraordinary. And as for the rest of it…"

He pauses, and I feel him looking at me like he's seeing every jagged, afraid piece of me and choosing me anyway.

"You will never be alone again. Whatever this becomes, whatever truths we uncover, I'm in it. With you. Always. Just like it's meant to be."

My breath catches. "What do you mean?"

His eyes soften, that impossibly rich green catching the last glimmer of sunset like dew clinging to grass at twilight.

"I've been waiting for this moment since the day I saw you on the street and in that office," he says, voice low and steady. "Waiting for you to stop pretending. To stop running. To stop denying *me*." His thumb brushes my cheek. "I don't care about anything else anymore. Just you."

"What are you talking about?" My voice is barely a breath. I feel like I know but I am too scared to voice it.

"This." And then his lips brush mine, soft, sure, inevitable.

The sun sets. And the world unravels. Somewhere beyond this bubble I hear gasps from all over. My attention is too focused on Cae. The kiss detonates through me, not gentle or gradual, but instant and *searing*. A jolt, hot, sharp, primordial. Magic explodes in my chest like a second heartbeat awakening. A golden thread surges between us, stitching something invisible and eternal, tying my soul to his.

Everything disappears, sound, thought, fear, except for the heat of his mouth, the press of his body, and the sudden, wild awareness that I'm not just kissing him. I'm becoming something else.

A deeper hum rises in my blood. My skin shivers, vibrating with energy I can't contain. When we part, I'm gasping. Shaking. I feel as if I've stepped out of my own body and into something *other*.

He leans in, resting his forehead to mine, grounding me again. "I can feel you," I whisper.

He smiles, but there's something reverent behind it. "I've felt you for so long."

There's a flash, light clicking and we both glance over to see Rina, camera in hand, tears shining in her eyes.

"You've felt it too," he says, never looking away from me. "You can't deny that you're mine. Not anymore. That we're fated. We're meant to be, forever."

Tears slip down my cheeks. I'm shaking, not from fear, but from knowing. This truth was always there. Waiting. And that terrifies me.

I shake my head slowly. "I—"

His jaw clenches. "You don't get to say no. Whatever's happening, we'll figure it out. I'm not letting go." He lifts my hand to his chest. "And don't forget, we have our date tomorrow."

Somewhere nearby, someone gasps softly. Lyra, maybe. Maybe Elowen. But I can't turn away from him.

"I—" I start again, but the word splinters as pain sears through me.

It hits like lightning. No, worse, like lightning woven with fire and wind and pressure that shouldn't exist inside a body. I stumble, clutching my stomach, the breath ripped from my lungs.

Cae's expression collapses into panic. "Vera?"

Another surge slams into me, fiercer. My knees give out. I fall to the earth, my hands and knees sinking into the grass. My vision fractures, shards of violet, gold, white-hot silver, colors I've never seen before, bleeding into the edges of my sight.

"I can't—" I gasp, barely able to get the words out.

"Vera, talk to me." His voice is raw, terrified. "I can feel your pain, gods, it's everywhere."

His voice is frantic now. "Rina! Nero!" But I barely hear him. Light floods behind my eyes. The ground falls away. Magic erupts out of me, around me.

Something cracks in the air, like the sky itself splitting. I can't tell if it's inside my body or if the sky is really ripping apart. A strange weight pulls at my shoulder blades, searing, burning, stretching and then a rush of wind. A shift.

I can feel Cae's hands on me, warm and grounding, desperate to keep me here. But I'm leaving. Fading. Voices blur into silence, shapes smear into light. I reach for him, but my fingers slip through the air like mist.

The world dissolves around me. For a moment, there's nothing but weightless dark, until two figures emerge through the haze.

The first girl has pale, straight hair the color of moonlight. Her face is delicate and long, a scattering of freckles across her nose. When her eyes open, they flash violet, like mine, but without the gold. The second girl appears beside her, her thick curls a deep burgundy that catches glimmers of unseen light. Her skin glows warm and olive, her violet eyes are set in an expression of fierce determination even in her confusion.

Both of them are staring at me. Their mouths move, but I can't hear what they're saying. I feel their panic—*their need*—as if it's my own. They reach for me, but just as our fingers might touch, they dissolve into the black.

And I'm falling again. With one last thought, I wonder—*Is this the prophecy?* Would I really die before my nineteenth birthday?

And who waits beneath the veil.
She remembers.

Acknowledgements

I want to sincerely thank my beta readers for their time, thoughtful feedback, and honesty, especially for pointing out when something felt redundant or needed more clarity. Your support and guidance helped shape this story into what it is today.

And to my husband for always listening and keeping me grounded and providing insight into my stories when I need it!

And to my readers: thank you for picking up this book, for letting yourself be transported into this world, and for sharing in Vera's journey. Your enthusiasm and support mean the world to me.

Hi! I'm Ali Wren, an independent author who loves blending adventure, suspense, and romance. With a background in biological anthropology, I enjoy weaving real-world science into my stories, where the men fall fast and hard and the women are strong, smart, and unstoppable.

When I'm not writing, I'm a mom, a science enthusiast, and an advocate for alopecia awareness. My *Veiled Prophecy* series grew from a dream into a rich fantasy world full of magic, danger, and adventure. A place where imagination knows no bounds.

I'd love to connect! Follow me on TikTok, Instagram, and Facebook @aliwrenauthor for updates, behind-the-scenes content, and more.

Keep Scrolling for a sneak peek at Book 2 in The Veiled Prophecy Series: *Veilbound*

Sneak Peek: Veilbound

I feel a burning all over me. Deeper than skin, like fire awakening in my bones. It pulses across my back and wraps around my right wrist, hot and insistent. I try to move, but I can't. My limbs are heavy. Useless.

Somewhere, far away, I hear voices. Muffled. Familiar. *Rina... Caelum...* They're talking, but their words are just out of reach, like echoes drifting across a lake at night. I try to breathe deeply, to fight through the weight, but the world slips out from under me.

When I open my eyes again, I am, somewhere else. Somewhere impossibly beautiful.

A forest stretches around me, vibrant and alive. The air hums with magic. Ahead, a glowing lake ripples like liquid crystal, refracting a perfect rainbow across its surface. Four-leaf clovers blanket the forest floor, their edges kissed with stardust. Rocks and tree trunks are draped in glowing moss, its veins lit with gentle gold. Bioluminescent flowers peek through the clover, blooming with soft violet and blue light.

I must be dreaming. Nothing this wondrous could be real.

I take a step forward, barefoot and silent. I'm wearing a flowing white dress, light as air, the fabric whispering around my ankles with each movement. A breeze dances through the trees, lifting my hair, guiding me forward.

The lake malls to me. I crouch beside it, enchanted. As I reach toward the glowing water, something catches my eye. My wrist. Something new.

I turn my hand over slowly and gasp. It's *the symbol.* The one I painted, combining the Thornevale crest with Elowen's. The same brushstrokes. The exact colors. But here, it glows softly, like the mark was etched beneath my skin with threads of starlight.

I raise my other hand, fingers trembling as I trace over it.

A voice, soft and melodic, breaks the stillness behind me. "Do you like it?" Startled, I spin to my feet. The woman from my dream the other night stands before me.

She wears a dress like mine, flowing and celestial. Her long hair falls in waves of deep violet and rich brown, cascading over her shoulders. Her eyes glow, violet and ancient.

"Who are you?" I demand, though the awe in my voice softens the edge.

"I am Aetherielle," she says gently. "It's nice to meet you, Veralyn."

My breath catches. "This isn't real. I... I've seen you before, in another dream."

She smiles. "You did. I couldn't reach you then, not fully. But now that your powers have awakened, the veil between us is thin. I've been watching you since the day you were born." She steps closer, her presence malming. "Last night was significant," she says, her tone laced with reverence. "And I'm sorry for the pain. When the Moon Goddess gifted me with my powers, I remember that burn. It is both a burden and a blessing."

"This is insane," I whisper. My fingers curl instinctively around my wrist, still glowing.

"Do you like your fated mark?" she asks again, softer this time. "I saw what you painted. It was beautiful. Sacred. I asked the gods to make that your mark and Caelum's. You are both chosen. Your bond is rare, powerful. The realms will depend on it. On you." I look down at the mark again. It shimmers gently beneath my touch.

"I love it," I whisper. "But I'm scared. I don't know what's happening to me."

"I know, my daughter," she says with such tenderness it makes my throat tighten. "But you will. Trust those around you. They will guide you through the dark."

I meet her eyes. "Someone's after me. Who is it?"

Her expression hardens. "That we cannot see. He wears a mask an ancient one, crafted to block even the Sight. No seer can find his face. He hides in shadow and weaves his plans in secret."

"Does he know where I am?"

Aetherielle nods solemnly. "Yes, he knows where you, but we do not know his plans. That is all we've been able to discern."

My heart sinks. "How do I stop him? How do I find the answers?"

"You are already walking the path," she says, voice steady. "You're closer than you know. That's all I can tell you now. I must send you back, Veralyn. Remember, you were destined for something great."

"No, wait!" I step forward, panic rising. "I have more questions—please—"

But she's already fading, her smile soft and sad. Her form scatters like dandelion seeds in the wind. I turn, heart pounding, and look back at the lake. The colors blur. The light dims. The magic dissolves into mist.

My eyes open to soft light spilling through my curtains. I'm lying on my side, facing the wall. The same dress from last night clings to me, wrinkled and still faintly warm from the fire that bloomed inside me last night.

I try to catalog everything I'm feeling. Fear, confusion, wonder, relief but also the pain from last night is gone. No more burning. The moment I shift, something hard pokes against my backside. I freeze. Slowly, I turn my head.

Caelum.

His green eyes are locked on mine, glowing softly with golden flecks. Even in their brightness, I see the shadows beneath them, dark circles telling me he didn't sleep much, if at all. A slow smile curves his lips, but it doesn't quite reach his eyes.

Stay tuned for updates on Veilbound and Whiskey & Lies: Book Two of Whiskey Tango Foxtrot series!